# Heart

## *Of*

# Marley

*T.K. Leigh*

HEART OF MARLEY

Published by Carpe Per Diem / Tracy Kellam, 25852 McBean Parkway # 806, Santa Clarita, CA 91355

Edited by: Kim Young, Kim's Editing Services

Cover Design: Cat Head Biscuit, Inc., Santa Clarita, CA

Cover Image Copyright Iulian Valentin 2014

Used under license from Shutterstock.com

ISBN: 090519694
ISBN-13: 978-0-9905196-9-0

To all the Marleys of the world…

You're stronger than you think you are…

# *PROLOGUE*

## *Six Years Ago*

*Cam*

MY HEART WAS RACING as I heard Marley's cries emanating from our bedroom. I knew what I had to do to protect her and get her away from all of this. I couldn't let *him* hurt her anymore.

Our lives used to be the picture of perfection…quaint raised-level home, white picket fence, huge back yard, and two loving parents…until Dad died three years ago just after our eighth birthday. Mama loved us, but the drugs and alcohol that she sought comfort in to cope with the heartache of losing her soul mate diminished her ability to act like a parent. I became the only one who would look out for us. I was Marley's last line of defense…her last hope.

I stood in the corner of the living room of the apartment that we had called home for the past few months. We had spent the last several years jumping from place to place, never staying for too long. Every time we moved, Mama promised that she was going to clean up her act and not tell *him* where we were. Then the withdrawal symptoms kicked in and she would cave, begging him for drugs, money, or both. She put her own selfish needs ahead of her children's well-being. I just couldn't comprehend how any parent could do that. Then again, I didn't know anything about addiction.

When *he* came into our sorry excuse for a bedroom that evening, I knew what he was going to do. He had been doing that very thing nearly every night since New Year's Eve three years ago. I wanted to fight him, but nothing ever worked. If I tried to get in his way, he would just knock me out and take what he wanted from Marley regardless. That night, I had bigger plans. When he ordered me out, I followed his demand.

Over the years, I began to hate myself for not being able to stand up to him and protect Marley. I never knew what hate was until he walked into our lives. Now I welcomed hate. I tasted hate. I breathed hate. All because I loved Marley.

I hadn't seen my mother in days. I had no idea when or if she would ever return, but that was okay. For what I needed to do, she shouldn't be there.

Tiptoeing past the couch and toward the front door, I opened the drawer of the entryway table. I saw a flash of light from the reflection of the street lamp on the metal of the gun barrel. *Can I really do this?* I asked myself. *Will I go to jail for the rest of my life?* Would *they send an eleven-year-old to jail?* I no longer cared about the potential repercussions. He had to be stopped. I would gladly spend the rest of my life behind bars to save Marley from her current prison.

Grabbing the gun as quietly as possible, I felt the weight in my hands. It was as if it weighed fifty pounds instead of less than two. I checked the safety and released it, secretly thanking my mother for thinking that it was a good idea, during one of her drug-induced hazes, to show me how to use a gun. She said that I was the man of the house now and I needed to learn to use a weapon to protect our home. Little did she know that the only thing I needed to protect us from resided within those four walls.

I retreated from the foyer and began making my way down the hallway toward the bedroom that I shared with Marley. Each sound seemed to be amplified tenfold, nervous energy flowing through every inch of me. My breathing increased and my entire body trembled…not with fear, but with pure rage at the thought of what my other half had been enduring nearly every night since Dad died.

Taking a deep breath, I placed my hand on the doorknob and turned it. I pushed the door open and surveyed the scene in front of me, my tongue caught in my throat.

"What do you think you're doing?" a booming voice slurred, not moving from his position.

"Get off of Marley," I quivered weakly.

"Leave! Now!" he ordered.

"I'm not going anywhere until you promise to leave my sister alone."

"Fuck," he hissed under his breath before he raised his imposing frame and stalked toward me.

Looking around his rotund belly, his white tank top stained, I gave Marley a reassuring nod as she grabbed the thin sheet off the bed and wrapped it around herself. Her quiet cries shattered my heart and erased the last bit of faith I had in the human race. Lifting the gun, I aimed it at him, cringing at the sight of his unbuttoned pants and the belt held firmly in his hand.

*Just pull the trigger,* I said to myself. *Pull it and free Marley. Free Marley… Marley… Marley…*

My nostrils flared and my vindication returned. All I saw was red. I had heard people speak of out-of-body

3

experiences before, but I never knew what they were talking about…until that moment. I seethed with fury. Before I knew what was happening, I pulled the trigger. Again. And again. And again.

I watched his disgusting body fall to the ground, his mouth agape and eyes wide as he clutched his stomach and leg.

Looking down at the gun in my hand, I immediately snapped back to reality.

"Cam…" Marley exhaled through her sobs. "You just shot him."

I ran to the bed, her frail body illuminated by the full moon, bringing attention to the scars and bruises on her legs. Wrapping my arms around her, I tried to comfort her the only way I knew how.

"To the moon and back," I whispered. It was our code. Her way of knowing that no harm would come to her.

"From the stars to the ocean, Cam," her sweet voice squeaked out in response.

"He's never going to hurt you or anyone else again." I rubbed her back, mindful of the scratches and welts from where he had used his belt on her. "I'll never let anything bad happen to you ever again, Mar."

I held her all night long, comforting her sobs and soothing her fears when she woke up screaming. I kept the gun clutched in my hand as I watched over her, keeping one eye trained on the body that had lost blood throughout the night, making sure that he didn't move. I would hear him moan out and beg me to call for help, but I refused. I wanted him to suffer and feel pain that was worse than what Marley had endured those past three years. I wanted his death to be slow and agonizing.

Once the sun rose, bathing everything in light, the reality of what I had done set in. I knew that I had to tell someone. The only person I could think of was my grams. Rummaging through my mother's things, I finally found her address book and made the phone call that would be the start of our new lives.

# CHAPTER ONE

## *PEACE*

### *Six Years Later*

*Cam*

"MARLEY? WHAT ARE YOU doing out here?" I asked, peeking out of my bedroom window to see my twin sister lying on the roof of our house.

"Thinking, Cam."

"Can I come and think with you?"

She tilted her head and I could see the sadness within her brilliant blue eyes. "Of course…if boys know how to think." She giggled at her dig at me.

Shaking my head, I carefully climbed out the window, crawling a few feet to where she lay right outside her own bedroom window. When we came to live with our uncle Graham and aunt Terryn all those years ago, we shared a room. After a while, they thought we were getting too old to have the same room and had a wall built in our formerly spacious bedroom. It took time to adjust to the new arrangement. Marley despised the separation, hating that I wasn't there to calm her down when the nightmares found her. And they always did, even though six years had passed.

About a month after the "Great Wall of Bowen", as

Marley referred to it, was erected, she began sitting out on the roof every chance she could. *"I can forget about everything out here, Cam,"* she would say to me. *"Being here and staring at the stars reminds me that the world is a bigger place and my problems are insignificant in the grand scheme of things."* She always had a way of putting things that made me feel better about our past. The guilt for not protecting her all those years still ate away at me, but her smiling, readjusted face put my concerns at ease, even if only for a fleeting moment.

Settling down on the roof next to Marley, I grabbed her hand in mine.

"Do you think Grams is happy now? Do you think it hurt when she…?" Her voice trailed off.

The past few weeks had been difficult for her…for both of us. The matriarch of our family had lost her battle with breast cancer. The doctors said she had six months to live. That was nine years ago. That was why we couldn't go live with her when we finally got away from *him*. She had fought her disease tooth-and-nail since getting her diagnosis. One day, she just stopped fighting. It hit both of us hard, but it affected Marley more than me.

"I think she's happier now. You saw how much…" I stopped short, the image of the weakened version of my grandmother that I had seen over the past few months still ingrained in my memory. The hardest part was watching her health fade over the months after she had begun to refuse any more treatments. I resented her for making that decision. I still remember having that dreadful conversation with Mama during one of our weekly court-approved supervised visitations just a few months ago.

*"Cameron, baby,"* she said to me. *"You can't take your anger out on Grams. She doesn't have much time left. Treasure each and*

*every moment you can spend with her while she's still here. This is her decision. She has fought this disease long and hard for the better part of the last decade of her life. She's ready to go and be with your dad now. Let her go…"*

And I had, at least I thought I did. Grams was the first close relative that I had lost since Dad was killed by a drunk driver when I was eight. I don't think I'll ever forget the solemn look on Mama's face when Uncle Graham dropped us at her house outside of Columbia for our visitation time two weeks ago. At that moment, I knew Grams was gone. And for the first time I could remember, I actually thought about death and how dying would feel. I wondered if Grams felt the same pain that I felt in my heart at that moment. I hated how much it hurt to lose someone I loved. And I knew I never wanted to lose anyone again.

"I think she's finally at peace," Marley said, breaking into my thoughts. She squeezed my hand and, out of nowhere, a light streamed through the night sky and disappeared into the ocean. "See, Cam. Look! Grams is okay." She raised her hand and wiped the tear that she was trying to hide from me off her cheek. "Remember what she would always say when we went to go visit her? And when we would talk about Dad?"

I nodded my head slightly. "The shooting star…"

"She's okay, Cam!" she exclaimed, her normal vivacious self returning after having been absent for the past few weeks. "Grams is okay. She said that's how we would know she made it to wherever she was going and that she was looking down on us." She rolled over and gave me a quick kiss on the cheek. "I feel better knowing that, don't you?"

Smiling, I gave Marley the answer she needed to hear. "I do." I wished I could believe it.

She nudged me and I turned my head toward her. Raising her eyebrows, she said, "Say it. I can't say my part unless you say your part first."

"To the moon and back, Mar."

"From the stars to the ocean."

We remained on the roof, contemplating life and how that precious gift could be ripped from you when you least expected. I often wondered what my life would have been like if that drunk driver had never killed Dad. Would we still be a happy family like we were before his death? Or would Mama have eventually found her way toward drugs and alcohol anyway? Would he have left her if she did? And would Marley have suffered abuse nearly every night for three years, the horrors still haunting her to this day?

"Do you think we'll always have this, Cam?" she asked several hours later as we pointed out the constellations to each other, making up new ones as we went.

"Of course we will, Mar. We're unbreakable...inseparable...indivisible..."

"Don't start quoting the *Pledge of Allegiance* now." She laughed and the sound filled the night sky over Myrtle Beach, the only other noise that of the crashing waves of the ocean a few blocks away.

"What I meant to say is that nothing can change this. No one can ever touch this."

"Even a beautiful brunette named Brianna?" she teased, pinching me.

"No. Not even a beautiful brunette named Brianna. She has a boyfriend, anyway. She's dating Mason," I said sadly.

"Not anymore," she responded, her voice sly.

"Well, how about a tall, gangly guy named Doug?" I asked, changing the subject to Marley's relationship status.

"It's not serious between us. We've only gone out a few times." Her answer was hesitant and I knew it was because she was scared of becoming intimate with anyone, her fears of having her trust betrayed still present.

"I doubt I'll be able to ask Bri out," I said, clearing the air. "I mean, she dated my teammate and friend. They were together for nearly two years."

"Word is that he cheated on her…with Jessica Harper, I think. Apparently, Grady was hitting on Diana Greene and, well…Jessica and Diana are pretty much attached at the hip."

"So are Mason and Grady," I replied. "But Grady has a reputation, and not a good one. So much for being the police chief's son."

"From what I've heard, Mason's getting a bit of a reputation, too. He's getting around. So this is the perfect time for you to finally make your move on Brianna. Be her knight in shining armor," she said dramatically, her blonde hair waving in front of her face.

"Every time I see her, I clam up. It's like my tongue is dead weight in my mouth and I can't put a coherent thought together."

"Just grow a set already, Cam!" she exclaimed. "She could use someone like you in her life."

"I know. I just suck at this stuff."

"You need to make the first move, especially with Bri. She's not like a lot of girls at school."

"Look at my kid sister, dishing out relationship advice."

She punched me playfully in the arm. "Younger by five whole minutes."

"But five minutes, nonetheless, Miss Bowen."

I could feel her roll her eyes at me. That was the thing

about having a twin. We felt each other. Even when I wasn't near Marley, I could still feel her...her heart, her soul, her livelihood. Everything she felt, I felt. Everything that upset her, upset me. There was a connection between the two of us that not many other people would understand or grasp, and it was that connection that amplified the guilt for what would happen later in the school year.

# CHAPTER TWO

## *PERFECT*

*Marley's Journal*

*August 12*

WE BURIED GRAMS TODAY. I still don't know how to feel about it. I miss her smile. I miss her laugh. I miss her voice. But mostly, I miss her heart. I feel closer to her than I do to anyone else…besides Cam, of course. Grams was the one who was horrified when she found out what Cam and I had to go through after Dad died. She was beside herself with guilt over it all, wishing that she had pushed harder to stay in touch with her daughter, our mama, but she had already begun to fight the cancer that would slowly kill her.

Those years after Dad died and before we were sent to live with Uncle Graham, my dad's brother, and Aunt Terryn still haunt me. And I think they still haunted Grams up until she died. I've tried to move past it all and, over the last few months, put on a smile for Grams so that she could go to her final resting place knowing that I'm okay. But that's not the real me and I think she knew it. Her sickness took a toll on her and she no longer had the strength to call me out on everything like she had been doing the past few years. She's one of the few people who could see through the façade.

I appreciate everything that Aunt Terryn and Uncle Graham have done for us, but I sometimes feel like I have to put on a show and a smile. Uncle Graham is a pastor in the local Presbyterian Church, and Aunt Terryn was a high school beauty queen with a substantial trust fund. She's now a stay-at-home mom and takes care of my two little cousins, Meg and Julianne. God is his religion; beauty and pageants are hers. I go to church every Sunday, and put on a smile and allow people to objectify me in the multitude of pageants that Aunt Terryn signs me up to compete in. She can't comprehend why I hate these things.

I don't mean to sound ungrateful. They've both tried so hard to make sure that we became well-adjusted teenagers and, for the most part, we are. But I still wake up screaming. I still cower in fear every time I hear footsteps outside my bedroom door. I don't fit into the mold in which they want me to be. So I put on an act. I smile. I wear a nice dress and wave in all the pageants. I work hard at making sure the public perception of me is fucking perfect because if they all knew what was going on inside my head every hour of every day, they would realize how far from normal I am. And I want to be normal. But what is normal?

My one constant is Cam. He knows. He sees the pain. He sees the torment. He sees the fear. He still hears my cries during the night and climbs out of his window and into mine, comforting me as he did all those years ago. I thought that after six years, I'd be okay, but I'm not. Maybe if I were allowed to go into therapy, I would be. But then word would get out that their niece had psychological problems and they would never hear the end of it. So Uncle Graham tells me to pray to God and everything will work out in the end. Aunt Terryn says that my mood swings are just a result of me being a hormonal teenage girl, and not because I suffered from sexual and physical abuse on a nightly basis for three years of my life. That has nothing to do with it. No one would still suffer from trauma over six years later, would they? (Cue me rolling my eyes.) Everything is swept under the rug so that they don't have to hear people whisper about their maladjusted, crazy niece. That would cause quite the stir at the Sunday church potluck and the Wednesday afternoon ladies tea.

Cam is my life. He's actually the one that encouraged me to start keeping a journal to express my feelings. I don't think I'd still be here today if it wasn't for him. Up until Grams died, I felt that living with the constant nightmares of my past was a curse, but the pain I felt from losing her was unlike anything I had ever experienced. And I've experienced a lot of pain. At that point, I realized that if anything happened to me, Cam would feel that pain. I hate the thought of him enduring any pain at all. Because of Grams' death, I've found new life. I've decided to treat every day as a blessing, as a gift. That's how Cam looks at everything. I need to do that, too.

I just wish it wasn't so damn hard to act like everything in my life is fucking perfect when it's anything but.

# CHAPTER THREE

## *BRIANNA*

*Cam*

"YOU'RE NOT GOING TO spend every Friday night of our senior year of high school working, are you?" Marley huffed as she plopped down on my bed a few weeks later. She seemed to finally be bouncing back after Grams' death. I was thrilled to finally see the old Marley again.

Shrugging, I looked at her through the full-length mirror on my bedroom door. "I'm not going to work *every* Friday, but I do need to keep saving money for college."

Her happy expression turned sad once more. I had forgotten how much she was dreading finishing high school. She knew that we would most likely be going our separate ways once we graduated. I hated the thought of not seeing her every day, too, but I wasn't taking it nearly as hard as Marley.

"Cam," she said in warning. "I told you…"

I put my hands up in defense. "I know. I'm sorry, Mar." Sighing, I joined her on the bed. "But you have to come to terms with it eventually. There is a chance that we won't go to the same college. You know that, right? You need to go somewhere that's going to be good for what you want to do, and I need to go somewhere that's got a great political science program."

15

Holding her head high, she waved me off. "I'm not going to think about it because then it won't happen."

Marley always had this thing where she would will something away. It never worked, but no one would ever stop her from doing what she wanted. I can't even count the number of times that we had been down at the beach and the sky started turning gray in the distance, storm clouds rolling in. Everyone else knew that the sky was about to open up and a typical summer thunderstorm would soon drench all of us, but that never discouraged Marley. She stood her ground. *"I'm willing that it won't rain so it's not going to,"* she had said with the most serious expression she could muster. It always rained, but that never discouraged her from trying the same exact thing the next time.

Grabbing my wallet off the dresser, I glanced at her before heading downstairs. "To the moon and back, Mar."

"From the stars to the ocean, Cam."

"I mean it, Mar. No matter what."

She plugged her ears playfully. "La, la, la, la," she said in a sing-song manner. "I can't hear you."

I shook my head and took one last look at her before heading out for work. I snapped a mental shot of my sister, my other half. I couldn't help but think how truly blessed I was to have her in my life. I often heard people talk about soul mates, always referring to finding the love of their life. My sister was my soul mate. I couldn't imagine my life without her.

"You better get going, Cam, or you'll be late. And if I were you, I'd be on time tonight…especially tonight." She winked.

I narrowed my gaze at her. "Why? I mean, I'm never late, but why are you being so…weird?"

"I'm a theater geek. I'm *always* weird," she retorted dramatically. "But I just so happen to know that a certain someone will be going to dinner with her mom and step-father tonight at the fine establishment at which you happen to be a waiter. Maybe you'll be lucky enough to get their table."

My eyes went wide and I rushed down the stairs, darting past the living room of our large two-story house.

"'Bye, Aunt Terryn! I'm off to work!"

"Cam! Cam! You need to give me a kiss good night," a child's voice called out with a slight lisp. I turned around and saw my younger sister, Meg, running toward the door, my even younger sister, Julianne, not far behind. It didn't matter that they were technically our cousins. In my mind, they were my sisters.

"Come here, you little bugger," I said, lowering my six-and-a-half foot frame to their level.

"Have fun at work, Cam!" Julianne said as she wrapped her arms around me, planting a wet kiss on my cheek. "When can I work?"

I released my hold on them, smiling fondly. "Enjoy your childhood while you can, munchkin."

"Will you bring me home a can… can…?"

"Cannoli?" I asked Meg.

"Yes. That's what I want. A cannellini!"

I laughed at her angelic voice pronouncing that word. "I'll see what I can do. But you do realize that one's a delicious dessert and the other is a bean, right?"

"Cameron, darling. Be nice. They're still learning," Aunt Terryn said from the kitchen, where she was preparing dinner.

"I was just playing." I turned my attention back to the two blonde-haired, blue-eyed little girls in front of me, their hair and coloring identical to my aunt. "If there are some left tonight, I'll do my best to bring one home for you. But you'll have to wait until tomorrow to eat it. I won't be getting home until after your bedtime. Okay?"

They both squealed with delight. They were more excited about me getting a job at Renaldo's than I was. It was the most popular Italian restaurant in town and was run by a married couple...Anita and Renaldo. Everyone loved them. When you were there, you were family and were treated as such.

We had been going to Renaldo's as long as I could remember and, when Marley and I turned sixteen, Aunt Terryn and Uncle Graham wanted us to get a job so that we could improve our college applications. I didn't mind, actually. It gave me an excuse not to have to go to church every Sunday. I wasn't against religion, but it always irritated the piss out of me that neither Marley nor I were put in therapy after going through what we did. We were told to look to God and all would be okay. Waking up several times a week from Marley's cries reinforced my belief that it was *not* all okay. I didn't know if it ever would be.

"Have a great night at work, darling." Aunt Terryn met me at the door and planted an affectionate kiss on my cheek. "Drive safe."

"I will." My keys clutched in my hand, I bolted from the house and hopped into the Jeep Wrangler that Mama helped me buy, starting the engine. During the short drive to the restaurant, Brianna's beautiful brown eyes flashed in my mind as anxiety (and probably hormones) ran through me.

Entering the kitchen, pots clanging all around, the familiar aroma of garlic and tomatoes greeted me.

"Hey, Anita," I said, poking my head in the staff room to see what tables were mine for the night.

"Hey, Cam. Darcy's out there now. A few of her tables are finishing up and then they're all yours."

"Thanks," I said, finding my locker and putting my wallet and keys inside. I was about to walk out when I remembered my sisters' pleas before I left home. "Oh, Anita, if it's not too much trouble and if there are any left tonight, can I steal a cannoli for Meg and Jules?"

A gentle smile crossed her face. "Of course you can."

I was about to head out when she called to me again, "Cam, one more thing. I had to get rid of a few staff members yesterday. Do you think you'll be able to work tomorrow afternoon?"

"I'm sorry. I wish I could, but it's Saturday. Marley and I have visitation with…"

"Oh, Cam," Anita interrupted me immediately. "I should have known. Don't worry about it. I'll find someone else to cover."

Shrugging my shoulders, I said, "I'm just sorry that I can't pick up the hours." I turned out of the office and went to get some side work done before having to take over my tables for the evening.

I finished my prep work in record time and slowly took over for Darcy so she could leave. After several hours had passed and I had given up any hope of seeing Brianna, the hostess alerted me that she just sat a new party in my section.

"Hi, my name's Cam," I said, looking down in my apron in search of my order book. "I'll be taking care of you…" I trailed off, my eyes meeting those beautiful brown eyes and all I could do was stare. Words always seemed to escape me whenever I was in her presence.

A sudden loud throat clearing startled me, bringing me back from her full lips. I turned my attention to her step-dad, who looked somewhat irritated that I was checking her out.

"Good evening, Mr. and Mrs. Grayson. Can I get you something to drink?" After jotting down their drink order, I winked slightly at Brianna and made my way across the large, bustling restaurant to the beverage stand, trying to control my heartbeat. She was the only girl I had ever met that made my heart explode from excitement and nerves at the same time.

I grabbed their drinks and returned to their table, concentrating as hard as I could not to trip and spill their beverages everywhere. I wasn't a clumsy person, but I didn't want to take any chances around Brianna.

"So, Cam," her mother said when I approached the picture-perfect family. Mrs. Grayson was one of those women that appeared to never age. Her features were still soft and vibrant, which contrasted with the smug look that seemed to be permanently glued on her face. She kept her dark hair short and I never noticed one strand out of place. "Your uncle tells me you're thinking about going the lawyer route like Bryant here." She gestured to her new husband.

"Yeah. I really enjoyed my Governments class this year…" I stopped short at the scowl on both of their faces from my mention of that class, which was taught by Brianna's biological father, Mr. Monroe.

"My uncle's been helping me narrow down my options for undergrad," I said, trying to recover from my earlier blunder, "but I'm also trying to keep in mind where Marley's going to go."

"That's probably not a smart move," Mrs. Grayson sneered. "That girl's a ticking time bomb waiting to happen. You, on the other hand, have a very bright future, Cameron."

There was an awkward silence at the table while she

looked at me in a condescending manner, my temper flaring. Avoiding her eyes, I settled my gaze on a Venetian scene that was painted on the wall by their table, doing the best I could to not respond to her remark.

"Please, dear," Mr. Grayson soothed. "Now's not the time."

I nodded in appreciation. I always liked Brianna's step-dad. He had an aura about him that just exuded warmth and compassion. He was quite a few years older than Brianna's mother. His hair was graying in a distinguished way that I'm sure attracted many women to him but, for as long as I can recall, he had only been interested in one woman. He married Mrs. Grayson a few years ago and treated Brianna with all the care and affection as he would his own daughter. He was an attorney who practiced law prior to being appointed a judge, an office he retired from several years ago. He now chaired the board of trustees at our lovely educational establishment.

Her mom stayed at home and made everyone else's business her business. I was fairly certain that most of the rumors regarding the adults in my town started from her lips. From what I knew, she divorced Brianna's father when Brianna was just six years old. She was happy to continue collecting those alimony payments until something better and more fruitful came along...like a judge that seemed to have more money than sense. As I turned and stared into her bitter eyes, I had to remind myself to play the nice, genuine southern boy that I was brought up to be.

"Are you ready to order?" I smiled my most charming smile at them, absently wondering how such a spiteful person could raise a daughter with as caring and beautiful of a soul as Brianna.

After scribbling down their order, I excused myself and

went behind the counter to drop off the ticket at the kitchen. As I was about to round the corner to go check on a few of my other tables, I nearly bumped into Brianna, surprised to see her standing in front of me.

"Hey, Bri," I said sheepishly, attempting to readjust my composure as I ran my hands through my sandy hair.

"Hi, Cam."

"What are you doing? Your parents…" I looked around her, trying to determine if they could see us from behind the brick pillar where we were standing. I could faintly make them out sitting side-by-side at their booth, her mother's expression that of disgust. Apparently, Renaldo's was not up to her too-good-for-everyone-else's standards.

"I just wanted to come and apologize for my mother's behavior. I don't know what came over me when I thought that she would actually act like a decent person for once in her life. I guess I was wrong. I was just hoping she would put her arrogance aside for one night for me. I'm sorry for what she said about Marley."

"You don't need to apologize for her, Brianna. You shouldn't have to."

"I know." She shrugged. "But I wanted to."

"Why did you want them to bring you here?"

She crossed her arms in front of her chest and rolled her eyes. An irritated expression crossed her face, which was completely at odds with her pleasing and delicate features. "They wanted to celebrate me starting my senior year of high school. Well, they mostly wanted to celebrate me being selected as a finalist in the Jessamine Pageant this fall. I think my mother filled out the application and forged my signature, though." She gestured with her head back at her table. "And Bryant's on the committee so I think it was a given that I'd be selected. I don't want to be around for the fallout that will happen when I don't win."

I could sense her unease with the topic. The Jessamine Pageant, named after the state flower of South Carolina, was a local event that happened each spring in Myrtle Beach where high school senior girls vied to be crowned Miss Jessamine so they could go on to compete in the Miss South Carolina Pageant. It was more a competition between the parents than the actual girls involved.

"Why don't you think you'll win?"

"Because I'm not the prettiest, most perfect, most talented girl in school." She looked down at her feet. "Your sister is. She'll win this thing, hands down."

"I don't know if she even put in an application, to be honest. I think she's been a bit pre-occupied lately."

"Cam!" I heard a voice call out from behind the counter. "Your order's up at table forty-one."

I met Anita's eyes and nodded in her direction before returning my attention to Brianna. "I'm sorry. I need to get back to work." I shifted nervously from foot to foot, reluctant to leave her presence.

"It's okay. I should get back to my mother before she accuses me of trying to sabotage their meal or something else ridiculous." She began to head away.

"Brianna!" I shouted abruptly.

She halted in her tracks and looked over her shoulder at me.

"I get off at ten. There's a bonfire down at the beach tonight. Meet me there?"

A wide grin crossed her face. "I'd like that. See you soon, Cameron."

I watched her sway her hips as she walked back to her table, my entire being alive at the way my full name rolled off her tongue in that sensual, but endearing manner. I was falling hard for that girl, even though I had

23

yet to kiss her or even ask her out. I had a feeling that was all going to change tonight.

# CHAPTER FOUR

## *NORMAL*

*Marley's Journal*

*August 29*

I SHOULD BE HAPPY. I should be thrilled. I have been selected as a finalist in the Jessamine Pageant, Myrtle Beach's most disgusting display of conformity that exists. I've watched this pageant for the past few years. I've had friends who were chosen as finalists and they were always so excited about the opportunity. Not me. I feel like a puppet up there, smiling because it's expected of me. I've learned to simply go through the motions, but that's not who I truly am.

I wish I were a normal teenager. I know that I appear to be one on the outside, but that's a front. Even Cam's begun to believe it. I think I've put on an act for so long that he believes the Marley he sees every day is the real Marley. Part of it is. There are moments of happiness and joy that I feel, especially when I see how content Cam is. His successes are my successes. His failures are my failures. His moments of absolute joy are my moments of absolute joy. And that's enough for me.

I hate to admit it, but some days I miss my mama…my real mama. The woman she was when my dad was still alive. We were so happy when we were a family. Dad was a mechanic. I remember sitting for hours in the garage at our modest house on the outskirts of Columbia, South Carolina. To this day, I still miss the smell of oil and grease. That smell feels like home. It feels safe. It feels pure.

He loved cars. We had a half-dozen old cars sitting in our yard that he wanted to fix up and make road-worthy. When he wasn't at the shop fixing someone's BMW or Mercedes, he was at our house, working on his own Mustang or Charger that he just had to have. Mama loved it, too. They met at a dirt race track, and their love for cars and all things fast was the pinnacle of their devotion.

Dad's family never approved of his profession or his choice in life partner. It still irritates me when I'm sitting at our fake family dinner and I hear Uncle Graham speak about him and how it was his choices that led him to his untimely death. His own brother. Dad came from a long line of lawyers, judges, politicians, and pastors. As a Bowen, you followed the law or God, nothing else. Dad was a bit of a rebel, and I think that's why I admired him so much, even when I was just a little girl.

*"When can I learn how to drive, Daddy?"* I remember asking him when I was barely seven years old.

*"You're too small, pumpkin. Your mother would kill me if I let you drive before you're sixteen."*

I huffed and plopped down on my hot wheels. *"That's not fair. I want to go fast like you, Daddy!"*

He took a sip of his beer and gazed down at me with the love that only a father could give a daughter. *"You will. Don't worry. I'll take you driving long before you turn sixteen."* He winked and I wish I had taken a snapshot of that image because I would fall asleep with it underneath my pillow just so I could feel love.

Don't get me wrong. Cam loves me. For the past nine years of our lives, it's been him and me against the world. Even when Uncle Graham and Aunt Terryn took us in and treated us as if we were their own children, we still had trust issues. Cam got over those fairly quickly once he was reminded of the happy times that we spent together during holidays with Dad's side of the family.

That's the thing about Cam. He's always been quick to forgive and forget, but that's not me. I remember. I remember the pain. I remember the horror. I remember the shame. I still feel all those things, even though I know I'm not supposed to. Having a niece with emotional problems is not the way to win pageants.

They do care about us, but I know taking us on has been a burden to them. Not a month after they agreed to take guardianship of us, Aunt Terryn found out that she was pregnant with Meg. The ladies here in town came over to tell her what an amazing thing she was doing. We became their charity case. Cam never saw it, but I did.

I started to get entered into pageants, Aunt Terryn playing the "Her mama can't raise her, and she's had such a rough life so she should win" card. And I usually did win, but Aunt Terryn never thought of the emotional repercussions to me from being paraded around like a sex object…

A sex object…

A sex object…

That's how I felt all those years ago. And that's how I still feel to this day.

I wish it would stop.

I wish I didn't feel this way anymore.

But I do. And I have no one that I can talk to about this. Or maybe I just don't want to talk about it. I could tell Cam anything and everything, but I worry that this would put a damper on his relationship with Aunt Terryn and Uncle Graham, and I hate the thought of that. I love how desperately he wants a healthy pseudo-parental relationship. We kind of have that with Mama, but we only get to see her once a week. I know that Cam craves more, and I can't bear the thought of taking that from him.

I guess I shouldn't complain. We could have ended up in the foster care system and been separated eventually, but that didn't happen. Aunt Terryn and Uncle Graham gave us food, something we hadn't had on a regular basis for years. They put a roof over our heads. They gave us stability. They gave us family. They gave us love. But sometimes I wonder whether it's all an act for them, too. Did they just do it so that all the parishioners at church would think that Pastor Bowen was such a humanitarian? Did they just do it so that Aunt Terryn could pull the sympathy card during pageants, ensuring that I won so that she, essentially, won, too?

I'm so sick of having to brush everything under the rug. Everyone here does it and no one says anything. This is normal. This is what is expected. I don't know how much longer I can forget and hide my past. I feel like I'm on a boat that's sprung more and more holes over the years. Every day that I'm forced to be someone I'm not is another leak in my boat. I fear that, one day, it'll be too much and I'll no longer be able to save myself from the raging storm that will pull me under.

Part of me is looking forward to going away to college so that I can finally be me again. I miss the real me, even though she comes out to play once in a while, normally when I'm on the roof with Cam. He's the only one that understands and loves me unconditionally. I don't want to think about not being at the same college as him. I'll go wherever he goes. I have no direction in life. He does. I can find a course of study anywhere. Anywhere that I feel safe and loved, and that's with Cam by my side. Cam is my normal, and I need normal.

Tonight was one of those moments of normalcy that I've begun to look forward to and crave over the past several years. I felt as though I didn't even have to put on an act. I could be me and not be judged.

I left the house shortly after Cam did and headed to my job at a clothing boutique at the mall.

"Hey, Aunt Terryn," I said, flying down the stairs, noticing that I had spent too much time figuring out what to wear and was now running late. "I'm off to work. I'm going to the bonfire at the beach after, but I'll drop my car off at home first and walk."

She raised her eyebrows at me. "Do you think that it's a good idea for you to be walking alone at night?"

"I'll be fine. It's only a few blocks. If it makes you feel better, I'll have Carla pick me up."

She raised herself off the floor where she was engaged in a rather intense arts and crafts project with Meg and Julianne, and walked toward me. Planting a kiss on my forehead, she said, "As long as you're comfortable walking, I'm comfortable with it, too."

Nodding, I began to head out the door.

"Oh, darling, what did your letter from the Jessamine Committee say?" she asked, although she probably already knew. She was one of the chairpersons of the committee, after all.

I plastered on my best appreciative smile. "I'm a finalist!" I squealed with fake enthusiasm. It was expected of me to want to participate in these pageants just like all of the teenage girls of Myrtle Beach who came from well-to-do families, like I now did. It's a bit ironic to know that it was these pageants that taught me all the skills I needed to pretend to be someone else. I learned how to smile wide for the judges. How to answer a question with the response that would earn me the most points. And how to be the girl everyone expected me to be.

"That's so great, sweetie!" She hugged me, bringing me back from my six-year period of deception.

"I have to go or I'll be late." I pulled out of her forced embrace.

"Of course, Marley. Have a good night at work."

I rushed out of the house and jumped in my sporty little Mustang that I bought with some of my pageant winnings. Within a record ten minutes, I pulled into the busy mall parking lot. For the first few hours, my shift went by with no excitement to speak of as I straightened up the clothes that had been thrown around during the Friday afternoon rush. About an hour after I got back from my break, I sensed a presence approach as I stood at a table, folding a bunch of t-shirts. Feeling a hand on my shoulder, I grabbed it in mine and pinned it behind the stranger's back, spinning around to face him...but it wasn't a stranger.

"Doug," I exhaled, my eyes growing wide as I released him from my hold. "I'm sorry. You know that I don't like it when people sneak up on me." I lowered my head and avoided his gaze. I had lost count of the number of times I had pinned him in that exact hold over the years.

"I know. That's why I did it. I like a girl who can take on a guy. But don't let it go to your head. If you weren't a girl, I'd have you on the ground in two seconds flat after that move."

My eyes scanned his tall frame, settling just below his waist as I raised my eyebrows in a playful manner. "Oh, really? Pretty sure I can get you laid out in less than a second, Douglas."

He instinctively backed up and covered his crotch with his hands.

"That's what I thought." I spun back around to continue my mindless chore of straightening the store.

"Are you going to the bonfire tonight?" he asked and I could feel his nerves from a few feet away.

"Maybe. Why do you ask?" Turning to face him once more, I placed my hands on my hips and smirked at him, heat rising in my cheeks in response to his attractive face, his formerly boyish features having grown more and more mature over the past year. Doug always dressed very well and tonight was no exception. His khaki shorts fell from his hips in such a way that made my heart speed up, especially when he lifted his hand and ran it through his dark hair, causing his polo shirt to rise up and expose a thin strip of his abs. I met his green eyes and tried to continue playing hard to get, but it was becoming more and more difficult, especially when he took several deliberate steps toward me and looked at me as if he wanted to consume every inch of me.

We had been playing this fun cat-and-mouse game for the better part of our junior year. There was something about him that I had been drawn to for as long as I could remember. He was my brother's best friend, which could make it a bit awkward if we were to date seriously, especially if things didn't work out. Then again, there was a reason my brother trusted him above anyone else he knew. If he was good enough for Cam, he was certainly good enough for me. He had always been the typical southern gentleman, holding the door open for me at school or when a big group of us would go somewhere to hang out. I would have been lying if I said that I didn't enjoy our past year of flirting. But relationships scared me. With relationships came intimacy and my past still haunted me, forcing me to refrain from getting too close to anyone.

"I want to take you," he said, his voice husky. "I mean...not take you in the sexual sense, but take you to the bonfire. With me." His expression turned from one of lust to one of unease and I could sense that he was embarrassed.

Always the one to try to rectify an awkward situation, I placed my hand on his shoulder and drew my body close to his. At five feet, eight inches, I was one of the tallest girls in my class, but Doug still towered over me by more than a half-foot. Standing on my toes, I whispered in his ear, "I'd love for you to take me, Douglas. Pick me up at my house at ten." I pulled back and winked before walking away from him. I could feel his eyes trained on my hips as I swayed them. And I was swaying them for him alone.

The rest of my shift passed painfully slow as I grew more and more excited about going to the bonfire with Doug. We had been out together numerous times in the past but it was always with other friends. Granted, we would be heading to the bonfire where approximately a hundred of our classmates would be but, this time, I was going with him and not simply seeing him there. As I was leaving the store after we closed, I couldn't help but think that maybe a normal, high school relationship was what I needed to finally be what I had wanted to be for so long... Normal.

I pulled up in front of my house a little after nine-thirty and ran inside to make myself look presentable. Changing out of the jeans and top that I wore to work, I found a white sundress to wear, making sure my back was fully covered. I applied lotion to my olive-toned legs and sprayed a bit of perfume behind my ears. Adjusting my long blonde hair so that the waves framed my face in a carefree manner, I grabbed a light blue cardigan and a pair of flip-flops before bounding down the steps.

Almost instantly, there was a quiet knock. I glanced at the clock and saw that it was quarter to ten. Pulling back the door, I was surprised to see Doug standing there.

"You're early," I commented.

"Yeah," he agreed, shuffling his feet, visibly nervous. "I saw you pull up with your car. Then, just a minute ago, I saw the light in your room go out and figured you were ready. I took a risk and hoped I was right."

I beamed at him. "Well, looks like you were." I stepped onto our front porch and locked up behind me, throwing my house keys into my hobo bag. "Don't worry. I don't think it's weird or anything that you were staking out my house," I joked, clutching onto his outstretched arm, walking down the steps toward his car. "Creeper."

Blushing, he turned to face me. "Sorry. I was just excited, I guess. I didn't want to waste another second of tonight."

Butterflies swam in my stomach as I processed the words that came out of his mouth. There was an electricity between us that had never been there before...or, at least, that I had never noticed. Maybe it was because I finally realized I wanted to stop with the cat-and-mouse game and let him catch me. Part of me had a feeling that he had already caught me ages ago, but it just took my brain this long to figure it out.

The intensity in his gaze caught me off-guard and I was a mess of nerves and hormones...never a good combination, especially in a darkened car. "Do you want to just walk?" I asked hopefully. "It's only a few blocks and, chances are, you'll never find a spot in the public lot anyway."

"Okay," he agreed, leading me past his car and toward the main street going out to the beach. The mood was tense, the silence between us uncomfortable as we awkwardly enjoyed each other's company.

"Thanks for asking me to come. I mean, tonight... I mean, for asking me to go to the bonfire with you. Not for asking me to come. That doesn't sound right." My face flamed red with embarrassment.

He smiled at me and winked. "No but, if you ask me, it sounds good."

I halted in my tracks, completely frozen in place. *I can do this*, I said to myself. *He was just joking. He doesn't mean anything by it. It's just a harmless joke, Marley. Just a joke.*

He noticed my reaction and turned to face me on the street. "I'm so sorry, Marley. That was completely inappropriate. I don't know what possessed me to say that. That's not the way my mama raised me. I really am a good guy. I normally wouldn't joke like that. You've got to believe that I didn't mean anything by it. Please." He slumped his shoulders, the formerly confident Doug replaced by a Doug that was full of remorse. "I understand if you don't want to come with me."

My eyes grew wide, more in irony than dread or concern.

"I mean, you don't have to go to the bonfire with me. God, I really hate that word right now."

I giggled. "Me, too." I raised my head and met his pleading eyes. I could tell that he was bracing for me to turn around and walk away from him, but that was the last thing I wanted to do.

"Come. Say it with me. Come..." I said to him. "It feels good." Throwing my head back to look at the stars

34

in the sky, I shouted to the heavens, *"Come!"* I raised my arms like an angel and spun around, screaming the word over and over again. I must have looked like a spectacle, but I didn't care. I didn't want one word to come between what could blossom into a good thing with Doug.

I slowed my spins, but the sky kept moving even when I stopped. I attempted to regain my balance, but soon found myself tripping over my own feet.

Two arms were around me instantly, preventing me from falling to the ground. "Whoa. Careful, Marley Jane."

I closed my eyes and basked at the sound of his voice calling me Marley Jane. Cam called me that all the time, but there was something so warm, affectionate, and thrilling about my first and middle name rolling off Doug's tongue. Focusing my gaze on his, I was met with his brilliant green eyes.

"Hey," I breathed.

"Hey."

"You still haven't said it."

He scrunched his eyebrows at me. "Said what?"

A grin crossed my face. "Come."

He chuckled, and the way his body shook made me want to melt into his arms so that our two bodies were entwined as one, never to be separated again. Leaning down, his breath was hot on my neck. My spine tingled.

"Come, Marley Jane," he whispered.

My eyes fluttered in the back of my head, overwhelmed with the effect that his body and voice had. This was completely new to me. It was exciting, exhilarating, and petrifying at the same time.

I licked my lips as I searched his eyes to prepare myself for his next move. I could tell he was conflicted with how to act. *Time to take the bull by the horns and grow a set*, I said to myself.

"What are you waiting for? An engraved invitation?"

"For what?" he asked in earnest.

"To kiss me."

"Are you sure?"

"If I didn't want you to kiss me, I wouldn't have asked you to. So kiss me, Doug. I know you want to. You've wanted to since we dissected that frog in Biology class last October."

He tightened his hold on me and before I could add any more quips, his lips were pressed firmly against mine. I ran my hands through his thick hair as he kept my body close to his, supporting me, making sure I was steady on my feet, even though the touch of his lips on mine made me feel anything but grounded. I felt as if I was floating in the air, the sensation of his caring and gentle movements opening up my heart to new feelings and emotions.

He pulled away from me and I was left panting. "That was some kiss," I commented.

"You're right about one thing."

"Oh, yeah? What's that?"

"Well, you were right that it was some kiss. But you were most certainly wrong about me wanting to kiss you since dissecting a frog in Biology."

A disappointed look crossed my face at the thought that he didn't actually want to kiss me.

He nuzzled my neck and nipped on my earlobe. "I had been wanting to kiss you since we were paired up on that astronomy project in Earth Science in ninth grade." He planted a sensual kiss on my neck before raising me so that I was standing straight once more. Winking, he grabbed my hand in his and said, "See. You were dead wrong, Marley Jane."

I tried to hide my excitement as we walked the few blocks toward the beach, but it was useless. Out of nowhere, a light streaked from the sky and into the ocean. I gasped in shock.

"What?"

I pointed toward the shore. "It's a shooting star," I said, my voice low and contemplative.

He stared at me as if waiting for me to elaborate.

"My grams," I began. "She had this thing. She would always say that was how we would know our relatives who passed before us made it to wherever they went when they died. She said the shooting star was their way of letting us know that they were happy and were watching over us." I continued walking on the beach, the heat of the approaching bonfire warming my skin. "Maybe that's Grams' way of saying that I'm doing something right."

He nudged me. "I hope it's Grams' way of saying that she approves of me."

"It's not her approval you have to worry about. Or have you forgotten that I have a *very* protective twin brother?" I winked as we greeted a bunch of familiar faces that were huddled around the fire on the sand, coolers and beach chairs making a maze of the area.

He rested his hand on my hip, his arms warming me in the cool summer night. "Perhaps. I have a feeling he'll be more than okay with us. I already asked him."

I turned to face him. "When? Why?"

"Well, he's my friend, and I didn't want him to think I was like half of the guys we go to school with that make comments to him about your legs or chest or anything else. I've never done that. And I *won't* ever do that. I just wanted him to know that my intentions weren't to just add another notch on my belt and that I do care for you.

A lot. More than I think you realize, Marley Jane."

That's all he ever had to do and I couldn't stay angry or upset at him. His apparent admiration and devotion to me was shocking and comforting at the same time. For that brief moment in time as I raised myself onto my toes and planted an innocent, but affectionate kiss on his lips, effectively announcing our relationship to everyone at the bonfire that night, I felt as if I could finally move on from my past. I felt as if I was finally normal.

# CHAPTER FIVE

## *CATCH YOU WHEN YOU FALL*

*Cam*

I NEVER WANTED TO leave work so badly but, at the same time, stay at work so desperately that I could ever remember. I had no idea what came over me when I asked Brianna if she wanted to go with me to the bonfire tonight.

I lived just a few blocks from the beach so I went home first, dropping off the cannoli that Anita gave me for Meg and Julianne.

"Hey, sweetie," my aunt said, walking down the stairs wearing her bathrobe.

"Hey. I'm not staying," I whispered in hushed tones, trying not to wake up anyone that was sleeping. "I'm meeting a few people at the beach."

"Good. Marley's down there already."

"Oh really?" This was news to me. Although she typically had a rather full social calendar so it shouldn't have come as a surprise, this summer was different for both of us with our grams being sick. "With who?"

Aunt Terryn grinned. "I was putting the girls to bed when she came in so I missed her, but it looks like Doug came to pick her up." She gestured to the front windows overlooking the street. I followed her gaze to see my best friend's black Pontiac sitting out front.

"Okay. I'm just going to change real quick and then head out. Love ya."

She smiled her perfect smile at me, her blue eyes sincere. "I love you, too, Cameron."

I ran up the stairs as fast as I could. I hated the thought of Brianna sitting in her car in the public lot waiting for me for too long. It would be a horrible first impression, although I'm pretty sure her first impression of me was back in sixth grade when I arrived in Myrtle Beach as the new kid at the middle school, story after story of who Marley and I were spreading amongst the students like it was newsworthy. I guess at the age of eleven, a new student is the height of excitement. Two new students is like Christmas come early, especially when they're fraternal twins.

Once in my bedroom, I stripped out of my black pants and polo shirt that was the uniform at the restaurant. Hastily gliding on some deodorant and tossing on a white button-down shirt and khaki shorts, I slid into a pair of flip flops, and was downstairs and heading out the door toward the beach in just a little more than a minute.

The streets of Myrtle Beach were calm that Friday night. A friend of ours had been hosting these bonfires at his parents' beach house every weekend all summer, but this was the first one I was able to attend. Ever since school let out in May, Marley and I had been spending every free moment possible with our grams. When we weren't with her, we still avoided parties, our minds preoccupied with her deteriorating health. Even on the Fourth of July, when everyone else was dancing and laughing at the bonfire, we stayed at home, watching the fireworks from the safety and security of the roof of our house just a few blocks away from the festivities. I

40

wouldn't have wanted to celebrate the holiday any other way.

The sounds of the bonfire filtered through the air as I approached the public parking lot, searching for Brianna's vintage orange Volkswagen Beetle. I could just imagine how her mother reacted when she pulled up in her driveway with that car. In my opinion, having grown up with a dad who was a car enthusiast, it was a piece of art. Spotting it, my breath caught at the sight of the beautiful brunette's long legs hanging out of the driver's side as she applied lotion, the moon illuminating her slender frame.

I approached with caution, not wanting to startle her. She appeared to be rather entranced in the act of rubbing her legs. There was something strangely erotic and comforting about the simple gesture, and I was secretly jealous of her hands. I wanted those to be my hands on her skin, caressing her, rubbing the silky lotion into her sleek legs.

Sand crunched under my footsteps and she looked up, a heartfelt smile greeting me.

"Cam," she breathed, placing her feet on the ground and walking up to me.

"Thanks for agreeing to meet me here," I responded nervously, my eyes glued to her beautiful pink lips.

"Thanks for asking me."

We stared at each other for what could have been seconds or hours while I tried to figure out how to proceed. I had been out with girls before, but never in an intimate or romantic setting. I had hung out with Brianna on numerous occasions when we were in middle school and she was invited to my sister's parties, but this was different. I didn't know why I never dated anyone. Girls flirted with me and I was an attractive-enough guy. I guess it all went back to my protective nature. I knew how apprehensive Marley had been about pursuing a serious relationship. Keeping her happy and comfortable had always been my top priority. I guess giving Marley a shoulder to cry on or an ear to listen to had become a full-time job, not leaving much time for anything else. I just hoped it was enough for her.

"Want to go check out the bonfire?" Brianna asked, waking me from my thoughts.

"Sure. Sorry. I drifted off there for a minute." I held out my arm for her to hang on to and led her across the sand toward the smoke and orange hue that was illuminating the night sky.

"It's okay. I'm used to it," she replied as a gust of wind blew from the shore, throwing her off balance.

"Whoa!" I cautioned, reacting quickly and wrapping my arms around her to steady her, enclosing her in my embrace. It was the closest we had ever been to each other. It was the closest I had ever been to *any* girl my age, besides Marley.

Looking down into her eyes, the glimmer of the ocean making them dance, my breathing increased from the depth I could see.

"You okay?" I asked quietly.

She kept her gaze glued to mine and nodded. Her lips parted slightly and her sweet breath caressed my skin. Nothing I had ever experienced in my life felt as warm and inviting as having Brianna's body pressed against mine.

"Cam…" she exhaled.

"Bri…" I replied, my voice soft as my eyes roamed her angelic face from her big brown eyes, to her small button-like nose, and finally settled on her full, pouty lips. I wondered what they tasted like.

"What are you waiting for?"

Nervous energy flowed through me in response to her sultry tone. "What do you mean?"

She titled her head toward me, her mouth just a breath away from my neck. "Kiss me, Cam. I know you want to. Or, at least, I *think* you want to. *Do* you want to?" she asked, her face flashing red in embarrassment.

"Of course. Do *you* want to, though? I mean, I don't want you to want to kiss me just because you think *I* want to kiss *you*. If you don't, I'm okay with not kissing you. Well, I'm not okay. It'll suck to not kiss you when I've been thinking about it since freshman year, but you don't have to kiss me if you don't want to."

She ran her fingers through my disheveled hair and my heartbeat increased dramatically. "I want you to kiss me," she said, a wide grin on her face. "And I plan on kissing you back." The most adorable scowl crossed her face. "I'm not so sure there should be this much discussion before a first kiss, Cam. It takes the spontaneity out of it a bit, don't you think?"

"Can I get a do-over?" I asked.

She nodded her head, smiling excitedly. "Help me up and then you can catch me again."

"Okay," I said, raising her body. "I just hope I can still salvage our first kiss." I winked at her.

"I have faith that you can, Cameron," her sweet voice assured me. "Are you ready to catch me?"

I met her eyes. "I'll always catch you when you fall."

She swooned in a dramatic manner, falling into my arms. My eyes roamed to her lips as she moistened them with her tongue. Lowering my head toward hers, I kept my hand firmly planted on the small of her back, holding her in place. I brushed my lips with hers and she moved against me in perfect synchronicity. Sliding my tongue across her lips, she opened her mouth in response. Our tongues met and I couldn't remember ever feeling so aroused.

I ran my hand down the contours of her frame, holding on to her hip and bringing her body closer to mine. I felt her shiver and her breathing increased as my tongue continued to caress hers. Pulling back, I knew I needed to stop before I could no longer hide my need for her.

"We should probably go join the party, don't you think?" I asked, looking down into her eyes.

She nodded and I helped her steady herself. Grabbing her hand in mine, I turned to head to the bonfire, Brianna at my side.

"Please tell me that I just witnessed the first kiss," I heard before I saw the blonde hair of my sister running toward us. "Did I?" she asked excitedly.

I could feel my ears turn red in embarrassment. "Maybe."

She grabbed my other hand and walked the rest of the way with us. "I think I did. I know you haven't kissed before so unless you two were sucking face at the restaurant earlier...gross, by the way...I totally witnessed the first kiss." She looked past me toward Brianna and winked. "And it's about freaking time, Cameron Michael."

I shook my head and glanced at Brianna. "Sorry. I can't do anything about her. She's been harping on me to finally make the first move with you all year, even when you were still dating Mason."

"*She* is right next to you...and he's right. He's liked you since freshman year. It's about time he made his move, isn't it?"

Brianna grinned and nodded fervently. "Yeah, especially considering I had a thing for him since seventh grade Geometry class."

Marley laughed and the sound brought a smile to my heart. "The Pythagorean Theorem is a big turn-on for me, too. Oh, baby. The word hypotenuse does things to me." The two girls giggled.

At that moment, everything was perfect. I had a beautiful girl whose kisses lit my entire body on fire. I had a best friend and sister who was finally past all the trauma she had endured early on in life. And we were about to start our senior year of high school. I had a feeling that it was going to be a year I'd never forget…

# CHAPTER SIX

## *FORGIVENESS*

*Cam*

"CAMERON, CAN YOU GO make sure that Marley is up?"
Aunt Terryn asked the following morning when I walked
into the kitchen.

"Sure. Where's Uncle Graham?"

She slammed the refrigerator door shut, startling me.
"He is playing in a golf tournament today. He said it was
for the church and was necessary."

I narrowed my eyes at her. "So are *you* taking us
today?"

She shrugged her shoulders, beating eggs in a glass
bowl somewhat roughly. "I guess I don't really have a
choice, do I?"

"I'll drive us so that you don't have to."

"No." Her voice was firm. "Absolutely not. Out of the
question."

"Okay. We can try to reschedule, maybe see if Uncle
Graham can take us during the week or something
instead. I'll call Mama and ask her if she can take a day
off."

Shaking her head, she said, "No. I appreciate your
understanding, but I need to learn to move past this. It
still pisses me off to no end that she abandoned you kids,

46

but I can't let that interfere with her attempt to make amends for her past and to form a relationship with you and Marley. You need a mother and so does your sister."

"We have one. Well, technically, two."

She smiled, standing on her tiptoes to kiss my cheek. "You're a good kid. Whenever I get irritated with the situation, I just look at you and Marley and realize that she must have done *something* right before your father was killed."

"It was a group effort," I responded, trying to lighten the tension in the room. "I'll go wake up Marley, but I may need some of this." I grabbed a mug and poured some coffee into it, fixing it the way that I knew Marley liked it.

I excused myself and ran up the steps, knocking on her door. "Mar, time to get up."

A girlish giggle sounded from beyond the wall.

"Mar, are you okay in there?"

She giggled again.

"I'm coming in so you better be decent." Hesitantly, I turned the knob, surprised to see Marley sitting at her vanity, the biggest grin on her face that I had ever seen. "What are you so giddy about?" I asked. "Still on cloud nine after your kiss with Doug?" I set her coffee down in front of her.

"No," she said coyly. "I mean, yes. But that's not what I'm excited about. And it's none of your business anyway." She spun in her chair, attempting to avoid my eyes as she pulled a piece of notebook paper out of her bag, her smile illuminating the entire room.

"Did he leave a love letter in your purse?" I plopped down on her bed and lay back, placing my hands behind my head.

"It's not a love letter. It's an 'I really like you so I

47

slipped a secret note in your purse when you weren't looking' letter." She raised her eyebrows at me. "You should take some tips from Doug to use with Brianna."

"Don't worry about me. I've got my own moves, and there is no way I'm sharing them with you or Doug. Hurry up and get ready. Aunt Terryn has to take us today."

Marley's joyful expression quickly turned severe. "Do you think that's such a good idea?"

"No, I don't, but Uncle Graham had to go play in some golf tournament for the church so she's stuck. She doesn't want to deprive Mama of her weekly time with us because of her opinion of her."

Marley looked down and toyed with her fingers in her lap. "Do you blame her, though?"

"I don't," I replied, sighing. "It took me a while to forgive Mama, but I think her spending three years in prison and having us taken away from her was punishment enough. You see how she looks at us every week." I sat up and gave her a questioning look. "You *can* see it, can't you?"

"Yeah, I guess," she conceded, turning her eyes from me. "I just wish it's as easy for me to forgive her as it is for you. You're a better person than I am, Cam."

"I'm not a better person, Mar. I'm just moving on with my life and taking it one day at a time. Same as you. Same as Aunt Terryn. Same as Uncle Graham. And same as Mama."

She got up and walked toward the bed, sitting next to me. I wrapped my arms around her. "Some days are easier to forgive Mama than others," I admitted.

She pulled back and scrunched her eyebrows at me. "What do you mean? I thought you *had* forgiven her."

"Yeah. But the way I look at it, forgiveness is an

ongoing process, at least for me. Some days, I feel that I need to carry the hate around and not forgive her or anyone else because of everything. Those are usually the days when I hear you screaming and crying in your sleep. I hate that, Mar. I wish I could take the nightmares away."

She visibly cowered and I could sense that she was uneasy about the direction our conversation had turned.

"You don't have to put on an act in front of me, Marley Jane." I pulled her into me once more, calming the fears that pervaded her for the better part of the past decade of our lives. "You don't have to hide from me."

"I'm not hiding from you…"

"Just everyone else then?"

"Maybe. I just don't want to let anyone down. I keep thinking that if I do normal things, like date, maybe I can finally be normal. And I felt that last night, Cam. When Doug kissed me and I was shouting 'come' at the top of my lungs…"

"Wait. What?" I interrupted.

She blushed, laughing. "It's a funny word and we were both nervous and kept saying come, but the way it was said, it could have had a double meaning. I could tell that he wasn't being himself because of it, and that bothered me. So I shouted it over and over again. And then I made him say it, too. It was a wonderful ice-breaker."

I planted a kiss on her forehead before getting off her bed so she could get ready in peace. "Another one of your theater tricks?" I glanced back at her and saw the Marley that very few people had the good fortune of seeing.

"You bet your ass it was." She winked.

"Okay. Get ready."

"Cam…" she said, her voice soft.

I turned around and met her brilliant blue eyes. I knew

exactly what she wanted when I saw the expression on her face.

"To the moon and back, Mar."

"From the stars to the ocean, Cam."

# CHAPTER SEVEN

## *MAMA*

*Marley's Journal*

*August 30*

WEEKLY VISITATION WITH MAMA was today. It started out just like any other Saturday, except Aunt Terryn had to take us instead of Uncle Graham. There has always been a great deal of animosity and distrust between Mama and Aunt Terryn, with good reason.

The two-hour car ride from Myrtle Beach to the suburb outside of Columbia was filled with tension, and I could see Aunt Terryn's knuckles turning white from the harsh grip she had on the steering wheel. I wondered if her jaw was going to lock in place due to the severe look on her face, her teeth grinding every few minutes. I just prayed that a cat-fight didn't break out. I had a feeling it wouldn't, not when our court-ordered case worker was required to be at all of our visitations.

"Marley Jane," Mama exhaled, raising herself off the couch as we walked into the living room. "Cameron Michael." She headed toward Cam and me, and pulled both of us against her small and slight body, hugging us. I inhaled and smelled the scent that could only be described as Mama. It was a mixture of baby powder, jasmine, and innocence lost.

"Hey, Mama," Cam said, planting a kiss on her cheek.

"Are you kids hungry? You must be after that long drive." She looked at us before her eyes settled on our aunt standing behind us.

"Terryn… What an unexpected surprise. Can I get you anything to drink or eat?"

Cam and I both turned to stare at her. "No, Grace," she responded curtly, obviously mustering all of her energy to remain cordial. "I just wanted to drop them off and ensure that Mrs. Gibson was, in fact, here." She gestured toward our middle-aged case worker crocheting on a rocking chair in the corner of the modest living room. "I have plans to meet up with some friends, but I'll be back at five o'clock sharp for them."

Mama smiled agreeably at her. "I wouldn't expect anything less. Enjoy your day in Columbia," she responded, her voice exuding the southern hospitality we were all accustomed to. She ushered both of us away from the front door and into the kitchen. "Now, tell me how the bonfire was last night."

The hours passed with ease as we sat on the back deck of Mama's small house just outside of our state capital. The air was thick with a late summer humidity, but that didn't bother us. Every so often, Mrs. Gibson would poke her head outside, apparently making sure that Mama wasn't firing up the crack pipe or injecting a needle in her arm.

I understood the court's reasons for ordering supervised visits at first, but once she had shown that she had cleaned up her act and obtained gainful employment, I thought they would re-evaluate their original decree. I had a sneaky feeling that the animosity Aunt Terryn had toward Mama played a factor in it. I wouldn't be surprised to have found out that she encouraged Uncle Graham to make a few phone calls to the judge, a fellow parishioner, who was assigned to this case. It didn't bother me too much, but I could tell it was hard for Mama to constantly have a reminder of the dark time in her life judging her actions.

"I'll be right back," Cam said, interrupting my thoughts. "Nature calls. Anyone need a water while I'm in there?"

I shook my head and closed my eyes, basking in the warm Carolina sun.

"I'm all set, sweetheart," Mama said.

I heard the screen door open and close, the only other sounds that of the occasional fly buzzing around my head and squeal of children playing in the neighborhood.

"Marley Jane," Mama said in hushed tones once we were alone.

I took caution at her voice. Opening my eyes, I looked at her kind and loving face, and could sense a hint of urgency in her demeanor that wasn't there seconds beforehand.

She clutched my hand in hers and gazed at me affectionately. Taking a deep breath, she began, "I was warned not to tell you this, but I think it's wrong to keep it from you."

I straightened my spine, my heart racing at her words and tone. "What is it, Mama?"

"I could get into a lot of trouble for saying anything. Your uncle and aunt wanted to keep you in the dark, but I think you should know. I think you *deserve* to know." She closed her eyes and when she opened them, I saw what Cam was talking about. I saw the remorse. I saw the pain. I saw the hurt. Most of all, I saw the confused and broken-hearted woman that my mama was when my dad died all those years ago. I saw the grief and shame she must have been living with day-in and day-out, knowing that she put herself in a comatose drug-induced haze while her boyfriend did whatever he wanted with a little girl.

"It's about Buck," she said gravely.

My eyes grew wide at the mention of that name. It had been years since I had last heard it, telling the social worker what he did to me. At first, I hated that Cam didn't kill him, but I figured spending a lifetime rotting away in a prison cell was retribution enough.

"What about...*him?*" I asked, unable to bring myself to even say the name.

"Sweetheart, he was granted parole."

My chin began to quiver at the thought of that monster roaming the streets. I could just picture his larger-than-life body leaning on a lamp post outside of the nearest school yard in a rundown area of town. I still remember the first time I saw him. He was so nice and inviting, offering to teach me how to play softball. He slowly ingrained himself into our family, looking after us while Mama was on another one of her drug relapses. Then he changed. He changed me. He changed Cam. And he changed Mama. He preyed on all of us. He promised Mama drugs, feeding her addiction so that he could feed his. Cam and I paid the ultimate price.

"I'm sorry, Marley," Mama said, bringing me back from my thoughts. "I don't know how it happened. I don't even know how he was up for it. He shouldn't have been eligible for another fifteen years. Part of me thinks this whole war on drugs has something to do with it. Why keep child predators in prison when people who are busted with an ounce of marijuana are, apparently, a greater danger to society?" She rolled her eyes, her disdain for our justice system obvious.

"I was going to keep my mouth shut, but I just had a bad feeling in my gut that something horrible could happen if I didn't at least warn you. Call it maternal instincts." She looked away. "I wish I had those instincts all those years…" Trailing off, she caught her lip in her teeth, attempting to hide her emotions.

"It's okay, Mama." I looked straight ahead, trying to summon the strength to be the bigger person. "I forgive you," I said quietly.

"What, Marley?" I could hear the surprise and relief in her voice.

I turned toward her and saw the tears flowing freely down her face from her silver eyes. "I'm letting go of my resentment and bitterness. It's too big of a burden for me to continue to carry. It took Cam to make me see that this animosity was holding me back. And I don't want to be held back anymore. I want to be a normal teenager. And I think forgiving you is the first step I need to take."

"Oh, come here, Marley Jane." She held her arms out to me and I climbed on her lap, remembering all the times she would rock me to sleep when I was a little girl. "I've been waiting to hear those words come out of your mouth for years. I know it's going to take time, but I'd really like for us to go back to the way things were before…"

"Me, too, Mama…except I'm not going to play My Little Ponies with you."

She laughed and, for the first time, I felt at ease with her. I put her needs ahead of mine.

"Sorry. Am I interrupting?" Cam's voice broke through the intense atmosphere.

I wiped my eyes, as did Mama, and she released me from her embrace. I got up from her lap and sat back in my lounge chair. "Nope. Not interrupting. We just had a little mother-daughter bonding. That's all. You have a penis, so you weren't invited."

"Marley Jane Bowen!" my mother scolded in complete exasperation. "I taught you to act like a lady. Do you want me to wash your mouth out with soap?"

I glanced at her and smiled. It was good to have my mama back.

# CHAPTER EIGHT

## *NEWS*

*Cam*

AFTER FINALLY GETTING BACK from our weekly visitation with Mama, I dragged myself into my room, thinking that it was probably time to start going through the stack of college applications that were sitting on my desk. Just as I was about to print my name on the first one, I heard a gentle knock on the wall, followed by the sound of Marley opening the window in her room. Shaking my head, I knew what she wanted.

Opening my own window, I climbed onto the roof and made my way toward Marley as she lay on her back, gazing at the night sky. After lying there in silence for over twenty minutes, I could tell she wanted to talk, but didn't know where to start.

"So it looks like you and Mama reached a turning point today," I said, breaking the ice.

Out of the corner of my eye, I noticed her wipe her cheek.

"Are you okay, Mar?" I inched toward her, grabbing her hand in mine. Nothing would prepare me for the words that were about to leave her mouth.

"Buck's out," she said, her voice barely above a whisper.

Shock and confusion covered my expression. "What do you mean?" I asked with a raised voice.

"Shhh…" she said, sitting up and looking at me. "Quiet or they'll hear us." She gestured down below to the lower level of our house.

"Who cares? They're both more than aware that we sit out here."

She shook her head. "No. It's not that, Cam." She lowered her voice and her eyes had a fury and magnitude that I had never seen before. "Mama told me. She said that Aunt Terryn and Uncle Graham didn't want us to know…didn't want *me* to know. Mama listened at first, but she told me today while you were in the bathroom. She said she had a bad feeling in her gut that something horrible would happen if she listened to them and didn't say anything."

Sitting up, I pulled Marley's body into mine as I processed what it meant. "He's not allowed to come near you. You don't have to worry about him hurting you again, Mar. I swear to you."

"I know," she said calmly, her lack of emotion somewhat surprising. "I get what you were telling me about forgiveness now. I don't forgive him for what he did and I never will, but I *can* accept it for what it was and move on from it. I can stop carrying the burden of hate I had toward Mama for her lack of judgment. I felt normal last night and I want more of that. I felt normal today, too. I like that Mama and I have turned a corner."

"Good. I'm glad. It's been a long time coming, if you ask me."

It was silent for a moment while we stared at the ocean.

"Do you know where he is?" I asked a few minutes later. "Buck… Did Mama say where he was or what happened?"

"No. All she said was that he was granted parole about six months ago, even though he shouldn't have been up for another fifteen years or so."

"That sucks. If you ask me, our parole board shouldn't be elected officials."

"I didn't know that."

"You really should have taken Governments with me this past year."

She laughed. "The only reason you took that was to suck up to Brianna's father because he teaches it."

"Maybe." My eyes went wide. "Mar..." I turned to face her. "Her step-dad... He's a former judge! Surely he would be able to access that information and could tell us what happened! Hell, maybe he could even get it revoked!"

"Cam, I'm not supposed to know. Mama will be in the doghouse with Aunt Terryn and Uncle Graham if they find out she said anything. And you know that the first person Mr. Grayson will call is Uncle Graham. It's not worth it."

"I guess you're right," I replied dejectedly, lying back down on the roof, Marley following my lead, the sound of Guns N' Roses blaring from a car as it zoomed toward the shore. "Do you think you could at least find out where he lives? That way we'll know whether he's nearby or not."

"I'll ask Mama next weekend and see if she knows. I'm certain that the court would have sent notice to Uncle Graham, so there's got to be an official document in this house somewhere, unless they got rid of it."

"I'll try to snoop around some time after school this week when Aunt Terryn takes the girls to dance class," I offered.

She groaned in irritation. "Freaking dance class.

They'll just be put through the wringer like the rest of us. I wish I could stop it."

"What do you mean?" I asked.

"Nothing, Cam," she exhaled. "Don't worry about it."

"If something's bothering you, I *do* worry about it, Mar. You know that."

"I know. It's just the amount of pressure that these families put on girls. Look at little Julianne. She's not even five and she's already in dance class. Did you see the costume she wore at the recital a few weeks ago? And all the makeup that was plastered on her face? There's this horrible expectation placed on girls to look pretty and act in a certain manner. They'll go through it, too, Cam. And it breaks my heart to think that Meg and Jules won't be able to do anything to stop it. They'll get suckered into the limelight and the pageantry, not wanting to look at Aunt Terryn's disappointed face if you say that you don't want to compete anymore. And she'll say that so-and-so's daughter, your friend, loves the competitions and the pageants. So you feel guilt. Guilt at the thought of letting her down because this is what she did when she was growing up. And guilt for thinking that you're not the perfect little girl you're supposed to be. I just wish I could stop it. But I can't."

I had no idea how to respond to this. Marley was one of the smartest and most observant girls in school. She saw the spectacle of the pageants and competitions that girls begged to participate in as what they really were…a contest between the moms to gain bragging rights among their close-minded circle of friends.

"You could quit, Mar. Tell people how you really feel about it all."

She shook her head. "If I pull out of the Jessamine Court, they'll just replace me with someone else. My opinion won't stop it. We're all powerless to change anything. I'll suffer through this last year of high school knowing that I can leave this all behind me in college and start over again...with you."

"Mar..." I said in a cautioning tone. "We've talked about this. You need to go where you need to go, and I need to go where I do."

She grabbed my hand in hers and turned to meet my eyes. "I *will* go where I need to go. Wherever you are and are happy is where I need to be."

I couldn't help but smile at her words. Marley and I had been through everything together. We had held each other's hands through all the turmoil and dysfunction of the early years of our lives. We supported each other and laughed together as we blossomed into our teenage years. I was more than aware we had a bond that most kids my age would think was strange. I wouldn't give this connection up for anything. Marley was my other half. She was my heart. She was my light. She was my best friend. She was my voice of reason. She was my everything. And I knew I was all those things to her, too.

"To the moon and back, Mar."

"From the stars to the ocean, Cam."

# CHAPTER NINE

## *HYPOCRISY*

*Marley's Journal*

*August 31*

THIS TOWN EMBODIES HYPOCRISY. I can smell it in the air. I can feel it as the wind brushes my skin. I can taste it in the water. And I can see it when I look around at the people of my uncle's church every Sunday. Hypocrites. "Pray to God," they say. "And he'll free you of your sins." What about other peoples' sins? And what if their sins still haunt me? What do I do about that?

I'll tell you what you do, Marley. You go to church. You sit in the front pew with your aunt, the pastor's wife, their two kids, and your brother. You smile. You shake hands with your fellow parishioners. You nod when they say how far you've come since you first stepped foot in this town, beaten, bruised, and tormented. Of course they didn't know the truth. They didn't know you were abused every day. Such dignified people don't talk about such things. No. They simply thought our drug-addicted mother could no longer take care of us. You bite your tongue when they say that they prayed for you to find your way. Little do they know that I'm still as lost as I ever was.

I had never gone to church when I was growing up. As far as I could remember, it wasn't until Cam and I came to live with our aunt and uncle that we had ever stepped foot in a house of God. They both tried to infuse religion into our lives, but I don't think it's worked. I'm not saying I don't believe in God. I just wonder how this all-loving, all-forgiving being could possibly allow a man to harm a little girl. Where was God when that was happening?

Listening to my uncle preach from his pulpit today, my body was in the poised position that I had mastered over the last six years…back straight; legs crossed at the ankles; small, yet pleasant smile on my face. All eyes of the church were not only on my uncle, but also on us. Any bad behavior on our part reflected poorly on him. Be well-behaved. Be gentile. Be perfect. Be anything but what you truly are. It wasn't just me, either. Looking around the church, every last person was pretending to be someone they weren't. Jessica Harper, the school slut, sat across the aisle from me, praying and nodding in agreement with my uncle as he spoke of saving yourself for marriage. She couldn't even save herself for a week! But there she sat, her body in the same position as mine, her legs crossed at the ankles…even though we all knew they were spread wide open the night before.

We were all puppets. Every single one of us. The cycle had been going on for years and we'd all been powerless to stop it.

A loud grunting sound brought me back from my thoughts and my entire body stiffened, the air sucked from my lungs.

I felt a hand grab mine and looked to my left, meeting my brother's silver eyes. He squeezed and gave me a reassuring nod. I hated the guttural sound of a man clearing his throat. That's what *he* always did. It brought me back there...to that horrible time in my life when all these peoples' God was nowhere to be found. My uncle always told me that He has a purpose for everything, even in horrific events. I wonder what His purpose was in allowing a grown man to molest and beat me every night. I don't see what it could possibly be. I don't think I ever will.

I heard the sound again and all I could see was a sweaty body on top of mine. All I could hear were my screams echoing in my head. All I could smell was the scent of nicotine and stale beer. My chin quivered and I felt as if I was losing control of everything. All it took was one sound, one vocalization from a human throat, and I was back in that dingy apartment.

As my uncle spoke of God's plan, I couldn't take it anymore. I bolted from the pew and ran down the aisle, gossiping eyes glued to me as I retreated from the sanctuary and into the church basement, locking myself in the ladies' room. I could feel the whispers of the congregation on my skin as I splashed water on my face, trying to shake the memories.

I hated how the smallest things set me off, forcing me to return to that horrible time in my life. It always seemed to happen just when I thought I could move on and have a normal, teenage life. As much as I tried to convince myself that I was moving forward, it was almost like the world was reminding me that I was still living in the past...like someone was trying to keep the fear and torment inside of me.

A gentle knock sounded as I peered at my reflection in the mirror, the image of a degraded eleven-year-old girl staring back at me regardless of the fact that I hadn't seen that person in over six years.

"Mar? It's me. Are you okay? Wait. Let me rephrase

that because I know you're *not* okay. Do you want to talk about it?"

Taking a deep breath, I tried to pull myself together so that Cam didn't see me so unsettled. It always worried him when I freaked out because of a memory. I hated the thought of constantly dragging him down because of my relapses. How much longer could he possibly be my lifeguard?

I opened the door and met his concerned eyes. "I'm fine, Cam. I just needed a minute. I'm sure Aunt Terryn is already on damage control, telling everyone that I have my period or something to explain why I left...other than the truth. God forbid anyone actually knew the truth!"

"Want to get out of here?" he asked, raising his eyebrows.

I glanced at the clock on the wall of the church basement, noting that the service wouldn't be over for another twenty minutes. There was no way in hell that I could go back in there.

Smiling, I nodded.

"Good. We're both going to get into so much trouble, but I don't give a fuck."

I placed my hand over my chest in faux shock. "Cameron Michael Bowen," I said in my playful gentile voice, "how dare you say the word fuck in a house of God! I do declare." I batted my eyelashes at him and my heart warmed at the smile on his face. I knew that no matter what I was going through, I could get through it as long as I could look at Cam and see him smile.

"Come on, Mar. Let's go break a few rules. Go big or go home! And I'm pretty sure you don't want to go home. Am I right?"

I nodded once more and before I knew it, Cam was hauling me out of the church basement, the potluck organizer glowering at us in disgust because we were ditching early. Cam must have noticed her displeasure and he turned around quickly. "Oh, Mrs. Dumond?"

I looked over his shoulder at her smug grin.

"I do hope you enjoy your Sunday potluck, but Marley and I are unable to attend. You see, Marley was molested and abused nearly every night for three years right after she turned eight, and certain sounds set her off. So, if you feel the need to spread lies and rumors about why we left, think about how you would feel if that were your daughter." There was a brief pause as her jaw dropped open in shock. "Brush that under the fucking rug, if you will."

He spun around and grabbed my hand, pulling me out of the church and toward his Wrangler. After opening the door and helping me in, he ran around to his side and started the engine, looking at me with a grin of satisfaction on his face. "I'm breaking *all* the rules today, Marley Jane. No matter what, we're going to get in trouble so let's make it worth it. What do you want to do?"

My eyes beamed with excitement. "Want to go on a road trip?"

He put his car in first and drove out of the church parking lot. "You bet. But, first, we need to make a few quick stops to stock up on provisions." He winked and I could finally shed the person I was forced to be for the last half-hour while I sat within those four walls of judgment.

# CHAPTER TEN

## *LIFE*

*Cam*

"ARE WE ACTUALLY GOING to do something, or are we just going to drive around town all day?" Marley huffed.

I looked into my rearview mirror at the back seat of my Wrangler, Marley's hand firmly enclosed in Doug's, and shook my head. "Mar, patience. We're leaving now."

She winked at me and reached into the front seat, grabbing Brianna's arm. "I'm so glad you were able to get out of the house."

Brianna smiled nervously. "Anything to escape for a minute."

"Where are we going?" Doug asked.

"Road trip."

"Go big or go home!" Marley exclaimed, repeating my words from earlier.

"We're going to Charleston. It's our last Sunday before starting school. We may as well enjoy the lack of homework while we can!" I pulled onto the interstate and headed south, the wind rustling through the open-top of my Jeep.

"How did you get away from church and everything today?!" Brianna shouted, glancing at Doug.

I chuckled. "Doug's Jewish. You didn't know that?"

Her face turned red. "No. I'm sorry, Doug. I had no idea."

He shrugged. "It's okay. It's not a disease or anything. And I get more holidays than all of you! My family's not really that Jewish. I mean, we do some holidays, but it's mostly for the food. I'm a sucker for a latke."

We all erupted in laughter and, for a little while, everything felt perfect. The miles between Myrtle Beach and Charleston passed with ease as we fought over who got to control the radio, Marley constantly leaning from the back to try to find Madonna, singing at the top of her lungs when she finally stumbled across a radio station playing *Vogue*. I laughed at Brianna and Marley and all their hand gestures as they sang along with the "Material Girl".

After a fun-filled two-hour drive with musical accompaniment that ranged from Janet Jackson to Metallica and everything in between, I finally pulled off the interstate and drove through the historic streets of downtown Charleston. Finding a public lot off of Market Street, I parked the Wrangler and our small little party went in search of amusement on that sunny, warm August day.

"Where to first?" I asked as we walked down a narrow cobblestone sidewalk, a horse-drawn carriage going by as it gave out-of-towners a tour of one of the most haunted cities in South Carolina.

"You know where," Marley replied, raising her eyebrows at me.

Groaning, I glanced over my shoulder at Doug, his eyes trained on Marley as if something horrible would happen if he looked away. "Hope you like to shop. Marley's got a thing for the central marketplace."

"It's fantastic, Cam!" she protested. "Where else can

you look at table after table of homemade goods, instead of that crappy commercial stuff you get everywhere else? I'm all about supporting the little guy. And I plan on supporting them with my latest paycheck!"

"Fine. But if Doug and I have to suffer through this, can we at least eat first?"

"I suppose."

"Actually," Brianna said, finally joining in on the conversation, "I'm kind of hungry, too. It *is* past noon."

"That settles it. We eat first. Crab House, Mar?" I asked, looking back over my shoulder.

She nodded in agreement. "Is there anywhere else? You know I'm a creature of habit."

I led the way across Market Street toward the Crab House. The hostess sat us at a table outside and we finally relaxed for the first time all morning.

"So," Doug said, breaking the ice a bit, "is there a reason y'all played hooky from church today?"

I noticed Marley's back become rigid and she gave me a cautioning look. Even if she hadn't, I wasn't going to say anything. It wasn't my place. "No reason." I shrugged. "I figured it was too nice a day to waste it in some church basement, socializing with people we hardly know."

"Yeah," Brianna said, rolling her eyes. "Marley and I will have enough of that in the coming months with all the functions we have to be at for the Jessamine Court."

I turned to her. "Your step-dad's on the committee with my aunt, isn't he?"

"Yeah." Her voice was quiet and I could sense that she didn't like speaking about her step-father so I tried to change the subject.

"How's your father been? Is he teaching at the school again this year?"

She swallowed hard, her carefree demeanor still replaced by agitation. I could only assume that she was nervous about skipping out on her Sunday obligations with her family, as well. We would all pretty much be in the doghouse when we got home, with the exception of Doug. He definitely had the most liberal and understanding parents in town.

"Yeah, he is. And at Coastal Carolina University, too."

"He seems to have his fingers in lots of pockets, doesn't he?" Doug commented.

"He sure does," Brianna replied.

"Whatever happened between you and Mason?" he asked.

Marley elbowed him. "Douglas! It's rude to ask a lady about her ex-boyfriend when she's in the presence of the new man in her life."

"It's okay," Brianna interrupted. "I'm sure I'll be getting that a lot once school begins. We dated for nearly two years so it's definitely been the break-up of the year."

"When did y'all end it?" I asked, trying to hide my unease.

"After Fourth of July. You guys weren't around much because of your grams so you were out of the loop. Long story short, he's not the same Mason I knew from first grade. It was more of a relationship out of obligation anyway, considering his mom's best friends with my mom so she kind of forced me to date him. Every time I mentioned breaking it off, she would get all short with me and blame me for trying to sabotage her friendship. Sometimes I wonder who the adult *is* in our house."

I grabbed her hand and her solemn expression was replaced with one of joy and hope.

"Well," Marley's boisterous voice broke through the tense atmosphere. "Look at us! Does this count as a double date?" She turned to Doug, his eyes wide at her mention of the word "date". "I mean, it would have to count as a date first, I guess. I mean, if you'd want to date. I mean..." She took a deep breath. "Are we dating, Doug? I don't want you to think that we have to date just because we finally kissed."

He smiled at Marley and I could see the overwhelming affection he had for her. Given her past, I grew nervous at the prospect of her dating anyone, but I knew Doug better than any other guy with whom I went to school. He was the only one I knew who would treat Marley the way she deserved to be treated.

"I'd like to think so," he said. "I mean, that is if you *want* to date me. I don't want to say we're dating if you're not dating me, but I'd like to think that I'm dating you."

"Okay." Marley nodded. "You can date me. I approve. Because I am *so* dating your ass." She giggled.

"Please don't seal the deal in front of me," I interrupted, not wanting to watch my best friend and my sister kiss right before our lunch arrived. There were some things I'd rather not see.

He winked at Marley. "I'll get you later, Marley Jane." Leaning over, he whispered something in her ear and a grin crawled across her face, making her entire being glow.

I raised my eyebrows at her and she blushed. This was the Marley I knew from all those years ago. Whenever she shut down or had an "episode", as my aunt referred to them, I would take her far away from everything. I'd help her forget about the expectations placed on her shoulders and the old Marley would come out of the shell she had been forced to live in for the past six years. Barely anyone knew the real Marley. Doug saw her on occasion, and so did a few of her close friends from school. I should have counted myself as lucky for being able to spend time with the real Marley because she began to slip farther and farther away over the months to come.

~~~~~~~~~~~

"YOU REALLY LOVE YOUR sister, don't you?" Brianna asked, clutching on to my hand as we maneuvered our way through the crowds of people in the central market that spanned several city blocks, stopping at nearly every table for Marley to *ooh* and *ah* over different pieces of jewelry and homemade trinkets.

"Of course I do."

"I think it's cute how well you get along."

I shrugged. "We've been through everything together," I explained, my voice pensive.

"So…" she said, slightly hesitant. "What's the real story?"

I glanced at her, wanting further explanation.

"I mean, I've heard the rumors. We don't hear them as much as we did when you and Marley first arrived in our sleepy little beach community in sixth grade, but I still hear them once in a while."

"What do they say?" I knew it shouldn't surprise me that people talked about why there was a court order requiring us to live with our aunt and uncle, but it still irritated me that no one had anything better to do than gossip about other people's struggles.

"Well, you can take your pick, really. That you and Marley were more than your parents could handle so they left you, and your aunt and uncle, being the saints they are, took you in."

I shook my head in disbelief.

"Let's see…" She wrinkled her forehead, deep in

thought at the ludicrousness of it all. She felt it, too. "There's also the rumor that your father was some hot shot in the movie industry, and he left your mom for some famous actress and she went off the deep end. And, of course, your aunt and uncle, being the saints they are, took you in... Notice a common theme, here?"

I nodded. "I'm starting to."

"You should because every rumor ends with your aunt and uncle being saints."

"Saints in public, maybe."

"I know what that's like," Brianna muttered under her breath. "Put on a smile and pretend that everything in your life is like it should be so no one becomes suspicious that there's something wrong."

I stopped dead in my tracks. "What do you mean by that, Bri?"

"Nothing," she answered quickly, avoiding my gaze. "I just... I'm sorry. I never should have opened my mouth. Everything in my life is fine. I just..." Her chin quivered and she took a deep breath. "I guess I just wish things were as simple as they were before. My mom and step-father don't get along with my dad, and they use me as a pawn in their game of who's better. My mom took my dad back to court, and both sides slung false accusations at each other. Who do you think it affected? Not them. Me. At least I'll be able to get away from it all for a bit when school begins because I'll be busy with theater and all the pageant stuff. I'll finally be able to escape...I hope."

"But you got out today," I said, trying to lighten the mood. "I can't think of anyone else that I'd want to get grounded for." I nudged her gently and she turned to meet my eyes.

"Either can I."

We stopped walking in the busy central market and faced each other, people attempting to maneuver around us. I didn't care that we were blocking their passage. At that moment, it was as though Brianna and I were the only two people in the universe. I bent toward her and she raised herself onto her toes. Closing my eyes, I poised my lips over hers, the electricity I felt from being just a breath away from her mouth igniting me. I didn't even have to kiss her to feel an overwhelming sense of fulfillment.

"Kiss me, Cam," she begged.

Licking my lips, I placed my hand on the small of her back and pulled her tall, slender body into mine. She whimpered…not in pleasure, but in pain. My eyes flung open and I saw a look of discomfort on her face. "What is it? Are you okay?"

She nodded quickly. "I'm fine."

"Are you sure?" I asked, eyeing her dubiously.

"Do you think I'm lying to you?!" she exclaimed. "If I say I'm fine, I'm fine!" She spun on her heels and began to walk away from me.

Exhaling loudly, I wanted to kick myself. Thankfully, I'd had enough experience with Marley's breakdowns and outbursts that I knew I could fix this.

Running through the crowd of people in the market, I caught up to her and grabbed her hand, spinning her around to face me. I could still see the terror and burn on her face.

"I'm sorry, Bri. I don't think you're lying to me. I shouldn't have made you feel as though I thought that. I get it."

"I just strained my back yesterday at dance class. That's all." She looked away, confirming my initial suspicion that she was hiding something from me...especially considering I knew that she had dance class every Wednesday, not Saturday. She typically worked at the gym on Saturdays.

Leaning down, I placed a gentle kiss on the top of her head and inhaled her scent, letting out a small moan.

"Smell something you like, Cameron?"

I groaned in response to her sensual voice. I wanted nothing more than to leave that public market and go somewhere that it could just be Brianna and me.

Opening my eyes to gaze down at her, I was happy to see a playful smile on her face. "I sure do, Bri..." I stopped short when I observed a familiar-looking silhouette in the distance walking toward us. Shaking my head, I tried to convince myself I was seeing things, thinking that it would be too much of a coincidence if it turned out to be true.

"Shit. Marley..." I said under my breath. Scanning over the heads of people, I was thankful for my towering six-and-a-half-foot frame for the first time in my life.

"What? What is it, Cam?" Brianna asked as I pulled her through the crowd of people, officially on Marley damage control.

"Hopefully nothing, but I can't risk it. I'm sorry. I can't really explain."

The fuzzy silhouette came into view and my heart dropped.

"*Marley!*" I shouted at the top of my lungs, everyone in the market continuing on with their business, except for Marley...

And Buck.

He stopped in his tracks and met my eyes. I shuddered at the sight of a woman on his arm. He looked dramatically different than he did all those years ago. He was more muscular and he no longer had a glaze about his eyes. His brown hair was graying in places, but he was clean-cut and shaven, wearing a crisp polo shirt, khaki shorts, and loafers. He looked rather distinguished, like someone who was finally moving on with his life. The thought filled me with peace and rage at the same time. Peace that I didn't kill him. Rage that he had moved on when my sister was still sentenced to live in the past.

I broke my gaze from his and met Marley's eyes. His eyes followed mine and my heart shattered in my chest at Marley's reaction. From ten feet away, I could feel her entire world crumble as she met those eyes that she had hoped to never see again. She let out a sob and grew weak in the knees, losing her balance. Doug steadied her and I pushed through the crowd of people, the mere feet between us feeling like thousands.

Finally reaching her, I wrapped my arms around her and quickly ushered her out of the crowded market, rubbing her back as she wailed, her entire body convulsing as I had never seen before. Approaching a relatively deserted alley, I turned to Brianna and Doug. "Can you just give us a minute?"

They halted and nodded their heads. I could see the look of concern and confusion on their faces. I wished that I could explain exactly what happened, but I couldn't do that. I was probably already in deep water with my aunt for what I said to Mrs. Dumond at church. No one was supposed to know the truth. I absently wondered if that had caused Marley more trauma than the actual events of her past.

Pulling her farther down the alley, I glanced over my shoulder and turned to face her when I was certain that we hadn't been followed. "Talk to me, Mar," I said, wrapping my arms around her trembling frame. "Please. What's going through your head? I need to know. Don't keep it inside."

"He has a girlfriend?!" she screeched. "How?! He never should have been released!"

"Shhh…" I attempted to soothe her sobs. "It's okay. He doesn't know where you live. He'll never hurt you again."

She leaned back and stared into my eyes. Wiping her cheeks, she said, "But what if he does it to someone else, Cam? What if it's all an act? It was an act with us and Mama at first. Don't you remember? He was the perfect gentleman and then the monster that lies beneath appeared out of nowhere. What if he's doing it again? What if that woman has a daughter? What if he marries her and *they* have a daughter? Will he do it to his own child? I can't just…"

"You have to, Marley. Believe me. I know what's going through your head right now. I feel it. It hurts me, too. But you can't take matters into your own hands. It's not right. Karma will eventually come for him, just like it will finally pay you back for all the shit you've been through. I know it, Mar. You're going to have the most amazing future because of all the horrible things you've had to endure in your past. Please. You need to see that. Live for your future. Don't shelter yourself with your past."

She buried her head in my chest and took several deep breaths as she clung on to me. When her breathing began to even out, I knew her momentary terror had passed. "How do you always know just what to say to calm me down?"

I planted a kiss on her head. "Simple. Years of experience."

She pinched me playfully in my side.

"Ouch! Not so hard, Marley Jane!"

She giggled and the sound brought a smile to my face. I

grabbed her hand and led her down the alley. Glancing at her, I asked, "Secret spot?"

She grinned and nodded her head enthusiastically. "Yes! Do you have enough stuff?"

I shrugged. "We can always rent some gear when we get there."

"You're digging into your college savings, aren't you?"

"What fun is looking at money in the bank? Life is marked by experiences, small moments of time. *That* we can take with us. I'd rather live a life full of moments than be surrounded by meaningless possessions, wouldn't you?"

She nodded contemplatively and I wished I knew what she was thinking at that moment.

# CHAPTER ELEVEN

## *SECRET SPOT*

*Marley's Journal*

*August 31*

"WHERE ARE WE?" DOUG asked as Cam pulled up to a small building at the entrance of a campground on the beach about twenty miles south of Myrtle Beach that we had discovered about a year ago. He had just gotten his Wrangler and wanted to take it for a drive.

We'd always loved hanging out at the beach, but living two blocks away didn't give us much freedom to disappear when we wanted to. This campground became our place. It was where we went when we needed to get away and be ourselves and not who everyone else expected us to be. Well, at least me. Cam didn't hide who he was from anyone. He didn't have to.

"It's our secret spot," I explained as Cam and Brianna ran inside to grab a few things we would need.

"Are we staying the night?"

I nodded fervently. "Go big or go home." That seemed to be the motto of the day. "If we're all getting grounded, may as well enjoy it. Am I right?"

Doug nudged me, winking. "I'm guessing all the stereotypes about the preacher's daughter or, in this case…niece, are true. You rebel, you."

I grinned in response. "You know it."

Cam and Brianna came back to the Wrangler and, within minutes, he pulled in front of our normal spot. We all chipped in and helped unload the blankets and food that he had picked up at the general store.

After setting up a few tents on the beach, we then got to work at starting a fire.

"Do you guys do this often?" Brianna asked, surprised at the efficiency with which Cam and I were able to build and light a fire.

"From time to time," he responded. "We haven't been here that much lately."

"Well…except a month ago on the night we found out that Grams died," I interjected quickly.

"Yeah," he agreed. "But that was different. We're not here to mourn tonight. We're here to have fun." He raised his eyebrows at me.

"Marshmallows!" I shouted. "There's a fire! With a fire, there must be marshmallows! They go hand-in-hand!" I rummaged through the supplies and grabbed the bag of marshmallows, chocolate bars, and graham crackers. "I hope you like s'more kisses, Douglas." I winked.

"Marley," Cam cautioned, "I really don't want to think about you and Doug kissing right now, okay?"

"Fine. We won't kiss in front of you if you and Brianna don't kiss in front of me. Deal?"

"Deal."

Brianna laughed. "You two crack me up. Now give me a marshmallow."

I handed out the sticks and passed the bag of marshmallows around. "S'mores make friends, ya know."

I could feel Cam rolling his eyes.

"What? They do! It's a proven fact!"

Doug wrapped his arm around my shoulder and I leaned into him. "There must be a story here, isn't there?"

"Yes. There is."

"Care to share, Mar?" Cam asked.

"Well, when we discovered this place last summer, we set up camp pretty much in this same exact spot. Just down the beach a bit, there was a family with two kids. The sun had just begun to set so there was still a lot of activity on the beach…people running, playing Frisbee, stuff like that. Well, these two little kids stumbled onto our little campsite and saw that we were roasting marshmallows for s'mores." I paused and slid the gooey marshmallow off my stick and into my mouth before placing on another one and starting to roast it. "Their parents came running after them and apologized for their kids barging in on us, thinking that we were dating. Gross, by the way. No offense, Bri."

"None taken." She grinned.

"That's when I explained that we're twins," Cam said, continuing with the story. "Turns out, this little boy and girl were twins, too, and we invited them to make s'mores with us. As Marley was preparing them for everyone, she kept saying 'S'mores make friends' over and over again. The little kids starting saying it, too. To this day, she says it every time we have s'mores…and M & M's."

"Well, yeah, because M & M's definitely make friends. Offer someone some chocolaty goodness and they will most certainly say 'thank you' and not 'fuck you'. It's scientifically proven."

Everyone erupted in laughter.

"I'm not so sure about it being scientifically proven," Cam said.

81

"Okay. Well, it's Marley proven, so that's close enough," I replied lightheartedly.

"Whatever, Mar," Cam said, bringing his attention back to Brianna.

I felt Doug's lips just a breath away from my neck. "I like the idea of Marley proven," he whispered. "I like it a lot."

I melted into his arms. "Me, too." I sighed, trying to calm down the butterflies dancing in my stomach.

The hours passed as we sat around our campfire and roasted marshmallows, talking about everything and nothing at the same time. Normally, I would have been hesitant to be at the secret spot with anyone other than Cam, but something about being there with Doug and Brianna felt so, well...normal. It was as if they were meant to be there with us.

When we arrived at our school all those years ago, Brianna and I had become friends almost instantly. A few years ago, when her mother re-married, she grew somewhat distant and aloof, probably because of all the drama at home. She was no longer the outgoing, carefree girl that she once was. That was around the same time she began dating Mason. Rumors circulated about what caused a change in her, but I was the last one to ever listen to a rumor, having heard quite a few good ones about myself.

Regardless, I had always remained close with her. She was probably the only girl in school that I would have considered telling what happened to me.

I felt a nudge on my head and my eyes flung open. "Oh, I'm sorry," I said to Doug. "I must have fallen asleep." I yawned, my eyes heavy with exhaustion.

"It's okay."

"Yeah, Marley. That's the way to win a guy. Drool all

over him while you snore."

I picked up a shell from the beach and chucked it across the fire at Cam. "I was *not* snoring." I turned to Doug. "Was I?"

"Nah, you weren't. And even if you were, I'm sure it would be the most adorable sound in the world."

"She snores, Doug. And it is *not* adorable. It's loud. I can feel the wall shake between our bedrooms."

"Stop exaggerating, Cameron Michael." I leaned my head back on Doug's shoulder, reveling in his comforting warmth.

"Do you want to go lie down?" he asked softly.

"I probably should. I'm a little tired."

He nodded and helped me stand up, growing nervous when he saw the two tents. "Ummm, why don't you and Brianna each take a tent and Cam and I will sleep out here." He turned to Cam. "Does that work for you?"

"That's what I was planning," he responded.

I shook my head. "Well, that doesn't work for *me*," I said, facing Doug, his hand enclosed in mine. "I can't ask you to sleep outside. Not when there's plenty of room in there…with me."

"Marley, I don't mind. I know you want to take things slow…"

"And we are. But you can still sleep in the same tent as me."

"Are you sure?"

I nodded. "I've never been so sure about anything before in my life."

He glanced at Cam, almost as if asking permission if it was okay for him to share a tent with me.

Grabbing his chin, I forced him to look at me again. "You don't need my brother's permission to sleep with me… I mean, sleep in the same tent as me…"

"She's right, Doug," Cam's voice broke through the tension. "Don't worry about me. But if you hurt her…"

"I know, I know." Doug's eyes remained glued to mine as he answered my brother. "You don't have to ever worry about me hurting her. I'd never be able to live with myself if I did."

I grinned and pulled him into the tent with me.

"Ummm… I can't sleep in this skirt," I said to him. "Are you going to be weirded out if I sleep in my underwear? Don't worry. I'm wearing boy shorts so it's like I'm sleeping in my gym shorts."

"Are you going to be okay with that? I really don't mind sleeping outside, Marley."

"Doug…" I said in warning as I slowly untied my linen skirt and let it pool at my feet before stepping out of it, wearing just a tank top and my underwear. I pulled the legs down a bit to make sure it covered the secret I had kept from everyone. "You're not sleeping outside."

His chest began to rise and fall in an increasingly arrhythmic pattern. "Damn, Marley Jane," he said quietly. "I really like your legs."

I giggled and allowed him to pull me into his body. "You still owe me," I murmured against his neck.

"Owe you what?" he whispered.

"A kiss. You said you would get me later. Now's your chance. I've been waiting all day for you to get me, Doug."

He groaned and I felt his body grow rigid against me. I also felt something else become hard. His lips brushed mine and I could taste chocolate and Doug as he slipped his tongue into my mouth. Deepening the kiss, I ran my hands through his dark, messy hair as he pulled me closer to him, shivers running through me at the sensation of his strong hand placed on my lower back.

"Doug," I exhaled, pulling out of the kiss. "We should probably sleep. I'm not ready to…"

"Marley, I have no desire to sleep with you. I mean, not that I don't want to, but…" He sighed and, even in the darkened tent, I could see his face turning red. "Dammit. Do you have any idea how tongue-tied I get around you?"

I giggled. "I have an idea."

"What I meant to say is that I'm one of the good guys and I have no intention of rushing you into anything."

I placed a kiss on his cheek. "Thank you." I crouched on the ground and unzipped one of the sleeping bags. "How about we snuggle, though? Can we do that? I've always wanted to spoon with someone."

He unzipped the other sleeping bag and flattened it, placing it on the ground. "Of course."

I lay down and he covered both of our bodies, wrapping his arms around me. For the first time I could remember, I fell asleep surrounded by the comfort of a guy's caring embrace.

# CHAPTER TWELVE

## *NIGHTMARE*

*Cam*

AFTER WATCHING MARLEY DISAPPEAR into the tent with Doug, I turned to Brianna.

"Cameron," she said sweetly, sensing my unease. "You're also not going to be sleeping outside." She winked and grabbed my hand, pulling me into the tent with her.

"I'd be lying if I said I wasn't hoping you'd say that."

She beamed as she wrapped her arms around me, crushing her lips against mine, her kiss sudden and unexpected. There was something about kissing Brianna that was so pure and perfect. I knew that it was a high school romance and probably wouldn't survive our first year of college, but at that moment, as I felt her body against mine, I didn't want to wake up to another day where I couldn't look into her smiling eyes or feel her soft lips against mine.

She pulled away, panting. "Sorry."

"What are you apologizing for?"

"I had been wanting to do that all day. It's been pure torture."

"You're telling me." I lowered myself to the ground and slipped into one of the sleeping bags. Brianna followed suit. We lay there, a breath away from each other, our eyes locked. "I promise I don't snore. At least I don't think I do." I grinned and inched toward her, my adrenaline spiking when she closed the distance between us even more. The only thing separating us was the down of the sleeping bags.

"It's okay if you do. I don't mind," she said. "I want to get to know all your little quirks. I already know some of them."

"Oh yeah?" I asked, brushing one of her brown tendrils behind her ear. She closed her eyes momentarily and basked from the contact.

"That's one of them," she said, her voice contemplative. "I remember when you first arrived here. You and Marley were new and interesting. I noticed how you always took care of her. One day, when we were all standing outside after school, waiting for our parents to pick us up, a piece of Marley's hair fell out of her ponytail and you pushed it behind her ear. It was sweet. That was the first time that I saw you do it. I think you had only been here for a month or so. I like how you take care of her. How you don't try to be someone you're not just so that guys at school won't make fun of you. I think it shows that you're comfortable in your own skin. I wish I could be more like that."

"Well, I guess I had to grow up pretty fast after my dad died all those years ago."

"It shows," she responded. "You don't act like the typical seventeen-year-old. Hell, I know some twenty-seven-year-olds who act less mature than you do."

We shared an intense look and I sensed that there was something going on with her. I couldn't quite put my finger on it, but I had an awful premonition that she was trying to hide something…maybe even from herself. Or maybe I was just so accustomed to Marley hiding everything that I had begun to expect it from everyone else, too.

"So," I said, lightening the mood. "What are some of my other quirks that you noticed?"

She wrinkled her nose as if she was deep in thought and I wished I had a camera so I could snap her photo. She looked absolutely beautiful, the playful expression on her face reminiscent of the Brianna I knew in middle school.

"The way you sneeze," she admitted.

"What do you mean?"

"I can always tell when you're about to. And I'm not just talking about the usual, opening your mouth and waiting for it. You close your eyes and rub your nose in the most adorable way, like there's a genie in there that you're trying to release."

"My nose is like a magic lamp?" I asked, laughing.

"Well, yeah. And it's the cutest thing ever."

I planted a kiss on her forehead. "I'll try to sneeze more often then, especially if you like it."

"I do," she admitted. "I like everything about you." Her voice grew quiet and pensive as she toyed with the button on my shirt, avoiding my eyes.

"Bri..." I cupped her chin and tilted her head so she was gazing into my eyes. "I like everything about you, too."

She smiled in response.

I gently caressed her graceful face, savoring the feel of her creamy skin on my hand. Lowering my head to hers, I hovered over her lips, readjusting both of our bodies so she was lying on her back.

I pressed my lips against hers, coaxing her mouth open as my hand found its way into her sleeping bag, roaming her stomach. I heard an unzipping sound and broke away from the kiss to see Brianna opening both of our sleeping bags. She grabbed my head and forced my mouth back to hers as she wrapped one of her long legs around my waist.

"Cam…" she exhaled.

"Are you two making out in there?!" I heard Marley shout from the other tent.

I groaned. "Ignore her, please," I said softly, crushing my lips back to Brianna's.

"You totally are!" Marley giggled. "I can hear your sloppy kisses all the way over here, Cameron Michael. Girls don't like it wet. They like it soft."

"I've got it under control, Marley Jane!" I shouted back before returning my attention to Brianna. "Now, where were we?"

"Right here," she responded, pulling my body flush with hers.

"Oh, Bri," I moaned, my hands grazing her frame. I moved from her lips to her neck, tracing my tongue against her collarbone. My fingers poised on the button of her shirt, I peered at her, silently asking permission. She nodded and I nervously began to unbutton it, my heart racing the entire time.

I lowered my head back to her body as she kept her legs wrapped around me, her hands clawing into my back as she gently thrust against me. I made my way down her stomach, her body throbbing against mine. I began planting kisses on the arm she had wrapped around me, stopping abruptly.

"Bri, what is this?" I asked urgently upon noticing a dark bruise on her bicep.

Her eyes grew wide in shock. "It's nothing, Cam," she responded quickly.

My eyes went to her other arm and I saw another bruise in the same spot.

"You can tell me, Brianna."

"I *did* tell you, Cameron," she hissed, lowering her sleeves and buttoning her shirt, her fingers trembling. She zipped up her sleeping bag and turned her body so she was facing away from me. "It's nothing." Her body continued to shake as she tried to muffle her sobs.

Lying back on the ground, I ran my hand up and down the side of her body, thankful when she didn't push me away.

"I'm sorry, Bri…"

"Me, too."

I comforted her the way that I used to comfort Marley all those years ago, wondering what happened to her to have resulted in two dark bruises on her arms. Her breathing finally equalized and I knew she had fallen asleep. I kissed the top of her head and wrapped my arm around her, drifting off to sleep.

~~~~~~~~~~~

I HAD NO IDEA how long I had been asleep before a loud scream woke me. I bolted up in my sleeping bag, scanning the tent.

Brianna rolled over. "What was that?" she asked drowsily.

"Cam!" I heard Doug shout.

"Fuck. Marley!" I ran out of my tent and into the other one to see my sister screaming and crying. "What happened?" I asked him, wrapping my arms around her quivering frame as she sobbed into my chest.

"Nothing! I was asleep and then she started flailing and shouting something about leaving her alone and to get my hands off her! I wasn't even touching her!"

"Can you just give us a minute?" I looked at him, trying to assure him with my expression that I believed him.

"Okay." He dejectedly turned away before glancing over his shoulder at me. "I'd never hurt her or touch her if she didn't want me to."

"I know you wouldn't."

He shook his head and left the tent.

"I'm sorry, Cam," Marley said through her tears. "I didn't mean to tear you away from getting laid. Gross, by the way."

I chuckled at her sense of humor even when reliving the nightmare of her past. "Marley, I wasn't getting laid. And you don't need to apologize to me. I'll always be here for you. You know that. To the moon and back."

She wiped her cheeks. "From the stars to the ocean."

I rubbed her back, feeling the grooves of her scars through the thin fabric of her tank top. "Was it the dream again?" I asked after several minutes.

She nodded. "Yeah. He was there," she whispered. "In that bedroom. But he looked like he does now and not like he did back then. And that woman he was with was there with him, and she was pregnant, Cam. She watched as he did those things to me. The whole time, all I could hear were a baby's cries."

"Shhh…" I soothed her. "It was just a dream. He can't hurt you, Marley."

"But what if he hurts someone else? Is he going to tell them that he's not to blame and he has to do it because he was born that way? Like he told *me*? That it was *my* fault?"

"It wasn't, Marley. What's it going to take for you to see that?"

"A miracle," she mumbled.

"I know things haven't turned out the way you would have liked, but it will get better. One day, you'll wake up and realize that you're a stronger person because of what you had to go through."

She took a deep, steadying breath. "I'm glad that I can talk to you about all of this and you don't judge me. You should become a shrink. I think you'd be good at it."

I laughed. "I don't know about that. I think I'd get too attached to my patients."

"Think about it, at least. The world doesn't need another lawyer. You'd waste your good soul. And your incredible heart."

"Okay, Marley Jane. For you, I'll think about it."

# CHAPTER THIRTEEN
## *NO GOD*

*Marley's Journal*

*September 1*

"ARE YOU READY TO face the music?" Cam asked, turning to me as he pulled the Wrangler into the driveway of our house, the street peaceful in the pre-dawn hours. After I woke up screaming, we all decided that we should probably get home and try to sneak in before the sun rose.

"What's the worst that could happen?" I responded. "They ground us? Go ahead. We start school tomorrow anyway. We won't have time to go out with our friends, not with all of the crap we have to do."

"Well, I hope it was worth it."

"To be normal for a day? It was *definitely* worth it."

We both remained in the car, neither one of us moving just yet.

"Hey, Cam?"

"Yeah?"

"No matter what, promise that you'll always stand by me." My eyes met his.

"When have I ever not stood by you, Mar?"

I shrugged. "You always have. I just need to make sure

93

that you always will."

"It's you and me against the world. To the moon and back."

"From the stars to the ocean," I whispered, my voice empty. Inhaling slowly, I placed my hand on the door and opened it. "Better get this over with."

Cam nodded and followed me out of the car and up the front steps of the house, the sky turning a pink hue as the sun began its slow ascent. We walked into the eerily silent, darkened house, and I thought maybe Aunt Terryn and Uncle Graham hadn't noticed that we never came home last night. It wouldn't have been the first time but, normally, Cam and I snuck out after they had already gone to bed. This time, not only did we not come home, we ditched church. I wondered which would be seen as the graver offense of the two.

As we tiptoed past the front entryway and saw no one sitting in the living room, we almost thought we hadn't been caught.

"Shhh." Cam placed his finger over his mouth, trying to hush my heavy steps.

Suddenly, a light turned on in the kitchen. We both snapped our heads in that direction to see our aunt and uncle sitting there, severe expressions on their faces.

"Cam. Marley," my uncle said. "Have a seat."

Glancing at Cam, he gave me a reassuring nod and we took several cautious steps into the kitchen, sitting down at the table across from them.

I looked deep into my uncle's sapphire eyes, his brown hair disheveled, as if he had just woken up. "Where were you?" he asked, his tone as calm and soothing as ever.

"Charleston," Cam replied quickly. He found my hand beneath the table and squeezed it, letting me know that he would take the blame for everything.

"What were you doing there?" he asked, his irritation starting to show. I contemplated whether he was simply putting on a show for my aunt.

"Helping Marley forget for a while."

"Did you even think what kind of effect your actions would have?!" my aunt inquired, her face flashing red in anger. "The entire congregation was staring and whispering after you both left! In the middle of the service, I might add! How could they look up to your uncle as a leader when it now appears that he can't control his own family?!"

"I'm sorry," I said, lowering my head. "I just needed to get away for a minute. I had a memory and I couldn't be there."

I could feel my aunt's judgmental eyes on me as she glared, then turned her attention back to Cam. "Mrs. Dumond told me what you said to her before you left. Do you have any idea how embarrassed I was? Not only did you both leave church, making all of us look bad, but now one of the elders thinks that Marley was…" She trailed off and the silence in the room was excruciating.

I raised my head and could tell that she was trying to find a way to finish her sentence. "You can't even say it, can you?" I asked quietly, my entire being seething with anger and frustration. "Why can't you? Neither one of you have ever been able to actually say the words…not that I can remember, anyway. Maybe if you finally say it, then you'll realize that it was a horrible thing! That I should have been put in therapy years ago to deal with it! Instead, I was forced to be paraded around like another freaking home grown beauty queen!" I quickly shot out of the chair and leaned toward both of them.

I was done keeping it all inside. I had kept quiet for ages. Something inside of me snapped and the anger, rage, and agony that I had been keeping at bay, only allowing Cam to see, was raging over me like lava. It burned me, and the only thing that extinguished the fire was letting the words flow from my mouth.

"Say it!" I screamed, my face not even an inch from hers as she stared at me in shock. "I was molested! Raped! Beaten! Ruined! At the age of eight! How would you feel if that were Meg?! Or Julianne?! Would you brush that under the rug, too?! Would you get them the help they so desperately needed?! Or would you be too concerned about what your friends would say then, too?! Would you destroy any chance they had at a healthy, happy future so that you could save face in front of your tea-drinking, past-their-prime teen beauty queen has-beens?!"

I felt a hand on my shoulder and turned to see Cam standing next to me, his eyes soothing as if trying to put out the flames inside of me. But they were lit. Nothing could stop it. The fire was spreading with each passing moment.

"Mommy?" I heard a quiet voice say. I tore my eyes from Cam and saw Meg and Julianne standing in the doorway in their pajamas, clutching their bears. They looked scared and I knew it was because they had overheard my screams.

"Meg," my aunt said, attempting to regain her broken composure. "Please take your little sister upstairs. I'll be up shortly to help you change into your play clothes."

"Is Marley in trouble?" Meg asked.

"That's none of your concern. Now do as you're told and I'll be sure to take you both down to the pier later for ice cream."

All she had to do was mention ice cream and the girls quickly followed her demand.

The tension in the kitchen could be cut with a knife as we all glared at each other. Wanting to be the bigger person, I looked deep into my uncle's conflicted eyes and said, "I'm sorry I left church. It's my fault. I convinced Cam to play hooky with me. I had an 'episode'," I explained, using air quotes. Heading out of the kitchen, I knew it was now or never. "Maybe if I got the help I needed when I needed it, I wouldn't have these 'episodes'. Instead, the only people I could ever talk to about it was Grams and Cam. They've been my therapists, but it still doesn't make up for not getting professional help."

"You *did* get help, Marley Jane," my uncle said in his pacifying voice. "All the help you've ever needed is right in front of you. There's no greater healing than the power of God."

My gaze narrowed on him. "There is no God."

# CHAPTER FOURTEEN

## *BEFORE*

*Cam*

"HEY, MAR," I SAID, climbing onto the roof later that Monday after doing some damage control on her behalf with Aunt Terryn and Uncle Graham.

She glanced in my direction and nodded slightly. "Hey, Cam."

Sighing, I lowered myself to the roof and lay back to stare at the sky over Myrtle Beach at dusk. "Did you really mean what you said before?"

Turning her head, she asked, "What part?"

"About God. Do you really not believe in God?"

She exhaled loudly as she considered my question. "I don't know, Cam. Some days I do. I don't know if it's God, but some days I do feel as if there is a higher power of some sort up there, making sure that I'm on the right path. Other days, I feel completely alone and without direction. I always hear Uncle Graham talking about how important it is to look to God for guidance when we're troubled. But when I'm troubled, that's when I feel nothing, Cam. I don't feel God or any other higher being at those times. Isn't that when He should be there? When I need Him or Her most?"

"Maybe God's busy doing other things at those times.

Maybe you're on His list and He's trying to get to you, but He has bigger fish to fry at the moment. Did you ever think about that?"

She raised her eyebrows. "Do *you* believe in God?"

"I wouldn't say I believe in God, but I do know there is some higher power, some driving force out there, some sort of light in a world that would otherwise be dark. So I guess you could say that I'm a firm believer in the light."

A streak of lightening flashed on the horizon followed by a loud clap of thunder, startling me. Marley, however, remained unmoving.

"You're a good person, Cam. You're so level-headed. It seems like nothing ever gets to you."

"Shit gets to me. I guess I've learned to process everything over the years." It was silent for a moment before I spoke again. "Have you been writing in your journal like I recommended?"

"Yeah. I started right after Grams died. It helps. In a way, it feels like I'm writing to her, but I definitely put a little more in there than what I would tell her. I'm pretty sure she doesn't want to hear about the size of Doug's junk."

"Marley Jane!" I exclaimed, playfully pinching her arm. "Neither does your brother!"

She giggled and I could tell she was slowly returning to me after her outburst that morning. I had gotten used to things over the years. Marley's emotions always took you on a wild roller coaster ride, the ebb and flow often unexpected and sometimes tumultuous. But during those moments that things flattened out, and the ups and downs of her life were on an even keel, even if for just an instant, those were the times that I treasured. I wouldn't trade those rare memories for anything in the world. Those were the times that I saw the real Marley...the girl that forced me to play Barbie's with her, the girl that convinced me the mud pie she made for me was really chocolate. The way her eyes brimmed with enthusiasm and mischief at the same time, you couldn't help but believe her, knowing that she would squeal with excitement and delight when you pretended to take a bite of her 'chocolate' pie.

"Remember the tree house?" she asked, bringing me back from my own memories. I could hear the lump in her throat.

"How could I forget? You hounded Dad for months to build you one."

"Remember going out there after he died, but before Mama lost the house?"

I nodded, finding Marley's hand and grabbing it. "Yeah, I do."

I felt her body tremble beside me as big, fat rain drops began to fall. "I think it would have been the best tree house on the block."

"The way Dad doted on you, it would have been a tree *mansion* by the time he was done with it."

Losing my father was hard enough when I was just eight, but having to be faced with the constant reminders of his life made it even more difficult. The worst was looking out our back window at a tree that he had begun to build a house in for Marley and me. The night that Mama had explained to us that Dad had gone to heaven and wouldn't be coming back, I remember glancing out there and seeing Marley sitting on the lone wood plank that he had set up as the foundation of the tree house. Nearly every night that we lived in that house, we would go out there and simply lay down and look at the stars.

"This reminds me of that," I said softly. "Of those nights in the tree house."

The sound of thunder boomed around us and we remained on that roof, not caring that we were both drenched from the late summer downpour cloaking the town.

"Me, too," Marley said. "I think that's why I like coming out here so much. It reminds me of 'before'. It makes me feel closer to Dad. I always swore I could hear him talking to me in that tree house and, some nights when I'm out here, I can still hear him."

"What does he say?"

She turned to face me and almost broke into tears. "That he's proud of you. That he can't believe how much of him he sees in you. That he's happy you don't let anyone or anything influence your decisions. That he's thankful you've never abandoned me. And that he's glad you finally got the Wrangler you always wanted…but he's much more impressed with *my* choice of car."

"Hey, now!" I laughed. "Don't knock the Jeep! It's a classic!"

"So is my Mustang!" she said, her teeth beginning to chatter from the rain and wind.

Raising myself off the roof, I pulled her up with me. "Come on, Marley Jane. You can't be sick for the first day of your senior year of high school. You're shivering." I helped her into her window and followed, grabbing a towel out of the bathroom and wrapping it around her before doing the same to me.

Once I was sure that she had warmed up, I turned to head to my own room.

"Hey, Cam?" she said, getting my attention.

"Yeah?" I looked over my shoulder at her.

"Thank you."

"For what?"

"For being my normal."

101

# CHAPTER FIFTEEN
## *LOSING CONTROL*

*Marley's Journal*

*September 2*

TODAY WAS THE FIRST day of school. It felt refreshing to be able to walk through the school campus and see friends. There was something about the socialization that happened in the hallways before class that always grounded me in some sense of normalcy. It was like this no matter where you went to school. And I wanted more of that...ordinary, normal, teenage averageness.

"Marley Jane Bowen!" I heard as I strolled through the halls between first and second period. I turned around and saw two of my fellow Dance Squad girls and good friends standing behind me.

"Carla!" I squealed, wrapping my arms around her and Kristen as if I hadn't just seen them at the bonfire on Friday. "I can't believe we haven't run into each other yet." I linked arms with them and we must have looked like quite the sight walking through the hall, all of us adhering to the cookie cutter mold...blonde hair, blue eyes, tall, skinny, our plaid uniform skirt hiked up to make it more fashionable and less "church-choir".

"Where are you off to now?" Kristen asked.

Pulling out my schedule, I wrinkled my nose in obvious displeasure. "Ugh. Cam must have registered me for this one. Governments. He keeps saying that I need to know more about how our government works."

"I'm in that, too!" Carla responded excitedly. "Isn't Brianna's father teaching it? Man, looking at that fine specimen of a man, she has some good genes!"

"Carla!" I said in shock. "He's, like, four times your age."

"Ummm… No. He's forty. We're only talking about a twenty-two year age difference. That makes him entirely do-able."

"You're disturbing sometimes. You do know that, right?" I shook my head and walked down the noisy, crowded hallways with my friends on either arm.

Mr. Monroe, Brianna's father, is *that* teacher at our school. The one all the girls flirt with or wink at. The one that all the guys would love to grab a beer with when they finally become old enough to drink. From what I know about him, he comes from a very wealthy family in Georgia. He met Brianna's mother when he moved up here to attend graduate school. He was a teacher's assistant and she was one of his students. Four months later, they were married. Eight months after that, Brianna was born. Their marriage was a victim of snobbery and stereotypes, and was doomed for failure. Obviously, it was based on lust, and their unhappiness and animosity toward each other has only increased over the years, mostly because the former Mrs. Monroe was angry when Mr. Monroe continued with his education and went on to get his doctorate, instead of simply signing his trust fund over to her.

Their constant bickering has put Brianna in a bit of an awkward spot the past few years. While Mr. Monroe is one of the most beloved teachers, Mr. Grayson, her step-father, is the chairperson of the board of trustees of this school, and pretty much runs the show here. He tried to have Mr. Monroe removed from his teaching position, but the board voted unanimously against it...well, almost unanimously. Rumors circulated about Mr. Monroe smoking pot with a few students, or touching one of his female students in an inappropriate manner. I'm more apt to believe the latter rather than the former, although any touching was probably welcomed and invited.

The bell rang and we bolted down the corridor, not wanting to be late on the first day of school. I was already grounded for playing hooky from church. I didn't want my aunt to add to that punishment.

"So I saw you sucking face with Doug!" Carla shouted just as Kristen threw open the door to the room and the three of us stumbled in, all eyes turning to us as we made our grand entrance.

"Miss DuBois, Miss Galloway, and Miss Bowen," Mr. Monroe said, turning away from the dry board and looking at us with his warm hazel eyes. Surveying his tall stature and athletic build, I could see why all the girls would find him attractive. He was the epitome of tall, dark, and handsome. And while I knew he was forty, I didn't think he looked a day over twenty-five, his features rather young, similar to that of many of the guys I had met when I went to visit college campuses last spring.

"The bell rang already, did it not?"

"It did," Carla said, throwing her hair over her shoulder and placing her hand on her hip in a flirtatious manner. I almost thought I saw her hike her skirt up even more.

"I'll allow your tardiness to slide today because it's the first day, but starting tomorrow, it will result in detention.

Do you understand, ladies?"

"Yes, sir," I responded as my friends pouted, hoping it would win his heart. It didn't.

"Good. Please find a desk. A seating chart is being circulated at the moment." His eyes remained glued to me as we all nodded our heads in unison.

Carla and Kristen scrambled in front of me and grabbed the last two remaining desks toward the back of the class. I was relegated to the only desk left...dead center of the front row. The worst desk there was.

Sighing, I made my way to the desk and slid into it, opening my backpack and grabbing a notebook. The classroom remained eerily quiet as I shuffled things around. Finally ready to begin, I looked up and was met with hazel eyes once more.

"Miss Bowen, a little modesty in your choice of tops may go a long way in the future. Or do I have to report you for taking liberties with the school dress code?"

I immediately placed my hand over my chest, noticing the neckline of my loose t-shirt had dropped dramatically. While we did have to wear a uniform, we were allowed to wear our choice of white top. Apparently, my choice today was a little too revealing. My face flushing red in embarrassment, I readjusted my shirt so that it was more, in his words, modest.

"No, sir."

His lips turned into a strange smile. "Good girl." He looked at me with a disquieting gaze and I shifted in my desk, hating the attention I was getting. Opening my notebook, I avoided his eyes and began writing the date on the first blank page I came across, making a mental note to begin to dress in a way that would no longer bring attention to myself.

The forty-eight minute class dragged on mercilessly as

my mind wandered to everything...ditching church the other day, driving to Charleston and seeing Buck in the market, going to our secret spot and falling asleep in Doug's arms, waking up screaming from another nightmare, looking at the confused expression on Doug's face, and telling my pastor uncle that there was no God.

I began to feel guilty for saying those words to him. How would I feel if my own family thought that my profession was worthless?

Granted, I didn't really have a profession. I didn't think folding t-shirts and hanging clothes in a boutique clothing store really counted as one...at least not to me. That wasn't what I saw myself doing in the long run. I guess that had always been my problem. I didn't know where I saw myself in twenty years. Hell, I didn't even know where I saw myself in twenty *days*.

Actually, that wasn't entirely true. I saw myself here, sitting at this desk, finally done with the first of my official obligations as a member of the Jessamine Court. It was less than three weeks until they would make the official announcement and present the twelve of us to the entire town in an elaborate display of sexism at its finest.

"Miss Bowen?" A voice woke me from my thoughts about the spectacle that awaited me at the end of the month.

I looked up from my notepad where I had unknowingly scribbled several expletives around a sketch of a girl dressed in a pageant gown, and was met with a somewhat stern expression on Mr. Monroe's face. You could hear a pin drop in that classroom.

"Yes?" I squeaked.

"I'm waiting for your answer."

"Ummm... My answer to what?"

He sighed in an irritated way. "Is this class too boring

for you, Miss Bowen? I thought, as your class president, you might take more of an interest in how systems of government work. But alas, in high school, it appears that class office is simply a popularity contest, isn't it? As long as you have a pretty face and charismatic charm, you'll win. Isn't that true?"

Crossing my arms in front of me, I glared at him. "Not necessarily, although it helps, doesn't it? Look at Bill Clinton. If I was old enough to vote, he would have gotten it based on looks alone."

Stifled laughs surrounded me and I looked across the aisle at Brenda McLean, winking at the shocked expression on her face.

"That's precisely why you need to be in this class, Miss Bowen. Over the next several months, all of you people will be turning eighteen. You will now have a say in who you elect and what your government does. You all need to be educated so that you can make a wise decision when you go to vote for the first time."

He spun around, returning to the dry board. "Now that I finally have Miss Bowen's undivided attention, perhaps she'll be so kind as to grace us with an answer to my previous question before we got off topic."

"Which was?"

I noticed his annoyance with me return. "While you were preoccupied with your little art project there…" he sneered, glancing to my notebook and I quickly covered my sketch with my hand, "we were discussing different systems of government. Our system here in the United States is what, Miss Bowen?"

"A democracy."

"Ah… So the beauty queen *does* have a brain."

I gave him a contemptuous smile. "Beauty and brains is a rare combination these days, but I've been blessed with

107

both."

Hushed voices echoed in the room and I could feel Mr. Monroe's previous irritation turn more into anger and, possibly, embarrassment. I had a feeling that this was a man who liked control and wanted everyone to agree with him no matter what.

"Miss Bowen, please see me in my office after class."

"Yes, sir," I replied in a sing-song manner.

The bell rang a few minutes later and I took my time collecting my things, hoping to prolong the inevitable punishment that would await me for speaking back to one of my teachers. Following the crowd out of the classroom, I slowly made my way toward the administrative wing, heading down the quiet hallway to Mr. Monroe's office. I was about to turn the corner when I nearly ran into someone walking rather quickly toward me.

"Brianna?" I said, noticing her downturned head.

She stopped abruptly and raised her eyes to look at me.

Scrunching my eyebrows, I surveyed her agitated demeanor. "Are you okay?" Lowering my voice, I asked, "Did you get in trouble for staying out all night on Sunday, too?"

"Yeah, that's it," she said sheepishly, pushing down the sleeves of her cardigan.

I followed her hands and could almost make out faint scratches and bruising. Grabbing her arm, I went to pull up her sleeve.

"Miss Bowen!" a voice bellowed out, forcing me to turn my attention away from Brianna. "Do you need a written invitation? Because, I assure you, my temper will only increase the longer I have to wait."

"Coming, sir," I replied meekly, looking at Brianna's nervous expression as I kept her wrist clutched in my hand. "We'll talk later," I said to her before dropping her arm and heading toward Mr. Monroe's dark, windowless office.

"Have a seat, Miss Bowen," he said, gesturing to a chair on the opposite side of his mahogany desk that appeared to be more of a mission statement than a surface on which to do paperwork.

I followed his request, growing nervous when I heard the click of the door behind me. As he walked around me and sat behind his desk, his vexing eyes remained glued to mine and I couldn't help but feel incredibly creeped out by him.

"Do you know why I asked you to come here today?"

"Yes, sir," I responded, trying to exude all the southern charm that I had learned from my aunt over the past several years. "I was out of line in class today. I apologize for my behavior and lack of judgment. It won't happen again."

It was silent for a moment while he appeared to process my words, caressing his chin with his folded hands. "You see, Miss Bowen, while I do appreciate and admire people who have the courage to stand up for what they believe in, I find your method of trying to bring attention to yourself quite juvenile."

"I was not trying to bring attention to myself," I protested.

"Then leave the sarcastic comments for your devoted followers, Miss Bowen. Your brother may find your sense of humor endearing, but I do not."

"I'm sorry, sir. I'll keep that in mind in the future."

"He's not always going to be around to cover for you. He's not always going to pick up the pieces for you. Don't you want to be an individual instead of someone who is so dependent on another person that they barely have their own identity?"

I was completely taken aback by his words. "I have my own identity," I murmured.

"Do you? By all means, please enlighten me. I've been trying to ascertain who the real Marley Bowen is for years."

I fidgeted with my skirt, wishing that I hadn't rolled the waist to make it shorter. The way he was staring at me made me want to cover every inch of my body with heavy armor. I could see how other girls at school would find it endearing and attractive, but they didn't have the past I had. Then again, I knew I was overreacting, as I was prone to do whenever in awkward private situations like this.

"I'm only seventeen. I don't *know* who the real Marley Bowen is. But I will say this about her. She doesn't always do what's expected of her. Not anymore." I stood up from the chair and grabbed my bag, looking down at him. "Are we done here? I'm already late for my next class, sir."

"Yes, we are…for now."

I turned away and went to open the door, only to find that he had locked it. My hands grew unsteady and I quickly unlocked it, throwing it open and practically sprinting down the hall.

I hated that my past still made me think the worst of everyone. He was a teacher, for crying out loud. Why did I automatically assume that he locked the door to his office for some perverse reason? Was I more messed up than I originally thought? Since spotting Buck in Charleston over the weekend, I felt as if I was losing control over everything. I needed to get it back.

# CHAPTER SIXTEEN

## *WHEELS TURNING*

*Cam*

"So what's this I hear about you banging Brianna?" Mason, her ex-boyfriend and one of my basketball teammates asked, coming up to me as I sat down at my regular lunch table to wait for Doug.

"You guys broke up." I shrugged, scanning his muscular stature. "And we're not having sex. Even if we were, it's none of your business."

He slammed his fist on the table, startling me.

"What the hell's gotten into you?" I asked. "You've been hanging around with Grady a bit too much."

"That has nothing to do with it. I'm just not keen on the fact that she moved on already. We dated for two years."

"And how long during those two years were you sleeping with Jessica Harper?"

His dark eyes flamed. "None of your fucking business."

Grady, another one of my teammates and Mason's sidekick, approached, his dark hair disheveled. I could almost smell the faint aroma of pot around him. "Heard you're dating Mason's ex. Did she ask you to be her escort to the Jessamine Court introduction?"

"Yeah, she has."

111

"Marley's in the court, too, isn't she?" Mason asked, his fierce expression softening a bit.

"Yeah."

"Who's she taking?" he asked, his eyebrows raised.

"Don't get your hopes up…either one of you," I cautioned my teammates. "She's kind of seeing someone."

Both of their eyes grew wide in unison. "Who?"

"Me," Doug said, sitting down next to me and taking a bite out of his sandwich.

"You're shitting me," Mason retorted. "Marley Bowen is dating *you*?"

"Don't sound so surprised," he said. "I'm living proof that girls like nice guys and don't want to always date someone who looks at them like a piece of meat like you two assholes do."

"Hey," Grady interjected. "Plenty of girls have been unable to resist my charm."

"Yeah," I agreed. "Until you got them in bed, then sent them packing."

"That was, like, one girl!" he protested. "Diana Greene. People don't call her 'dirty Diana' for nothing."

"And you guys wonder why I never wanted you to date Marley." I rolled my eyes at them.

Grady shrugged. "Whatever. She'll get bored with Doug, I'm sure."

"Don't count on it," a familiar voice interjected. I looked at Doug and smiled when I saw Marley sit down next to him and place an affectionate kiss on his neck. "And even if I wasn't dating him, I wouldn't go out with either one of you, so don't waste your time or energy."

I snickered at Marley's boldness.

"I heard you already got in trouble this morning," Mason said snidely.

She looked down at her yogurt, avoiding his eyes. "Maybe. Nothing I can't handle."

"What did you do?" I asked.

"Nothing, Cam." She glared at me. "I may have been a bit snarky to Mr. Monroe during my Governments class that *you* signed me up for. I'm not happy with you at all right now."

"It's an important class, Mar. You'll thank me later."

"Don't hold your breath," she mumbled.

"Let's go, Grady," Mason said. "See you at practice after school." He retreated from our table and I wondered how Brianna could ever date a prick like him.

"What was that all about?" Marley asked.

"He's just pissed that I'm dating his ex, even though he treated her like crap the whole time."

She scanned the cafeteria before leaning across the table. "Have you seen her yet today?" she asked in a quiet voice.

"Yeah. Third period. She's in my History class," I replied. "I think she was late this morning because she was supposed to be in my first period Spanish class, too, but she never showed up. Why?"

"No reason," she said quickly. "I ran into her when I was heading to Mr. Monroe's office and she seemed a little, well…off."

"I think her mom let her have it pretty bad when she got home yesterday. She was a bit out of it in class this morning and you could tell that she was still a little agitated."

"She was in homeroom," Doug offered.

Marley scrunched her eyebrows at him. "She was?"

"Yeah. But about a minute before the bell rang, she got called out to Mr. Grayson's office…or maybe her dad's. I can't remember. All I remember was that it was

113

something about a family emergency. Mason walked her down there because she appeared to be a little worried. I don't think our homeroom teacher has heard that they've broken up yet."

"I hope everything's okay," I said.

"I have to go." Marley shot out of her chair, leaving her half-eaten yogurt on the table.

"Where are you going?" I called after her as she began to walk away.

"Nowhere. I just… I have to go. I'll see you later, Cam." Determined, she walked out of the cafeteria toward the theater wing. I could almost sense the wheels turning in her head.

# CHAPTER SEVENTEEN

## *SIGNS*

*Marley's Journal*

*September 2*

THE THING ABOUT BEING a victim of abuse is that you can sometimes sense when someone else is suffering through it. You see the signs more clearly than most people, usually because it's the same things that you tried to hide…sometimes the same things you're *still* trying to hide.

Then again, sometimes you feel so alone and isolated that you wish you had someone to talk to about what you went through, so you try to see something that's not there. It's a fine line.

All I *did* know, as I was leaving the cafeteria after hundreds of red flags started popping up, was that I had a very good idea about where Brianna was. It was where I always went when I was having an "episode". Walking through the empty halls, I pulled open the door that led up to the catwalk of our school's state-of-the-art theater. Climbing the narrow spiral stairs, I emerged onto the truss, thankful that I never had a fear of heights. *I guess I'd have to be scared of dying first*, I thought to myself.

I took a step onto the catwalk and Brianna must have

sensed the shift of weight. She looked up from where she was sitting overlooking the theater fifty feet below us.

"Hey, Marley."

"Hey, Bri," I responded, taking several cautious steps toward her.

Sitting down next to her, I dangled my feet over the side, poking my legs through the safety grates that were there to prevent anyone from falling down below.

I had always been able to read people. Something about Brianna's aura led me to believe that she was at war with herself…almost like she wanted to scream at the top of her lungs but, at the same time, stay mute. I had my suspicions that something was going on, but I had no idea what. I wondered if things weren't quite over between her and Mason, as much as she probably wanted them to be. My heart began to break for her and I knew what I had to do, regardless of my aunt's insistence that I pretend it never happened.

"Has Cam ever said anything about why we moved here?" I asked her. Like the rest of the town, she most likely knew absolutely nothing.

"No, he hasn't."

I kept my eyes trained forward and nodded. "My dad died when we were eight. I loved him. Well, of course I did. He was my dad. We had such a strong connection. He was a mechanic and loved cars. When I was just a little girl, I remember telling him that I wanted a Mustang when I got older and could drive." I smiled at the memory.

"He was coming home from work one night and was killed by a drunk driver. It was Memorial Day weekend. Cam and I had just turned eight a few weeks beforehand. Mama had postponed our birthday party to have it that weekend. Instead of celebrating our eighth birthday with friends and family at a back yard Low Country Boil, we mourned my father and threw his ashes out to sea."

I looked down when I felt a hand meet mine.

"Mama was having a hard time with Dad's death. He was her soul mate...her one true love...her everything. She shut down and turned off. I always wondered what a broken heart felt like. Looking at my mama, I knew that she was suffering from one. They loved each other so fiercely. Whenever I was around them, I physically felt the love they shared. After he died, I no longer felt that. Part of Mama died in that car wreck, too.

"I remember Cam having to help me get ready for school the first day of third grade in September because our mama was too drunk to wake up. You'd think that, with her husband having died because of a drunk driver, she would stay far away from liquor, but she didn't. She stopped going to work and we eventually lost the house that we had grown up in. We were forced to move from apartment to apartment...places that weren't fit for habitation, but it was all she could afford.

"One day, a man appeared on our doorstep and, for a brief period of time, everything seemed like it was going to get better. Mama stopped drinking and using drugs. She cooked. She cleaned. She even got a job so that we could move into a better place. Then, one night, she fell off the wagon and started using again. I remember seeing her put the needle in her arm as we sat there watching TV on a Friday. She said it was her medicine and that she needed it. He didn't do anything to stop her. It was almost like he encouraged her...almost like he had simply been biding his time, waiting for her to slip up and start using again.

"Cam and I shared a room. There wasn't much space, but we didn't mind. After being allowed to stay up to watch the ball drop that New Year's Eve, we went to sleep. Hours later, I woke up to someone climbing in bed with me. Someone that weighed much more than Cam."

Brianna gasped and squeezed my hand even harder.

"I looked across the bedroom at Cam's bed, hoping that he would come help, but he wasn't there. I was so angry with him for abandoning me, for not doing anything even when he could hear my screams and cries for help. It happened over and over, almost every night. I would go to school during the day and be subjected to abuse at night. Every few months, Mama would sober up enough to realize that something was going on and would get us away from him, promising to never let him know where we ended up. But once the cash ran out and she needed drugs and alcohol, she would break down and call him. No one at any of the schools we went to ever did anything. Kids were coming in without having eaten in days, so when a little girl comes to school with a few scratches and bruises, no one says anything. I wish someone noticed it, though. If they did, I wouldn't have had to live that nightmare for nearly three years."

I turned to look at her and saw the tears forming in her eyes. "One night, Cam had enough of listening to my cries. So instead of putting up a fight and trying to protect me when *he* came in, he left the bedroom. Not even five minutes later, he returned with my mama's gun and shot him. Mama went to jail for a little bit for child endangerment and neglect. Guardianship of Cam and me was granted to my aunt and uncle until we turn eighteen. And that's the real story of why Cam and I came to Myrtle Beach."

I stared straight ahead as I tried to hold back the tears I felt from sharing my story with someone. It had been years since I had spoken those words. It felt alarmingly

118

therapeutic.

"I'm sorry that you had to go through that," Brianna said, breaking the heavy silence.

"Me, too. I wish someone had noticed something off about our home situation early on. That way, I wouldn't have had to live the nightmare for as long as I did. I wish that someone had seen the signs, had heard the desperate pleas for help that I was shouting with my eyes."

I glanced at her and noticed her tense up. "I get it, Bri. I know what you're going through."

"What?" Her voice grew loud. "What do you think I'm going through?"

I tried to stand my ground. I could only imagine what she was thinking at that moment, knowing that all her attempts to cover up the pain and torment had been for nothing. "I'm not sure, but I have a feeling. And, well, I just wanted to let you know that I'll listen if you ever want to talk about it. Your secrets will always be safe with me, just like I know mine will be safe with you."

"Does Doug know?" she asked, obviously curious.

"No, he doesn't. Besides my aunt and uncle, and Cam, I don't think many people know the truth."

"They make you hide it, don't they?"

"Yeah, but there's only so long anyone can possibly be expected to keep it inside. I'm glad that I finally shared it...with you."

"Why not Carla or Kristen? I know how close you are with both of them," she said.

"I know, and I love them both dearly, but if I told them, it would be turned into the latest Hollywood blockbuster before the final bell of the day." I met her gaze once more. "I trust you, Bri. We have a unique friendship that I wouldn't trade for anything. I feel like I can tell you anything and you won't use it against me or to benefit you."

"I would never be able to betray anyone like that…even if I hated them."

"That's why you're the perfect girl for my brother. You're a lot alike in that way. He has a good heart, and so do you."

"But what if he finds out? About me? I mean, if there *was* something going on, how will he react? I don't want to hurt him, but I don't know… I just can't say anything, Marley. I wish I could, but I can't."

"Believe me, I know how you feel. Take your time. Learn who you can trust and who you can't. Then slowly begin to share with those that you can. Those people who will never judge you for something you had absolutely no control over. Even if all you need is someone to just sit with and remain completely silent, sometimes that helps, too."

"Like you and Cam and the roof?"

I giggled. "Yeah. Like the roof. This could be our roof, Bri."

She wiped her cheek. "I like the sound of that."

# CHAPTER EIGHTEEN

## *PURPOSE*

*Cam*

I PULLED UP IN front of our house after basketball practice, wondering what Brianna's Beetle was doing parked alongside the road. Practice had been a bit awkward. Coach had to break up a few scuffles between Mason and me. He had this mania in his eyes, almost like he had this obsession with Brianna. Like if he couldn't have her, no one could.

Entering the house, I was surprised to see Marley and Brianna playing with Julianne and Meg.

"Your boyfriend's home," Marley said in a teasing manner.

Brianna looked up from where she was constructing a log cabin made of play-dough with Julianne. Her smile completely melted my heart. Any fight I got into with Mason and Grady was absolutely worth it just to see her smile.

"Hey," I said.

"Hey," she replied.

"Do you like Cam?" Meg asked, always the nosey one.

She grinned, her eyes remaining locked with mine. "Yes, I do. I like him a lot."

"Have you kissed?" Julianne asked, butting in on the

121

conversation.

Brianna's eyes went wide, unsure of how to respond.

"That's none of your business, munchkin," I said quickly, saving her from having to answer my inquisitive sisters. Turning my attention back to Brianna, I lost myself in her brown eyes.

"Well, this is awkward," Marley interjected. "Go shower, Cam. Bri came to see you, not me, and I think she'd prefer if you didn't smell like the boy's locker room."

Meg giggled. "Yeah. Boys are smelly."

"They sure are," Marley replied. "And gross."

"Is Doug gross?" Julianne asked.

I noticed Marley's ears turn red, the signature Bowen indication that we were embarrassed. Grinning to myself, I retreated up the stairs just as I heard Marley respond that Doug was anything but gross.

Dashing into the bathroom, I took the quickest shower of my life, not wanting to keep Brianna waiting for too long. Once I was satisfied that I no longer smelled like I had just gotten out of basketball practice, I threw on a pair of shorts and a t-shirt before running down the stairs, nearly pummeling into the six-foot frame of my uncle as he was walking in the front door.

"Sorry, Uncle Graham."

"Where are you running off to?" he asked.

"Nowhere, really. I was just going to go for a walk with Brianna, if it's okay."

"Hi, Pastor Graham," she said sweetly, sidling up next to me as we stood in the foyer. "I was sick this morning and wanted to talk to Cam about what I missed in class so that I don't fall behind in my studies."

Shaking his head, he walked away. "Miss Monroe, if you want to see my nephew, you don't need to lie about it. Have a nice walk on the beach, kids. Just don't tell your aunt I let you go, Cam. Technically, you're still grounded."

"Yes, sir," I responded before grabbing Brianna's hand and leading her out of the house.

"I hope I didn't get you in trouble," she said quietly as we crossed the street toward the shore.

"No. He tries to act strict, but there's not a lot of follow-through. Last time we did something that landed us in hot water, we were grounded for a month. It lasted a whopping three hours."

"Really?" she asked.

"Yeah. We were grounded around four o'clock in the afternoon. By seven, Carla and Kristen showed up at our house and he allowed Marley to go to some study group with them that they had probably just made up. I'm pretty sure it was during summer, too."

Brianna laughed. "Let me guess. Marley convinced him."

"Yup," I said in agreement. "She's always had a knack for getting people to listen to her, no matter what. That's probably how she won the election for class president."

"That, and people love her. She's easy to get along with. She's caring and compassionate. And genuine. You know what you get with Marley, even though she puts up a front."

"What do you mean?" I turned to her as we walked along the beach. "Do you really think she puts up a front?" *I* knew that she did, but I never thought anyone else was able to see through it like I could.

Taking a deep breath, she faced me, grabbing both my hands in hers. Closing her eyes, the wind whipped her hair and a look of complete ease washed over her face. At that moment in time, she appeared to finally let herself go and stopped pretending to be the girl she was told she had to be by her mother.

Opening her intense eyes, she said, "Marley told me."

"Told you what?" I asked, confused.

"About what happened to her. About what you did to protect her."

"What? Why?"

Releasing one of my hands, she shrugged and continued walking along the shore, pulling me with her. "Because she said she could trust me. Because she wanted me to know. Because..." She stopped short, turning to face me once more.

"What is it? You can tell me."

She searched my eyes, the silence deafening as we stood on the sand, the storm brewing off the coast throwing her a bit off balance. "Because..." she began again, attempting to control her long brown, wavy hair, "sometimes things suck and you just want someone to know what you went through."

A loud crack sounded and the sky opened up, drowning us both with a September storm typical of those in the late summer.

"Come with me!" I shouted over the rain. "Let's get you home."

She closed her eyes and shook her head. "No. I want to stay here, Cam. Do you feel that?" she asked, raising her arms and basking in the torrential downpour that was soaking both of us.

"No! I don't. All I feel is the rain!"

Brianna opened her eyes and looked at me with the most intense expression I had ever seen on her innocent and pure face.

"Well, I do, Cam! I don't know how to describe it, but I feel something out here! With you! It's something I've never felt before! I feel..." She closed her eyes briefly, her chest rising as she looked at me again, contentment covering her face. "Happy. But it's so much more than happy. I feel at ease. I feel completely unfettered."

"You don't feel wet?!" I shouted over the thunder.

She laughed. "No. I definitely feel wet...and maybe a little cold, but it's worth it to have this other feeling, Cam."

"You've been spending far too much time with Marley in the theater department."

A sly smile crossed her face and I saw what she was talking about...one look and I knew that something had changed in Brianna. Don't get me wrong. I was always attracted to her, but when she was dating Mason, she became a bit of a shy girl, completely at odds with the outgoing friend of Marley's that would be over nearly every day with Carla and Kristen. Right then, I saw a glimpse of the old Brianna, her smile wider than I had seen in years. I couldn't help but think that Marley had something to do with it.

"Maybe so. Maybe knowing that I'm not alone has released the tiger inside."

"When did you ever think you were alone?"

Her eyes grew hooded and she sauntered up to me, making my entire being harden under her powerful gaze. "That doesn't matter, Cam," she said, her body a breath away from mine. "None of it does anymore. All that matters is this moment. Right here. Right now. I want more moments like this. Promise me we can have more of this."

I swallowed hard, completely turned on as I tried to keep my eyes focused on Brianna's face and not her wet shirt that was becoming somewhat transparent. "I'll give you anything you want, Bri."

125

"Cam…" she said breathlessly.

"Yes?"

"I want you to kiss me. Kiss me like you mean it. Kiss me like you've never kissed any other girl before. Kiss me with so much magnitude that it makes me forget…"

I crushed my lips against hers, stopping her from finishing her thought. I had always been respectful the few times that we had kissed over the past several days. This kiss was completely different, though. It wasn't soft or timid. It was passionate and ravenous. Our bodies intertwined as we devoured each other. I craved her more than I could remember wanting anything before in my life.

"Cam," she said, tearing away from the kiss and staring at my heaving chest.

"Yes?"

"What did it feel like?"

"What? What are you talking about?"

She avoided my eyes and looked out at the ocean, the waves growing strong and tumultuous with the storm that was soaking us. "When you pulled the trigger and shot him, what did it feel like?"

Running my hand through my wet hair, I took a deep breath. "It felt… It felt vindicating and remorseful at the same time, Bri. I knew I had to do it, but I still can't forget the look on his face when he fell over. I remember watching him for hours as he begged me to help him and I wondered whether he would ever die…whether I *wanted* him to die. I knew that I didn't. He did horrible and disgusting things to Marley. Did he deserve to die for it? I don't think so. And I'm glad he didn't die."

She snapped her eyes back to mine. "He's not dead?"

I slowly shook my head. "No, he's not. I shot him in the stomach a few times and in the leg. I was only eleven so I did the best I could."

"What happened?"

I looked at the sky and began to get nervous when I noticed lightening streak the horizon. "Here. Come with me." I grabbed her hand and led her down the shore toward a small alcove hidden from the beach by trees, sheltering us from the storm.

"What is this place?" she asked as I lowered myself to the ground. She followed suit, sitting next to me.

"Somewhere I come to think. No one knows about it. Well, I'm sure they do, but no one ever really comes here. Of course, you know about it now, but I'm okay with that."

"Really?"

I grinned, wrapping my arm around her drenched body, trying to warm her in the chilly evening air. "Really."

"So…"

"Right. Buck."

"That's his name? He sounds like a scumbag," she commented.

I shrugged. "Yeah. He was charged with a handful of offenses…rape, child endangerment, assault. He was sentenced to forty years, eligible for parole after twenty. Well, Marley found out that he was released about six months ago after only serving five years. And when we were in Charleston on Sunday…"

"That man." She gasped in shock. "The one that was staring at her…?"

I nodded slowly. "Yeah. I needed to get her out of there. I've spent the last decade of my life trying to protect her. And I have a feeling that I'll be spending the next decade of my life doing the same thing. So I guess it's a good thing that you know about it because trying to save Marley from herself is sometimes a full-time job."

"What do you mean, save her from herself? She's not…?" She gave me a knowing look.

"No!" I exclaimed quickly. "She's definitely not suicidal or anything, but she has good days and she has bad days…and then she has really, *really* bad days."

"And nightmares?"

I nodded. "Yeah. Really bad nightmares. You saw the result of that. But that's not even the worst of it."

"What is?" she asked.

"The hopelessness that finds her." I paused for a moment and thought about how to explain it. "When we got home early Monday morning, our aunt and uncle were waiting for us. Monday was a really, *really* bad day," I explained. "She told Uncle Graham that there is no God."

Brianna simply nodded in response. This was not the reaction I had expected from her. I actually thought that she would be slightly aghast at the notion, but she remained rather unmoved by the idea.

"You don't think that's a bit rash?" I asked her.

"I don't know, Cam. Do you blame her for thinking there is no God? I can see how she would feel let down and abandoned. She had to endure more horror and trauma than anyone I know. Where was God on those nights?"

I stared straight ahead. "I know. I hate to admit it, but I feel the same way sometimes. I guess I just have to remind myself that I don't see the big picture yet. Maybe God ignored her constant screams and cries for help for a bigger purpose. Maybe she was meant to endure that trauma for a reason. I can't dismiss what I hear my uncle preach about on Sunday. About God's purpose. Even if it's not God, per se, there's got to be a reason for it. If there isn't, what point is there?"

She leaned into my body and I felt a warmth I couldn't remember experiencing before in my life. "There has to be a point," she murmured, and I couldn't help but feel uneasy about what her words could insinuate.

# CHAPTER NINETEEN

## *BENEATH THE MASK*

*Marley's Journal*

*September 20*

I HAD BEEN DREADING today since receiving my letter from the Jessamine committee naming me as a finalist in this year's display of grotesque perversion that had become a yearly tradition in this town. Nearly every other girl that had been chosen as a finalist was excited and would talk in animated voices about what they were going to wear to the formal Jessamine Introduction Gala. I, however, felt none of that excitement. To me, it was more something I had to do out of duty and obligation than something that brought me joy.

Today was picture perfect. The sun was shining and the temperature was pleasant. I opened the windows to my room to allow the salty ocean air to blow through as I went about getting ready for the big event.

A hurried knock sounded on my door and my aunt burst through. "Are you almost ready? Doug will be here any minute, Marley. You can't be late."

I huffed as I sat down on my vanity chair, allowing her to manhandle my hair and coerce it into some sort of style worthy of a reluctant beauty queen.

"What have you been doing up here all morning?" she continued, barely even taking a breath. "Are you trying to sabotage your chance of winning this? All those other pageants and contests were child's play compared to this one. This is the one that could earn you a spot in the Miss South Carolina Pageant. Don't ruin this for yourself by showing everyone that you don't care."

"I'm sorry, ma'am," I responded quietly. I had no energy left for fighting her. It was futile anyway.

"I need you to be excited about this opportunity. It will reflect poorly on me as a member of the selection committee if my own niece isn't enthusiastic about this."

"I am excited," I lied. "I guess I'm just nervous. That's all."

"Oh, Marley Jane," she comforted, her tone softening. "You have nothing to be nervous about. Today is just a day to introduce our finalists to the town, to show them that you're all worthy to be Miss Jessamine, even if you don't win…but you'll win. I know you will."

I simply nodded as she finished pinning my hair back, allowing a few of my waves to fall in front of my face.

She took one last look at her work and her expression dropped. "Marley, do you have a cardigan to wear with this dress?"

I shook my head. "No. It's too warm for a sweater, Aunt Terryn."

"Yes, but…"

I lowered my eyes, knowing what she was referring to. I had no problem letting people see the scars from the years of abuse, but the notion horrified Aunt Terryn. Then they would ask questions and would talk about poor little Marley Jane Bowen.

Heading toward my closet, I found a light white shrug that complimented the sleek emerald green knee-length

131

dress that Aunt Terryn brought home for me a few days ago when she found out that I had yet to get a dress for today.

"That's much better," she said, relief washing over her. "Put your face on, Marley Jane. This is important."

"Yes, ma'am," I said as she turned to leave.

I took several steadying breaths. "I can do this," I said to myself. I kept repeating those words over and over again as I gazed into the mirror, putting my makeup on as Aunt Terryn had taught me all those years ago. Opening my drawer, my eyes settled on my mirror compact...my life vest for the past few years. I flipped it open and stared at the razor blade it contained, the sharp edges beckoning me...inviting me...telling me that it could release all the pain, even momentarily.

"You okay?" I heard as I was about to pick up the blade. Snapping the case shut, I turned to see Cam standing in the doorway. He saw the expression on my face and quickly closed the door, pulling up a chair and sitting next to me.

"Stupid question, huh?"

I nodded. "Yeah. Definitely."

"Just turn it off, Mar. It will be over before you know it. I'll be there for you. And so will Doug."

I looked at him, ready to snap under the weight of the mask I had been forced to wear. "Doug's expecting to see the Marley he knows that's excited about all this ridiculous pageantry. It's getting harder and harder to be that Marley, Cam. I don't know how much longer I can pretend to be someone I'm not. What if he sees the real Marley and doesn't want to be with me anymore because of it?"

He planted a gentle kiss on my forehead just as I heard the doorbell ring. "Then I'll kick his ass. Believe me, I think he knows who you are more than you realize. And maybe you should let him see the real Marley because that's the Marley I love."

"Only because you *have* to love me."

He shrugged. "I don't have to. I see lots of brothers and sisters that can't stand each other. I'm glad that's not the case with us. Now finish up. I'll go stall Doug and calm down Aunt Terryn."

"Thanks, Cam."

He sent me a warm smile and left me to finish getting ready. As I put the final touches on my makeup, my eyes kept wandering to that compact. It was tempting me, promising to dull my inner turmoil.

Flipping the case open, I swiftly raised my dress and dug into the skin of my inner thigh with the razor, tracing the word that had been carved in my flesh for the past few years. I exhaled, allowing my pain to leave me momentarily, and felt at ease for the first time all day. Quickly placing a bandage on my most recent bodily mutilation, I readjusted my composure.

Checking my reflection to ensure that my makeup was applied perfectly, I stared back at the Marley everyone else knew...hair coifed, makeup impeccable, emotional and physical scars covered so no one could see the truth.

Making my way down the stairs, I heard Doug and Cam talking in the living room. As I entered and my eyes settled on Doug, I felt as if all the air had been sucked out of the room. I had seen him in formal attire before. Hell, we went to our junior prom together. But today, as he stood in my living room in his khaki dress pants, light green dress shirt with the top button undone, and his dark hair damp from the shower, I felt completely speechless and weak in the knees. I think he felt the same way by the ardent, yet lustful stare he was giving me, his mouth slightly agape.

Swallowing hard, he said, "Hi, Marley."

"Hi, Doug," I responded calmly.

"You look… Wow. I don't think there's a word that expresses how… Just wow…"

"I like wow." I sauntered up to him. "You look wow, too," I whispered in his ear.

"I really want to kiss you right now, but I think your aunt will kill me if I ruin your makeup."

I pulled back and rolled my eyes. "Probably."

"Shall we?" he asked, holding his arm out for me.

"Absolutely." I grabbed his elbow and allowed him to lead me out of the house. Turning back and looking at Cam to see an odd look of satisfaction on his face, I asked, "Are you riding with us?"

"No. I'm picking Brianna up at her father's house and then we'll be over there. Her mother thought it would look bad if I just showed up there because I'm supposed to escort her, so she let her stay with her dad last night."

"Well, you should go get her so you're not late."

"I'm right behind you guys."

"Good. See you there."

Doug led me out of the house and supported me as we walked down the steps of the front porch toward his Pontiac. He opened the door for me and helped me sit down, his eyes lingering just a few seconds longer on my legs.

"See something you like, Douglas?" I asked coyly.

His face flamed red in embarrassment. "I… Well… Yes, Marley Jane. I see something I really like," he responded. "I see some*one* I really like." He leaned down and planted a tender kiss on my neck before closing the door and running around to the other side to get behind the wheel.

Cranking the engine, he turned to look at me. "You look amazing, but I think there's something missing."

I scrunched my eyebrows in confusion. "What? Did I forget something?" I surveyed my attire and made sure I had all the accessories that Aunt Terryn said she painstakingly selected for me to wear with my dress.

"This," Doug said, pulling out a small rectangular box.

"What is this?" I asked, my heart thumping in my chest.

"Your something missing." He beamed at me. "Open it."

With shaky hands, I removed the beautiful red ribbon that was tied around the black velvet box, gasping when my eyes settled on a breathtaking silver bracelet with emerald stones inlaid throughout.

"Doug," I exhaled. "It's gorgeous. You didn't…"

"I wanted to, Marley. I know today's difficult for you."

"What makes you think…?"

"I know you better than you think I do. You don't have to pretend around me. I've watched you since you arrived here all those years ago, trying to finally work up the courage to talk to you. I know when you're sad, or angry, or upset, or trying to make everyone else happy. So today, and every day forward, if you ever feel like you're all alone or you need a reminder of the real Marley, look down at your wrist." He unclipped the bracelet and placed it around me. "And pretend that it's my hand holding you or my arms around you…reminding you that you're not alone. That the Marley that is hiding layers beneath this mask you've been wearing is the Marley that I…"

"That you what, Doug?" I asked, a quiver in my voice, tears forming in my eyes from his sweet words.

"That I wish more people could see. Because that

Marley is worth knowing."

"Oh, Doug." I flung my arms around him and hugged him tighter than I can remember hugging anyone in my life. It was one thing for Cam to say something similar, but hearing it from someone who was interested in me in a romantic sense made my heart melt. And it made me hopeful that I could finally bury my past and stop being the girl I had been forced to be the past few years.

"We should probably get going."

I released my hold on him. "Yeah. You're probably right." I readjusted myself and put on my seatbelt. For the duration of the short drive to Brianna's step-father's house, my eyes remained locked on the beautiful bracelet around my wrist.

Pulling up in front of the valet stand at the entrance to the gates of their palatial estate on the beach, I stepped out of Doug's car and he held my hand as we walked up the path toward the entrance.

"You have to go inside the house first, right?" he asked.

I simply nodded and he could tell I was uneasy about everything.

"It'll be okay, Marley. Just smile and picture everyone naked."

I laughed heartily, completely not expecting those words to come out of Doug's mouth.

"I'm not so sure that's such a great idea. I'd probably be giggling the entire time." I smirked at him. "Maybe I'll just picture *you* naked and leave it at that."

His eyes grew wide.

"But then my complexion will be all flushed, and my aunt will not be pleased with that. Maybe I'll just repeat your words in my mind when you were about to tell me that you love me, but chickened out."

He stopped abruptly as we approached the pillared

entryway. "What makes you think that I love you?"

I shrugged. "It's just a feeling I have, Doug. I guess that when you go so long without being loved and someone finally *does* love you, you notice it. Like after my dad died and the only person in the world that I felt loved and cared for me was Cam. I studied the look in his eyes. You have that look, too, although it's more intense and primal. And, no, I don't think it's too soon. I mean, we've known each other for years now. We didn't jump into a relationship quickly. It wasn't hot from the start and then nothing. It's been warm since day one and has only become warmer and warmer. And that makes your non-declaration of love worth it. For the record, I don't love you, too."

He pulled my body into his, groaning, gently caressing my back. "It's taking all my willpower not to kiss you right now."

I looked up into his eyes and, for a moment, we were the only two people on the planet. I could forget about my past and my present as I stared into Doug's eyes.

"Marley Jane, I don't love you so much."

I gently brushed my lips against his. "I don't love you so much, too."

"Come on, beautiful. Cinderella can't be late for the ball."

"Actually, I think she *was* late for the ball," I commented, allowing him to lead me into the extravagant house, my heels clicking on the marble tile in the cavernous entryway. "And she still got the prince. At least I got to come with the prince… I mean, I arrived with the prince. Holy hell, I still hate that word."

He leaned toward me and his warm breath danced on my neck, sending shivers up and down my spine in an exquisite way. "Come. Say it."

Our eyes met.

"Come," I breathed.

"Marley!" I heard a voice call. I spun around and saw Mr. Grayson's imposing figure standing by the staircase. "The girls are upstairs. Your escort will wait for you by the winding stairs leading to the lawn out back." He raised his eyebrows at Doug as if ushering him away.

He turned to me once more. "See you soon. I don't love you."

"I don't love you, too."

"Come, Marley. This way," Mr. Grayson ordered, leading me up the stairs as I giggled at his use of the word.

"Douglas seems to be a very nice boy, doesn't he?" he commented, making small talk as he navigated through the hallways of his stately home.

"I think so."

"I'm glad to see you happy. And to finally see Brianna happy, as well. I think your brother is good for her. At least now she's able to spend time away from her father."

"What do you mean by that?" I asked quickly.

He stopped abruptly in the hallway. "It's not my place to say anything. It's important for her to have a relationship with him, but... I shouldn't have said anything. Please forget about this."

"Okay, Mr. Grayson. And, for the record, I'm glad you married Bri's mama."

He grinned his dazzling smile at me. "So am I, Marley. Now go wait with the rest of the girls." He gestured to the door in front of us. "I'll see you shortly."

I opened the door and was met with the sound of excited female voices talking about what they were wearing.

"Marley!" Carla and Kristen squealed, running up to

me and practically tackling me to the ground.

"Hey, girls," I responded enthusiastically.

"I am just so stinking happy that we're all on the court together! It's going to make senior year so much better," Kristen began, talking a mile a minute.

I plastered a fake smile on my face, not wanting them to see any displeasure. If they saw it, the gossip mills would be running full force about how darling Marley Bowen was irritated with the thought of being put on display for all to look at, and then it would get back to my aunt. We certainly couldn't have that.

"It sure is," I responded, mirroring her elation at the prospect. I scanned the sitting room, noticing Brianna by herself in the window alcove, staring out at the sprawling gardens down below. I was surprised that Cam had gotten there before me.

"Excuse me for a minute. I need to go powder my nose."

I walked across the room. "Hey, Bri."

She looked up at me and I could sense that she was shaken up over something.

I sat down next to her, neither one of us saying anything.

"I wish this house had a catwalk, too," she said, breaking the silence.

"I'm sorry."

"Your brother's too sweet sometimes. I put on my face and pretended everything was okay, like I'm supposed to. That's what hurts the most sometimes. Having to lie and deceive the people that I care about."

I nodded, knowing all too well the burden she was carrying. "You'll find strength to let them in eventually. Like when I told you. That was the first time I had told that story since the trial. It actually felt good to share it.

You should try it."

She took a deep breath. "I wish I could."

"I get it. Believe me, I completely understand. It's this fucking town."

"Not the entire town," Brianna interrupted. "There are some good people. People you can be the closest version of yourself around. Like you. And Cam. The ones that see this for what it is. A way for our parents to show off in front of each other."

I glanced down at my arm, feeling the strength and love wrapped around my wrist.

"That's beautiful," Brianna commented.

"Doug gave it to me."

A genuine smile crossed her face. "He's perfect for you. You should think about telling him, Marley. He deserves to know."

"I know he does. But I'm just worried that he won't want to be with me anymore once he knows that I'm not… Well, that I'm…"

She grabbed my hand. "Doug's not like that. I know that. *You* know that. What's stopping you?"

"My guess it's the same thing that's stopping you. Fear. Not wanting them to change the way they act around you. Not wanting them to look at you like you're a victim, the sympathetic looks that you'll receive once it's out there."

"Ladies!" a shrill voice sounded. We turned our attention to the doorway where my aunt stood, as well as a handful of other women that I had seen at functions over the years.

"It's time to begin. The order you're to be introduced is on the door. Please line up accordingly. Your escort will be waiting for you at the bottom of the steps leading out to the gardens. You will walk unaccompanied down the stairs. Your escort has been instructed to offer you their arm, then you will proceed up the center aisle and onto the stage. Once you are all introduced, Mr. Grayson will make a brief speech and then you will all be photographed for the area newspapers. Now, remember to smile and make us proud."

Brianna and I shared a look before we raised ourselves off the bench we were sitting on and walked toward the door, finding our position amongst the twelve girls. I groaned when I saw that I was dead last. I always hated that.

"Marley!" Carla squealed. "You're the grand finale!"

"I know! Isn't it great?"

"The judges must really like you," Savannah, one of the other girls, remarked. "The last few years, at least as long as I can remember, the girl who eventually went on to win this was introduced last. It must be the lucky position!"

"Well, that's how I feel," I responded with a fabricated smile. "So lucky to be here." I was happy that the only person who could sense my sarcasm was Brianna. She turned around and giggled at me before we were led out of the room and toward the back doors, all the important people of our beach community in attendance as they mingled and tried to play the game of who's better than whom. It always happened at these events. The one-uppers, as I liked to call them.

My mind blanked out as I heard Mr. Grayson begin to introduce all of us girls, one by one, complete with small snippets of information that were supplied to him. I wished that I could have sabotaged what was on those cards in his hand. I was pretty sure that would have made this a much more enjoyable experience…for me, at least.

I could just hear Mr. Grayson's voice in my head. *And*

*next, ladies and gentlemen, is Diana Greene. She is very active in giving back to the community…or at least giving head to the community. She has been very influential in the student body at McMillan Preparatory School, mostly in persuading all the teachers to continue to give her passing grades when she should be failing. Her oral skills are impeccable, ladies and gentlemen.*

I stifled my inappropriate laughs just as I felt an elbow nudging me. "Marley," my aunt hissed. "We're waiting."

"Shit. Sorry."

Forcing a smile across my mouth, I made my way down the steps, my eyes focused solely on Doug as he waited at the bottom. I completely blocked out everything else that was going on around me…the prying eyes, the voices, everything. The only thing that mattered was Doug and being near him. His presence calmed me when I was seconds away from cracking and letting everyone see what lay beneath the façade that had become Marley Jane Bowen.

"Hi, Marley Jane," he said softly as I approached.

"Hello, Douglas." I grabbed his arm and allowed him to escort me across the sprawling lawn and up to the stage, my eyes remaining glued to his the entire time. It hit me like a tidal wave. Doug was my peace. He was my calm. He was my home. The look of admiration in his eyes reminded me of the expression on my dad's face when he would look at me. I never wanted to stop gazing into Doug's eyes. I never wanted him to stop looking at me with that amount of devotion. With that look, I could get through anything. Finally.

# CHAPTER TWENTY

## *DEMONS*

*Marley's Journal*

*October 31*

THIS PAST MONTH HAS been one of the best that I can remember. Ever since the Introduction Gala all those weeks ago, I feel like a different girl...a new girl...a changed girl. And I think it's Doug's not love that's done that. I think about him a lot. Probably more than I should, but I can't help it. Isn't that what not love is supposed to be like? Aren't you supposed to have that person on your mind all the time? Because I do! I never saw myself getting close to someone, but there's just something about Doug that almost makes me want to finally tell him about my past, despite my aunt's request that I remain silent.

"Almost" is the key word here. I know that, at some point, I will have to. I'm just hoping that it's in the future...the distant future. I'm worried that the truth will break his heart, and I'm not sure I'm ready to do that.

We've been back in school for nearly two months and I'm happy to have that routine in my life. Get up. Get dressed. Go to school. Sit in class. Go to dance. Go home. Go to work when I'm scheduled. Cue heart flutter when

Doug unexpectedly walks through the doors of the boutique at which I work. We spend nearly every free moment together, which doesn't seem to be a lot these days with all of my extra obligations for the Jessamine Court. But when I want to roll my eyes as I listen to the committee speak about what an honor it is for us to be chosen, I look down at my wrist and feel Doug's not love. His not love is what gets me through those moments.

As I made my way to my Governments class this morning, I grinned when I saw Doug standing outside waiting for me. Walking up to him in his Halloween costume that consisted of hospital scrubs and a stethoscope, I faked passing out as I leaned against several lockers.

"Doctor Mullins, I feel faint. I think I need you to administer mouth-to-mouth."

He curved toward me, his arm placed against the wall as he hovered over me. "We can't have you feeling faint now, can we, Marley Jane? We need you to keep breathing."

His lips brushed mine and spine-tingling chills spread through my body. Over the past few months, I had grown accustomed to his kisses, but each kiss was still different and unexpected. Each kiss still made me want to melt into a puddle at his feet, forcing me to become a blubbering mess.

"I'm so in not love with you, Douglas," I exhaled as he ran his fingers against the contours of my body.

"And I'm so in not love with you. And you look rather hideous today in that getup. You really should not have worn that. I am all sorts of not turned on right now."

I giggled, my face blushing as his eyes roamed my body in the tight little nurse's costume I wore. Halloween was the one day of the year that we didn't have to wear our school uniforms as long as we wore a costume. Pretty much the entire student body dressed up, enjoying the one-day reprieve from conformity.

"Well, good. Because I certainly did not want you to find me attractive today. Because then you would kiss me and I certainly do not enjoy the feel of your lips on mine. It repulses me."

He leaned toward me again, his mouth just a breath away, warming my lips. "Oh, really?" he asked, his voice husky.

"Really," I croaked out as the bell rang. He remained unmoving. "Doug, you're going to be late."

"You're worth it." His lips met mine just as the sound of someone banging on a locker startled both of us. We turned to see Mr. Monroe towering over us, his face severe.

"I'm sorry. Was I interrupting?"

"I apologize, sir," Doug said, moving away from me.

"Be on your way, Mr. Mullins. Miss Bowen needs to get to class."

He nodded and left, looking over his shoulder at me and winking.

I couldn't help but grin in response, my heart ready to burst with not love.

"Miss Bowen?" a voice brought me back to the present.

"Sorry, sir. It won't happen again." I tried to walk past him and into the classroom.

He stepped in front of me, preventing me from doing so. "You see, that's the thing. I have a feeling that it will happen again. And again. And again."

I looked at him, remaining silent.

"No response? Where's the smart-mouthed Marley Bowen that's normally present? Or does Douglas bring out the obedient nature in you?" He grinned at me as if he was trying to make a joke, but I couldn't help but feel extremely uncomfortable. No wonder Brianna's mother left him. I wouldn't want to remain married to a man that looked at every girl, legal or not, as if she was a conquest.

"I'm trying to turn over a new leaf, sir," I said, a sardonic smile on my face.

"Ah," he sighed. "There's the Marley Bowen I'm used to. Go on then." He gestured to the classroom. "One toe out of line in class today and I won't hesitate to make you stay after school…as you should be doing anyway, but I'm in a forgiving mood."

"Yes, sir. Thank you, sir."

I entered the classroom, my hands shaking from the feel of his eyes burning my body, unable to brush the feeling that perhaps Mr. Monroe had something to do with Brianna's unusual behavior. He had always been a bit odd. The girls at school swooned over him, but I just had this feeling that he had demons inside that he hid with the mask he wore…just like me. I was able to take the mask off on occasion, and maybe he did, too, and Brianna received the brunt of it.

Sitting at my desk, I attempted to pull the skirt of my costume down.

Mr. Monroe cleared his throat, getting everyone's attention so that he could begin his lecture. "Now that the school year is underway, it's time to talk about what you'll be required to do for your senior project in this class."

Groans sounded throughout the room.

"As we've talked about in the past, the basis of all government systems is law and order. Different governments base their laws on different principles. Here in the United States, we base our statutory code on the common law system. Years and years ago, before laws were codified and written down as such, what was right and what was wrong was determined by custom. We still do that to this day. Generally, that's what a law is. It's a customary way of dealing with certain situations. We see customs every day. Some we agree with, some we don't.

"What I want you to do is find a custom, law, ordinance, or committee resolution that you disagree with on the local level here in Myrtle Beach. It could be anything that you feel strongly and passionately about. You will research this custom or law, you will find out the history of it, and you will write a paper about your findings and argue why that custom or law should no longer be in effect, or how you would change it to greater benefit society. You will give an oral presentation of your argument in the spring."

"Mr. Monroe?" a voice said. The class turned their heads to see Brittany Hamilton with her hand raised. "So, it can really be anything?"

"That is what I just said, Miss Hamilton."

"See, I heard this rumor… Well, Courtney told me about her sister who's in a sorority or something at one of the colleges, and she said that her sister said that they have to have a guy live in the house so that it's not considered a whore house or something like that. Would that count?"

We all turned to look at the exasperation plastered on Mr. Monroe's face and I chuckled.

"I suppose…so long as you actually find the law or resolution and it is, in fact, true and not some fraternity boy's way of being able to sleep in the same house with several women. Lucky bastard," he said under his breath, the class erupting in laughter at his comment.

His eyes remained fixed on mine as if he was gauging my reaction. I had learned to simply remain neutral in this class. I did not want to draw attention to myself, but it seemed that, no matter what, he found a reason to look at me.

"Now, everyone grab your things and quietly head to the library. We'll be spending the class period up there so you can start to research a topic for this project. And, from now on, every Friday, you are to report directly to the library so that you're able to work on this during our class period. I'm being generous in permitting this so I expect you to all blow me away with your final presentations."

"Marley!" I heard Carla shout as the class grabbed their bags and began to shuffle out of the room toward the library. I stopped and waited for her and Kristen. "Want to pair up with us?"

"I think this is supposed to be an individual project."

"So? We all pick the same law or whatever and work on it together, but make sure our papers are just different enough so that Mr. Hottie doesn't catch on...or maybe he does. I wouldn't mind having to stay after class with him."

I rolled my eyes. "Thanks for the offer, but I actually think I want to do this one on my own."

"What do you think you're going to do?" Kristen asked.

I shrugged. "I'm not sure yet. I'll figure something out." I couldn't tell them what I had planned. This was the perfect opportunity for me to finally say something. I had every intention of looking into all the traditions in place that surrounded the Jessamine Pageant and sound a call for change. I should have made a stand earlier.

# CHAPTER TWENTY-ONE

## *UP*

*Cam*

"YA COMING, MAR?" I shouted up the stairs, waiting, as usual, for my sister to emerge.

"Be right down. Keep your goddamn pants on!"

"Marley Jane!" my aunt scolded. "Watch your language! There are children present!"

"Sorry," I heard her mumble. She was most certainly *not* sorry.

She bounded down the stairs wearing the same costume she had on earlier, although it was now a bit shorter and slightly more revealing.

"Looking good," she commented, scanning my vampire costume. "Are you going to suck Brianna's blood tonight?" She raised her eyebrows at me as she pinched my arm. "Or maybe she'll suck something of yours," she joked, whispering in my ear so no one could overhear her.

"Mar, that's none of your business."

She made a slurping sound and my face turned red in embarrassment, although it was great to see the carefree version of my sister. Ever since the Introduction Gala several weeks ago, she had been more outgoing and at ease in her own skin. I only hoped it was Doug that brought this Marley back to me.

"You're sick."

"Maybe, but you still love me."

I rolled my eyes. "Maybe."

"No. You do. Don't even try to deny it. You'd be lost if you didn't have me for a sister."

"Sure. Are you ready to go, Nurse Ratched?"

"Reading *One Flew Over the Cuckoo's Nest*, are you?" She raised her eyebrows at me. She had been hounding me to start reading more for months now.

"Perhaps. I figured I might as well start with that book. Call it research for dealing with crazy people…like you."

"Let's go, Cameron, before I permanently disable your ability to have children. Goodnight, Aunt Terryn," she called out in her sing-song voice.

"Goodnight, kids. Have fun. And if you drink, don't drive. Stay at Doug's. It's okay."

I nodded. "Of course. Thanks."

"You bet."

I led Marley out of the house and we hopped into my Wrangler. Turning down the road, I noticed her expression. "Okay, Mar. Spill it."

"She hates me."

"Aunt Terryn does *not* hate you, Marley. How could you even say such a thing?"

"Because she's always so nice to you. And she's nice to me when you're around. But… I don't know. I have this feeling that, if I wasn't doing all this pageant shit, she'd never speak to me."

"You're overanalyzing everything, just like you always do. Stop assuming the worst of people. She loves you. She's done so much for you…for both of us. I know that sometimes it's a bit hard to figure her out. One second, she'll be cold, and the next, she'll be giving you

150

permission to sleep over your boyfriend's house..."

"It's not hard to figure her out," Marley interrupted. "She's bipolar."

I shook my head, laughing. "No, she's not. I just think she's confused about how to raise us. She's not our mom, but she's expected to fill that role, even though Mama's still in the picture. I think that's why we see the difference in behavior on occasion. It's like sometimes she remembers that she's supposed to be the mom; other times, she wants to be the fun aunt."

"I can't wait to be the fun aunt," she said, cutting the thick atmosphere. "I'm going to spoil yours and Brianna's kids!"

"Mar, we've only been dating for a few months. Don't rush us. It's a high school romance anyway. Those relationships never work out."

"But they can, can't they?"

I could sense her concern about it. The thing about Marley was that when she loved, she loved with every fiber of her being and she couldn't imagine life without the object of her affection. It was all or nothing with her. It was hot or cold. It was black or white. There was no in between.

"Of course they can."

She smiled. "Good."

I pulled up in front of Doug's parents' house, already seeing quite a few cars there. "So much for having just a few people over," I said to Marley as I put the car in park. It was a good thing he lived in the middle of nowhere with not many neighbors. The properties were huge out this way so no one would even hear the party going on.

"Yeah. I warned him about telling Carla and Kristen, and the rest of the girls, but he figured it's his senior year and it was time to have one huge party while his parents are out of town. I think his older brother's home from U.S.C. this weekend, too, so he invited a few of his buddies over."

"This is going to be quite the party then. Are you sure you're okay with it? There's going to be a lot of people, Marley."

"Cam," she said, turning to look at me as we walked up the driveway to the house. "You can't always worry about me and how I'll react. I know you won't always be around to pick up the pieces. I see that now. I get that being my brother and dealing with me has become a burden on you. I don't want to hold you back, so please don't worry about me tonight. You just have fun with Brianna." She winked as she grabbed my hand and pulled me the rest of the way toward the house, drunk bodies dancing on the lawn.

"I'm your brother. I'm always going to worry about you."

"I know. I just don't want it to come before your own needs…if you know what I mean." She giggled and I simply rolled my eyes at her.

As I watched her make her way through the party, smiling and hugging girls that I never remembered seeing her talk to before, I couldn't help but think that this was one of her good days. But I knew that for every up, there was an even worse down. Marley had been up since the Introduction Gala. An awful premonition formed in the pit of my stomach that when she finally fell from the high she had been on, it would be so far that no one could possibly bring her back. I hoped with everything that I was wrong.

# CHAPTER TWENTY-TWO

## *NO POINT*

*Marley's Journal*

*October 31*

THINGS WERE GOING SO well for so long. Everything seemed so...normal. I knew I had this obsession with normal, but I couldn't help it. I should have known that it was too good to be true, that there was no way I could continue on the high that I had been on. Doug's not love wasn't enough to chase away the demons like I thought it would.

As I maneuvered through the living room of Doug's house that was packed with dancing bodies, people were calling my name left and right. I recognized some of the girls as having graduated with Doug's brother, Justin, so I enthusiastically hugged them, regardless of the fact that I had no idea who they were. This was what girls did, right? We would hug and pretend that we were the best of friends, then turn around to secretly gossip about them behind their back.

"I hear you're dating Doug!" one of the drunk blondes slurred.

"You heard right!" I shouted back.

"Shots! We must do shots to celebrate!" a tipsy redhead

exclaimed.

"I'm not twenty-one," I stated.

She rolled her eyes. "Like that should stop you. Come. I insist. As a former member of the Jessamine Court, of which you're now a member, you must do a shot with me. Trust me. You'll need the alcohol to get through that spectacle." She looked at me and her previous level of enthusiasm was replaced with an expression that I couldn't quite label.

"What do you mean?" I asked quietly.

"She means that she's had too much liquor and she's now running her mouth. Isn't that right?" a tall, skinny brunette said in warning.

The redhead shook her head. "Of course you would say that. You didn't win." She turned her attention back to me. "Lacey Richards." She held her hand out. "I won three years ago."

"I'm Marley-."

"I know who you are. Be careful, Marley Bowen. And trust no one," she whispered into my ear so no one could overhear her. "Now! Shots!" Lacey grabbed my arm and led me through the crowd of people toward the kitchen, her words repeating in my brain as I tried to figure out what she could possibly mean.

"Here. Drink this." Lacey handed me a plastic shot glass filled with a clear liquid. I held my nose to it and nearly gagged from the smell.

"What is this?"

"Tequila. It helps you forget."

I glanced around the party and was unable to find Cam. Shrugging, I brought the shot to my mouth. "You only live once, right? May as well make it count."

"That's right, Marley."

I looked into her small hazel eyes and I could sense that

she had the same opinion of the pageant that I did. I threw the shot back, choking through the burning sensation of the liquid. I had never really drank before so the taste of the tequila was quite a shock to my system.

Once the fire grew dull, I felt a warm sensation coat my stomach and travel through the rest of my body. I knew that alcohol had a tendency to remove your inhibitions and helped you to not really care, but that was what I always wanted. I wanted to stop caring about my past.

"Another round!" I shouted to cheers and whistles.

"I don't think that's such a good idea, Marley Jane," a sensual voice sounded.

I spun around and looked into a pair of blazing green eyes.

"Doug," I exhaled, practically tackling him to the ground as I threw my arms around him, planting a deep kiss on his lips.

"Whoa. Take it easy there. You're making me spill my beer."

I giggled. "So sorry, Douglas. I understand that having a full cup of beer is much more important than kissing the girl that you're in not love with." I winked.

He threw his beer to the ground and pulled me into him, his mouth pressed against mine before I could even protest. His hand roamed my frame from my hip to my shoulder. Pleasure ran through me, making me become completely unhinged and as if I was not myself. I tried to draw his body even closer, but nothing was able to extinguish the fire inside caused by my need for him.

He released his hold on me, panting. "Damn, Marley Jane. How much have you had to drink?"

"I only did one shot. I just really missed you today." I stood on my toes and kissed his neck. "I was left rather frustrated before second period. That kiss just didn't do it

155

for me."

"Well, how about that one?" he asked, referring to our most recent exchange. "Was that one better?"

I scrunched my nose in a playful manner. "The jury's still deliberating on that. I'll let you know when they reach a verdict. Of course, you could try to butter them up and show off your skills during the process."

He laughed. "I love your mouth, Marley."

"Don't you mean that you *don't* love my mouth?"

He slowly shook his head. "No. I mean that I love your mouth. And the body attached to it."

We stared at each other, the tension between us hot and carnal.

"Here. Come with me." He grabbed my hand and led me away from the kitchen and up the stairs, my heart racing in my chest as we walked past couples making out in the hallway.

"Where are we going?" I was sure he could hear the nerves in my voice.

"My room. I mean, if you want to. I just really want to spend some time alone with you. We can keep the door open. I promise I won't try anything."

"I want you to try something, Doug." I was surprised at the words leaving my mouth, but I knew that making out with my boyfriend while his parents were out of town was another rite of passage. It was normal. I needed normal. So I permitted him to lead me down the hallway on the second floor of his house, toward his darkened bedroom.

Throwing the door open, he allowed me to enter in front of him. Nerves coursed through me when I heard the click of the lock. I spun around, the look he was giving me a mix of desire and admiration.

"Have I told you today how beautiful you are?" he asked me, his tone serene.

"I think you were about to," I started, "before Mr. Monroe interrupted you giving me mouth-to-mouth, which was a medical necessity at that moment."

A smile crossed his face and he pulled me into his body, his hand placed firmly on the small of my back as he deliberately led me across his room. "How about now? Are you still feeling short of breath?"

Biting my lower lip, I nodded fervently. "Oh, yes. I'm definitely light-headed."

"Well, the doctor is in." Lowering me to his bed, he crawled on top. "Marley, I…" He stared at me and pushed one of my blonde curls away from my eyes.

"Yes?"

"I am really in not love with you," he said, his voice warm and full of reverence.

My body heated in response to his words. "I'm really in not love with you, too. Doug…" I closed my eyes, summoning the inner strength I needed. "I want you to show me how much you're in not love with me." I narrowed my gaze at him in a knowing manner.

"Are you sure?"

I swallowed hard. "Yes," I replied nervously, trying to convince myself that I could do this. Doug had been so incredibly patient with me when I knew he must have been rather frustrated at this point. Any of the other girls at school would have already slept with him. I knew I was different, but it was a normal thing to want to become intimate with the boyfriend I had been dating for several months. I *needed* the normal.

"We don't have to, Marley. I don't want you to think that you have to do anything you're not ready for."

"I know." I grabbed his head and brought his lips to mine. "I want to," I assured him. I just didn't know if I could follow through.

Groaning, his soft lips met mine and he explored my mouth as he had been doing nearly every day for the past few months. But that kiss felt so much more electric as my mind raced, thinking about what we were going to do. I was excited and scared at the same time.

He tore his lips from me and trailed kisses down my neck. I tilted my head, giving him better access as his hand roamed my body, his motions nervous and inhibited.

"Doug," I moaned. "Take my dress off."

He hesitated. "Are you sure?"

"Will you stop asking me that? I wouldn't ask you if I wasn't sure. Now, unzip me." I sat up on the edge of the bed and instantly felt Doug's hands lower the zipper of my nurse costume, thankful that the darkened room hid the scars. I wasn't ready for that conversation just yet.

Standing up, I let the dress pool to the ground and stood in front of him in just my white lace bra and boy shorts.

His eyes grew heated and I could tell that he wanted me...probably more than he had ever wanted anything before. Straddling him, I pinned him to his bed and brought my lips to his once more, his hands remaining glued to my hips.

I ran my fingers through his hair and he flipped me onto my back. He dragged his tongue across my collar bone, lowering his body down mine, stopping briefly at my chest. Gazing up at me, he raised his eyebrows. I nodded, my heart beating loud in my chest. He lowered the cup of my bra, continuing the exploration of my body with his mouth.

I threw my head back and moaned as I wrapped my legs around him.

He crushed his lips against mine and his hand trailed

down my midsection, grasping onto my leg. He began delicately thrusting against me and I released the grip that my legs had on his waist.

"Do you feel what you do to me, Marley?" he asked, his voice raspy.

"Yes."

He continued his movements and I closed my eyes as his tongue circled my neck, his teeth tugging on my earlobe. He grunted and I tensed up, but he didn't notice it. I squeezed my eyes tighter, the image of a man moving on top of me making me tremble. Memories flooded back and I returned to that time in my life.

"Doug," I said quietly as he continued moving against me, each motion pushing me deeper and deeper into my past. "Doug," I repeated as he kept licking and sucking. My heart raced and flashes of everything I had endured played like a movie in front of my eyes. I tried to remind myself that I was free, but nothing worked. The burn and pain became too much.

"*Get off me!*" I shrieked, pushing against him, shooting off of the bed as my entire body shook.

"My god. Marley, I'm sorry," he said, his apologetic eyes meeting mine.

"*No, you're not!*" Throwing my dress on, leaving it unzipped in the back, I quickly retreated from the room, dashing down the hall and out of the house.

I had no idea where I was going, but I knew that I needed to go as far away as possible. Running down the street, the full moon the only light, I reached the end of the road, my eyes settling on a simple tree house in the yard of a property for sale. Climbing up the ladder, I collapsed, curling into a ball, and cried harder than I had ever cried in my life.

The realization that I would never be normal washed

over me and I hated everyone. I hated Buck for what he did to me. I hated my aunt and uncle for thinking that God was the answer to everything. I hated Doug for loving me. And I hated Cam for being normal. I wanted to be normal, and his ability to be what I wanted and craved with every fiber of my being was like a knife to my heart.

If I couldn't be normal, what was the point?

# CHAPTER TWENTY-THREE

## *FALLING*

*Cam*

"HEY, HANDSOME," A SWEET voice said, sidling up to me as I watched Marley talk with a group of girls. I looked to my left and my eyes fell on Brianna in a short and tight flight attendant costume.

"Wow. You look…"

She raised her eyebrows at me. "Good enough that you'd think about joining the mile high club?"

I nodded slowly. "But you had a flapper costume on at school. I liked that one, too."

"Oh." She looked away. "I just thought that maybe you'd…"

I grabbed her chin and made her stare into my eyes. "It's hot. But I'm worried about having to fight off all the guys here who are drooling over you because of how amazing you look."

She planted a kiss on my lips. "You're the only one I want drooling over me."

"Well, then…mission accomplished."

"Good!" She clapped her hands. "Want a drink or anything? Doug said we could crash here if we wanted to."

I hesitated. "I don't know. I mean, I don't know what

161

Marley's going to want to do and if she doesn't feel comfortable…" I trailed off, hating that I was disappointing Brianna by putting Marley first. "You know what? I'll have a beer. I need to stop constantly thinking of Marley before me."

Brianna held my hand and led me toward the kitchen. "No, you don't. I think it's sweet that you always do that. She needs it, Cam. But you need to live your own life, too."

"May as well start doing that with a beer."

Brianna grinned and filled two red cups, handing me one. "Want to go sit outside by the fire pit? It'll be less noisy," she said over the loud cheers and singing that was going on all around us.

"I'd like that." I led her from the kitchen and out the back door, the cool air refreshing after having been inside the house that was sweltering from all the warm, dancing bodies. Supporting her as we climbed down the steps of the back deck, we made our way across the sprawling lawn and toward a stone fire pit. Just a few feet away, drunk high school and college students were stripping into practically nothing before hopping in the hot tub.

"Wanna go for a dip?" Brianna asked.

"I'd rather not."

"I was hoping you'd say that," she retorted, sounding somewhat relieved.

"I mean, don't get me wrong. I'd love to be in a hot tub with you, Bri, so long as it was just us. I'm having a hard enough time trying to not punch every guy in the face who's looking at your legs. If you got in that hot tub with a bathing suit on, I don't know what I'd do."

She lowered her head. "I'm sorry. I can go change."

I stopped abruptly and pulled her body into mine, lowering my lips to hers as she moaned into my mouth.

My hand grazing her back, I gently pushed against her so she could feel how turned on I was and she gasped.

"Don't you dare go change."

She giggled. "Okay." Her teeth began to chatter.

I shrugged out of the black jacket that went with my vampire costume and slung it over her shoulders. "As much as I hate to cover you up, you need to keep warm. My aunt will have my ass if you get sick and can't make it to the Thanksgiving Day parade in a few weeks."

She rolled her eyes and I grabbed her hand, leading her to the fire pit. "Yeah. God forbid only eleven girls are on that stupid float instead of twelve."

"It's a rather grave offense," I joked.

"It is to some people."

We sat on the stone benches, the warmth of the fire heating our skin in the chilly fall night air. Everyone else was either in the hot tub or in the house drinking and dancing. It was just Brianna and me, and that's how I liked it.

"This is my favorite time of year," she said, drawing a long breath.

"Oh yeah?"

"Yeah. All the leaves changing color. The burning smell in the air. Everything going to rest for the winter knowing that, in spring, it'll be a rebirth…a new start. Makes me hopeful for my own new start, I guess."

"Like in college?"

"Yeah, like in college," she replied rather softly.

"Have you been accepted anywhere yet?" I asked.

"A few places. I'm still undeclared as far as my major goes. It just seems like a whole lot of pressure to put on a seventeen-year-old to ask them to decide what they want to do for the rest of their life. I have no idea what I want to do. All I know is that I want to get out of this town."

"You and Marley both," I muttered. "You guys are a lot alike."

"Please don't tell me that's the only reason you're attracted to me."

"God, no," I said quickly. "I mean, you're both fed up with this town, but I guess a lot of people we go to high school with are. Who wouldn't look forward to finally being able to go to a new place and have some independence? That's what college is all about, isn't it?"

"Yeah. I guess."

"You're nothing like Marley. Believe me."

She reached over and grabbed my hand in hers, not saying a word. She didn't have to. In that one simple gesture, she spoke volumes. We sat there for a while, listening to the crackling of the fire in front of us.

"Know what I like about you, Bri?" I said finally, facing her. "You're selective with your words. You don't speak much so when you do, I know it's important. I'd rather hear three meaningful words out of your mouth than three thousand insignificant ones."

"Like... I love you?"

My heart stopped in my chest when I heard those three amazing words leave her mouth, surprised at her forwardness and inhibition in saying them.

"I don't care if you don't feel the same way about me. I'm pretty sure that you don't..."

"What makes you think that?" I interrupted her.

She shrugged and pinched her lips in that adorable way she always did when she was thinking hard about something. "How could you? I mean, we've only been dating for two months. Love doesn't happen that quickly. I've been crushing on you for as long as I could remember, even when I was dating Mason. And I always loved you as a friend. But now I love you as more than a

164

friend." She smiled, a carefree expression crossing her face.

"There you are, Bri." My voice was quiet and thoughtful.

"What?"

"There's the Bri that I knew in sixth grade. I knew you were in there somewhere beneath this hard exterior that you've had up the past few years." I leaned toward her and hovered my mouth near her lips. "Because that's the Brianna that I fell in love with."

"Oh, Cam," she sighed, reaching up and running her fingers through my shaggy hair. "I hope you're not just saying that because…"

"I've loved you for longer than I think you realize, Bri."

"Really?"

I grinned wide. "Really."

"Cam!" I heard a voice shout, tearing me away from Brianna's lips. We both turned to see Doug running down the slope of his back yard, panicked.

"What's wrong?"

"It's Marley."

I eyed him cautiously. "What do you mean?"

"I took her up to my room so we could be alone…"

My nostrils flared and he could sense my rage over his admission.

"It's not what you think," he interjected quickly. "I had every intention of being respectful, Cam. Honest to God. But things got a bit heated and one thing led to another and, well…long story short, she completely freaked out and then ran. I've tried looking everywhere for her and I can't find her. I don't know where she could be and I figure you've got to have some crazy twin-sense, right?"

"She wouldn't have gone far. Let's go." I grabbed Brianna's hand and led her, rather quickly, up the back yard and into the house. After a few minutes of navigating our way through the crowd of people, we finally pushed past the front door and piled in my Wrangler. I took off down the road, driving slowly in case she was walking in the darkened night.

"Cam, I'm so sorry," Doug said as my eyes scanned the street. "I just… I'm a complete ass. I would never do anything to hurt Marley. I thought everything was okay and then, the next thing I knew, she was screaming at me. I don't get it."

I sighed, glancing at him, slamming on the brakes when I drove past a vacant property for sale, noticing a tree house in the side yard.

"What is it? Do you see her?" Doug asked anxiously.

I pulled the parking brake and we both jumped out of the Wrangler at the same time.

"Call it my twin-sense," I responded as I helped Brianna out of the back.

We all ran across the expansive lawn, slowing down when we saw Marley's trembling body curled up in the small doorway to the tree house. Approaching with caution, I noticed Doug stop dead in his tracks as his eyes settled on my sister's exposed back that was illuminated by the full moon.

He turned to look at me, questioning. I felt Brianna tense up beside me when she saw what had shocked Doug.

"Is it…?"

My eyes met hers and I simply nodded.

"Oh, god…" she exhaled, her chin quivering.

I headed toward the tree house, climbing up the short ladder. "Marley…?"

"I'm sorry, Cam. I tried. I really did. I've tried so fucking hard to be normal and to forget, but I can't. I want to so fucking bad. I just can't do it. I want to go back to how things were before Dad died! I want my fucking tree house! Why can't I have that back?" Her sobs echoed through the empty yard and my heart broke for her.

I sat next to her, pulling her into my arms. She held on to me as if letting go would mean letting go of her very existence. "It's okay, Marley Jane. Let it out. Stop keeping it inside."

"Marley?" We both looked to see Doug hesitantly standing at the bottom of the ladder.

"Hi, Doug," she said, wiping her tears.

"I never meant to…"

"I know you didn't. I'm sorry."

"I'm the one who's sorry," he said quietly.

Squeezing Marley's hand, I said, "I think it's time."

She looked at me, her eyes growing wide. "I don't know if I can…"

"I *know* you can. He needs to know."

# CHAPTER TWENTY-FOUR

## *THE TRUTH*

*Marley's Journal*

October 31

I KNEW THIS DAY would eventually come. I had ignored the reality of what a relationship would mean for me…and for Doug. His love set me free, or so I thought. But no amount of love could erase the past or free me from the demons that haunted me. My existence was a ticking time-bomb and, at some point, no one would be able to find a way to deactivate me.

"Marley?" Doug said, sitting down next to me in the tree house after they had found me. "Are you okay?"

I stared into his confused eyes and wished that I could tell him the words that he needed to hear, but I couldn't. Shaking my head, I said, "No, Doug. I haven't been okay since my eighth birthday."

I felt a squeeze on my hand and looked at Cam. "I'll give you guys some privacy. Unless you want me to stay?" He raised his eyebrows at me.

"No. I can do this."

He leaned over and planted a kiss on my temple. "I know you can, Mar." He climbed down the ladder and made his way back to Brianna, wrapping his arms around her.

"Your back…" Doug said quietly.

"It's not as bad as it used to be…"

"What happened?"

"Everything. Everything that a little girl should never have to endure happened to me, Doug."

"Please, Marley. Just tell me. I need to know. I don't ever want to hurt you again."

"I know." Taking a deep breath, I met his eyes that were awash with concern and sorrow. "When I was eight, my father died. Mama was depressed and turned to drugs and alcohol. We lost our house and had to move to some shitty neighborhoods. One day, a man saw me playing in the school yard while we were waiting for our mama. He taught me how to throw a softball. Mama never showed up so Cam and I had to walk home. He must have followed because, a week later, he appeared on our doorstep. He began to date Mama and, for a minute, she stopped drinking and doing drugs. That didn't last. He began supplying her drugs, ensuring that she would be passed out nearly every night."

A tear fell down my cheek as I recalled that first night. "It was New Year's Eve. Mama invited him over to celebrate. She drank and I remember seeing her stick a needle in her arm. She said it was her medicine. I was too young to realize that she was shooting heroin. We stayed up to watch the ball drop. Mama was already passed out so he put us to bed and I fell asleep pretty quickly. I don't know how long he waited, but in the middle of the night, I felt someone climb into my bed."

Doug wrapped his arm around me and pulled my body into his, his grip tightening on me as he listened.

"I had no idea what was going on. I was so confused. All I knew was that whatever he was doing was the most

169

painful thing I had ever felt in my life. He kept saying that he had demons and that this was the only way he could release them. I tried to fight him, but it never worked. He would use his belt on me whenever I attempted to get away from him."

"How many times?" Doug asked, his voice barely above a whisper.

I looked into his eyes and could see tears forming. "Practically every night for three years."

He let out a small sob and pulled me even closer.

"Cam had to listen to my screams and cries for help nearly every night. Our mama was always unconscious from the drugs so she never stopped it. She was too drunk or coked-up to realize that anything was going on, except every few months when she promised to get her act together. She would see the welts on me and the bruises on Cam's face and would take us away to somewhere new. Then the withdrawal symptoms would set in and she'd call him, begging for drugs, and he'd be back in our lives. Until Cam couldn't take it anymore and found my mama's gun and shot him."

"So he's dead?"

I shook my head. "No, he's not. He was sent to prison, but he was released recently. After that night, Cam called my grams, who called the police about everything. We were sent to a home. They tried to split us up, but I would throw a fit whenever they took him from me. When I kept trying to hurt myself, the people running the home eventually caved in and let us stay together. Cam was the only one who could stop it. I guess he still is."

"What do you mean, Marley? Do you still try to hurt yourself?"

"I haven't in over a month. It takes my mind off everything, but since you told me that you're in not love with me, the pain of my past isn't as bad. I have a reason to keep breathing."

"You've always had a reason to keep breathing, Marley Jane, even if I wasn't in not love with you. You have people who love you…your aunt and uncle, and Cam. You must realize that."

I shrugged. "I suppose. I guess sometimes I just want to turn it off and be at peace."

"Do you really think that hurting yourself is the way to do that?"

"Sometimes I do. But I haven't felt that way in a while because every time I do, I think of you. And I look down at my bracelet." I glanced at my wrist. "And I feel your not love and I know that I have a reason to keep breathing. Doug, you're my reason to keep breathing." Tears began to stream down my face in response to my admission to him.

"Oh, Marley," he exhaled, planting a kiss on the top of my head. "I'm so sorry you had to go through that, but I swear I will never hurt you. We can take our time. I'm not going anywhere. I promise."

"Good." I pulled out of his embrace, wiping my cheeks. "You better not look at me any differently now that you know the truth. I'm still the same Marley."

"No, you're not," he said thoughtfully. "Now maybe you can be the *real* Marley around me a little bit more."

"What do you mean? I *am* the real Marley around you."

He raised his eyebrows at me.

"Okay. Maybe I haven't been the most genuine version of myself."

"Just stop pretending. I'm in not love with you more than you can possibly imagine, and that means all the parts of you."

"Like what?" I gave him a sly smile.

"Well, for starters, I really like your lips. The words that leave them on a daily basis make me laugh and fall a little bit more in not love with you."

I leaned in and gently brushed my lips with his. "What else?" I murmured against him.

"Your smile, regardless of the pain it tries to hide. And maybe that's why I like it so much because, regardless of your past, you've found a reason to continue on and smile. I just hope that I never do anything to make that smile disappear. I fell in not love with that smile years ago, Marley Jane, and I never want to go a day without seeing it on your beautiful face."

I crushed my mouth against him, running my hand through his hair, deepening the kiss. "What else?" I panted.

"Your heart, Marley Jane," he said softly, his eyes intense. "It's been broken and betrayed in the worst ways imaginable. But, against all odds, it found a reason to keep beating. It proved that it was capable to love and receive love in return."

"Don't you mean not love?" I interrupted.

He chuckled. "Of course. I stand corrected."

It was silent while we sat in the tree house, the leaves rustling in a gentle breeze as his hand caressed my scarred back.

"You're stronger than you think you are, Marley. Never forget that, okay?"

I simply nodded, wishing I could actually believe that his words were true.

# Chapter Twenty-Five

## *Breakable*

*Marley's Journal*

*November 21*

THREE WEEKS HAVE PASSED since I told Doug the truth. Three weeks have passed that he's treated me as if I'm about to break at any second. Three weeks have passed that I cringe when he looks at me. They always say that the truth will set you free. Not for me. The truth has erected bars around me. I walk through the halls of school, worried that people are talking behind my back. Granted, that could be because I ran through Doug's house with my dress about to fall off after my "episode", but I still can't help but feel as if everyone is treating me differently...especially Doug. I hate that. I want it to stop.

I am so sick of being asked if I'm okay. Every time Doug sees me, those are the first words out of his mouth. It used to be *Hey, beautiful girl* or something like that. Now, it's *How are you, Marley?* And not just a normal *how are you*. It's a sympathetic, compassionate, "walk on eggshells because the crazy, molested bitch might crack and shoot all of us at any second" *how are you*.

The same was true today as I headed toward my second period Governments class. I considered spinning around and walking away when I saw Doug there. I couldn't stand his kindness and empathy.

"Hey, Marley," he said, his eyes scanning my body as if he was worried that I was about to pull out a gun and start shooting. "How are you?"

I huffed. "I'm fine, Doug." I pushed past him. "I have to go or I'll be late. Our class meets in the library on Fridays. I keep forgetting."

"I'll walk with you."

"You don't have to. Your class is on the other side of the building."

"I just want to make sure you get there safely."

I faced him, my eyes on fire. "Stop it. You promised you weren't going to do this."

"Do what?" he asked, taken aback.

"This. What you've been doing all month! You're treating me like I'm about to crack. I'm not delicate so stop treating me like this, Doug. I'm sick of it!"

I began to walk away and he reached out, grabbing my arm.

"Marley, I'm just worried about you…"

"Well, stop!" I hissed. "And get your fucking hand off me!"

He released his grasp, surprised at the tone of my voice. As I retreated from him, I felt a hint of guilt for behaving that way, but I brushed it off. I continued past the library, not caring about the potential ramifications of skipping class. I didn't want to be around anyone. I just wanted to be alone.

I ran to the theater department and climbed the spiral stairs up to the catwalk, happy to have a moment of peace. But I still felt the hurt. It had been there since Halloween. Nothing was stopping it. Doug's changed behavior was eating me up as the realization washed over me that he no longer looked at me with the adoration that was once in his eyes. Now there was a look of sorrow and condolence in his expression.

Rummaging through my bag as I sat on the catwalk, I found what I was looking for. Sliding my skirt up, I saw the red marking on my inner thigh. It had grown dull over the past few months, Doug's not love having muted my need to release the anguish through that blade.

Grabbing the razor, I dug into my skin, the physical pain taking my mind off the horrors of my past. I traced over the word that I had cut into my thigh the night that I won the Junior Miss Myrtle Beach Pageant nearly two years ago...*Ruined*. The word was a reminder to me that no matter what I thought, my life was forever ruined.

Letting out a breath, I carved the word over and over again, each time drawing more and more blood, my inner demons releasing through the act. Finally feeling sated, I placed the razor back in its hiding spot and grabbed a few bandages, covering up my blood-stained thigh.

A loud door closing startled me and I quickly readjusted my skirt and hid the bandages in my bag. Looking up, I saw Brianna in the doorway, her hair disheveled and a look of complete fear and panic on her face. Taking a deep breath, she attempted to readjust her demeanor, running her hands through her hair to fix it.

"Hi, Marley."

"Hey, Bri. Rough morning?"

She laughed slightly and rolled her eyes. "Rough couple of years is more like it." She made her way toward me and sat down. "How about you?"

I shrugged. "Rough few weeks, I guess. I feel better now, though."

"How?" She met my eyes, pleading with me to tell her

how to make the pain stop.

I hesitated. No one knew about my cutting, other than my aunt and only because of the pageants. Of course, she told no one about it and pretended it didn't happen. I insinuated something to this effect when I told Doug about my past, but I didn't go into any details. I was pretty sure he would be horrified if he knew the extent of my need to self-mutilate. This was the one thing I had that no one knew about. This was the one thing I had that was all mine. And I hated the thought of Brianna hurting herself thinking that it would help. I knew it was destructive. I knew it was abnormal. But, at the same time, it was liberating when I felt the blade dig into my skin and release all the anguish that had built up since the last time I cut. It was the only thing that could release the hurt and trauma.

"Nothing, Bri," I replied. "Sometimes having a minute alone to forget is the best medicine."

"Do you want me to leave?" she asked, about to get up.

"No. We can be alone together. I don't mind."

She nodded and stared straight ahead. It was silent for a brief moment before she spoke again.

"Doug's acting differently toward you, isn't he? I noticed it during lunch the past few weeks. He used to have this heat in his eyes like he was ready to just attack you… In a good way, of course."

I giggled. It felt good to talk to Brianna about it. "Yeah. Now it's like he's walking on glass around me. I hate it. I'm the same exact Marley I was before I told him, but he's not the same Doug."

"That's what I'm afraid of, too."

# CHAPTER TWENTY-SIX

## *ANSWERS*

*Cam*

"AUNT TERRYN! I'M HOME!" I called out, walking into the foyer of our house after getting home from school.

Looking around, I wondered where everyone was. "Uncle Graham?" I continued past the living room and kitchen, and into the back hallway, pausing outside a closed wooden door. Knocking softly, I listened for any movement.

My heart racing at the thought of getting caught, I carefully opened the door to my uncle's office. I strode to his desk, taking out a paperclip and picking the lock of the drawer. When I promised Marley that I would see if I could find out where Buck lived, I was thankful when she never brought up the subject again. Over the past few months, I had tried to brush off my own anxiety about the situation, but nothing worked. I needed to know.

Flipping through file after file, I became despondent when all I ran across were folders full of bills, report cards, and community service programs my uncle's church sponsored. Just when I was about to give up, I stumbled across a folder marked with a set of digits, almost like a case number.

Opening it, the contents made me sick to my

stomach…photos of Marley's beaten body, transcripts of her sealed testimony during the trial, reports of previous accounts of Buck's abuse. I almost put it all back, not wanting to look at any more reminders of the past that still tormented Marley. Then, my eyes settled on a Notice of Release, accompanied by what appeared to be correspondence between Buck and my uncle.

"What the…?" I seethed with anger at the thought that he had been writing to Buck while he was in prison. Furious, I continued snooping through the file, my blood boiling as I scanned the transcript of Buck's parole hearing to see that my uncle testified on his behalf, saying that he had found God, had repented for his sins, and was no longer a danger to society. Because of my uncle, Marley's abuser and tormentor was now free. Turning back to the Notice of Release, I jotted down the address on a piece of spare paper, quickly locked the desk, and ran out of his office and up to my room.

I didn't think that I could ever look at my uncle the same way again. I understood that he divined strength and power from God and his church, but I couldn't comprehend how any man, no matter whether a man of the cloth or not, could forgive his own niece's abuser and encourage the state to release him, then try to cover it up. I knew instantly what I had to do. I had to go check on Buck for myself.

Looking at the address I had scribbled on a piece of paper, I pulled out a local map, surprised again that he lived no more than thirty minutes away from us. As I hastily highlighted the route, I heard the front door open, followed by Marley's heavy footsteps running up the stairs.

Tossing a few items into my backpack, I knew I needed to come up with some excuse for leaving the house.

"Hi, Cam," Marley said, throwing the door to my room open and plopping down on my bed. "Working tonight?"

"No. You?"

"Yeah."

"Where were you at lunch today?" I asked, trying to hide my nerves. "Doug was worried."

"He should be," she spat.

"What's going on with you guys?" I eyed her with a concerned look.

"Don't worry about it, Cam. It's nothing. I'm just a little anxious about the Thanksgiving Day parade. That's all."

"It'll be fine, Mar." It was silent and I could tell that there was something else on her mind. "Spill it."

"Did you see the feature on the Jessamine Pageant in the paper?" Her voice was quiet and edgy.

"Yeah? What about it?"

"Just…what if Buck saw it and is able to find out where I live because of it? What if he's…?"

"Marley, you need to stop dwelling on this. I'm starting to see why Uncle Graham and Aunt Terryn didn't want you to know."

"What?!" she exclaimed before lowering her voice. "How could you side with them, Cam? How could you even say that I shouldn't know he's out there roaming the streets, possibly victimizing another girl like he did…?"

"Marley, you need to have faith in the justice system. He must have been granted parole for a reason," I said, unable to even believe the words coming out of my mouth. "Perhaps he truly did see the error of his ways and was able to get the help he needed when he was locked up."

"Do *you* think he did?"

I shrugged. "I have to. It's the only way I can refrain from hunting him down and finishing the job that I started six years ago." Our eyes met and I hoped that she couldn't see the truth behind my lies. "I have to go, Mar."

She scrunched her eyebrows. "I thought you didn't have to work."

"I don't. I have plans."

"With Brianna?" she asked in a flirtatious manner.

"No. With a few of the guys. It's a school thing. Brianna's working tonight."

She narrowed her eyes at me. "You're a horrible liar. You expect me to believe that you're working on school stuff on a Friday night?"

"I'm not you, Marley. I don't mind doing homework on Friday."

She shook her head and raised herself off my bed. "Okay. Whatever, Cam. Have fun studying on a Friday night, loser."

I chuckled, inwardly hoping she wouldn't see through my deception.

Grabbing my backpack, I headed out of the house and jumped in my Wrangler. I took out the map and scanned the route I had highlighted. I felt awful for keeping this from Marley, but she needed to continue moving forward instead of dwelling on her past. Still, I needed peace of mind. Cranking the engine, I drove away from the beach and inland to Conway.

As I sat on Buck's street, my eyes trained down the road at his two-story house in a very middle-class section of town, I absently wondered where he worked and whether he lived with anyone. I hoped that he was living with his parents, a pathetic excuse for an existence at the age of forty-six, but I had a feeling I wasn't going to get my wish.

Hours passed and I remained there, unable to leave. I was desperate for answers. Glancing at my watch, I noticed that it was nearly eleven o'clock. Marley would be home from work and would be wondering where I was. Just as I was about to give up for the night, a car drove past me and pulled into the driveway of Buck's house. Fishing the binoculars out of my bag, I looked through them, spotting the man that ruined my sister.

He ran around the car and opened the passenger door, helping a woman to her feet before planting a sensual kiss on her lips. It was the same woman we saw with Buck in Charleston two months ago. They walked to the front of the house and she grabbed a set of keys from her purse, unlocking the door as if she lived there, too.

Marley couldn't know.

# CHAPTER TWENTY-SEVEN

## *INNOCENCE*

*Marley's Journal*

*November 27*

TODAY WAS THE DREADFUL Thanksgiving Day parade here in our sleepy little beach community. I remember moving here and being so excited about watching the parade. Everything back then was exciting...even the "Little Miss" pageants my aunt entered me in. The parents would "ooh" and "ah" over how adorable we all looked with our fluffy pink dresses, hair in curls, makeup on, making us appear more mature than we were. They would laugh as we walked down the stage with all the attitude we could muster, posing in front of the judges like we had been trained. They would cheer when we won. That first pageant when I was named the winner and the spotlight was on me, I was so excited...especially when I saw the proud look on my aunt's face.

A few years ago, the innocence of it all changed. We were stuffing the chests of our dresses, wearing high heels, and posing in a provocative manner. Most girls had no problem with it. If I didn't endure what I had at an early age, I probably would have enjoyed these pageants, too. Most of them do offer us girls a chance to do something constructive. I love dancing. I love singing. I love the community service that is attached to the pageants. But I don't love people judging my body. I feel objectified, but I don't have a choice. *Sex sells. Sex wins.* Those were my aunt's exact words when I questioned why I had to wear a bikini during the swimsuit portion, and why I had to wear a gown with a slit in the side that went from Florida to Maine. And she didn't even blink twice when she said it.

Sex may sell and sex may win, but sex destroyed me.

And it still destroys me. Every day when I look at Doug, I see his hesitation around me. I can only take so much more of it before I crack. I'm at my breaking point. Cutting has helped. Of course, carving *Ruined* over and over again wasn't enough. I needed fresh blood. I now sport a nice new "tattoo" on the inner thigh of my other leg. I tried to stop, but I just couldn't. The demons inside me were shouting and the only thing that could quiet the voices and dull the pain was more cutting.

This morning, as the homey smells of pumpkin and cranberries wafted through my house, I sat in front of my vanity, doing all I could to make it stop hurting. No matter how deep I cut, nothing was working. Tears streamed down my face, ruining my makeup, but it wasn't enough.

Taking a deep breath as I stared back at my reflection, I wondered how much longer I was going to have to feel like this. Wondering if I'd ever have the courage to draw the one line that could end it all.

"Marley!" I heard my aunt's voice shout, bringing me back from my thoughts. "We need to go."

"Coming!" I said, placing my razor in its case and throwing it into my purse. I hesitated, wondering if I had time for one last cut.

"Marley! *Now!*"

I resisted the urge and quickly fixed my makeup before heading downstairs to see my aunt standing by the front door, her face fixed in the irritated expression that I had come to expect from her.

# CHAPTER TWENTY-EIGHT

## *THANKFUL*

*Cam*

"WHY DO YOU THINK Aunt Terryn is letting us spend the weekend at Mama's?" Marley asked after the parade as I drove from Myrtle Beach toward Columbia. "And agreed to no more supervised visits?"

"I think she's finally coming to terms with the fact that Mama's served her sentence and is trying to move on with her life." I didn't tell her that the reason probably was due to her husband's role in permitting Marley's abuser to roam free. She'd have been considered quite the hypocrite if she still held a grudge against our mama for her part when her husband was the reason Buck was now a free man.

She reached from the back seat and squeezed Brianna's arm. "I'm glad you're coming."

"Me, too," she replied. "I haven't met your mother yet."

"You'll like her," I said. "And she'll love you. What's not to love?" I winked before glancing at Marley in the rearview mirror. "Did you invite Doug?"

She leaned back against the seat and crossed her arms in front of her chest. "No, I didn't."

"Marley…" I said, my tone cautioning. "You've got to

stop."

"So does he, and that's all I'm going to say on the topic."

I shook my head before turning up the music. After a quiet drive, we arrived at Mama's house. She greeted us all warmly as we walked inside, the smells of Thanksgiving surrounding us. It reminded me of all the Thanksgivings we had when Dad was still alive.

"Gosh, look at you kids," she said, hugging me and Marley. "Every time I see you, I swear you grow another inch, Cameron. And you, Marley Jane... You're becoming such a beautiful young woman." She pulled back and stared fondly at the two of us, her chin quivering. "You two look so much like your father. He would be so proud of both of you." We shared an intense moment before Mama broke her gaze from us.

"Now, you must be Brianna!" she said enthusiastically, pulling her in for a hug. "Cameron has told me so much about you but, I have to say, you're much prettier than he's been letting on." She winked at her.

"Thank you, Mrs. Bowen. Thanks for having me."

"Are you staying the weekend, dear? You're more than welcome. I have plenty of room."

"Thank you, Mrs. Bowen. I hope it's no trouble."

"None at all."

The afternoon flew by as we all sat in the living room watching Christmas movies, the smell of turkey growing stronger and stronger with each passing hour. Finally, by the time my stomach couldn't handle it any longer, Mama called us into the dining room.

My mouth watered when I saw the feast that she had prepared for us...turkey, cornbread stuffing, sweet potato pie, green bean casserole, and her homemade cranberry sauce.

She handed me a set of carving knives that I remembered from my childhood. "Cameron, baby, since you're the man of the house now, you get to do the honors."

"I'm not the man of the house, Mama. I'm not eighteen yet."

"Oh, my sweet boy," she said, placing her hand affectionately on my arm. "You became the man of the house the minute you began to look out for your sister when no one else could. Now, carve that turkey."

"Yeah, Cam," Marley piped up. "I'm staaaarving over here." Her voice was dramatic and I couldn't help but grin.

I stepped up to the turkey and grew slightly nervous. "I've never really done this before. I hope I don't fuck it up."

"Cameron Michael!" my mother exclaimed, whipping her cloth napkin at me. "Don't swear like that in front of a lady." She leaned toward Brianna. "I taught him better than that, sugar. I assure you."

"It's okay, Mrs. Bowen. I'll make sure to teach him a lesson later."

We all erupted in laughter and my mama fanned herself. "I like this one, Cameron, baby. You better keep her around."

"I hope to," I responded, my eyes meeting Brianna's. As I gazed around the table at the three most important women in my life, a warmth spread through me. I was finally able to have a real Thanksgiving with my mama...something I hadn't had since we were seven.

I refocused my attention on the turkey in front of me and heard a soft sob. Looking up, I saw tears falling down Marley's cheeks. "What? Am I doing this wrong?"

She shook her head. "No. It's not that. It's just... You

look so much like Dad right now, Cam. Seeing you standing in front of a turkey with his old carving knives… I just miss him. I always see him in you, but I really do today…" She took a deep breath as she attempted to get her emotions under control. "So do him proud and cut that bird like he would have."

"Marley, your father was absolutely horrendous at carving a turkey," Mama commented.

She laughed in response. "I know. But what fun is Thanksgiving if the turkey isn't good and butchered?"

"One completely butchered carved turkey coming up then. I'm glad Dad set the bar so high."

"Oh, he did, baby," Mama said. "But I think you'll live up to his standards."

After carving the turkey and dishing out servings to my small family, we gorged on the decadent food. Once we were all stuffed from the feast and had cleaned up, a knock sounded on the door.

"Marley, sugar, can you answer the door for me?" Mama said as we were relaxing in the living room.

"Okay, Mama." She got up and went to the front door, pulling it back.

I was surprised to see Doug standing there. I think Marley was even more so.

"Doug, what are you doing here?" she asked.

"Marley, don't be rude," Mama scolded, a satisfied expression on her face. "I invited him."

She spun around, her eyes on fire. "Why?"

"Because, baby girl, Thanksgiving is all about being with the people you love and that you are thankful to have in your life."

"Fine," she huffed, plopping down on the couch and crossing her arms in front of her chest, her irritation loud and clear.

"Thanks for inviting me, Mrs. Bowen," Doug said politely, hesitantly sitting next to Marley, his eyes awash with compassion as he surveyed her.

Out of nowhere, as Bing Crosby sang *White Christmas* on TV, Marley screamed, "Stop looking at me that way! Just stop!" She hovered over Doug, her chest heaving in rage.

"What way?" He was clearly taken aback by her outburst.

"The way that makes me feel like..." She trailed off, her chin quivering.

"Like what?"

"Like a helpless victim that's still living in the past! I know I am! I don't need your eyes reminding me of that!" She ran from the room, her footsteps heavy as she flew up the stairs and slammed the door to her bedroom.

He turned to us, his eyes wide. "What did I do? I don't understand. She's been pushing me farther and farther away for weeks without so much as an explanation." His voice became contemplative. "I miss her."

"It's the way you were looking at her," Brianna offered.

"What? What's wrong with it? I just want to make sure she's okay."

"This is exactly why she was hesitant in telling you about everything," I explained. "You want to know what set her off when we were at that home, waiting for the court to grant guardianship to our aunt and uncle? The way people would look at her. All the caseworkers and social workers looked at her as if she was a helpless victim, and for someone who felt helpless for years, it's the worst feeling in the world. She is not a helpless victim, Doug. Yes, she's a victim. More importantly, Marley is a survivor. So treat her like one. Please."

He shook his head dejectedly as he processed my

words. "I'm sorry. I never…"

"I know," I said, cutting him off. "You need to treat her the same way you did before you knew. She's trying to shed her past. Now whenever you look at her and she sees the changed expression on your face, she's reminded of the worst time in her life. She doesn't need that. She needs someone who will look at her in a way that makes her want to fight for a future."

"I'm trying. It just seems that no matter what, she's pushing me away."

"The thing that you have to understand about Marley is that she has highs and lows. Before the Halloween party, she had been on a high for so long that when the bottom dropped, it fell far."

"What makes the bottom drop?"

I shrugged. "It could be anything. Reminders of her past, of having her trust betrayed. Marley doesn't trust easily, but she trusts you. I know she does."

"Go talk to her, Douglas," Mama interjected. "Staying down here and toiling over the situation won't give you any answers. The only person who can give you that is sitting up in her bedroom. She's probably beating herself up over her behavior, but she's too proud to admit that she made a mistake. Go remind her of what's at stake if she keeps pushing you away."

# CHAPTER TWENTY-NINE

## *TOGETHER*

*Marley's Journal*

*November 27*

MY MAMA ALWAYS HAD a way of putting things that made me feel like complete shit but, at the same time, love her even more. I felt like complete shit when she told me that the purpose of Thanksgiving was to spend the day with those that we love and are thankful to have in our lives, and it was mainly because I had been treating those people like crap lately, myself included. And that realization made me love my mama more than I thought possible.

After my dramatic scene of screaming at Doug, I stormed up the stairs and threw myself onto the bed. I never understood why Mama had bedrooms for Cam and me at her house, considering we were never really permitted to stay the night, but I was thankful for the privacy tonight so I could stew in solitude.

Reaching into the back pocket of my jeans and finding my compact, I took out the razor, about to lower my jeans. A sudden knock startled me and I quickly put the blade back in its hiding place.

"Marley, open up! Please."

191

"No. Go away, Doug!" I shouted.

"I'm not going anywhere until I can talk to you."

"You talk to me every day in school," I replied sarcastically.

"I'm talking about the real Marley. The Marley that's excited about shooting stars. The Marley that finds the significance in the insignificant. The Marley that has had unspeakable things happen to her, but has learned to move past it. The Marley that loves with her beautiful, albeit stubborn, heart. That's the Marley that I…"

I rushed to the door and opened it, staring into his intense green eyes, the passion and fire behind his gaze palpable. The sympathy that had covered his expression the past several weeks was no longer there. In its place was a heat and electricity that I had never seen before.

"That you what?"

He leaned in, his lips poised on mine. "That I love," he whispered.

My heart raced in my chest at his voice uttering those words. "I thought you didn't love me a lot," I murmured against his mouth.

He grinned and gently pushed me into my room, closing the door behind him. His lips moved against mine as he explored my mouth for the first time in nearly a month.

And, for the first time in nearly a month, I didn't feel the pain anymore. I felt a much more healthy emotion…love. I felt it in the way he lightly, but firmly, led me toward the bed. I felt it in the way he held my back as he lowered me down. But, most importantly, I saw it in his eyes. He no longer looked at me as if I was ready to shatter into a thousand tiny pieces at any second. He gazed upon me with a look that was hard to label. It was so much more than love, devotion, or tenderness. He admired me with a look of complete reverence. At that moment, I knew I was staring into the eyes of a man who would never do anything to hurt me.

"Show me your love. I need it, Doug," I begged him, unable to stop the pleas that escaped my mouth. The burning rage and anguish inside me was replaced with an overwhelming sensation of rapture. I wanted to give my heart, my entire existence, to him because I knew he would guard it with his life.

He pulled back, his eyes wide with concern. "Are you sure? We don't have to. I don't want you to think..." He trailed off. "I don't want a repeat of what happened last time." He avoided my gaze and I could tell he was conflicted.

"I want to. I need the normal, Doug. You're my normal." I pressed my lips against his. "I've been thinking about this day for a long time. I've been thinking about doing this with *you* for a long time."

"If it becomes too much, Marley, let me know and we'll stop, okay?" He looked at me, his eyes searching mine.

I nodded.

"I need to hear you say it. Please. Just so I know."

"Yes, I will. I promise."

"I don't want you to think that you have to do this for me, Marley. I'm happy to wait as long as you need. I'm not going anywhere."

"I'm not. I want to do this for me...and for us."

He groaned and tightened his hold on my body before flipping over onto his back, pulling me on top of him. "You're in control, Marley."

I raised my eyebrows at him in a flirtatious manner. "I like the sound of that." I began to circle my hips against him, shivers running through my body at the feel of him between my legs.

"Kiss me, Marley Jane," he begged softly, his voice raspy.

I lowered my mouth to his. "I've missed this."

"What?"

"Kissing you. I'm so sorry, Doug."

"Don't be. I'm the one who's sorry. Now, kiss me."

"Yes, sir." I giggled and my mouth moved against his, our tongues meeting.

A small moan escaped as his hands roamed my body, finally settling on my hips. I pulled out of the kiss, panting, and stood up, unbuttoning my jeans.

I was about to lower them to the ground when the red scars on both legs caught my attention.

And Doug's.

"Shit!" I exclaimed, attempting to raise my jeans back up, hating that I hadn't thought about him seeing the marks.

Doug grabbed my arm and stopped me. "Marley," he said softly. "What is that?" His eyes roamed to my thighs. "Is that…?" He swallowed hard. "Did you…?"

I simply nodded.

"Why?"

"You wouldn't understand," I hissed.

"But I want to, Marley." His voice was sweet, regardless of my tone. "Don't push me away again. Please. Just help me understand."

Nervous at how he would react, I gingerly lowered my jeans and stood in front of him so he could see the scars that I had carved into my body. Sitting down next to him, I grabbed his hands in mine. "Because this pain takes my mind off my past, at least for a little while."

"How long…?" He swallowed hard.

"A few years. I only do it when the pain is unbearable."

He fought back his emotions and his voice wavered.

"Why was the pain unbearable this time?"

"Because I didn't have you anymore," I admitted. "I tried to feel your not love when I looked at the bracelet you gave me, but every time I looked at it, all I could see were your eyes that viewed me as a helpless little girl."

His chin quivered. "Please tell me this isn't my fault."

"It's not. I don't want you to think that. I just... I tried to stop and I couldn't. Your not love dulls the pain. It's the only thing that does. Even cutting doesn't make it stop hurting...not like your not love does."

He leaned in and kissed me with such passion that I could physically feel his affection for me in that simple act. "You can be so exasperating and so incredible at the same time. But let's get one thing straight, Marley Jane. I'm completely head-over-heels *in love* with you. Okay?"

I grinned. "I love you, too, Douglas Evan." I fell over onto the bed with him and pulled him on top of me.

He roamed my body with his mouth and, for the first time in the presence of a guy, I felt completely at ease and venerated by his motions. Lowering himself between my legs, he glanced up at me as if asking permission. I nodded and he slid my panties down. Delicately kissing each of my inner thighs, he said, "I promise that I'll help erase the scars, Marley...both physical and emotional."

My chin quivered in response to his words and I let out a quiet sob. He quickly raised himself up and wrapped his arms around me.

"I'm sorry," I said. "I'm sure crying before sex is such a turn-on." I wiped my cheeks.

"I'm okay with it. And we're not having sex, Marley."

I pulled back, a pout on my face. "Why not? I thought..."

"This is so much more than sex for me."

I smirked in a playful manner. "Douglas, do you want

to make love to me?"

His eyes searing into mine, he simply nodded and pressed his lips back to my mouth.

Thousands of unique and unexpected sensations coursed through my veins as Doug slid out of his clothes. I never thought I'd ever be able to feel comfortable with the act of sex, but the thought of what we were about to do didn't just excite me. It thrilled me.

He fished a condom out of his wallet and rolled it on before sitting back down on the bed. Grabbing my hips, he pulled me on top of him, surprise etched across my face.

"I told you. You're in control."

"I don't really know what I'm doing," I confessed.

"Neither do I."

"You've never…?"

"Nope. We'll figure it out together."

Nodding, I placed my legs on either side of his waist, my eyes remaining glued to Doug's, and our two bodies became one.

"Are you okay?" he asked as I momentarily stilled my motions, trying to acclimate myself.

"I'm better than okay," I exhaled, leaning down and nibbling on his earlobe.

"I love you, Marley Jane Bowen."

"And I love you, Douglas Evan Mullins."

As we found our rhythm, our eyes locked the entire time, I no longer thought of my past. Intimacy no longer petrified me. It excited me. I just hoped it always would.

# CHAPTER THIRTY

## *CHANGE*

*Marley's Journal*

*December 1*

IT'S AMAZING HOW MUCH love can change a person. As I walked through the halls earlier today on the first Monday back after Thanksgiving break, I felt as if a weight had been lifted off my shoulders. I felt free. I felt at peace. Above all, I felt loved. Even when Doug wasn't walking me to class, I felt his devotion to me.

Approaching my Governments class, I grinned, my face blushing when I saw Doug leaning against the lockers just outside the room. Sauntering up to him, my lips lingered against his neck and I whispered, "Good morning, Douglas."

"Good morning, Marley Jane. You look quite ravishing today."

I planted a kiss on his lips before getting lost in his emerald eyes.

"There's this glow about you, and I can't quite put my finger on it."

I giggled in response. "Maybe because I spent the weekend having sex with my hot boyfriend."

"Miss Bowen!"

We both turned our heads in surprise to see Mr. Monroe standing just a few feet away. Apparently, he had witnessed our entire exchange.

Licking his lips, his eyes surveyed my body in the unusual way that he seemed to look at every female. "Do you need a reminder of this school's policy regarding public displays of affection?"

"No, sir," I responded meekly. Bowing my head and turning away from Doug, I walked past Mr. Monroe and into the classroom. I could feel the burn of two sets of eyes on me, one gazing in adoration and the other a confusing feeling.

Once I was settled, my notebook and text book on my desk, I raised my head to see Mr. Monroe standing next to me. He leaned in, his mouth just a breath from my neck. "See me after my lecture."

"I have class."

"It is not optional, Miss Bowen," he growled. "Your lackadaisical attitude has been wearing on my patience all semester. Do *not* test me."

"Yes, sir." I swallowed hard. I never wanted a class to drag on as much as I wanted that one to. I was nervous about what awaited me when I went to see Mr. Monroe once the bell rang. I couldn't shake the feeling that he had it out for me, and the only reason I could come up with was because my brother was dating his daughter. But why?

The bell rang after a class that seemed to last only eight minutes instead of forty-eight.

"Miss Bowen," Mr. Monroe said as the rest of the students filed out. "Come with me."

"I'll just pack up my things and head that way. You don't have to wait for me."

He crossed his arms in front of his chest and his shirt

stretched from his flexing biceps. "I don't think so, Miss Bowen. It seems every time I look, you're allowing some guy to put his paws all over you. Not on my watch. Now, come with me."

"Doug's my boyfriend. He's the only one I let put his paws on me, sir," I explained as I slung my bag over my shoulder.

"Still, I've promised your aunt and uncle that I would look after you."

"What?!" I exclaimed, shocked at his confession. "Is that why you've been a complete ass to me all year?"

He spun around to face me, his eyes overflowing with a bizarre combination of fury and amusement.

"Pardon my French, sir," I added, keeping my head high.

"You think I'm an ass?" He raised his eyebrows at me.

"Well, yes. You do have a tendency to be a bit of a controlling prick, since we're being honest with each other."

Shaking his head, he softened his hard expression, and I could have sworn that I heard a laugh escape. He led me toward the administrative wing, the noise that typically pervaded the hallways of the classroom corridors nonexistent. As we turned the corner and approached his office, Mr. Grayson walked toward us, his usual charming smile on his dignified face.

"Hi, Mr. Grayson," I said cheerily.

"Marley," he replied in greeting before turning his attention to Mr. Monroe. "Adam."

"Bryant. If you'll excuse us, I have some business I need to attend to with Miss Bowen. She violated this school's prohibition against public displays of affection."

I glanced at Mr. Grayson, putting on my most convincing look of remorse.

"Then, please, allow me to take her off your hands, Adam. You have much more important things to do, like grade papers. All I have to do is sit in my office and count my money, as you so aptly like to point out is the only thing I do for this school."

I giggled at Mr. Grayson's obvious disdain for Mr. Monroe.

A firm hand gripped my shoulder and I tensed up at the contact, my heart racing. "No. I also need to speak with her regarding her senior project."

"I'll send her your way once I'm finished." Mr. Grayson winked at me, a jovial expression on his face.

"No need, Bryant," Mr. Monroe responded before turning to me, his eyes intense. "Go to my office, Miss Bowen," he demanded. "I'll be with you shortly."

I stood locked in place, my legs unable to put one in front of the other.

"Now," he growled.

I snapped to and, in a daze, continued down the hallway and into Mr. Monroe's office, nervous energy coursing through me from the tone of his voice and the awkward exchange between Mr. Monroe and Mr. Grayson.

Hushed voices echoed down the corridor and I struggled to decipher what the two men were saying, but their voices were too low. All I knew was their anger and hostility toward each other was clear as day in the hissing that I could make out. After several uncomfortable minutes, I heard footsteps walking toward the office. I readjusted my position in the chair and faced forward, trying to pretend that I hadn't been attempting to eavesdrop in on their conversation.

"Now, Miss Bowen, where were we?" he asked, closing the door and sitting behind his desk. "Ah, yes, you were calling me an asshole."

I rolled my eyes. "If the shoe fits…"

He sighed. "I understand that I may act in a displeasing manner on occasion but, I assure you, it's for your own benefit. Now, I apologize for making you think that the reason I wanted to see you was to scold you based on your behavior, which does need a bit of adjustment. However, I was your age once, too. I've made out with my fair share of high school girlfriends in the halls, too. Let's get to the real reason that I had you come here." His eyes narrowed on me and he licked his lips in that disturbing way he always did. "Brianna."

I scrunched my eyebrows. "What about Bri?" I asked guardedly.

"She's dating your brother."

I nodded slowly, alarm bells going off in my head. "Yes. And?"

"Have they…?" He raised his eyebrows.

My eyes grew wide at what he was referring to. "I don't know!" I exclaimed. "Did you really ask me to come to your office so you could find out if your daughter is having sex with my brother? Isn't that misuse of your position or something?"

"I'm worried about her, Miss Bowen. Her mother doesn't communicate with me and Mr. Grayson has, unfortunately, been able to block any attempt I've made at speaking with her here at school. I just want to make sure that she's being safe and smart."

"I bet you would," I muttered under my breath.

"What was that?" he asked cautiously.

"Nothing," I replied. "She's a teenager. I'm pretty sure she'd rather hang out with her friends than her parents. I know I do. If we're through here, I need to get to class."

"Just one more thing. I'd like to speak with you

regarding your proposal for your senior project."

I slouched in my chair.

"I just want to be sure that you're prepared for possible backlash if word gets out that you want the Jessamine Pageant discontinued."

"I didn't say I wanted it to be discontinued. I just want it to be seen as a celebration of feminism instead of a display of sexism. That's all. Right now, it seems to be a celebration of boobs and legs instead of the strides women have made in this country over the past several decades. That's what should be celebrated. Our brains, not our bodies."

A candid smile crossed his face. This was a side to Mr. Monroe that I had never seen before. "You know what makes you stand out from all the other female students here?"

I shook my head in disbelief at the sudden change in demeanor. "No, sir."

"Your passion, Marley. Keep that. Remember that. If you're passionate about something, you can make change happen. I know it." He grabbed a sheet of paper and scribbled something on it. "Here's a pass excusing you. I'll walk with you to your Physics class." He raised himself from behind his desk and opened the door. I stood up and followed him, the atmosphere somewhat awkward as he escorted me down the halls. I wondered how he knew my schedule.

As we approached my classroom, he turned to me. "For the record, Miss Bowen, I'm on board with your opinion of the Jessamine Pageant. I do hope we can work together to possibly change some things in this town." He spun on his heels, leaving me completely speechless and anxiety-stricken about the thought of working with him on anything.

# CHAPTER THIRTY-ONE

## *NEW PATH*

*Cam*

"WORKING TONIGHT, OR GOING to your bullshit study group?" Marley asked on the Friday before Christmas.

"It's not a bullshit study group."

She rolled her eyes as she lay on my bed, looking through some papers, making notes every so often. "Whatever, Cam. If you're banging Brianna, you can just tell me. I'm banging Doug."

"Marley! I do *not* need to know that."

She giggled.

"But I'm happy for you. That's a big step for you."

"That's a big step for anyone, Cam. So…" She raised her eyebrows at me, questioning. "You and Bri?"

"Not yet."

"Do you want to?"

I plopped down on the bed and opened my mouth, about to say something.

"Hold on," Marley said, preventing me from continuing. "I think this conversation is more aptly suited for the roof." She scrambled off the bed and opened the window, climbing toward our spot. I followed. Once I was situated, she turned to me. "Okay. This is better. Now, do you want to?"

*T.K. Leigh*

"Of course I do. I'd be crazy to *not* want to. She's beautiful, smart, funny, witty, amazing. She's the whole package."

"Then what's stopping you?"

"It's hard being a guy, Mar. I have to make the first move, and I don't want to do anything that she's going to hate me for later."

Marley grabbed my hand. "She won't hate you. Have you talked to her about it?"

"No. Not really. I mean, we flirt a lot." A smile crossed my face. "On Halloween, when she was wearing that smoking hot flight attendant costume, we joked about the mile high club. So it's out there, but I don't know…" I sighed and I knew she could sense that I wasn't telling her everything.

"What?" she persisted.

"There's something about her sometimes. It almost reminds me of you in a way."

She shot up and looked down at me. "What do you mean?"

"It's hard to put my finger on it, exactly. There's just something…I don't know…off. Or maybe I'm imagining it. She's definitely a bit more shy than most girls at school, but I kind of like that."

"She *is* shy," Marley responded. "And that's exactly why you should talk to her about it. See if she's ready. Want to know what helped me get over my fears of intimacy?"

I groaned. "Not really, but you're probably going to tell me anyway, aren't you?"

"You bet your ass I am."

"I really hate this conversation. I don't like the idea of my best friend and my sister… You know."

"Whatever. Anyway, Doug let *me* be in control. He had

204

never had sex before, either. So we both kind of figured it out together. It's fun that way. There's no pressure. There's no expectation to perform in a certain manner."

I raised myself off the roof. "Okay. I'm leaving. This conversation is officially over before I drive over to Doug's and kill him."

"Don't do that! I'll miss his…"

I plugged my ears. "La la la. I can't hear you."

Glancing back at her, I saw a huge smile on her face.

"Get your brain out of the gutter, Cameron Michael. I *was* going to say that I would miss his heart. Because that's what I'm in love with."

I paused, wanting to take a mental snapshot of Marley. She was in one of her "up" phases. I hoped that this one would last and would become her new normal. She deserved to live in complete happiness with lows that weren't so low anymore.

"But I like his cock, too."

"*Enough!*" I shouted, my face turning red as I crawled back through my window, the sound of Marley's infectious laughter like music in the chilly night air.

"Cam?!" she called out.

I spun around and met her eyes, a serene expression on her face. I knew what she wanted. I always knew what she wanted. "To the moon and back, Marley Jane."

"From the stars to the ocean, Cameron Michael."

I grabbed my bag and left, feeling guilty for keeping this secret from her. She had been so happy and at peace since Thanksgiving. We hadn't talked about Buck in quite a while and I wanted to keep it that way. But that didn't mean I couldn't keep digging.

"Cam! Cam!" Meg called out as I headed down the stairs toward the front door. She ran from the living room where she had been admiring our Christmas tree.

"Hey, munchkin."

"Santa's coming soon, isn't he?"

"As long as you're on his nice list."

"I've been good all year. I think I'm set." She grinned at me. "Are you on his nice list?"

I chuckled. "I hope so. I'm running out and I won't be back until after you're in bed so give me a good night kiss. Both of you." I crouched down and Meg and Julianne ran to me, wrapping their arms around my neck. "Good night, kiddos."

"'Night, Cam!" Julianne said.

I peeked my head into the kitchen to see my uncle sitting at the table, looking over a few letters. My eyes settled on what he was reading and I noticed the handwriting. I hoped it was an old letter and he wasn't still corresponding with Buck. I made a mental note to try to go through that file again soon.

"I'm heading out," I said, my expression flat.

"Okay. When will you be back?"

"I'm not sure. I want to get some work done before I head to Columbia next week. I'd rather not have to do school work when I'm with Mama."

"That's understandable." He returned his attention to the letter.

"Thanks, by the way."

He looked up at me. "For what?"

"For letting us spend our Christmas break with Mama. It means a lot to her…and to Marley."

"It's time that you and Marley form a healthy relationship with her, Cameron. Your sister needs her mother in her life. I'm not a fool. As much as I wish she had pulled herself together after my brother died, she never got the help she needed. She has now. She's seen the error of her ways and she's trying to make amends for

206

her past. That's all anyone is trying to do, really. God teaches us to forgive. I've forgiven her, just like I've forgiven Buck for what he did."

My spine straightened at the mention of his name. "You have?"

"He's served his time and is trying to move on from his past. I mean, he's *serving* his time..." He looked at me nervously.

My eyes narrowed on him and I reminded myself that he wasn't aware that I knew. "He's out, isn't he?"

He sighed, shaking his head as he folded the papers he was looking through, and began to retreat from the kitchen. "It's completely irrelevant whether he's out of prison or not."

"Why? Why do you think that?"

He spun around. "Because, Cameron. A man shouldn't have to be reminded of his sins for the rest of his life, not when he's made amends and begged God for forgiveness and to shepherd him on a new path. And we shouldn't be sitting here judging him when he made a mistake. God has judged him. That's enough."

"But what about Marley?" I asked quietly, hoping that she couldn't overhear us. "Why should *she* have to be reminded for the rest of her life? Where's *her* new path?"

"She has to trust God to help her move past it. He will help her find her way."

Shaking my head at the unfairness of it, I watched him make his way into our living room and plant a kiss on Meg and Julianne's head as they played with their toys.

Storming out of the house, I climbed into my Wrangler and sped down the streets of Myrtle Beach, pulling onto the interstate and stopping down the road from the house that I had sat in front of almost every night for the past several weeks. I couldn't tear myself away, no matter how hard I tried.

Nothing ever changed. I would see him come home from work. Apparently, he worked as a carpet cleaner these days. I hoped that the only homes he cleaned were vacant and he never came into contact with any families that had little girls. I refused to believe he was a reformed man, regardless of my uncle's convictions that God had judged him enough.

I remained parked on the street that Friday, just like I had done so many other times in the past. I watched his car pull up and he got out, walking toward the house. A few hours passed as I sat there, wondering if this was a waste of time. Suddenly, just before eight o'clock, he walked out of the house with that same woman on his arm. I wondered if she knew about his predisposition for underage girls.

He helped her into his car and within moments, they were heading down the street. Cranking the engine of my Jeep, I maintained a discreet distance as I followed them to a downtown section of town, where he parked the car and got out. I observed them enter an upscale restaurant, and I hated Buck for being able to go on a date with a rather attractive older woman.

I was about to leave and call it a night when I saw the hostess seat them at a table by the window. Shrugging my shoulders, I decided to stay and keep watch, and that's when I saw it…the light from the candle on the table reflecting on her ring finger. Buck grabbed her hand in his and kissed it in an affectionate manner. She smiled with an enthusiasm that a woman could only give if in love with someone. I punched the steering wheel at the thought that the bastard was getting married.

# CHAPTER THIRTY-TWO

## *UNWELCOME*

*Marley's Journal*

*December 19*

THE DOWNSIDE OF HAVING a job in retail is the busy Christmas season. From Thanksgiving through Christmas Eve, the mall is packed with holiday shoppers trying to find the perfect gift for that special someone.

As I pulled into the parking lot on the last Friday before the big day, there were barely any spots to be found. About to give up, I decided to drive across the street to a vacant grass lot that people used during busy times at the mall…like the Friday before Christmas.

Locking my Mustang, I hurried across the street, walked the extensive mall parking lot, and made my way into the crowded shopping center. When I entered the boutique clothing store that I worked at, I groaned at the disaster that greeted me.

"Hey, Marley!" Kristen exclaimed, running up and hugging me, completely ignoring the customer she was helping. "I'm so glad you got me a job here! It's the best ever!"

"You're welcome. Now don't make me look bad and try to actually work for your paycheck, okay?"

She winked. "You got it." She turned to walk back to the now irritated woman she had been helping and then stopped, facing me once more. "Oh, by the way, Doug came by looking for you."

My face flushed. "Really? When?"

"A few hours ago. He had some Christmas shopping to do and said he'd try to swing by before he had to get home."

"But he's Jewish."

"But *you're* not." She raised her eyebrows at me.

I groaned.

"What did you get for him?"

"Nothing yet. I've never had a serious boyfriend before so I'm at a complete loss about what to get him for Christmas or Hanukkah…or Christmaskah, as he's been calling it.."

"You have a brother, though. It can't be much different."

"I don't want to give him something that I'd give Cam. I want to give him something a little more meaningful."

She giggled. "I know what he'd like and it's definitely not something you can give Cam."

"Really? What?"

"Sleep with him. He'd love it. That's what I'm planning to give Mason for Christmas."

I scrunched my eyebrows in confusion. "You're dating Mason? This is the first I'm hearing of it."

"Oh, no. We're not dating. But I've heard he's good in bed. Carla and I are meeting him and Grady after I get off here tonight, and I'm probably going to give him his present then."

I rolled my eyes. "He's a pig. Stay away." I pushed past her, walking toward the back room to drop off my bag and start my shift.

She followed. "But seriously. Doug and you... You should let him fuck you."

I avoided her eyes.

"Unless... *Marley Jane! You've slept with Doug?!*" she shouted so half the store could hear.

I lowered my head, my entire face flushing red in embarrassment from the looks I was getting from a few of the guys I went to school with that were shopping in the store.

"Kristen," I hissed, my teeth clenched. "It's none of your business if I'm sleeping with him or not. What we do in private is exactly that. Private."

She crossed her arms over her chest. "Fine. But if you haven't, you can give that to him. And if you have, think about spicing things up. I think there's a store in the mall that sells fuzzy handcuffs and grape-flavored condoms."

I rolled my eyes and retreated into the staff room, wondering why the hell I was actually considering Kristen's advice. I did want to give Doug a present that meant something, but I had no idea what that could be. The more I thought about it, the more I realized that Kristen had a point. Doug and I had been sleeping together for almost a month, and, every time, he had been gentle and cautious, almost as if he was scared to do something that would set me off. What Doug needed was freedom. I needed the freedom, too.

Going back into the store and taking my place next to Kristen behind the cash registers, I leaned over and whispered in her ear, "So, what store sells those fuzzy handcuffs?"

She giggled and beamed at me. I hated and loved her at the same time.

The evening flew by as the line to check out seemed to never end. I barely had time to even take a break.

Thankfully, I managed to escape for a bit to go grab a few things from the store that Kristen had mentioned. I thought I would be slightly embarrassed to buy handcuffs, an eye mask, and body paint, but I wasn't. I was incredibly turned on just thinking about Doug using it all on me. A year ago, or even a few months ago, the thought of being restrained in any way would have caused me to scream and break down, but I trusted Doug with my heart. More importantly, I trusted him with my body, something I never thought I'd be able to do. Doug was my future. Finally realizing I had a future made my past seem insignificant in comparison.

As I was walking to my car after closing the store, all thoughts were of Doug. He never stopped by during my shift, which kind of disappointed me, but I understood that it was the first night of Hanukkah and he should celebrate with his family. I was in a complete trance as I contemplated the expression on his face when he opened his gift, my entire being overwhelmed with excitement and nerves at the same time.

Unlocking my car, I nearly jumped when I heard a deep voice call my name. Turning around, I scrunched my eyebrows. "Mason… Grady… What are you doing here? Kristen got off work over an hour ago."

"I know," Mason said. "She and Carla just left to go home. We were about to leave when we saw you. Not too smart to be walking all alone across an empty parking lot this late at night." His dark eyes narrowed on the bit of cleavage that was showing from my fitted black shirt.

Crossing my arms in front of my chest, I raised my eyebrows at them. "Get what you wanted from Carla and Kristen then? You two make me sick sometimes. They're real people with real feelings. I know they say they're not interested in a relationship, but maybe if you assholes acted more like Doug, my friends wouldn't feel like they had to sleep with half the school."

They both stepped toward me and I backed into my car. "Didn't anyone ever tell you that variety is the spice of life, Marley?" Grady said, licking his lips in a sly manner.

"I much prefer monogamy. That's my kind of turn-on. But that's me. There's plenty of other ways to spice things up, Grady."

I spun around and was about to pull the door open when I felt a hand on my shoulder. My gut reaction kicked in and I grabbed the hand, reeling around and pinning it behind the body attached to it.

"I like a girl with fight in her, don't you, Mason?" Grady asked coyly.

"Makes it more fun," he offered in agreement.

Grady pushed out of my hold with ease and they began to walk away.

Looking over his shoulder, Mason said, "Don't worry, Marley. One of these days, you'll get sick of boring old Doug. When that happens, I'll be happy to show you some real spice."

"Don't hold your breath," I spat out.

"We'll even put those handcuffs in your bag to good use," Grady interjected, his brown eyes scanning my body.

Climbing into my car, I tried to shake off the interaction. It wasn't the first time something like that occurred between us. It usually happened when they got bored with whatever girl they were sleeping with at the time. They certainly made the rounds. There were a handful of us that they always attempted to flirt with, but lately, their flirting had become more and more aggressive. Brianna had noticed it, too. Cam and Mason had gotten into quite a few fights when he had seen Mason grabbing or touching Brianna in the hallways, begging her to reconsider and take him back. I wondered if that was what caused her to close down on occasion. Maybe their flirting had turned into something else…something unwelcomed that she was forced to keep to herself to salvage her mother's friendship.

The thought consumed me as I drove from the mall and toward my house.

# CHAPTER THIRTY-THREE

## *MARLEY JANE*

*Marley's Journal*

*December 25*

MERRY CHRISTMAS! I'D BEEN nervous about today ever since listening to Kristen's brilliant, but nerve-wracking idea of giving Doug the gift of kink, as I'd been referring to it. I'm pretty sure Jesus would be turning over in his grave if he found out I was celebrating his birthday by allowing my boyfriend to tie me up and do what he wanted with my body. I wonder if Jesus had a kinky side. I'm probably going to hell for even thinking that.

I woke up late this morning and bounded down the stairs to see my mama sitting in the living room by the tree, reading a book. "Merry Christmas, Mama," I said.

"Merry Christmas, Marley Jane."

"Where's Cam?" I asked.

"He's upstairs. Brianna just called and said she wasn't feeling well so she wouldn't be able to make it today. I think he's a little disappointed."

I sat down next to her on the couch and she wrapped her arms around me. "I can imagine. I think he was really looking forward to giving her the gift he bought her."

"What did he get her?"

"She's had her eye on these pearl earrings. He saved all his tips over the past few months so he could buy them for her."

Mama shook her head, a brilliant smile on her face. "That's something your father would have done." She stared at me with a contemplative look. "Have I ever told you the story about how he proposed to me?"

"No."

"Well," she started as I rested my head against her shoulder, "I always went to the dirt track. I loved cars...the sound of the engine, the vibrations when they revved their motors. I just adored it. That's how I met your father. I had been seeing this guy who had this beautiful sixty-eight Roadrunner, and he would bring it to the track to race every weekend. One day, your father showed up with a sixty-six Firebird that was complete shit. I mean, it was the biggest piece of crap I had ever seen." She laughed at the memory and I could tell she was still heartbroken that he was gone.

"But that never discouraged him," she continued. "At first, he just watched the races. He checked out the cars, talked to the guys and, as the months went on, something would be different on that Firebird every single week. One day he showed up, and it didn't look like the same car it had been six months ago. He completely revamped it. He took his time and was patient. I admired his dedication. This wasn't just something he did to simply pass the time. It was something that he was passionate about. I wanted that passion in my life."

I sighed as I recalled my dad's exuberance for all things car-related. He loved us very much, but when he spoke of cars, there was a spark and vibrancy about him that wasn't there any other time. I would have wanted that passion in my life, too.

216

"One day, I approached him to talk about his car, and there was this magnetism there, Marley Jane. I couldn't remember feeling this way about anyone before. He told me how this was just a side project he had been working on, unbeknownst to his family, while he attended law school. I could tell that they did not approve of his fascination with cars and it killed me to think that someone had been discouraging him from doing what he loved.

"We started dating and I persuaded him to follow his dreams instead of do what was expected or demanded of him. You can probably figure out that this is why his side of the family has never really liked me. He dropped out of law school and became a car mechanic. He didn't make nearly as much money as he would have made as an attorney, but that didn't matter. You can't put a price on happiness. Every week, he would race his Firebird. And nearly every week, he would win. He would take those winnings and put them into a coffee canister. I always wondered what he was saving up for."

"I know..." I teased.

"Well, one Friday night after we got home from the track, he handed me the roll of cash that he had just won and asked me to go put it in the canister for him. This wasn't an odd request. I had done it on occasion. But that Friday night in May, over twenty years ago, I opened the canister and in it sat a black velvet box."

I looked up at my mama and saw tears flowing down her cheeks.

"I spun around and he was standing in the doorway of our bedroom, dressed in the most ridiculous suit I had ever seen. It was horrible, Marley Jane," she said, laughing and crying at the same time. "Well, he grabbed the canister out of my hands, got down on one knee, and asked me to spend the rest of my life with him." She glanced at her left hand and toyed with the simple diamond that still sat on her ring finger. "It wasn't big or extravagant, but I didn't care about having anything flashy. All I cared about was his love and passion. And I got to enjoy that for ten years."

"Do you still miss him?" I asked quietly.

"Not one second of any day goes by that I don't miss him, Marley Jane." She wiped her tears and her eyes settled on me. "Did you know that he's the one that picked out your name? We knew we were having twins, but they thought that you were both going to be boys. You can imagine our surprise when you popped out."

"I never knew that!" I exclaimed, my eyes growing wide, pulling out of her embrace.

"The second the doctor said that you were a girl, your father started sobbing like I had never seen him cry." She pulled me back into her arms and I looked up at her as she continued her story, "He wanted a little girl so badly, although he would never admit it. We had always said as long as you both arrived happy and healthy, that was all that mattered. Cam was always going to be Cameron Michael. You were supposed to be Declan Joseph."

"I was supposed to be a Declan?" I said in disbelief. "I'm glad I'm a Marley."

A genuine smile crossed Mama's face. "When the doctor turned to us after delivering you, we could sense that something was wrong. We were so worried that you weren't going to make it. When he said that you were a girl, your father grabbed you out of the doctor's hands and held you. He whispered 'Marley Jane' without giving it a moment's thought."

She brushed my hair out of my face. "He loved you very much. And I know he'd be so proud to know what a strong, beautiful, amazing woman that his Marley Jane has become."

"Thanks, Mama." I hugged her and thought how different our relationship was since just a few months ago.

"Good. Now that's out of the way, call Douglas and remind him to bring condoms with him for this weekend."

I shot out of her arms, my eyes wide with shock. "What do you mean? We haven't…"

"Marley Jane, I was not born yesterday. I am perfectly aware of what you two were doing up in your room when you were here for Thanksgiving. And you'd have to be a complete idiot to think that I didn't hear him sneak into your bedroom after I went to sleep. So let's not pretend. He's more than welcome to stay here the weekend and sleep in your bedroom with you. I'm not going to be one of those parents that ignores the fact that their child is having sex. I know you are. Just be safe."

"Yes, ma'am."

"And have fun."

I giggled. "Don't worry about that." I winked, bringing a smile to my mama's face.

Doug arrived a short while later, and Cam came down to join our small Christmas celebration. I could tell that he was upset about Brianna.

"I'm sorry that Bri couldn't make it," I offered as we were washing dishes, allowing Doug and Mama to get to know each other a little better, considering he was sleeping with her daughter and she knew about it.

"Me, too," he responded. "I just feel like she's been avoiding me."

"What makes you think that?"

He shrugged, keeping his attention on the dish he had been drying for the past few minutes. It couldn't be any drier if it had spent the last several months in the Mojave Desert.

"It's hard to say. I called her Friday night after I got home from my study group because we were planning to meet at the beach, and she didn't answer. Then, on Saturday, I went to the gym and she was working at the front desk, but she tensed up when she saw me."

He lowered his voice. "I noticed a bruise on her arm and when I asked her about it, she flipped out on me. It's not the first time that's happened. Maybe it's not over with Mason. Maybe they're still fooling around with each other."

My mind flashed back to Friday night and running into Mason and Grady. Brianna had been working at the gym that night. Did they go find her after they left me?

"Bri would never do that."

"Then what am I supposed to think?"

"Be patient with her, Cam. It's nothing. I think you're so conditioned to think the worst of everyone because of what we went through, you're trying to find something that's not there. Hell, I bruise all the time. All I have to do is bump into the couch the wrong way and I have a mark on my leg for weeks. As for her not calling, you know how her mother can be at times."

He nodded as he continued drying the same dish.

"*It's fucking dry, Cam!*" I shouted, grabbing it out of his hands and thrusting a wet one at him.

He chuckled. "I was wondering how long it was going to take you to do that." He nudged me.

"You suck sometimes."

We continued washing and drying the dishes in silence as the sound of Christmas carols rang through our house.

"Thanks, Mar," he said.

"For what?"

220

"For talking some sense into me. I know I'm overreacting. I just… It's just…"

"I get it, Cam. You love her. And you miss her. You don't have to explain it to me. You're preaching to the choir. But you have nothing to worry about with Bri. You should see the dress she got for the New Year's Eve Gala. All I'm going to say is you better stock up on condoms because you will definitely be needing some."

His face flashed red and I laughed. I loved embarrassing him.

"Or you can just borrow some of mine."

"Jesus, Marley Jane. Enough already."

I stood on my tiptoes and planted a kiss on his cheek.

"You irritate the piss out of me nearly every day," he said, "but I couldn't imagine a day without you."

"Merry Christmas to you, too."

After finishing the dishes, we went back into the living room and spent the next few hours watching Christmas movies with Mama. I rested my head on Doug's lap and propped my feet on Cam's.

"You've certainly got both these boys wrapped around your little finger, Marley Jane," Mama commented as she observed Doug caressing my head and Cam rubbing my feet.

I yawned and stretched. "Yup. I sure do." I looked into Doug's eyes and my heart began racing in my chest. "Want to go to bed?"

He nodded eagerly.

I shot off the couch. "Okay. See you tomorrow." I grabbed Doug's hand and practically dragged him up the stairs. Closing the door to the bedroom, thankful to finally be alone, I jumped on him, pressing my mouth against his, kissing him like it would be the last time I ever would.

"Damn, Marley," he said, tearing away from my lips.

221

"What's gotten into you?"

I brought my bottom lip between my teeth and shrugged, giving him my most coy look. "Nothing. I just missed you. And now that we're alone, I can give you your real Christmas present. That wallet was *not* your real present, by the way."

"I'm happy with the wallet. You don't have to give me anything else."

I pressed my finger over his mouth, hushing him. "Believe me. I think you'll want this." I winked as I slowly unzipped the black dress I had been wearing. Shrugging it over my arms, I allowed it to pool at my feet.

His eyes grew wide, his jaw dropping.

"You like?" I asked as he scanned my body, taking in my red lace bra, matching thong, and a garter belt clipped to my stockings.

He simply nodded. "I'm beginning to really like Christmas." He drew me into him as he devoured my mouth. His hands roamed my frame, leaving fire in its wake.

"Doug," I exhaled. "There's more."

"More? How could I possibly want anything else?"

I raised my eyebrows. "I'm just full of surprises today."

Grabbing his tie, I led him toward the bed and pulled him down on top of me. I wrapped my legs around him and forced his mouth against mine. I could tell he was unsure about how I would react to him being on top of me. It had usually been the other way around, but that needed to change.

Reaching for the bag that I had placed on the nightstand, I handed it to him. "Here. Open it."

"Can I open you first?"

I shook my head. "No. That one first. It'll make opening me more fun."

222

I could feel him harden against me as he reached into the bag and began to rummage through the tissue paper. He pulled out the first item he came across, his eyes narrowing in lust and uncertainty at the same time.

"Marley... You don't have..."

"Doug," I interrupted. "I trust you. I love you with all my heart and I know you love me. I want you to feel free to do what you like when we're having sex. I know we're both kind of new at this so we'll figure out what we both like together. I'd be lying if I said the idea of you handcuffing me wasn't a big turn-on. I got a little wet buying those."

He groaned and licked my lips as if begging for permission to enter. Grabbing my wrists in his hands, he raised them over my head as his tongue caressed mine. I smiled when I heard the click of the handcuffs.

He nipped on my earlobe and began lowering himself down my body.

"There's more," I exhaled.

"More?"

"Yup."

He returned his attention to the gift bag and pulled out the eye mask. "Are you sure, Marley?"

"Douglas Evan, if my kinky ass boyfriend didn't have me handcuffed to the bed right now, I'd slap him." I winked.

He laughed and raised my head, slipping the eye mask over my face, my world growing dark.

"Holy shit," I breathed.

"What?" He quickly removed the mask, his face awash with concern.

"Don't you dare! Put it back on. It's the coolest thing ever." I giggled. "It heightens the rest of my senses, especially touch."

He lowered the mask back over my eyes, his breath dancing on my lips. A sensual tingle spread through my body. "This is fucking hot. You need to try it sometime."

He didn't respond. It was completely silent except for my breathing. If I didn't know any better, I would have thought that I was completely alone...except for the sparks igniting deep within as I felt a finger find its way into my bra. I arched my back in response. I was completely unhinged and couldn't remember ever being so turned on in my life.

"Doug," I moaned. "I need you." Wrapping my legs around his midsection, I began bucking him. "Please."

"Okay," he said. "I'll always give you everything you need." I felt him climb off me, the familiar sound of clothes falling to the floor and a foil wrapper being opened echoing in the room. Fingers hooked through my panties, and he gingerly slid them down my legs. Bracing myself, I gasped in complete surprise when I felt his tongue on me. I threw my head back, unable to control my reaction. We had been intimate, but he had never done *that* before. It felt fucking incredible.

It didn't take long before the most amazing warmth spread through me. I tried to stifle my screams as my body began to convulse. My mind was a blank slate and if you were to ask me my name at that moment, I probably wouldn't have been able to answer you correctly.

In an instant, his lips were against mine, his tongue invading my mouth. I moaned, tasting me on him, making me burn for him with even more intensity.

"*That* was your Christmas present, Marley Jane, not the earrings. Although, I'm planning on doing that every chance I get from now on. You taste very yummy," he commented.

"Yummy?" I asked, giggling.

"Yup. Yummy," he answered as he slid inside me. "Remember, if it's too much, just tell me to stop, okay?"

"Shut up, Doug. It's not too much." I moved against him and he buried his face in my neck.

"I love you, Marley."

My chest heaved from the incredible sensation of experiencing Doug's love.

"I love you, Douglas. Always."

He brushed his lips against mine and murmured, "Always." His movements became uneven and, within moments, he clamped his teeth on my neck, stifling his own moans as he shook on top of me.

He took off the eye mask and looked deep into my eyes. "That may have been the best Christmas present ever."

I smiled the widest and most genuine smile I could remember. "Ditto."

He rummaged through the bag. "Ummm… Marley? Is there a key for these things?" he asked nervously.

My heart dropped to the pit of my stomach. "Of course there is."

"Are you sure? I'm not seeing one."

"*What*?!"

A grin crossed his face as he held up the key.

"Douglas Evan, if I wasn't handcuffed right now, I'd kick your ass."

"Well, we can't have that. Maybe I'll just have to leave you this way."

I smirked. "I'm okay with that," I replied as he kissed me, unlocking my handcuffs.

"Merry Christmas, Marley Jane," he said, pulling my body into his, his front against my back.

"Happy Hanukkah, Douglas Evan."

"I hope you had a good first Christmas with me."

"I sure did. The first of many."

"I hope so," he whispered against my neck, tracing circles with his tongue on my skin.

"We'll use the body paint tomorrow," I said sleepily and felt him harden against me once more.

# CHAPTER THIRTY-FOUR

## *A NEW YEAR*

*Cam*

I HAD NEVER BEEN so nervous as I was that night, getting out of my car and walking up the driveway to Brianna's front door to pick her up for the New Year's Eve Gala at the country club. There was this excitement in my body and I'd be lying if I said I wasn't eager to see how she looked, especially after all the teasing Marley had been doing over the past week.

When Brianna opened the door, my breath caught. She had always been beautiful in my eyes, but as she stood in the doorway wearing a mermaid-cut floor-length sapphire dress that shimmered when the light hit it, I thought she looked absolutely stunning. It was slightly revealing, but still tasteful and elegant. Her dark hair was curled and pinned up, leaving a few ringlets to frame her pear-shaped face. She wore a hint of makeup, her eyes popping from the shadowing.

"Wow," I mumbled under my breath.

"Do you like my dress?" she asked coyly, spinning around, tripping on her heels.

"Whoa! Easy there!" I stepped forward, catching her in my arms as she fell back.

Our eyes met while she remained enclosed in my

embrace, her silky skin soft in my hands. "Thanks for catching me," she exhaled breathlessly.

I nuzzled my face against her neck and inhaled her fruity scent. "I'll always be here to pick you up," I murmured into her ear.

I felt her body almost melt into mine as she processed my words. Pulling back, I met her brown eyes that were full of depth, pain, and compassion. I could look at her for hours and never tire of it.

"We should go before we're late," she said, snapping me out of the trance that her glistening eyes had me in.

I helped steady her back on her feet. "Of course." Giving her my arm to hold on to, I led her from her house to my Wrangler, opening the door and helping her in.

I ran around to the other side and got behind the wheel, cranking the engine. Glancing across the car at her nervously fidgeting in her seat, I grabbed her hand in mine. "You look absolutely beautiful tonight."

She blushed, turning her eyes from me.

"I mean, you're always beautiful. But that dress... I mean..." I took a deep breath. "I'm digging a hole again, aren't I?"

Leaning across the center console, her lips hovered over mine. "Yeah. But I think it's cute when you do that. I like that I fluster you."

"You do more than just fluster me, Brianna. You make me completely speechless."

"Good. Now kiss me."

"Yes, ma'am." I pressed my lips to hers, cognizant of the fact that we were in her parents' driveway. I had no desire to upset them by making out with her in front of their eyes, even though they were probably already at the gala. Tearing away after a simple yet affectionate kiss, I winked. "To be continued later."

She leaned back in her seat. "I hope so!"

I pulled out of her driveway and maneuvered the streets of Myrtle Beach, heading toward the country club.

"I'm glad you're feeling better," I said, breaking the heavy silence in the car.

"Oh, thanks." She hid her eyes, pulling her shawl tighter around her bare shoulders.

"Everything's okay, right?"

"Of course. What wouldn't be okay?"

"I don't know. I just worry about you sometimes. If you ever want to talk about anything, I'll listen. I'm not going anywhere."

She rolled her eyes in a playful manner. "Except maybe to Arizona."

"How did you hear? I just got the letter yesterday."

"News around this town travels fast. You should know that. I mean, we all had a feeling when the scouts came to watch you pitch last spring at the championship game, but to know that you got a full baseball scholarship... It's a big deal, Cam. You should be proud. I guess I'm just concerned about where that will leave us."

"Nothing will change, Bri. I don't even know if I'm going to go there yet. There's a lot I have to consider before making a decision. If I get into Georgetown, I'd like to go there. And with everything that's been going on with Marley, I have to think about her, too. I know she's been great lately, but I'm just worried that if the bottom falls out again, she'll fall deeper than she ever has."

Brianna leaned over and planted a kiss on my neck just as I turned into the country club parking lot. "You're such a good person. I'm the luckiest girl."

I pulled into a spot and killed the engine, facing her. "No. *I'm* the lucky one." Placing my hand on her cheek, I brought her lips to mine, my fingers grazing her luxurious skin. Hesitant, I slipped my tongue into her mouth, caressing her gently, my motions delicate.

She moaned and began to kiss me with even more vigor. Before I knew what was happening, I was clumsily lowering my seat and pulling her on top of me. I had never been so aroused in my life.

"Cam…" she exhaled.

I responded by tightening my hold on her, not caring that we were probably steaming up the windows of my Wrangler.

"Cam…"

I continued kissing her, rocking my hips against her.

She whimpered and I assumed she was enjoying whatever I was doing. Brianna was my first serious girlfriend, if you could call dating in high school serious. Still, this was the most intimate I had ever been with anyone before and I really had no clue what I was doing. I just let my urges guide me, hoping that she was enjoying it.

Pressing her body even harder against mine, I kept my hand planted firmly on the small of her back, savoring in the feel of her flesh against me as I continued exploring her mouth.

"*No!*" she screamed suddenly, shocking me. My eyes flung open to see her flailing against me. I quickly released my hold on her and she darted back to the passenger seat. Throwing the door open, she ran through the parking lot in the opposite direction of the country club as I stared in confusion at her reaction.

"Damn it!" I shouted, punching the steering wheel of the car. Taking a deep breath, trying to settle my nerves and hormones, I knew I needed to fix this. Leaving the car, I scanned the parking lot for any sign of her.

"Hey, Cam!" I heard Mason call out as he was heading into the gala with Kristen.

I spun in the direction of his voice and a playful grin crossed his face. "Brianna's looking hot tonight, isn't she?"

"Shut it, Mason."

"Just an observation, bro. Did you bang her yet?"

"No. And even if I did, I wouldn't tell you about it."

"Too bad. She's a good lay. You should get on that."

I ignored him and continued walking, finally spotting Brianna's shivering frame sitting on a bench, her hair dimly illuminated by the winter moon. Running in her direction, I slowed to a stop when she glanced back at me, tears streaming down her face. I couldn't remember ever feeling so guilty.

"Bri." I sheepishly ran my hands through my hair. "I'm so sorry. I got carried away. I... I just... I was stupid." I lowered myself to my knees, hoping she would see how horrible I felt. "Please don't think I'm like the rest of these assholes. I'm really not. It's just... You look fucking amazing tonight, Bri. And the feel of your lips... I lost myself. I promise that I'll never let it happen again. I don't care what it takes to earn back your trust, I'll do it."

She shook her head. "I'm sorry, Cam. I didn't mean to freak out. I just..."

I raised myself and sat down next to her, wrapping my arms around her.

She leaned her head against my shoulder. "I just don't like confined spaces. That's all."

"I get it. It was a sleazy move for me to make out with you in my car."

"I liked it, though," Brianna responded, the terror that was in her eyes just moments ago replaced with a flirtatious look.

231

"We don't have to rush into anything. I don't want to pressure you into something you're not ready for, Bri. Please know that."

She bit on her lower lip and I could sense that she was deep in thought. "How's Marley doing? With Doug, I mean."

I shrugged, trying to brush off what she was referring to. "They're good."

"No, I mean…" She lowered her voice. "With sex. And her past. She's okay?"

"I really hate talking about my sister's sex life. You have to realize how strange this is for me."

Her face remained fixed. "I know. I was just wondering if she's okay."

Shaking my head, I said, "I think she's more than okay."

Laughing slightly, she took a small breath. "Good. That's good to know." It was quiet for a moment before she spoke again. "I want to, Cam. It's all I've been able to think about since Halloween. No. I take that back. It's all I could think about since you kissed me."

"Really?" I raised my eyebrows.

Her gaze met mine and she slowly nodded her head. "Yes. I just…"

"We'll take it slow, Bri. I'm not going to force you to sleep with me if you're not ready. And I'm not going to leave you just because you're not ready. I love you for you and not for your body."

"Really?" She pursed her lips at me.

"Yeah. But, since we're being honest, I love your body, too."

She ran her hands through my hair and brought my head to hers. "I love your body, too," she murmured against my mouth. "And the heart that's inside of it. It's

232

so pure and light. I love you, Cameron Michael."

"I love you, Brianna Marie." My breathing increased as we remained unmoving on the bench, reveling in the warmth of each other's embrace. "We should probably go inside before our parents throw a tantrum," I said finally.

She sighed. "Okay. On one condition."

"Anything for you."

"I get to kiss you at midnight and we can watch the sunrise together on the beach in the morning."

"I'd love nothing more." I planted one more kiss on her lips and helped her up, leading her from the bench and into the elaborate country club that was decked to the nines in celebration of the Jessamine New Year's Eve Gala. Men wore tuxedos and all the women were dressed in extravagant gowns. A big band played jazz standards as people danced and enjoyed the last night of the year.

I grabbed Brianna's hand and led her to the dance floor, a Frank Sinatra tune filling the air. "Hope you don't mind dancing."

"With you? Never."

The hours passed with ease as I savored the feeling of Brianna's body against mine. As the night was coming to an end, I felt a tapping on my shoulder. I turned my head to see Mr. Grayson standing over us.

"May I cut in and enjoy one dance with my beautiful step-daughter?"

"Bryant," Brianna said, her face turning red in embarrassment.

"Of course, sir. I don't mind."

"No. I came here with you, Cam. And I'm going to dance with you."

"It's one dance. I need to use the restroom anyway. I'll be back soon." I kissed her neck and permitted Mr. Grayson to lead her across the dance floor.

After using the restroom, I made my way to the bar to grab a water. "Hey, Cam!" I heard Marley shout.

I spun around to see my sister walking toward me in a glimmering silver gown. "Hey, Mar. Having a good time?"

"Surprisingly, yes. For a stupid Jessamine function, this one is rather fun."

I narrowed my eyes at her. "How much have you had to drink?"

She opened her clutch and showed me four small empty vodka bottles. "Nothing, Cameron. The drinking age in this fine state is twenty-one. A Jessamine candidate does not drink before she's twenty-one. Such things are unheard of." She laughed and I couldn't help but join in.

"As long as you're not driving."

Her playful expression turned serious. "You know that I would never…"

"I know."

"And Doug drove me here. He didn't sneak any alcohol in. Well, he did, but it was for me." She winked. "Okay. I'm off to find Doug. See ya later."

I nodded and headed back toward where Brianna was dancing with Mr. Grayson. He sensed my approach and faced me, placing her hand in mine. "Treat my best girl well, Mr. Bowen."

"I always do, sir," I said politely as he walked away.

She let out a long breath, visibly relaxing.

"Miss me?" I settled my hand on her lower back, dancing with her once more.

"Always," she responded.

"Do you think the reason we all had to take ballroom dance in gym class was for these stupid functions?" I asked, trying to bring Brianna back from where she had gone to in her head.

"Probably," she rolled her eyes. "It certainly wouldn't surprise me."

"Me, either." I glanced to the far end of the room to see Mason and Grady eyeing someone as if they were planning their next conquest. Following their line of vision, I noticed that they were looking at Marley with an expression of intense heat, unbeknownst to her.

I saw her kiss Doug on the neck and excuse herself to head down the hallway toward the restrooms. My heart started racing when I saw Mason and Grady slink down the hallway behind her.

"Cam?" Brianna said, noticing that I was distracted. "Everything okay?"

"I'll be right back," I answered quickly, leaving her alone on the dance floor. As I was about to turn down the corridor to the restroom, I heard several grunts. "Shit. *Marley!*" I turned the corner, not expecting to be met with the sight that greeted me.

"Marley?" I couldn't stop laughing when I looked at my sister's slim frame standing over Mason and Grady, her heel digging into Mason's crotch while Grady was curled up in a ball, holding on to himself.

"Your friends are pigs. Kristen and Carla just left crying because of these two assholes. Not to mention they've been hitting on me forever, regardless of the fact that they know I'm with Doug."

"They're more just teammates than friends these days," I explained.

"Whatever. Now, boys…" She returned her attention to them. "If I hear that you try to hit on any of my friends again, you'll remember what will happen, right?"

They nodded quickly.

"I didn't hear you!" She kicked Grady hard in the balls and he let out a loud grunt.

"*Yes!*" he shouted.

"That's better. You're going to remember the pain you feel right now, correct? Because, so help me, if you come near me or any of my friends, or any of the other female population of our school with the sole intention of, and I quote, 'bang and hang', I will revisit this situation and you'll wish that I had ripped your balls off tonight instead of allowing you to walk out of here. Okay?"

They both nodded.

"What was that?" She dug her heel harder into Mason's crotch and kicked Grady again.

"*Yes!*" they both shouted.

"Goody!" She spun around and walked into the ladies room.

"Your sister's fucking crazy," Mason moaned.

"We're all a little crazy," I responded. "You touch her again, I'll let the entire school know that you got beaten up by a girl."

"I plan on telling them anyway," I heard from the ladies' room. The door opened and Marley emerged, grabbing on to my arm and pulling me away from Mason and Grady.

"Can I just say that I don't think I've ever laughed so hard in my entire life?"

"That felt good," she replied just as the band leader came on to announce that it was one minute until midnight.

"Come on, Mar. Let's bring in the new year." I pulled her onto the dance floor where we found Brianna and Doug speaking with Mr. and Mrs. Grayson. As we all counted down to midnight, I couldn't help but notice such a change in Marley since the previous year. She typically stayed locked up on New Year's Eve, the memories of that New Year's Eve when she was eight still tormenting her. But this year, as I looked at her, I realized that she had shed her past. She was no longer dwelling on it. She was looking forward to her future.

"Happy New Year!" voices yelled all around me as the familiar strains of *Auld Lang Syne* played. Two arms pulled me in and I gazed into Brianna's gorgeous eyes.

"Happy New Year, Cam," she murmured against my lips.

"Happy New Year, Bri." I pressed my mouth to hers and couldn't think of anything I'd rather be doing to celebrate the New Year. We all began to make the rounds, wishing everyone a happy New Year. Finally finding Marley, I wrapped my arms around her and planted a kiss on her forehead. "Happy New Year, Marley Jane."

"Happy New Year, Cameron Michael. I have a feeling this is going to be a year to remember."

"Me, too."

~~~~~~~~~~~

As BRIANNA AND I emerged from the country club several hours later, I turned to her. "Still want to watch the sunrise together?"

"I've been looking forward to this all night." She clutched my arm and I led her to my Wrangler, helping her in. I drove through the empty streets of Myrtle Beach and pulled into the public lot by the shore. Taking my shoes and socks off, I tossed them in the car before grabbing a few blankets that I kept in the Jeep.

Brianna grabbed my hand and we walked across the beach, the chilly sand refreshing on our feet. We approached the tree alcove and I laid down the blankets. She lowered herself on the ground and pulled me on top of her, our lips almost touching.

"Hey," she murmured.

"Hey," I replied as I nuzzled her neck, inhaling her hair.

"Smell something you like?"

I chuckled. "Yup. Apricots. And passion fruit. And Brianna. Best smell in the world."

Her eyes met mine and the innocence that was usually present in her gaze was absent. In its place was a look of unyielding desire. "Kiss me, Cam. Like you kissed me in the car before."

"Are you sure? I don't want to rush you…"

Cutting me off, she grabbed my neck and forced my lips to hers. Before I knew what was happening, she was deepening the kiss, parting my lips with her tongue. I moaned into her mouth, my heart racing as she ran her hands up and down my back. I pulled out of the kiss, panting from the intensity.

"Cam, touch me," she pleaded.

"Where?" I whispered.

"Here." She grabbed my hand and pressed it against her chest.

My eyes grew wide.

"You won't break me, Cam. I promise."

I nodded slightly, staring into her eyes as I ran my fingers across the fabric of her dress.

"Cam, unzip me. I want to feel your skin on mine."

"Are you sure? What if someone sees?" I glanced around, my concerns unfounded. Our secret spot was completely hidden from view. No one else knew about this private little slice of the beach.

"No one's going to see. And if they do, I know that you'll protect me," she whispered in my ear, circling her tongue on my neck. "You always do."

Groaning, I returned my lips to hers, clumsily fumbling with the zipper on the back of her dress, lowering it.

She pulled the dress over her head and lay back down as I gawked at her slender body in nothing but a bra and panties.

"Bri, we don't have to do…"

"Cam, did you ever think that maybe I *want* to? If you do, that is. I mean…"

I lowered my mouth to hers. "I love you, Brianna. I'll give you anything you want. I just don't want to have a repeat of what happened earlier."

She smiled. "Cam, I trust you. You're one of the good guys. You always have been. You do have a condom, right?"

I reached into the pocket of my tuxedo pants and grabbed my wallet, pulling out the foil packet. "Yeah." I shrugged. "Sex talk with Uncle Graham. He told me to always carry one on me, no matter what."

"Good."

She pulled my head toward hers and I trailed kisses across her collarbone, nervous and excited about being with her. This was the moment that every teenage boy dreams about. I was anxious about whether I even knew what I was doing, but when I saw the look of peace and pleasure on her face as I moved inside her, I knew I must have been doing something right.

As we lay there in the aftermath wrapped in a blanket, watching the sunrise, her delicate body intertwined with mine, my heart overflowed with a strange feeling of absolute adoration for the girl next to me.

# CHAPTER THIRTY-FIVE
## *MAKE A STAND*

*Marley's Journal*

*March 9*

SENIOR FEVER IS RUNNING through the halls of our high school something fierce these days. Nine weeks left of high school. Seven weeks until I finally turn eighteen, which just so happens to be the same day as the stupid Jessamine Pageant, but all the duties and obligations that go along with that don't seem so bad anymore, not with Doug at my side. Or under me. Or on top of me. One of these days, we'll try behind me. I'm not quite there yet, but I know I will be soon.

Today started out like a typical Monday morning as I sat in homeroom next to Cam.

Just as everyone was filling out graduation information, the intercom buzzed and Mrs. Pritchard, our homeroom teacher, scurried to answer the phone.

"Miss Bowen?" she called out after hanging up.

I looked up from my desk. "Yes, ma'am?"

"Mr. Grayson has requested that you go see him immediately."

I scrunched my eyebrows in confusion. "Why?"

"I'm not sure, dear. His secretary just called and asked

to see you. My guess is it has something to do with either the Jessamine Pageant or your choice of college. Here's a hall pass."

I grabbed my stuff, glancing at Cam. Neither one of us had chosen a college just yet. The only school that we had both been accepted to was U.S.C., which wasn't a bad school, but there were better places for him to go for his major, not to mention the full baseball scholarship he had been awarded. We had been arguing about this once the letters started to arrive a few months ago.

As I was walking toward the administration corridor, I couldn't help but think how far I had come since Grams died last August. Back then, I was horrified at the thought of going to a different college than Cam. While I would still miss him, I no longer needed him to constantly pick me up when I was down. I had Doug to do that. Ever since Thanksgiving, I hadn't experienced any more lows. It almost seemed like, with Doug, there *were* no lows. Maybe I finally had a new normal.

"Miss Bowen," a voice broke through my thoughts. I glanced up to see Mr. Monroe standing in front of me. "What brings you down here? Shouldn't you be in homeroom?" He raised his eyebrows at me, waiting for my response.

"I called her down here," Mr. Grayson said, walking up to me and smiling in the affectionate manner I had grown accustomed to. "It's rather important."

The two men glared at each other and I could have sworn I saw both of them stick their chests out in an attempt to appear more muscular and fearsome than the other.

"Well," Mr. Monroe finally said, "I also need to speak with her about her senior project. I'm sure it's more important than anything to do with your little pageant that isn't for two more months." He grabbed my arm and quickly ushered me into his office, locking the door behind him.

"Honestly, what's the deal with you two? Is it a competition all the time?"

"It's not a competition, Miss Bowen," he replied, sitting behind his desk. "I disagree with his methods of doing things, that's all. He shouldn't be calling you out of homeroom to discuss anything that isn't school related."

"Maybe he wanted to speak to me about college or recommendation letters or something like that."

He eyed me. "That's highly doubtful, Miss Bowen, but I appreciate your innocence. Now, I've been meaning to discuss this with you. What kind of work have you done on your project?"

I slumped into the chair. "It's harder than I thought it would be. I know the history of the pageant, how it started as a way to empower women. But now they have all these other parts of the competition that weren't there when the pageant was founded. They now put an emphasis on beauty instead of a woman's intelligence and strength. *That* should be the focus."

"*Make* that be the focus, Marley." His gaze bore into me. "Use your past."

My eyes grew wide, my heart thumping in my chest as disbelief covered my face. "I don't know what you're talking about, Mr. Monroe." My voice was cautious.

"I *know*, Marley. I know all about what you went through. If you want them to re-evaluate things, make a point."

I fidgeted with my fingers in my lap, looking down. "I can't," I said softly. "No one is supposed to know."

"Is that *your* decision or has that decision been made *for* you?"

My head shot up at his ability to see something I thought no one could.

"Do you really want to stay silent? Don't you want to be a voice of survival? The whole point of this project is for all of you to realize how difficult change can be. But what you also need to realize is that if you disagree with something, change happens at the grassroots level. The local level. Start small. Making people see that their ways are wrong or harmful, even to one person, is never an easy thing, Marley. It's the hardest thing in the world. But if you can get one person to re-evaluate their position, and that person convinces another, *that* is how change happens. That is how this country earned its independence. Could you imagine if our forefathers said 'It's too hard to fight against tyranny'? We'd still be subjects of the crown. Stand up for what you believe in."

I was completely speechless at his passionate plea. This side of him was completely at odds with the stern professor that lectured our class every day during second period, although he did come out on occasion.

"How do I do that?"

"Bring attention to imperfection and flaws, Marley. You are in an ideal position to do something. You're a finalist. Not one person chosen as a finalist has ever stood up for change, except for last year. The seed was planted back when Gabriella Knox tried to get the swimsuit portion discontinued."

"Another one of your students?"

A sly grin crossed his face. "My lips are sealed."

"Okay, so I have a platform to make a change. How do I do it? No one is just going to listen to me bitch and moan about the swimsuit portion or any of that. They've heard it all before."

"Here's how." He opened a file and threw a photo at

me. "How will they react if they see this, knowing that you've been forced to cover it up for years?"

Shocked, I looked down at a recent photo of my uncovered back, the scars of my past visible for all to see.

"How did you…?" My mind raced as I tried to determine when and where that photo could have been taken.

"Does it really matter? I have it. Your aunt covers it all up. You're about to turn eighteen. Make them see their beauty pageant for what it has, unfortunately, become. Make them really think about what all of this has done to you, Marley. What it could be doing to other girls in this town who are forced to remain quiet about their past and then are paraded around as if everything's okay. Force them to celebrate the achievements of women, not just their bodies."

"I think can do that," I said quietly, not believing the words that were escaping my mouth. I wondered if I could follow through.

"Good. Now, you're late for first period." He broke his gaze from mine and began to scribble on a hall pass. "You're off to French with Madame Pearl, correct?"

"Yes, sir."

"Here," he said, handing me the pass. "I'll walk with you."

"But I have to go see Mr. Grayson."

"You're not going to see him."

"You're very strange sometimes." I stood up and went to open the door, unable to because it was locked. I felt him approach behind me, his proximity making my entire body grow rigid. Reaching past me, he unlocked the door and pushed it open.

"Shall we?"

I turned my eyes forward and simply nodded,

wondering why Mr. Monroe always seemed to make me think that something was off about him. I wanted to know the real story behind him, and I knew exactly who would have answers.

French class seemed to last forever while I waited impatiently for the bell to ring. Finally, it did, and I bolted out of the room, dashing toward Carla's and Kristen's first period class just a few doors down.

"Hey," I said when I saw them saunter out. "Let's skip. I need to talk to you guys."

"About what?" Carla asked cheerily.

I lowered my voice. "Mr. Monroe. Come on. Let's go." I spun on my heels and knew their curiosity got the better of them when I sensed them on either side of me as we strode down the hallway and into the warm March air.

Plopping down on a picnic bench with a few other students who were either skipping or had study hall, I faced my two good friends. "What's the story with him?"

"Who? Hottie Monroe?" Carla asked.

"Yeah," I said, rolling my eyes at her boldness and impropriety. "I've heard the rumors. I'm sure y'all have, as well. But the two of you have a knack for wading through the bullshit and getting to the bottom of it. So... What do you know?"

They shared a look before they both turned to me. "So, remember Gabriella Knox?" Kristen asked excitedly.

I swallowed hard at the name. "Yes."

"Well, she took his Governments class last year, too. And he was 'helping' her with her senior project," Carla continued, using air quotes. "Something to do with the swimsuit portion of the pageant, which...God, what a prude. That's the part of the competition I'm looking forward to."

"Carla, focus. Before someone realizes we're skipping

245

and we have to go back to class."

"Right. Okay. So, apparently, Mr. Hottie had it out for her. Kind of like he has it out for you, Marley." She winked. "Anyway, she had to go to his office a few times, and there are definitely rumors floating around that certain things happened in his office. Some say consensual, some say not. Other rumors say that he waited until the night of the pageant and made his play then. Some say it was in the green room, like he locked her in there after everyone else had left. Others say that it was after the ball and he slipped something in her drink. She never said anything. Come to think of it, she denied it pretty fiercely, but Mr. Hottie and Mr. Grayson got into a heated argument at graduation and she just kind of disappeared." She raised her eyebrow.

"I think it was all part of the deal," Kristen interjected. "My brother, Chris, goes to U.S.C. with her and he said that she has this amazing apartment off campus and a gorgeous new Mitsubishi…a hot little red sports car. Her family didn't exactly have a lot of money. I think she was here on a scholarship. Mr. Monroe comes from quite a wealthy family. And don't forget, Brianna was the result of him sleeping with one of his students when he was a teaching assistant in grad. school. So… What does that tell you?"

"You think Mr. Monroe paid off Gabriella in exchange for her keeping her mouth shut?"

"No. I *know* that's what happened."

# CHAPTER THIRTY-SIX

## *MOVING ON*

*Cam*

BY EARLY MARCH, THINGS had gotten so busy with school that nearly a month had passed since I had been able to check in on Buck. Finally, on the Monday after spring break, I was able to sneak away for the night. At this point, I had been to his house so many times that I could drive there blindfolded.

I parked in my usual spot just up the street from his house and waited for his car to drive down the street. Around the time he always got home from work, I saw what appeared to be a new mini-van drive past me and pull into the driveway.

"Wow. He must have gotten a new car," I said to myself. "I would have opted for something a little bit more sporty and a little less soccer mom…" I trailed off, fear rushing over me. "Please, no."

I watched as he ran into the house, my mind trying to come up with some other plausible explanation for his recent car purchase. "Stop thinking the worst, Cam. There's no way." Suddenly, I noticed movement from his house, my heart dropping to the pit of my stomach when I saw him escort a pregnant version of the woman with whom he had been living to the mini-van. They drove past me and I debated whether I should follow them or go home. This had become a rather unhealthy obsession, and the anger only grew more intense now that I saw she was pregnant.

"Fuck it," I said, cranking the engine and tailing them through town, surprised when they drove toward Myrtle Beach and pulled into the parking lot of the mall where Marley worked. I prayed that she wasn't working tonight.

I kept my distance as I followed them into a baby store. Peering around the aisle, I noticed they were picking out clothes for a girl. I seethed with hatred and kicked a wall, several store associates turning to glare at me.

"Sorry. I didn't see where I was going."

They simply nodded and went on with organizing the store as I contemplated what to do and whether to finally come clean with Marley.

"Cam," a voice I had hoped to never hear again said. I looked up to see Buck standing a few feet away from me.

"Buck…" I furrowed my eyebrows in an attempt to feign surprise, not wanting him to know that I had become somewhat preoccupied with following his every move.

He sighed. "You've been keeping an eye on me, haven't you?"

"I…"

"It's okay," he interrupted me. "I don't blame you. If I were in your shoes, I'd do the same thing. I know you hate me, and you should. I shouldn't even be talking to you. I could get into a lot of trouble if anyone found out, but I needed to let you know how truly sorry I am for everything. If I end up going to prison again, it'll be worth it just so I could finally apologize to you."

"It's not me you should be apologizing to," I spat viciously. "Do you have *any* idea how severely fucked up

Marley is because of everything you did to her?" The pitch of my voice rose as I tried to subdue the lump forming in my throat.

He lowered his head, the formerly confident man that inundated himself in our lives nowhere to be seen. If I didn't know any better, I wouldn't believe that the man standing in front of me was the same person that ruined my sister.

"I can only imagine," he said solemnly. "I'm not going to stand here and make excuses for my behavior, but I finally know how horrible it was. I see that now." He gestured over to where the woman I had seen him with these past few months was sorting though a display of pink onesies. "It's a girl. I'm going to be a daddy. I get it now. I could never imagine anyone hurting my daughter the way…"

"The way you destroyed Marley?" My face flamed with anger and I felt the burn of pure disgust wash over me. "Well she *was* someone's daughter! Someone's niece! Someone's sister!" I hissed, my chin quivering with the memories of Marley's nightly screams and cries. "How do you know you won't relapse and do the same thing? To your own daughter? How…?"

"I would never be able to live with myself. I know it probably sounds like I'm just blowing smoke up your ass. That's not my intention. I don't expect you to forgive me. I have enough trouble trying to forgive myself. I'm just trying to move on with my life. To learn from this dark time in my life and prevent it from happening again."

"How?"

"I found a support group, thanks to your uncle. He put me in touch with a therapist…"

"Wait. What?" I was floored that he would encourage Buck to seek therapy when he refused Marley any help.

249

"I've prayed for forgiveness like your uncle asked when he came to see me in prison. And I tried to stay on that path as soon as I was released. For the most part, I have, but I'm only human. At times, I've felt weak and needed some sort of support for when I thought I was losing my way. He referred me to a group and we meet every day. That's where I go after work and before coming home."

It was silent while I processed what he was telling me.

"Please, Cam. Let me live my life. I have a life now. I don't feel the demons inside me. I feel like I finally have a direction with my fiancée and daughter. I beg you to stop living in the past."

"I'm not…"

"Then why have you been sitting outside of my house for months?"

I avoided his eyes and stared at the white tile floor.

"You love your sister. You always have. I'm sure she's trying to move on. Let her move on." He held his hand out to me and I hesitantly took it. "Have a good life, Cam. God bless."

I simply nodded, words evading me.

# CHAPTER THIRTY-SEVEN

## *SILENT NO MORE*

*Marley's Journal*

*May 9*

THE DAY I'VE BEEN dreading since getting that letter last August has arrived. The Miss Jessamine Pageant.

Today started off like any typical Saturday, apart from having a near heart attack when I opened my eyes to see Cam lying in my bed, staring at me.

"AAAAAGGGGHHHHH!" I screamed, punching him and pushing him off the bed.

He laughed at my reaction as I sat up and continued to kick him. "What the fuck, Cam?"

"Happy birthday to you, too, Mar."

"You're an ass. Did you want me to die of a heart attack before I turned eighteen?"

He looked at his watch. "Wait for it... Too late. It's 8:05. You're officially an adult."

I stood up and reached down, grabbing his hand, and pulled him to his feet, his frame towering over me by nearly a foot. "Happy birthday, Cameron Michael." I wrapped my arms around him.

"Happy birthday, Marley Jane. You ready for today?"

I looked up at him and a slight smile spread across my

face. "Surprisingly, yes. I'm actually looking forward to it. Now that I'm eighteen and will be moving to Columbia in a few weeks, I have quite a few things planned."

Cam pulled back, his eyes narrowing on me. "Like what?"

I pinched his side. "You'll just have to wait and find out. Trust me. This is one pageant of mine you do *not* want to miss. I have a feeling people will be talking about this one for years. My years of silence end today, Cam. I'm eighteen. No one can tell me what to do, how to dress, what to say or not say anymore."

"Are you prepared for the fallout? I mean, as much as you may hold a grudge against Aunt Terryn for certain things, she *did* provide a way for us to stay together. If it wasn't for…"

"I know! They didn't have to take us. We could have been put through the wringer in the foster system and separated, but we weren't. I *am* thankful to them for that, but… It's not just them. It's this entire town, Cam. Mr. Monroe got me thinking…"

"What? What do you mean?" He sat down on my bed and I followed.

"Our senior project. He was kind of the one that gave me the idea to do something today. He's right. I'm at a distinct advantage to say something and make a stand. He's talked at length to me about how change doesn't happen overnight. But last year…"

"You mean with Gabriella?" Cam asked.

"Yeah. She planted the seed. We all remember her stink about the swimsuit portion."

"She was practically crucified for that, Marley. Have you heard the rumors that went around about her?"

I shrugged. "I may have heard one or two."

"People said she lost her mind, that she went off the

deep end and demanded that Mr. Monroe sleep with her. That she blackmailed him and he just paid her off to make it all go away."

"What do *you* think happened?"

He sighed. "I don't know. You never know what to believe these days, it seems."

"It doesn't matter to me. They can talk shit about me all they want. Nothing could be worse than the truth, and that's exactly what they're all going to get today."

"You're sure about this?"

I looked Cam in the eyes and he could see the determination in my gaze. "I've never been so certain about anything in my entire life. I need to do this. To free myself from my past."

He planted a kiss on my forehead. "Okay. You may want to start packing your shit then."

"Most of it's already over at Mama's anyway. Two weeks from today, we'll be high school graduates. I can't wait."

"Me, either, Mar."

"Marley!" my aunt's voice cut through.

"Yeah?!" I shouted.

I heard footsteps coming up the stairs and she appeared in the doorway. "Good. You're up. Get a move on. Your hair appointment is at ten. Hurry." She spun around and retreated back down the stairs.

Cam and I shared a look. "Not even a happy birthday?" he remarked.

"Oh, Cameron Michael, you should know that pageants are much more important than birthdays. At least according to her they are. Now, if you'll excuse me. The queen must get ready for the ball."

He rolled his eyes and left, allowing me to prepare for my day in peace. As I was collecting my things and placing them in my travel case, I went through my mental checklist, making sure that I had everything I would need for the pageant.

Rummaging through the medicine cabinet in my bathroom, I stumbled across my mirror compact and my hand hovered over it. That had been part of my pageant kit for the last two years, but I was trying so hard to free myself from the chains of my past. Shaking my head, I slammed the medicine cabinet shut, leaving the compact where it was.

"Marley! We need to leave!"

"Just one minute!" I finished throwing my hair supplies and makeup into my kit. My eyes settled on my bathing suit and the reality of what I would have to do today washed over me.

"Fuck it." I ran back into the bathroom, found my compact, and quickly lowered my jeans. Digging the blade into my skin for the first time in months, I was able to momentarily release the anxiety coursing through me about what I was about to do.

"Marley Jane! Right now! Your appointment is in five minutes! Are you trying to be late?"

Hastily bandaging my legs, I readjusted my composure and grabbed my things, placing my compact in my purse. "No, ma'am. Just slow, as usual." I struggled down the hallway with my heavy cases, my aunt looking up the stairs at me with an irritated expression. *You'd think if she was worried about being late, she'd at least offer to help,* I thought to myself. *God forbid she break a nail.*

I heard the door to Cam's room open and he came running out. "Here, Mar. Give me the heavy one. I'll carry it down for you." I dropped my case and glared at my aunt. "Thanks for helping me, *Cam.*"

He leaned toward me. "Be nice," he whispered in my

ear. "It's not worth it."

I nodded. "You're right. I have bigger fish to fry today." Climbing down the stairs, I pushed past my aunt.

"Marley!" Julianne called to me. "Are you going to be a princess again today?"

"I'm not a princess, Jules."

"But you get to wear a crown! That makes you a princess."

I smiled at her innocence. I used to have the same excitement about the pageants before I realized it was just a way for the town's moms to compete amongst themselves over who produced the best offspring.

"Well, then, I hope I'll be a princess again," I replied, more for my aunt's benefit than anything. I needed her to think that nothing was wrong. I didn't need her overbearing eyes watching my every move.

"Me, too! I hope that I can be a princess one day."

I took a deep breath, wanting to scream at the thought of pure, angelic Julianne suffering the same torment that I had the past several years. I needed to make a stand. I needed to sound a call for change...for Julianne and Meg. They needed to be spared from being used as pawns, the perverts of the town ogling their adolescent bodies. I wanted their pageant experience to be one of empowerment.

"You already *are* a princess in my eyes." I looked at Meg who stood by her side. "Both of you are." I planted a kiss on both of their foreheads. "I'll see you kiddos later."

I walked out of the house and, in a matter of minutes, we pulled up in front of the salon to go through the normal routine of being waxed, clipped, trimmed, and primped.

"Marley!" my stylist, Liz, exclaimed as I walked in,

wrapping her arms around me. "Now, do you want to get the waxing over with first?"

I nodded. She knew how much I hated that part.

"Andrea will take you and then we'll have some fun." She winked and gestured to the petite blonde woman standing next to her. I followed her and stripped down for the humiliating process of having nearly every inch of me rid of hair. After the painful procedure, I was relieved to be sitting in my chair, having my hair done.

"Hey, Marley," I heard as I sat with a rejuvenating mask on my eyes. I took off the cloth and turned to my left to see Brianna there, having her hair styled, as well.

"Hey. I didn't know you were coming here."

She rolled her eyes. "Yeah. Me, either. Apparently, your aunt persuaded my mom that to have any shot at winning, I had to get my hair done here."

I busted out laughing. "That's the most ridiculous thing I've ever heard!"

She giggled quietly, glancing at the other end of the salon where my aunt and her mother were with their own stylists, getting their hair and makeup done as if they were the ones competing in the pageant.

"I know. It's not worth arguing over. I just need to get through this day and it'll all be over. Happy birthday, by the way."

"Thanks. My aunt completely forgot."

She turned away. "That sucks."

"Yeah. Tell me about it. Of course, if we forget Mother's Day tomorrow, we'll never hear the end of it. I'm glad she has her priorities."

Looking into the mirror as Liz was diligently curling my long blonde locks into a style that my aunt had demanded, I noticed a man walk in carrying a large bouquet of roses.

The girl at the front desk grabbed them, got up from her chair, and walked toward where Brianna and I sat. My heart melted at the thought that Cam had sent her flowers. Then the receptionist turned to me. "Marley, these are for you."

"What? Why?"

"Because Doug loves you," Brianna said enthusiastically. "And he would never forget your birthday."

I shook my head in disbelief. "I never expected him to do anything."

"It's a big deal, Marley. It's not every day you turn eighteen."

I grabbed the flowers and put them on the counter in front of me, opening the card.

*Happy birthday to the most beautiful woman on the planet. Every day, I fall even more in not love with you. Just kidding. I love you, Marley Jane. Always.*
*Love,*
*Douglas*

A wide grin crossed my face as butterflies swam in my stomach. It was hard to believe that we had been together for almost a year and I still grew excited when I thought of him. We would face our share of bumps in the road ahead, particularly because he would be going to Duke and I would be heading to U.S.C. since it was close to Mama, but I knew we would find a way to make it work.

"What's in the box?" Brianna asked, tearing me away from my thoughts.

My eyes settled on a black velvet box tied in the bow around the vase that I hadn't even noticed. My heart racing, I grabbed the box and slowly flipped it open, gasping at the beautiful diamond solitaire earrings. "Oh my…"

Brianna giggled. "He's been saving for those for about four months."

"He didn't have to do this for me."

"No. He didn't. But he did. Doesn't that make you feel good?"

I nodded. "It makes me feel better than good."

"You are one lucky girl, Marley," Liz said, staring over my shoulder at the earrings. "I need to find my own Doug. Does he have any brothers that are about fifteen years older?"

"No. He's the youngest, but his oldest brother is only twenty-three."

"Damn… Oh, well. I'll just keep looking."

I took the earrings out of the box and placed them in my ears, the light from the salon reflecting in the gorgeous stones. "I have a feeling this will be my best birthday yet."

Brianna reached over from her chair and grabbed my hand. "I think so, too."

Several hours later, I was finally primped and looking like a proper beauty queen.

"What do you have in your ears?" my aunt demanded as I walked to the front of the salon, ready to head to the country club where the pageant would be held.

"Earrings," I responded sheepishly. "Doug sent them to me with these flowers," I said, gesturing to the breathtaking arrangement of red roses…eighteen red roses for eighteen years. "Aren't they pretty?"

"Those do not go with your evening gown or your swimsuit, Marley. You can't wear them."

"But I just got them."

"Does it look like I care? You can wear them tomorrow

and every day after. Today, you need to wear the jewelry that I picked out and spent money on."

"Yes, ma'am," I answered. There was no way in hell I was ever going to take these earrings out of my ears. She would have to pry them from my cold, lifeless body.

I climbed into her car and we drove in silence the entire way to the country club, nervous energy starting to flow through me when we pulled into the parking lot. Grabbing my stuff, we made our way into the palatial building, every inch of it decorated with the signature white and yellow flowers for which the pageant was named.

"The green room is this way," she said, leading me to a spacious room that they had set up into a makeshift dressing and changing area, complete with snacks and beverages for us. She helped me unpack my things and hang up the dresses I had brought with me.

My stomach growling, I excused myself and began to make a sandwich.

"What are you doing?" my aunt asked just as I was about to take a bite.

"Eating."

She ripped the sandwich out of my hand and tossed it into the garbage. "You can eat after the pageant. I don't need to listen to all my friends telling me how much weight my niece has gained. I have to go meet with the rest of the judging committee. Do you think you'll be able to resist stuffing your face for the next few hours?"

"I don't know. Why don't you have my jaw wired shut so I don't have an option?"

"Don't get smart with me, Marley. This is important to me."

I sighed. "Yes, ma'am. I'll resist the temptation of turning into a fat cow so you can save face in front of your friends."

Her fierce eyes turned sincere and she sat down next to me. "Marley," she started, placing her hand on my arm in a show of feigned compassion, "I'm only doing this because I care about you. I just want you to be happy. I loved doing these pageants when I was your age. You always talk about wanting to be normal. Well, look around you. All your friends love doing this. This *is* normal."

Reminding myself of what I had planned for that day, I gave my aunt the most reassuring smile I could muster. "I know. I'm sorry. My blood sugar is just low."

"Have a carrot. I'll be back before the swimsuit competition to help you." She stood up and left the dressing room. My blood boiling, I turned my attention back to the catering table and grabbed the most fattening item I could find...cheese and butter crackers.

The next several hours passed in a frenzy of hair spray, glitter, and sequins as all twelve of us prepared for the opening act of this display of sexism...I mean, feminism. I sat in front of my vanity, staring at the mirror compact on the counter, trying to resist the urge to go to the restroom. It was taking all my resolve to not grab that razor. The only thing dulling the pain was the fact that after today, I would never have to be subjected to this carnival again. I needed Doug at that moment. I kept looking at my wrist and ears at the jewelry he had bought me that I still wore, regardless of my aunt's demands that I put on her pre-approved accessories. I focused on my wrist, willing the circle of hope, love, and devotion that hung on me to work the magic it had in the past.

But I'd never had to put myself on display like I was about to. Grabbing the compact, I glanced at Brianna on my right. "I'll be back. I need to pee."

She looked up from her sketchpad, her outlet for relieving the stress, and said, "Okay."

Just then, the door opened and the stout man that had been working on this as the stage manager entered the room. "Five minutes until curtain. Places, ladies."

Groaning, I placed the compact back on my vanity, hoping I'd have a break after the opening song and dance number to do what I needed to do.

"Ready?" Brianna asked, standing up from her chair.

"Let's get this over with."

She grabbed my hand and we headed to the elaborate theater. The stage manager made his way down the line, clipping mics to us. We looked like cookie cutter molds, all of us wearing the same black dress with a sequin belt. *Conformity at its finest*, I said to myself.

"Sixty seconds," the stage manager called and we all took our places behind the curtain.

Looking at Brianna, she nodded and we both plastered on the fake smile that was expected of us. The curtain opened and, like the puppets we all were, we broke into the routine that we had rehearsed over and over again during the past several weeks when pageant duties had a higher priority than school work. Scanning the audience, I found Doug's brilliant eyes as he sat next to Cam, and I felt at ease. I felt the peace that I had been needing to feel all day.

Finishing the opening number, we all scurried off the stage and into the dressing room to put on one of our formal gowns for the official introduction. The sound of twelve pairs of heels echoed down the hallway and we attempted to change as quickly as possible. Within a few minutes, we were all dressed and making our way back to the stage, where they would bring us out one at a time to introduce us. I had the unfortunate position of being last.

Then again, that would ensure that everyone in attendance would have to listen to what I had to say.

As each of the twelve girls were called to the stage and introduced, most of them replied with some bullshit charity that they wanted to bring attention to during their reign as Miss Jessamine. My aunt told me that my cause would be shoreline preservation. So she wouldn't catch on, I even memorized the words that she ordered me to regurgitate. Over the past few weeks, however, I worked on a completely different speech with the help of Mr. Monroe, who had become my unexpected ally.

I focused on my breathing as I heard Mr. Grayson call name after name. I felt a nudge on my shoulder and the stage manager gestured to me. "You're up."

I nodded and made my way from the wings and onto the stage, the bright lights making me feel so small, every eye focused on me.

"And our final contestant is Miss Marley Jane Bowen," Mr. Grayson's gentle voice said. I walked to where he stood, dressed in his tuxedo. "Marley will be attending the University of South Carolina this fall where she hopes to major in psychology."

My eyes remained fixed on my aunt as Mr. Grayson continued to read what was on the cue cards that I had given him. She pursed her lips in annoyance and I smiled at her reaction.

"Well, Marley. I wish you all the luck."

"Thank you," I said into the microphone.

"If chosen as Miss Jessamine, what cause would you be working toward during your reign?"

"As we all know," I began, my aunt relaxing in her chair at the opening words of the speech she had coached me on, "pollution has caused our shoreline to erode farther and farther each year." I closed my eyes, taking a deep breath before opening them again. "But that's not what I plan on bringing attention to." My gaze met Mr. Monroe's and he nodded slightly. "I would, instead, like to bring attention to the importance that child victims of abuse receive the help they need, whether it be counseling or intensive therapy. It's a cause very near and dear to my heart. When I was eight…"

My aunt jumped up and grabbed the microphone in front of her chair. "Okay. That's time."

I looked at the timer on the front of the judge's table. "I still have ninety seconds."

"Go on, Marley," Mr. Grayson said, giving me an encouraging smile.

"Thank you." I turned back to the audience, their curious eyes glued to me. "When I was eight, I was molested. I never received the treatment I needed. I'm still dealing with my past, but I've finally started to shed it. If society didn't place such a stigma on therapy, maybe I would have moved past my self-destructive tendencies earlier. If I win, I will work tirelessly to ensure that anyone who has been a victim of any type of abuse realizes that seeking professional psychiatric help is not a bad thing. Thank you."

Mr. Grayson turned and looked at me with more compassion than I had ever seen in his eyes. "Thank you for sharing your story, Marley. I know this must have been difficult for you. You're a strong girl. Ladies and gentlemen, Marley Jane Bowen."

I felt a unique sensation of relief as I took my place amongst my fellow contestants, their mouths open in shock…except for Brianna. She had a look of vindication on her face. It mirrored the way I felt. And this was just the beginning.

After the introductions, we all left the stage and made

our way back to the green room. I expected my aunt to come storming in, fuming, but she didn't. Instead, girls I went to high school with, but barely knew, came up to me and hugged me, thanking me for giving them a voice. It went on and on, and I didn't know what to make of it. As I was about to change into the dress that I would be wearing for the talent portion, I was met by Kristen's and Carla's tear-filled eyes.

"Marley," Carla cried, both girls wrapping their arms around me. "We're so sorry. We had no idea."

"It's okay, girls. No one really knew. I wasn't allowed to say anything, but I'm changing that."

They pulled out of the hug and wiped their cheeks before breaking down and crying again.

"My mom didn't want me to see a shrink, either," Kristen admitted through her tears.

"Wait. What? For what?" I asked, looking at her.

"My dad used to beat my mama. And me. And my brothers. After she filed for divorce, it was never talked about again. I always felt so worthless. And I think that's why I sleep with any guy that will have me. I hate the idea of rejection."

I placed my hand on her arm in understanding, a revelation washing over me. Because I was able to talk about my past, these girls were sharing the ghosts that they had been forced to forget. I wanted more of this. I had originally said I would major in psychology just to get a rise out of my aunt. Now, as I stood there, tears flowing down more faces than not, I knew what I would spend the rest of my life doing. I was going to help girls find their voices.

The stage manager came in to hurry us along in getting ready, and Carla and Kristen left to go change. I pulled on my long, black sequined gown that I would be wearing for the talent portion, wondering if my aunt would attempt to cut my performance short.

After an excruciatingly long time, I was called to the stage and heard Mr. Grayson announcing my name, saying that I would be performing a song from *The Phantom of the Opera*. I walked out to enthusiastic applause and approached the microphone at center stage.

"Thank you for the introduction, Mr. Grayson, but I've changed my mind. I'm going to do a song titled *Silent All These Years* by Tori Amos." I looked to the accompanist sitting behind the grand piano, whom I had worked with on my new song choice. He nodded and began playing the opening notes, my eyes glued on my aunt's. I wanted to laugh at the look of indignation on her face.

Standing in front of that crowd, I felt a huge weight lift off my chest. I normally hated being on public display for everyone to judge, pretending to be a fake version of myself, but that all changed. I was making a stand. I was finally able to be the real Marley Jane Bowen. Meeting Mr. Monroe's eyes, I could tell that he saw it, too. His words the first day of school, wondering who the real Marley Jane Bowen was, echoed in my mind, and it was because of him that I finally realized who she was.

I finished my talent portion to resounding applause, most of the judges standing in ovation…except for my aunt, naturally. I met Doug's eyes, and I could see the pain he felt for what I had been through. But in the pain, I saw my hope…my future.

I hustled off the stage, knowing that the swimsuit portion would be next and my aunt would be furious with me. Approaching the green room, a hand grabbed my arm and I was forced to look into my aunt's irate eyes.

"What they hell are you doing? Are you trying to make sure that no one votes for you? Are you trying to make me the laughing stock amongst my friends?"

"No," I answered calmly. "I'm just finally moving on from my past. I'm no longer going to pretend what happened to me was something I should be ashamed of. It has turned me into the woman I am, and I'm proud of who that is."

"Well, I'm not. This is ridiculous, Marley. After everything I've done for you…"

"What?!" I asked, my voice growing loud. "That you paraded me around so you could be buddies with all your high school friends again? So you could shove that I won in their faces? Oh wait. No, that's not right. That *you* won? I'm eighteen, but you've forgotten that today's my birthday. I'm an adult and I plan on making my own decisions, starting with speaking about my past in the hopes that it encourages other girls who have gone through the same thing to feel like they're not alone. I felt like that for years! I felt there must be something wrong with me because of what happened. And the worst part of it?! I thought it was *my* fault! Not my mama's! Not the sick fuck who had to get his rocks off with a little girl! Mine! And *you* made me feel that way! I'm thankful for you and Uncle Graham giving Cam and me a home, making sure we stayed together, but your obsession with these pageants has done more harm than good." I spun on my heels and ran into the green room.

She followed and thrust my swimsuit at me. "Put this on so I can apply the cover up. We don't need people seeing the physical scars. That's too much."

"Yes, ma'am," I said, smiling to myself on the inside as I slid into the small red bikini that she had picked out.

"And take those earrings off. I already told you. Wear the jewelry I picked out for you."

"Not a chance in hell, Aunt Terryn."

She huffed as she applied copious amounts of foundation to my back before stepping away to check her work. "That will do." She shoved the container at me. "Put this on your thighs. We'll discuss your transgressions later."

I grabbed the foundation. "I look forward to it," I sneered as she walked away.

Running through the green room, I found Brianna as she was adjusting her swimsuit. "Bri. Come here. I need your help."

"You're really pulling all the stops, aren't you?"

I shrugged. "Like Cam always says… Go big or go home."

"The way you're going, your next home will be a grave."

"If so, it'll be worth it."

# CHAPTER THIRTY-EIGHT

## *STRENGTH*

*Cam*

"YOUR AUNT LOOKS PISSED," Doug said to me after Marley's talent portion.

"Maybe," I responded. "But I've never been so proud of her. She's forcing all these people to open their eyes. Look around you." I scanned the audience, most of the women drying their eyes with tissues. "She's getting to them. I just hope it lasts. I hope they don't feel bad for a day, then continue on with how things have been."

Doug nodded. "Me, too."

Mr. Grayson appeared on the stage again and began announcing the contestants for the bathing suit portion of the competition. After a few girls, Brianna was announced and I hated that she was forced to be on that stage, wearing one of the tiniest bathing suits I had ever seen, for everyone to gawk at. She looked amazing, her slender frame shimmering from the oil that all the girls used on their bodies, but I'd rather her wear that when it was just us.

"Do you think Mr. Grayson's a bit creepy?" Doug whispered in my ear.

"What do you mean? He's always been so nice. He treats Brianna like his own daughter. You can tell how much he cares for her by the way he acts toward her. We should all be so lucky to have someone like him in our lives."

"I guess," Doug responded. "He's just got this heat in his eyes right now. And look at him." He gestured with his head. "He's adjusting his pants. You know why men do that." He raised his eyebrows at me in a knowing manner.

"He is *not* turned on," I said loudly before lowering my voice. "He's looking at Brianna, for crying out loud. That's sick. He's probably just itching from having to be in a tux for so long. I know I would be. I've adjusted my jeans a few times, too, and they're pretty comfortable. Does that mean I've got a hard-on for you?"

He laughed and several people turned to stare at us. "I know," he whispered, sighing. "It was stupid. I don't know what I was thinking." It was silent for a moment before he spoke again. "What do you think about the rumors about her dad? Do you think that's why his visitation with her was restricted?"

"If the rumors *are* true and he may have made a few misjudgments in sleeping with a former student…"

"Still a student at the time," Doug corrected. "And don't forget, he slept with Brianna's mom when he was a teacher's assistant and she was an undergrad student."

"Whatever. I doubt the rumors are true. He's so passionate about teaching. He's the one who persuaded Marley to make a stand today. I think she always secretly wanted to, but if it wasn't for his prodding, I don't think she would have had the courage. Apparently, they've been working together on this the past few months, making sure all the pieces were in place without anyone finding out, including my aunt."

"Really?" Doug looked at me, his eyebrows furrowed.

"I didn't know that. Don't you think that's a bit odd?"

"No. Not really. You haven't taken his class. He's always encouraging us to make a stand and to enact change. That's what he did with Marley."

"And Gabriella Knox," he muttered under his breath and I could tell he was on edge.

"I really doubt that rumor is true. There's no way. You don't know him that well." I turned my attention back to the stage just as Mr. Grayson was announcing Marley. Her tall, skinny body came into view as she walked in her heels to the center of the stage, stopping in front of the judges before following the choreographed pattern that all the girls had made. As she approached the end of the catwalk just a few yards away from me, my heart fell.

"What the…?" I quivered.

Quiet whispers echoed around me as the audience had the same reaction that I did. Then she turned around and people audibly gasped at the sight of her back, her welts visible for all to see. They had grown dull over the years, but the light hit her body in just the right way so that people could see the faint pink marks and grooves in her skin from where Buck had used his belt on her. Guilt overwhelmed me for keeping everything I knew about him from her.

She took her position in the line of girls and I couldn't stop looking at the red marks on her inner thighs. In a complete trance, I raised myself from my seat and bolted out of the theater, running down the corridor that led from the green room toward the stage just as all the girls were filing in. I pushed through them, my eyes settling on Brianna and Marley walking together.

"Mar," I said quietly, my eyes awash with concern.

She turned to Brianna. "I'll be right there."

She nodded, squeezing my arm affectionately as she

270

retreated into the green room.

"I don't understand. How come you never told me?"

She crossed her arms over her stomach and I shrugged out of my jacket, draping it around her shoulders.

"I needed this for me, Cam. It was the only way to stop the pain."

"How long?"

"A couple of years. I haven't done it since Thanksgiving. But I had to do it this morning because of the pageant. I'm getting better."

"What if something happens when you're at college? I'm heading to Georgetown and won't be around in case you take things too far and…"

She placed her hand on my arm. "I'm not going to, Cam. I'm shedding my past. I promise. You can't constantly worry about me. I get it now. You need to live your life, and that's not always going to be near me. At the beginning of the school year, I hated the thought of us being away from each other. You're my rock, but you've also been my crutch. It took Doug to make me realize that I'm worthy of love, regardless of my past. I hate the idea that things won't work out between Doug and me, but that doesn't mean someone else won't come along who will love me just as fiercely as Doug does."

Nodding, I wrapped my arms around her. "I'm proud of you, Marley Jane. You're definitely getting to everyone out there."

She pulled out of my chest and grinned at me. "Good. Mission accomplished. Now, let me go. I need to change into my evening gown." Handing me my jacket, she walked toward the green room.

"Hey, Marley?" I said.

She looked over her shoulder at me.

"To the moon and back."

"From the stars to the ocean." She disappeared into the room. I hastily walked down the corridor and made my way back to the theater, retaking my seat next to Doug.

"I'm sorry, Cam," he said. "I should have… I had the same reaction that you did when I first found out."

"It's okay. I don't blame you for wanting to keep Marley's secret."

Mr. Grayson took the stage again and began announcing the girls for the evening gown portion. I was thankful that this display was almost over. I was ready to get out of there and enjoy the afternoon before having to go to the Jessamine Ball later that evening.

Once all the girls were standing in a line in their evening wear, Mr. Grayson returned his attention to the audience. "Now, the moment you've all been waiting for… The crowning of this year's Miss Jessamine." Applause rang through the theater as my eyes remained glued to the nervous expression on Brianna's face and the fulfilled look on Marley's.

Mr. Grayson reached down and grabbed the envelope from the judging table and opened it. "This year's second runner up is… Miss Brianna Monroe!"

My eyes grew wide and I clapped enthusiastically for my girlfriend as she politely stepped out of line and walked toward Mr. Grayson, allowing him to kiss her on the cheek as two little girls came out with a bouquet of flowers for her. She walked toward the corner of the stage and her eyes met mine. I winked at her and she blushed.

"This year's first runner up is… Miss Jessica Harper!"

Doug leaned over. "Do you think she slept with half the judging panel like she slept with half the basketball team?"

I shrugged and continued to clap politely. "Who cares?"

"This year's winner and our Miss Jessamine who will go on to compete in the Miss South Carolina Pageant next month is… Miss Marley Bowen!"

I could sense Marley's shock from a mile away. She was so convinced that after all the stunts she pulled, none of the judges would vote for her and would think that she was making a mockery of their precious pageant. Instead, they saw it for what it was…a showing of strength. At that moment, I couldn't be prouder of my sister.

# CHAPTER THIRTY-NINE

## *THE CYCLE*

*Marley's Journal*

*May 9*

IT'S A NEVER-ENDING CYCLE. It won't stop. You think if it happens once, it surely won't happen again. The odds of probability are against it, right?

Wrong.

It will. Again. And again. And again. The past finds you. It reminds you that, no matter how far you've come, you're not as strong as you thought.

You're not as free as you thought.

I was so happy to have won the pageant. It was the first one I could remember being excited to win because I did so being the truest version of myself, and not the person I had been forced to pretend that I was those past several years.

Walking from the stage, all the girls congratulating me on my win, I tried to rid myself of them as quickly as possible. There was only one person I wanted to see at that moment. Finally clear of the backstage area, I ran down the hall, past the green room, and jumped into Doug's arms.

He lifted me up and spun me around before lowering

me down. He pressed his lips against mine and I curved my body into his, allowing him to run his hands up and down the exposed back of my evening gown.

"I love you, Marley Jane. I'm so proud of you."

"I love you, too," I said. "Thanks for the flowers and the earrings. They're beautiful."

"Not nearly as beautiful as you."

"Oh, Doug." I hugged him once more before noticing Cam standing off to the side, trying to give us our space.

I pulled away from Doug and walked up to Cam.

"Congratulations, Marley Jane," he said, embracing me. "Feel better?"

I nodded. "Much. I feel…free."

"Good. Are you prepared for the backlash?"

I shrugged. "I guess. Nothing I can do to stop it now. The damage has been done. But no matter what Aunt Terryn says, it was completely worth it."

"I'm glad."

"On that note, I really don't want to drive home with her. She'll sit in the car and scream at me. I don't think it'll be so bad if I just see her at the house, especially if Meg and Jules are around. Do you think you can have Bri or Doug drive you and I'll take the Jeep home? I was so focused on what I had to do today that I never thought of an exit strategy."

"I can go with Bri. We were planning on heading to her mom's house to sit by the pool for a few hours this afternoon before the ball, anyway."

I winked. "Sure you are. I'm sure the only thing you'll be doing is lying by the pool."

He thrust the keys into my hands. "See you later, Marley."

"Use a condom, Cam."

"What time should I pick you up tonight?" Doug asked

as I turned away from my brother.

"Eight? That'll give me time to either smooth things over with my aunt, or enough time that you'll be able to smell a rotting body."

He placed a kiss on my lips. "Just remember that you're a strong girl, and no matter what, you did a good thing today."

"Thanks, Doug. See you in a few hours."

He grabbed my hand and feathered his lips across it. "I look forward to it."

I spun around and retreated to the green room, taking my time gathering all my stuff. I had no desire to hurry home, knowing that the only thing waiting for me there was an indignant aunt. Part of me thought about hiding out at the country club for the rest of the day before the ball that evening. I just hoped that she saw today as what it was supposed to be…not a personal attack on her, but on the stereotypes and misconceived notions that have been doing more harm than good over the past several years, if not longer.

"Are you coming, Marley?" Carla asked as she and Kristen were carrying their stuff out of the room.

I looked around and noticed I was the last one there. I glanced at my area and I had barely made a dent in the mess in front of me. "I'll be along. See you tonight."

"Okay," Kristen said. "And congrats."

"Thank you." I heard the door close and I returned my attention to all my makeup scattered over the vanity. As I was packing up my kit, I heard the door open once more. The room went dark and a loud click sounded as if someone was locking the door.

"Hey!" I called out. "I'm still in here. I just need two more minutes and then I'll be gone."

I cautiously raised myself off my stool and tried to

maneuver through the pitch black room. Suddenly, I felt two hands grab me and push me, face first, to the ground.

"*Get off me!*" I screamed, fighting against the figure that had me pinned. "*Help!*" I yelled at the top of my lungs, my body writhing as my chest began to rise and fall in an uneven pattern.

"It's useless, Marley," a familiar voice crooned, the heat of his breath torturing my neck. "They're all gone," he murmured. "There's no one to hear you. There's no one to help you. There's no way out."

He ran his hand down my leg, ripping the slit of my dress. A tear fell down my cheek. I cringed when I felt his tongue on my face.

"I love the taste of tears. Each one is different. Tears of joy taste different than tears of sorrow. But my favorite are tears of fear. Call it an addiction."

"Why?" I closed my eyes, wanting to wake up and it all be a dream. It had to be. There was no way this could be happening.

"Have you ever wanted something you know is wrong? That you know is off limits, but you go for it anyway?" he asked, his husky voice growing agitated and neurotic. "It's a rush." His body quivered on top of me. "I've tried to stop, but I can't! Nothing works! It's no longer a choice for me! There are demons inside me and the only way to keep them at bay is to succumb to them when the urge strikes. I've had my eyes on you all year... Well, the past few years to be honest, but something or someone always got in the way. Not today."

I took a deep breath as I felt his hand roam my leg toward my inner thigh. I tried to refrain from crying, not wanting the sick fuck to get off on my fear anymore.

"You could get help," I whimpered.

"I have. I've tried everything. No amount of therapy

has worked. Well, no traditional therapy has. I have a new form of therapy…"

I gasped. "Brianna…"

"You always were a smart girl, weren't you?" He grunted and I screamed out.

"Please, stop," I begged, but it was useless. No matter what I said, he continued his assault, ignoring my cries. The harder I sobbed, the more he got off.

At that moment, I realized that the world was a cruel place. I was fooling myself to think that I could shed my past and only look toward my future. The past will always torment you, mocking you, shouting at you that you're weak. You're powerless to forget it. You're ignorant to think that you can move on from it.

I tried to shut it out and pretend it wasn't happening, but the pain was excruciating. Nothing could make it stop. Even when he was finished destroying my very existence over and over again, an existence that took me nearly seven years from which to come back, the pain only intensified.

Finally, I no longer felt his weight on me, and all I could do was curl up in a ball and pray for death. In death, I could finally find peace. There was no peace for me here.

As I lay on the ground, my body trembling, he pulled me up, tearing the arm of my dress, and walked me through the room. Opening the door, he scanned the hallway and ushered me out the back, handing me my bags and leaving me in the alleyway with the rest of the trash.

I needed to get out of that place. I threw my bags in the dumpster and grabbed my purse, running across the parking lot toward Cam's Jeep. Tears streamed down my face the entire drive home as the past hour replayed in my mind like a horrible movie. Parking in front of the house, it appeared lifeless. I walked inside and realized I was all alone. But there was no telling when someone would come home. I dashed up the stairs and into Cam's room, hoping to hide out there while I attempted to pull myself together.

Closing the door, I stared at my reflection in the mirror. I couldn't even stand the sight of me. I was so sick of everything. Of looking at my face. Of being me.

Screaming, I clawed at my face with my professionally manicured nails, drawing long scratches down my cheeks, exhaling when I saw the blood trickle down. It wasn't enough. With shaky hands, I rummaged through my purse and pulled out the mirror compact.

Sitting at Cam's desk, I lifted up my dress and lowered the razor to my inner thigh, ignoring the blood that was still there from the assault. I couldn't even stand to look at it. I carved over and over, but nothing worked. I etched new words on my legs, my arms, my stomach. Nothing released the pain. Nothing brought me peace.

Flipping over my hand, I stared at my wrist, wondering if I could really draw that line. As I continued to look at it, I noticed the drawer of Cam's desk was slightly ajar. A folder caught my eye and I put down the razor. Opening the file, my chin quivered as I stared back into the eyes of the first man to ruin me. Sifting through everything, I wanted to scream.

Secrets destroy. Secrets ruin. And this secret made me feel more betrayed than I ever had in the past. Betrayed by the one person who swore he would stand by my side...who would wipe away my tears...who would help fight the demons.

Cam knew. He knew where Buck lived. He knew that my uncle, my own flesh-and-blood, was the reason that

279

this sick fuck was out of prison. They still spoke! And often. As I flipped through all the letters, I felt as if my worst nightmare had become a reality. Then my eyes settled on a fuzzy black-and-white photo that the pedophile sent my uncle.

The rage inside grew to a fevered pitch and I knew what I had to do. I knew what would stop the pain. Cutting wasn't working anymore. I could only think of one thing that would help. That would bring me the peace I so desperately needed.

Grabbing the photo and the map with the route that Cam had highlighted, I stormed out of his room and into the garage, opening the safe that I was told to never open unless it was an emergency.

As I sit behind the wheel of my Mustang writing this, watching *him* walk into his house with his very pregnant fiancée, I'm convinced this is an emergency.

# CHAPTER FORTY

## *UNFORGIVEN*

*Cam*

"I'LL BE BACK IN a half-hour or so," I said to Brianna. "Don't worry. I promise I'll drive your baby with care. I just want to make sure Marley's okay."

She stood on her tiptoes in the entryway of her mother's stately home and placed a kiss on my lips. "I look forward to it. See you soon, Cameron."

I bolted down the driveway and into Brianna's Beetle, driving carefully along the coast of Myrtle Beach. Parking in front of my house, I noticed that my aunt and uncle's car wasn't there. I assumed they were dropping off Meg and Julianne at their grandmother's before heading to the ball for the evening.

Just as I was getting out of Brianna's car, Doug pulled up. "Hey," I called out.

"Hey," he said, meeting me. "Where's Marley's car? Is she here?"

"Where else would she be?" I responded, scanning the street for her red Mustang.

He nodded. "I just hope she's okay after getting yelled at by your aunt. I know she was a bit nervous about that."

"I'm sure she's fine." I entered the house and ran up the stairs, banging on her door. "Mar? Are you in there?"

No answer.

"Marley?"

Still no answer.

"Okay. I'm coming in so you better be decent." I opened the door, surprised to see the gown she was going to wear that evening hanging in the closet. "It doesn't even look like she's been here. If my car wasn't sitting out front, I wouldn't think that she had ever come home. Her stuff from the pageant isn't even here. Nothing is."

I ran down the hall and into my room. Approaching my desk with the intention of calling Aunt Terryn's mother to see if Marley had gone with my aunt and uncle to drop off the girls for some reason, my eyes fell on the photocopies I made of the file my uncle kept on Buck. "Shit," I breathed, my mind racing as a horrible feeling settled in my gut.

Snapping to, I looked at Doug standing in my doorway, a worried expression on his face. "Go to the ball. Find my aunt and uncle. They should be there soon. Tell them to go here. I have a bad feeling." I scribbled an address on a piece of paper and shoved it at him before running down the stairs.

"What? Why? I'm coming with you."

"No, you're not. And call Brianna for me and tell her I'm not going to make it."

"Cam. Please. What's going on?"

I stopped and looked at Doug, my shoulders dropping slightly. "I've been keeping tabs on Buck. It looks like Marley found out and now knows where he lives. I have a bad feeling that she's over there. Maybe I'm wrong, but…I don't know. Something feels off right now."

"How do you know?"

"Call it my twin-sense. I just know."

I ran out to my car and drove away from the shore

toward the house that I had staked out and observed over the better part of the past year. It killed me that I hadn't been honest with Marley from the start.

Spotting her car parked on the street, I jumped out and ran up to the house. Reaching the door, I peered into the front windows. Almost instantly, my gaze settled on a very frightened version of Buck, his body trembling. I followed his line of sight to see my darling sister...the light of my life, my other half...pointing a gun at him.

I threw open the front door, thankful that it wasn't locked, and shouted, "Marley! No!"

She spun around and her wild eyes met mine. Tears were streaming down her face as she held on to the nine millimeter with shaking hands.

"Marley," I said softly as I surveyed the room, noticing Buck's fiancée crying in the corner. "Please. Put the gun down. You don't want to do this. It's not going to change anything. It's not going to make you feel better. *I* didn't feel better. I felt worse. Please."

"No, Cam. I think it will. It will make me feel *so* much better," she said, her voice quivering but strong at the same time. It was unlike any tone that I had ever heard come out of her mouth. She wasn't herself. Something set her off and this girl pointing a gun at me was not my twin.

I began to examine her body, noticing that she still wore her pageant gown. It was torn at one shoulder with more ripping at the seams and the slit, exposing her leg almost all the way up to her hip. My eyes traveled the length of her leg and I saw bruising and redness in four thin strips midway up her thigh. There was even more bruising, marks, and scratches on her arms. On a few of the bruises there was a distinct crisscross pattern, as if the imprint of a ring. Her face was scratched and she had carved numerous words into her legs and arms. This Marley was completely different than the Marley I saw just a few hours ago.

"Marley," I said, my chin quivering at what all those marks could be from. They were certainly not all self-inflicted. "Why are you still in your dress?"

"Because it never stops, Cam!" Her chest heaved from her heartbreaking sobs, her expression manic. "No matter what! I can make a stand all I want, but will it end? *No!* Nothing I say or do will ever make it stop. There are thousands of sick, twisted men just like *him* everywhere." She gestured with the gun toward where Buck stood, shaking in fear of the weapon pointed at him by a seemingly irrational woman.

"I'll never be free of my past. It will always cling on to me and not let me go."

I swallowed hard, her inferences making it clear what happened to her in the last few hours.

"Who, Marley?"

She closed her eyes and inhaled deeply before returning her defeated gaze to me. "You already know the answer, Cam, but you've been too blind to see what's been right in front of you all along. And so have I."

I was completely baffled. Nothing made sense.

"Please, Marley. I need to know."

She shook her head and I could see her body shivering from the memory of what she had endured today and all those years ago.

"It needs to be stopped! And I'm starting with him!" Vengeance in her eyes, she took a step closer to Buck, clinging to the gun as if it were a life vest...her last hope of survival.

"Marley! No! You don't want to do this. He's turned his life around. He's sorry for what he's done, aren't you?" I met Buck's tear-stained eyes.

He nodded quickly. "Yes. I am. I'm so sorry for what I did to you. I know it doesn't mean anything, and that I hurt you and betrayed your trust, but you have to believe that I'm reformed. I would never harm another person or touch another girl in that way again. Please," he begged, sweat falling from his brow.

"He's trying to move on with his life, just like you're trying to move on with yours, Marley." My voice was soothing as I attempted to talk some sense into her.

She closed the distance between herself and Buck, her eyes crazed. "He's going to get married, Cam! He convinced her to marry him! And they're having a baby! She's pregnant, due to deliver the baby any day now!" She grabbed a picture of an ultrasound and shoved it at me. "It's a girl! What if he's lying, Cam? What if he hasn't turned over a new leaf? What if he's planning on doing the same thing to his daughter that he did to me? I can't live with myself if I don't do something to stop him. To stop all of it! *It needs to end*!"

"Please, Marley," Buck said, taking a bold step toward her. "I will not touch my daughter that way. I love her. Please. Let me know my daughter."

The atmosphere in the room intensified as Marley stared into Buck's apologetic eyes, the distaste that covered his being all those years ago absent.

"Please, Marley. Let me move on. You have such a bright future ahead of you, despite all the pain and suffering I put you through. Don't take that away from yourself."

A protracted moment passed before she shook her head in resignation and I could tell that Buck's words forced some sort of revelation in her. Her rigid body visibly relaxing, she gradually lowered the gun. Both Buck and I let out a long breath.

Then a smile crossed Marley's face. "I just can't take that risk, Buck." She raised the weapon and shot him in the chest.

He fell back, toppling over the coffee table as it shattered beneath his weight.

"Buck!" his fiancée shouted, rushing to him.

"No! Marley!" I ran to Buck, trying to stop the flow of blood as best I could with the little first aid training I had received. His fiancée cried and held his hand.

"Doesn't make you feel any better, does it?" I asked, glancing back at her before returning my attention to Buck, praying that he wasn't dead.

"You were right, Cam. I don't feel any better. Killing him won't stop it." Her voice was stoic and void of emotion as a look of tranquility crossed her face. It was the most at peace I had seen Marley since our eighth birthday.

I began to give Buck CPR, not knowing if that would help in the case of a gunshot.

"I get it now. I know what will finally stop my pain," Marley's sweet voice said as I continued my compressions regardless of the fact that I knew it was useless. He was dead.

"From the stars to the ocean."

A gunshot sounded and I jumped, turning to see that Marley was slumped over on the ground, blood streaming from her head. "*Marley! No!*" I screamed, the pain of that sight torturing my soul. I could feel my heart crumbling in my chest as I rushed to her.

"Marley," I sobbed, cradling her lifeless body against mine. "Please, Mar." I hugged her tight, hoping that my arms would bring her back to me. "You need to wake up now, Marley Jane. Stop playing. It's not funny anymore.

You made your point." I held her for as long as I could, warming her body when it grew cold over the hours that I sat in a strange house in a complete daze, flashing lights illuminating the night sky outside.

"Cameron, baby," a soothing voice said, waking me as I kept Marley clutched in my embrace. "You need to let her go."

I looked up to see my mama standing there next to my aunt and uncle. Brianna and Doug stood in the corner, holding on to each other, tears in their eyes as they watched me. I wondered when everyone had arrived. The last thing I remembered was hearing the gunshot that changed my life.

"Let Marley go," Mama said.

I stared at them, emotion overwhelming me at the thought of ever letting Marley go. "I don't know how," I sobbed out. It was the absolute truth. I had no idea how to let go of my sister. We had been together since before birth. There was no such thing as life without Marley. I couldn't even imagine a day where there was no Marley.

"You find a way to honor her memory," my uncle said, always the level-headed one. "That's what she would have wanted." My aunt nodded and let out a loud sob as she ran from the room.

I wanted to scream. I wanted to yell. I wanted to cry. Mostly, I wanted my sister back. My other half. My heart. But she was gone. Never to return again. Never to punch me when I was being an ass. Never to kick me underneath the dining room table when I stretched my legs into her space. Never to tease me about my relationship with her friend.

Looking down at her, I planted a kiss on her cheek. "To the moon and back, Marley Jane."

My heart shattered when she couldn't respond how she

usually did.

And that was the moment the realization washed over me like a tidal wave. She was gone...

# CHAPTER FORTY-ONE

## *REASON*

*Cam*

I WAS IN A complete daze that night and into the early hours of the morning as I sat answering question after question, while the police tried to put all the pieces together about what happened. I wish I could give them the answer they wanted to hear, but I couldn't. All I could say was that my sister snapped because she didn't get the help she needed when she needed it, and now she was gone.

Marley was gone.

My sister was dead.

My best friend killed herself.

No matter how many times I said it, I still couldn't come to terms with the cruel reality of it all.

"Now, I want to go back to one thing and then you'll be free to leave, Cam," Mr. Benson, Grady's father and the police chief, said, bringing me out of my thoughts.

"Yes?"

"You mentioned that Marley had said something to the effect that someone had hurt her."

"Everyone hurt her," I replied, my voice low and empty. "Maybe not directly, but everything in this town put another nail in her coffin until she couldn't take it anymore. That's why she's…" I couldn't even bring myself to say it out loud because then it would be true. Steadying myself, I stared into Mr. Benson's benevolent eyes. "All I know is that something happened to her yesterday after the pageant. I don't know what, but *something* happened that pushed her over the edge. That's all I can really tell you right now."

"Okay. Thanks, Cam. I'm sure you'd like to be with your family so I appreciate you taking the time to answer my questions. If you think of anything, anything at all, please call me."

Getting up, I started to leave the room. I reached the door and glanced at him. "It won't bring Marley back so I don't know why it even matters."

"Cam, I can't even imagine what you're going through," he soothed. "I'm not even going to pretend that I can sympathize with you because I most certainly cannot. But what I can tell you is that if we find out that something *did* happen to Marley, we'll catch whoever's responsible and bring them to justice. Isn't that what Marley would have wanted?"

Shaking my head dejectedly, I said, "What Marley would have wanted was to finally be at peace. I guess now she is."

I left the police station and hopped in my Wrangler. Everything about the short drive home seemed inherently wrong as I watched the sun rise in the east. There was an emptiness and desolation in the streets of Myrtle Beach, the vibrancy of our beautiful beach community replaced by bleakness. I could no longer feel Marley's spirit around me, and I had no idea how I could possibly be expected to survive without her. I had hoped, with everything in me, that last night was one giant nightmare…that I would wake up and Marley would come bounding into my bedroom at any second. But as I pulled in front of my house, I knew that I wouldn't get my wish.

Killing the engine, I couldn't muster the strength I needed to step out of the Jeep and into the house. As I sat there staring at the roof that reminded me of everything I had lost, a thousand emotions rushed over me...sadness, rage, hate, anger, resentment, desperation, and love. The love I had amplified those emotions a thousand times.

I punched the steering wheel and screamed, wishing it would make it hurt less. But it didn't. I didn't think anything would ever be able to take away the pain and guilt I was experiencing. For the first time in nearly seven years, I let it all wash over me. I stopped pretending that everything was okay when it was anything but.

Taking several deep breaths after letting out my emotions, I pulled myself together the best I could, unsure of what scene would greet me when I walked through the front door. As I climbed the steps to our porch, everything seemed grim and somber. I entered the house, surprised to see Brianna sitting on the floor of our living room, playing with Meg and Julianne.

"Hey," I said quietly.

Her head shot up quickly and an empathetic look crossed her face. Turning back to my sisters, she said, "Can you two color by yourselves for a few minutes while I go talk to your brother?"

Meg looked toward the hallway where I stood and I could tell that she had been crying. "Okay. We'll stay here and color." Her voice was subdued and lacked the innocence that she normally exuded when she spoke.

Brianna walked up to me and grabbed my hand, leading me up the stairs and into my room. Once we were alone, she wrapped her arms around me and I felt her body begin to shake against mine.

"I'm so sorry, Cam," she sobbed. "I'm so, so sorry."

Closing my eyes, I let the tears fall, not caring that I was crying in front of my girlfriend. She felt my pain, too. She had a bond with Marley almost as strong as I did.

"Why are you here?" I asked softly.

"I wanted you to feel some sort of love when you got home from the police station. And the girls' grandmother couldn't watch them this morning so I agreed to while your aunt, uncle, and mama…" She trailed off.

I nodded. She didn't need to tell me. I knew they were at the funeral home, making preparations.

"They came home a few hours ago to let the girls know what happened…" She brought her bottom lip between her teeth, trying to hide her quivering chin from me.

I pulled her into me once more in a feeble attempt to be the strong one.

"It's all my fault," Brianna lamented into my chest.

"No, it's not. It's everyone's fault. Everyone in this town is to blame here."

She shook her head. "No. I knew exactly what happened to Marley and I stood aside and let it happen again. I should have known."

I reeled back. "What do you mean? What do you know?"

Her eyes grew wide, a look of horror on her face. "I can't, Cam," she whispered.

"Why not?!" I shouted, my expression fierce. "My sister is fucking dead! She shot herself, Bri! If you really care about her like you say you do, tell me! What is it that she kept from me?! What is it that *you're* keeping from me?!"

"It's not something I can share with you! I want to. I just… I can't!"

I gripped her shoulders tightly, my face flaming with anger. "Goddammit, Bri! Just fucking tell me!" I shook her, my passion overtaking my rationale.

She fought against me and freed herself. "Don't you *ever* fucking touch me again, Cam!" she screamed, bolting from my room. As she was about to run down the stairs, she turned around. "I thought you were one of the good ones." She rubbed her arms and I could see a red imprint from where my hands were. I scrunched my eyebrows, noticing a faint bruise with a pattern similar to the ones on Marley's body. "You're just like everyone else." She spun around and flew down the stairs.

Slamming the door to my room, I collapsed onto my bed, my emotions overtaking me once more. I didn't know how many tears a person could possibly cry until they would no longer fall.

Hours later, I heard a gentle knock on my door. Opening my eyes, I noticed the sky was turning pink, the sun setting in the west.

"Come in," I croaked out, keeping my vision trained on the horizon, wondering how the world could keep turning even though Marley was gone.

"Cameron, baby."

I turned my head at the sound of that unexpected voice.

"Mama? What are you doing here?" I tried to hide my surprise at seeing her standing there. She looked so calm and level-headed. I expected her to be drowning her sorrows in a bottle somewhere like she did after Dad died. Hell, *I* wanted to drink to try to dull the heartache.

"I came to check on you, sweetheart." She made her way over to the bed.

I sat up, allowing her to wrap her small arms around me. It didn't matter that I was taller than her by over a foot. At that moment, I felt like the little eight-year-old boy that cried in his mother's arms after losing his father.

But this time, I was an eighteen-year-old young man that had just lost his sister.

"How are you doing, baby?"

I shook my head. "Not good, Mama. Not good at all. When will it stop hurting? How come I don't remember feeling like this when Dad died?"

She rubbed my back and attempted to assuage me. "You were too young to really feel that loss, Cameron. You cried a lot. We all did. But you had Marley to help you get through it." Her chin began to quiver as the words left her mouth.

"You loved Marley with everything you had. Just like I loved your father with everything *I* had. And that makes the pain even worse because you don't think you can possibly move on from the suffering you're feeling right now. But you will. You're a survivor, Cameron. No matter what obstacles life has placed in front of you in the past, you made it through. And you'll make it through this, too. It won't be easy. It'll hurt. Some days will be easier than others, but you'll find a way to keep Marley with you. She'll always be a part of you. Just because she's not here physically doesn't mean that she's gone forever. Remember those moments you had with her. Remember that connection, and I guarantee you'll feel her spirit."

I nodded slightly.

"Come on, baby. Come downstairs. You can't go through this alone. I made that mistake after your dad died. I pushed everyone away instead of allowing anyone to help me. It was the worst decision of my life because I lost you and Marley. Be with your family. They need you just as much as you need them. Meg and Julianne need their big brother."

"I'm not their brother."

Mama shrugged. "Maybe not by blood, but being a

294

brother is so much more than having the same parents. You have a connection to those little girls, and they're going through something that no six- and five-year-old should be going through right now. They keep asking when Marley will be home. Please. I think if they could just see you and hug you, it will make it easier on them when they finally realize that Marley won't be coming home."

I let out a loud sob at my mother's words, still unable to come to terms with the fact that I'd never hear the front door open, followed by Marley's heavy footsteps running up the stairs again. At that moment, I knew the world was a cruel place.

My mama grabbed my hand and led me from my darkened bedroom and down the stairs. The house was full of activity, light, and grief at the same time. My aunt sat at the table in the dining room on the phone, apparently keeping herself busy by planning Marley's memorial service. My uncle sat in the living room with several people I recognized from church, but couldn't remember their names.

"Cam!" Meg squealed when she saw me emerge. "Auntie Grace said she'd get you to come out and play with us! Do you want to play Chutes and Ladders?"

Remembering Mama's words, I plastered a weak smile on my face, trying to be strong for the girls. I needed my family now more than I ever had before. But the person I really needed was Marley. She was the only one who truly understood me. She was the only one to tell me that I was being an ass. She was the only one to assure me that everything would work out. I no longer had that voice in my head.

"Go grab your game and we'll play in the den to stay out of your parents' way."

She smiled, showing me where she had lost another tooth since I saw her on Friday, and ran up to her room in search of her board game.

Mama squeezed my arm in a comforting manner. "You're a good kid, Cameron. After your dad died, I often wondered if my life would have been better if I had never met him because my heart physically ached. Then I looked at you kids and I knew it was worth it. You'll eventually find something or someone that makes the pain you feel right now worth it. I promise you. It may not be today or tomorrow or even this year. But eventually, you'll realize this happened for a reason."

~~~~~~~~~~~

TIME PASSED MERCILESSLY SLOW as we all sat in the living room, not saying anything, well-wishers stopping by with a fruit basket or a casserole. Occasionally, I would see tears falling down Mama's face as she looked at me. I couldn't imagine what she was going through at that moment. I lost my sister, but she lost her daughter. She had tried to keep a strong front as we went through the motions of planning Marley's memorial, when I'm sure that all she wanted to do was cry. There were no expectations on my shoulders. I was able to let out my emotions, and I did. But my poor mother continued to smile and say she was fine, when it was clear that she was anything but fine.

What do you even say at this point? That you're sorry? That you should have known? "Sorry" just seems like such an inadequate word. Over the next few weeks, I knew I would be hearing that word a lot. *I'm so sorry for your loss. Is there anything I can do?* Yes. There's something you could do. You could bring my sister back. Empty

296

compassion. Empty assurances. Empty feelings. That's what I had to prepare myself for.

Now that Marley was dead, mourning her became the "in" thing to do. People came to our house in droves to tell us how sorry they were, although they didn't seem to be upset or saddened by her passing. To them, this was probably another way to maintain their status in the church or in the community.

All I could think as I listened to their fake condolences was how come they didn't find the compassion for her while she was going through whatever she was over these past several years? Everyone neglected the cry for help that Marley's actions were screaming at all of us. Her silence was deafening and we ignored it. Each and every person in this town dug her grave, myself included.

After the third day of having our house inundated with well-wishers, I couldn't take it anymore. "I'll be upstairs," I said curtly to my uncle as he grieved with a few parishioners of the church.

He grabbed my arm. "Cameron, you should stay down here."

"Why?" I seethed. "None of these people gave a shit about Marley when she was still alive. Now that she's dead, you know why they do? Because a dead teenager is newsworthy. They can all reminisce years down the road about the poor girl who put a fucking bullet in her head because no one thought it was important to put her in therapy. All these people care about is their perfect little world where little eight-year-old girls aren't raped and molested on a daily basis. People don't speak of such things. So Marley didn't speak of such things and it killed her. Now all these people, you and Aunt Terryn included, are trying to wipe clean their guilty conscience by coming here and saying how sorry they are for my loss. *My loss.*

*T.K. Leigh*

Not theirs. They don't feel the loss. Not like me, or Mama, or Meg or Julianne. Because they didn't lose anyone. So if you'll excuse me, I'd like to mourn my sister the way that I should be... Away from all these fake people who didn't care about Marley when she was alive." I pushed past him, ignoring the loud silence in our living room.

Dashing up to my room, I opened the window, climbing through the narrow opening to our spot. A chill set over my body as I lay down against the hard surface. The wind picked up and I could almost hear Marley's laugh. I could almost feel her hair blowing on my face. I could almost feel her tears fall down my cheeks. Until I realized that they were my own tears.

"Why did you do it?!" I shouted, staring at the darkening sky above me. "Why couldn't you talk to me? Or Mama? Did you not think that this would affect me? Did you not think about any of us? Why did you have to be so damn selfish, Mar?!"

I took a deep breath, trying to control my emotions to get through what I wanted to say to her. "How am I supposed to go on without you? Do you expect me to just keep going on as if nothing has changed? *Everything* has changed. I don't know who I am without you. I don't know how to even be *me* now. Such a huge part of me is missing."

Tears continued to fall as I listened to the calming sound of the waves just a few blocks away. "I still feel you out here, ya know? I always loved sitting on this roof with you, Marley Jane. Out here was where we could just be us. The us that we were before Dad died. You and your shooting stars." I shook my head, laughing through my tears at all of my sister's crazy ideas. The realization of it all overwhelmed me. "I guess you're the shooting star I

298

have to look for now."

Wiping my cheeks, I settled my cries. "I should have said something and made you get the help you needed, regardless of what Uncle Graham and Aunt Terryn thought. I should have gone behind their backs and put you in therapy. I have so much money saved up for college. I should have taken that money and put it to better use. I didn't mean to let you down, Marley.

"What made you snap this weekend? What happened to you? How come you didn't come talk to me before thinking it was a good idea to go kill Buck? I thought things were looking up, Mar. I really did. We just turned eighteen. We were about to go move in with Mama. Could you not wait two more weeks? You broke my fucking heart, Marley. Half of my heart is dark. Your light is gone."

I closed my eyes and pretended that Marley was next to me, staying silent as she contemplated the meaning of life. That was the only thing that mended the hole in my soul.

That night, I remained on the roof, clutching a pillow off Marley's bed to my chest, but sleep never came. Every time I closed my eyes, Marley's slumped over body flashed in front of me. Remorse overwhelmed me for rushing to Buck and not disarming her first. I was so worried she had killed him that I failed to protect her. I prayed with everything I had in me that it was all a horrible dream. That I would open my eyes and see Marley's smiling face lying next to me, her hair blowing in the wind, her face bright with laughter. Instead, in the morning, I opened my eyes to the cruel reality that was now my life. I never imagined what life without Marley would be like. Besides my mama, she was the only person I knew since the day I was born. Now that she was gone, I felt like I didn't know how to breathe. That I didn't know how to exist.

# CHAPTER FORTY-TWO

## *SCAR*

*Cam*

FRIDAY MORNING CAME AND I went through the normal motions. Eat breakfast. Brush my teeth. Shower. Get dressed. Instead of going to school, I was heading to the church with my family, all of us dressed in our best clothes. When saying good-bye to your world, you should look your best, right?

I sat there, in a complete daze, during the service. I heard my uncle's voice reverberate through the tall walls of the sanctuary, but I couldn't comprehend what he was saying. The one thing I kept hearing over and over was that this was God's plan. I couldn't understand that. How could a teenage girl killing herself possibly fit into *anyone's* plan? All I could think was that God must be a cruel bastard if he took my sister from me for some bigger purpose. I didn't give a fuck about what the purpose was. Maybe it was selfish, but I had a purpose for Marley's life, too. And that was having her by my side through all of our ups and downs, not having to say good-bye to her before she even got to graduate high school.

I contemplated all the life experiences I would now miss out on because Marley was gone. I'd never be able to see her at U.S.C. or have her come visit me at

Georgetown. I'd never be able to go out to a bar with her to celebrate our twenty-first birthdays. And I'd never be able to dance with her on her wedding day.

Unable to take it anymore, I abruptly stood up and bolted down the aisle. Throwing the large wooden doors of the church open, I inhaled deeply, trying to subdue the lump that had taken up permanent residence in my throat over the past week.

Collapsing on the stairs, I didn't care if anyone saw me sobbing uncontrollably. Nothing mattered anymore. Nothing could heal the scar on my heart.

I stared at the cars driving by, hating the people in them for no other reason than it felt good to hate. It felt good to judge them from afar. A loud creaking brought me back from my rage-filled thoughts and I glanced over my shoulder to see my aunt walking down the steps toward me. She sat next to me and I could see that her eyes were red from crying.

"How are you?" she asked, wiping her cheeks.

"Confused. Bitter. Angry. But mostly…heartbroken."

She nodded and another tear fell down her face. "I'm sorry. It's just hard for me to look at you and not see Marley by your side. You have the same eyes. And smile." Her lower lip trembled and I could tell that she finally had a moment where she could let her emotions take over, instead of having to keep it all inside as she had that week. We had barely spoken two words to each other as I brooded in my room and she entertained half of the town that stopped by our house.

"I am *so* sorry, Cam. I always had a bad feeling that something like this would happen one day."

I scrunched my eyebrows. "What do you mean?"

She stilled for a moment and I could tell she was torn. "This town, Cam," she admitted finally. "I've gone along

302

with everything for years, keeping my mouth shut and doing what was expected of me, just like Marley did. And it killed her."

Her eyes turned warm and contemplative. "I love your uncle very, very much. He has an enormous heart, but he's been stuck between a rock and a hard place since you and Marley came to live with us. There's not one thing that I can pinpoint it all to, but a mix of everything."

"Why couldn't you just make sure she got the help she needed? That we both did?" I asked, my voice shaking.

"I wish I had. Marley is the unfortunate victim of age-old prejudices and stigmas that have plagued this town for decades now. I once hinted at looking for a therapist for both of you just after you came to live with us. This was during our weekly Wednesday afternoon tea at Mrs. Monroe's house...well, Mrs. Grayson now. You should have seen the disdain-filled eyes looking at me at the mention of it. Her mother, that wretched woman, pulled me aside and spoke to me in such a way as I had never been spoken to in my life. She warned me about what kind of stink she would make if I followed through, threatening to have her friends on the church board remove your uncle as pastor. I'll never forget her words...
'*The people of the church need a leader, not someone who has a niece with emotional problems. God is the only one from whom you and your family should be seeking counsel*'."

Her eyes met mine and I saw the regret in them. "Your uncle has always been so devoted to his religion and the church that I shuddered at the thought of him losing this. Back then, I had no idea how grave the consequences of this decision would be. If I did, I never would have talked Graham out of putting Marley in therapy. *I* was the one that stopped it and convinced him that all the help and guidance Marley needed she could find in God. That was me, not your uncle. Even back in September, after Marley said that there was no God, he was willing to throw caution to the wind and get her the help she needed."

"So why didn't you?"

"Because of the pageant. It was purely selfish of me. I just… The pageants were so different twenty years ago. It was fun. All the girls were supportive and our mothers didn't even want us to participate. It's not like it is today. I see it all so clearly now. All these girls are entered into the pageants left and right just so that us moms can have something to talk about at our weekly tea or church potlucks. I was so jealous when all my high school friends were having children and were able to enter their daughters in dance class and all the 'Little Miss' pageants here in town. Graham and I had tried to conceive for years. We about gave up hope and were surprised to find out I was pregnant just a month after you and Marley came to live with us. So I was on the sidelines for years as I watched all my friends play dress-up with their daughters. They looked like they were having so much fun. I wanted that, too.

"Then you and Marley came into our lives and I saw my chance to be close to everyone again. I was so selfish that I didn't think about the possible repercussions of how Marley would feel when she was paraded in front of strange eyes and made to perform. I didn't care, but I wish I did. I feel that all of this could have been prevented and I swear to you, we're going to make it up to you, to your mama, and to Marley."

Staring ahead, I processed what she had just told me. I wanted to blame them so that it was easier, but I just couldn't do it.

"It's not your fault, Aunt Terryn," I said, meeting her

eyes.

She let out a quiet sob. "I knew you would say that, but it is. If Marley had gotten the help she needed…"

"She may have done the same thing. I just… As much as I want to blame *someone*, I can't. Killing Marley was a group effort, I'm afraid."

It was silent before she spoke again.

"Are you still going to move back in with your mama? You can stay with us as long as you want to," she said quickly. "But I understand if you want to move in with her."

I nodded. "I just don't know if I'm ready to move on. Leaving the house and moving in with Mama makes me feel like I'm ditching Marley. I'm thinking of going to U.S.C. in the fall instead of Georgetown so that I can be near Mama during the school year."

"Her room will always be here, and so will yours. And, of course, the roof."

I smiled at her words. "You better never get rid of that house now."

"I wouldn't dream of it."

"Good."

The doors opened again and people began to flood from the church in a solemn manner, quiet whispers sounding as sympathetic eyes met mine. Guilt covered all of their faces, but I knew it was only fleeting. After a week passed, they would go back to their lives. Hell, they would probably go back to their old ways in a few hours, and I hated them for that.

"Aunt Terryn," I said, turning to her.

She grabbed my hands in hers and simply nodded. "I get it, Cam. You go say good-bye to your sister the way you want to." She stood on her toes and planted a kiss on my cheek. "I love you, Cam. And I am sorry."

"Me, too."

I darted up the steps, stopping abruptly at the top when I was met with Brianna's beautiful brown eyes. I hadn't seen her since earlier that week when I lost my temper with her. I hated myself for not apologizing sooner.

"Hey, Bri," I said quietly, shuffling my feet.

"Hi, Cam. How are you?"

I shrugged, looking away, not wanting her to see how broken I was. "I'm okay."

She shook her head and a small smile crossed her face. "Liar."

I chuckled. "You got me."

There was an awkward silence between us as I tried to formulate my thoughts. "Listen, Bri…"

"Cam, stop. I know what you're going to say and I don't want you to. You were right to be angry with me. I'm angry with myself. I wish I had…" She looked to the sky as if trying to calm her emotions. After taking several deep breaths, she returned her eyes to mine and I could see how remorseful she was. It was genuine and pure. Everything I had come to expect from Brianna over the years. "I should have told you a long time ago. I'm going to have to live with this regret the rest of my life."

"What is it, Bri?"

"Brianna!" a booming voice called out.

We both snapped our heads and my eyes settled on Mr. and Mrs. Grayson, her father just behind them.

Her body tensed up and she returned her gaze to mine, her eyes narrowed. "There are things you need to know, but I can't tell you right now. Can you meet me at the trees where we…?" She blushed.

"When?"

"Eight o'clock?"

"Of course," I said.

"Thank you, Cam." She turned away from me, walking to meet her family.

"Brianna?" I called out.

She looked over her shoulder at me.

"I love you."

Her chin began to quiver. "I love you, too. I am *so* sorry, Cam."

"Brianna Marie! We're leaving. Now!" Mr. Monroe shouted at her and a sinking feeling formed in the pit of my stomach.

~~~~~~~~~~~

ALL AFTERNOON, OUR HOUSE was flooded with well-wishers that came to pay their last respects to the beautiful girl that was taken from me far too soon. Half of the high school showed up, most of the girls crying as they walked through the living room and wrote their good-byes on one of the many giant portraits of Marley that Mama had made for the occasion.

I sat in the corner with Mama and watched the rather strange dynamic between the teenagers and adults that mourned and socialized. Most of the adults had a look of fake compassion on their faces as they walked by all the photos of Marley smiling and posing for pictures after having won one pageant or another. Their noses were turned in the air as if they were belittling their integrity by paying their respects to a girl that was so clearly unstable that she took her own life.

"She was so beautiful, wasn't she?" Mama asked quietly.

"She was. She took after you."

A smile crossed her face. "You always know just what to say, Cameron Michael. You'll make some woman very

307

happy one day. Speaking of which…it looks like you and Brianna had a bit of a reconciliation today outside the church."

"I guess," I responded. "I overreacted last time I saw her and I don't know if she'll ever forgive me. I grabbed her arm and it left a mark, Mama. You taught me better than that."

"Yes, I did. But I also taught you to never hide your feelings. At least I tried to. Your emotions just got the better of you. It happens to everyone. Do you regret it?"

"The second I did it, I was ashamed of myself."

"As well you should have been. Brianna will understand." The sound of polite chatter and china dishes filled the room as Mama and I were content to remain in our own little world. "Have you spoken with Doug?"

"No. I'm a bad friend."

She gestured toward the doorway and my eyes settled on the broken frame of my best friend. "I know this week has been difficult for you. It's been that way for all of us, Cameron. Don't let it fester. There are other people, like Doug, who are experiencing the same pain you are. He loved Marley with all his heart. It's always good to share your pain with someone else. So go. Share your pain, baby."

I shook my head in disbelief that the woman sitting next to me was the same woman that neglected her children for so long. "How do you always seem to know what to say?"

"Years of remorse. Now go."

Squeezing her hand, I raised myself off the chair and walked across the room to where Doug stood, his normally tall stature shrunken.

"Hey," I said, shoving my hands in the pockets of my

dress pants.

"Hey."

"How are you? Wait. I'm sorry. I fucking hate that question."

He laughed slightly. "Me, too. I *really* hate that question these days. At least you haven't been in school this week. That's all I've been hearing. Every day. Everyone's been so concerned about how I'm doing, but they don't want to hear the truth. They just want to ask so they can feel like they actually care when they probably don't."

"Fake people," I muttered.

"Yup. They're mourning Marley because it's the cool thing to do right now. Next week, there will be a new fad and they'll move on and forget that Marley Jane Bowen ever existed. But not me. I'll never..." He trailed off and closed his eyes, trying to compose himself. "I'll never forget her," he continued, his voice barely above a whisper.

"Here. Come with me. I want to show you something." I gestured toward the stairs and led him into my room. Opening the window, I climbed onto the roof. He followed.

We sat there in silence, watching the last bit of daylight disappear behind us.

"So this is the famous roof?" he asked several minutes later.

I nodded. "Yup. This is it. Not too exciting, is it?"

"No, but I see why she liked to come up here. You can almost forget for a minute, can't you? Like you're in your own little world and it can just be you."

"I've slept out here the past few nights," I admitted. "I feel her out here. All I feel inside the house is regret and remorse. I hate that feeling. Out here, I feel Marley's spirit. I can hear her laughter when the wind blows."

"Do you hear her bellow at the rain to leave when she's out on the beach?"

I grinned fondly at the memory. "Yeah. I definitely hear that. Loud and clear. The rain doesn't listen, though."

"It never does. Stubborn ass."

Long moments passed before either one of us spoke again.

"She loved you, ya know," I said, breaking the silence. "I'll never forget the look on her face the morning after the bonfire all those months ago…"

"Which bonfire?"

"The one right before the start of the school year. I walked into her bedroom to bring her a coffee and she was sitting on her vanity with the biggest grin on her face because you left a love letter in her purse or something."

Doug grinned, his ears turning red. "Yeah. I remember that. You always had to bring your top game with Marley. Hell, I was thrilled when she noticed me. I know there were lots of ups and downs with us, but I'm glad we finally reached a point that she trusted me…with everything. I just wish I could have done something m-." He stopped short, a sudden movement in the sky catching our attention. "Holy…"

"Marley and her shooting stars," I said, wiping my eye. "She's okay. That's got to be her way of letting us know."

He nodded. "Then why do I still feel like this?"

I shook my head. "Maybe because we both know there's more to what happened to Marley. Something happened after the Jessamine Pageant and I'm going to find out."

"Are you sure, Cam?"

"No. I'm not sure of anything these days. But I refuse to believe that Marley would have done this unless something set her off. The day before, she was talking about how excited she was to graduate. Hell, she was working on her speech! That's not a girl who would kill a man before turning the gun on herself...unless she was provoked."

"I hope you're right." Doug turned to me, a look of unease on his face.

"I have to be."

~~~~~~~~~~~

SNEAKING OUT OF MY house just a few minutes before eight that evening, I made my way down the street toward the beach, thankful when I couldn't spot Brianna's Beetle in the public lot yet. Reaching the tree alcove where we went to be alone, I sat down to wait.

As I stared out into the darkness, the sound of waves crashing in the distance, I pondered what Brianna wanted to tell me. My mind ran through thousands of different scenarios as time passed with no sign of her. Concern washing over me, I checked my watch and saw that it was nearly nine o'clock.

Raising myself off the sand, I dusted my pants and headed back to the house, wondering if she stood me up because she was still angry with me about what happened earlier this week. Or maybe there was something more.

Opening the door to my house, I was relieved to see that most of the guests had left over the past hour. "Hey, Aunt Terryn. Has anyone called?"

She shook her head. "No. The phone hasn't rung all day. Why?"

"Nothing," I said quickly. "I had plans to meet Brianna at the beach and she never showed up."

"Her mother and step-father were supposed to stop by

311

today and they never did, either. But I think she left the church with her father."

"Her father? I didn't think she stayed with him much."

"Neither did I. Word is, Mr. Grayson and Mr. Monroe got into a bit of an argument in the church parking lot when she was getting into the car with her mother. Mr. Monroe grabbed her out of the car and threw her into his. He certainly has a bit of a temper."

"I gotta go, Aunt Terryn."

"Where are you going, Cam?"

"I just... I have to go."

I dashed out of my house and raced away from the shore and inland several miles, toward her father's home. Pulling in front of the large plantation-style house, I bolted out of my Jeep when I saw two ambulances in the driveway.

"Brianna!" I yelled, heading for the door just as I observed paramedics rushing out of the living room with a stretcher. "Is she okay?" I asked as they pumped air into her lungs.

"No. We've got to get her to the hospital before we lose her again."

"Again?" I quivered, stepping back to allow them to load her into the ambulance. My eyes settled on a nasty bruise and a welt on her head, blood tricking down her pale face.

"Yeah. Looks like she shot the sick prick before she tried to off herself with all those pills. He probably won't make it." He gestured toward the doorway and I saw another stretcher being rolled from the house and into the second ambulance.

Mr. Grayson followed close behind, his eyes frantic. "Cam! It's awful. I just don't... I never should have allowed her to come over here."

"Where are they taking her?" I asked, confused.

"To Memorial General." He placed his hand on my shoulder. "I'll give you a ride."

I glanced down, spying his wedding band. "No. I'll take my own car."

# CHAPTER FORTY-THREE

## *AWAKE*

*Cam*

I SAT IN THE emergency room waiting area for hours, my mind racing and trying to replay everything in my head, looking for a clue. I prayed that when the doctor came out, he would have good news. Mama arrived with Doug as soon as she heard, as did Aunt Terryn and Uncle Graham. It seemed the only times we saw each other lately was during tragic events. I hated that.

"Mr. and Mrs. Grayson," an authoritative voice said sometime after midnight.

We all raised our heads to see a man in hospital scrubs standing there. "I'm Dr. Avery. Your daughter is stable enough to see you now."

"What happened?!" I shouted. "Is she okay?"

Her mother glared at me. "Cameron, we'll go see her first. She's our daughter."

"No. She's *your* daughter. Not *his*," I fumed.

"Cameron, baby," Mama said, placing her hand on my arm. "You can go see her once they come out. That way, you'll have some privacy with her." She raised her eyebrows at me and I knew what she was saying.

I nodded and turned my attention back to Mr. and Mrs. Grayson. "I apologize. I'm just tired and emotionally drained. Please excuse my behavior."

A forgiving smile crossed Mr. Grayson's face. "Of course, Cameron. It's completely understandable." He excused himself and followed the doctor down the hallway, his arm around Brianna's mother's shoulders.

After an excruciatingly long time, they emerged into the waiting room where we were all eager to hear what they had to say.

"She's going to be okay," Mr. Grayson said rather stoically. "They were able to pump her stomach. They estimated that she swallowed a few oxy pills leftover from a recent back injury, as well as several dozen acetaminophen pills. She's lucky I got there when I did."

"Why were you there?" I asked.

He glowered at me, obviously irritated and perhaps unsettled by my questions. "As I've told the police, Brianna forgot her purse at the church and I brought it to her just in case she needed it." He faced everyone else. "She's resting at the moment. We appreciate all of your concern, but please come back to see her tomorrow. She's had a trying day."

They both stood there as if waiting for us to leave.

I remained unmoving, not wanting to leave that dismal place without seeing Brianna's chest rise and fall. I needed to know that she was still breathing.

Mama nudged me. "Come on, baby." She leaned into me. "At least make everyone think you're leaving. Okay?"

"Okay." I reluctantly walked with Mama out of the emergency room waiting area, leading her toward my Jeep. Doug followed us.

"What's going on? Do you think…?" he asked once he was certain no one could overhear.

I shook my head. "I don't know what to think, but

Brianna wanted me to meet her at the beach. She never showed up. When I got to her house, there were two ambulances. Her father was shot and she was, apparently, unconscious from a pill overdose. But there was a bruise on her head as if it had been slammed against a hard surface. I don't know. Maybe she fell, but something is off."

"Do you think Mr. Monroe…? And that's why Marley…?"

"I have no idea what to think, but I know that the one person with answers is lying in a hospital bed right now. And I'm going to sit by her side until she can give me those answers."

Mr. Grayson drove past us in his Mercedes and I opened the door to my car as if I was about to get in. Mama leaned over and kissed my cheek. "Get going then, Cameron. We'll come to check on you in the morning."

I threw Doug the keys and dashed back into the emergency room, thankful when the nurse at the registration desk gave me Brianna's room number and allowed me to go see her. Running through the hallways, I found her room and pushed the door open, my heart dropping when I saw how pale and lifeless she looked, her head bandaged, monitors measuring her vital signs.

Sitting down in the chair beside the bed, I grabbed her cold hand in mine.

"Cam?" she whispered.

"I'm here, baby." I caressed her skin.

"I knew you'd find me."

"Shhhh… Get some rest. I'll stay by your side all night. I'm not going anywhere."

"Good. Then he won't come back to finish the job."

My heart dropped into the pit of my stomach, wondering what her words could imply.

~~~~~~~~~~~

THE SOUND OF A soft giggle cut through my dreamless sleep. I startled awake, confused, before my eyes settled on Brianna's weak, yet smiling face as she lay in the hospital bed.

"You were snoring. And drooling."

I adjusted myself in the chair and wiped my face. "Sorry. I'm sure that's a big turn-on."

"You being yourself around me? Hell, yeah, it is."

I leaned over the bed and kissed her forehead. "I'm glad you're okay."

"How's my dad?" she asked, her eyes becoming impassioned and overflowing with unease.

I hesitated, unsure of how to respond.

A look of resignation washed over her face, her chin trembling. "He's dead, isn't he?"

I nodded slightly and she burst into tears. I wrapped my arms around her and soothed her sobs. Long moments passed while she attempted to get her crying under control, my brain still on overdrive about what the hell was going on.

"That bastard's had it out for him for as long as I can remember."

I pulled back and narrowed my gaze at her. "What were you going to tell me yesterday at the beach? It was that your dad hurt you, isn't it? And that he hurt Marley, too?" I needed to know that the person who hurt two of the most important people in my life was dead.

Tears welled in her eyes once more. "Not my dad. He would never... It was Bryant."

I shook my head. "Your step-father? But..." I trailed off as I scanned Brianna's body, hating that I hadn't put

317

all the pieces together earlier. "How long?" I quivered.

"Since they got married, really. I think my dad knew there was something off. He noticed bruises, but anytime he tried to confront him about it, Bryant threatened him. I was so scared and I wanted to say something, but he said he would find a way to pin it on my father and not himself. I didn't want my dad to get into trouble for something he had no idea was really even going on."

"Gabriella Knox…?"

"That was Bryant, too. He set my dad up. Bryant's a former judge. Dad was worried that he'd never get a fair trial. How could he protect me from a jail cell? So he agreed to pay off Gabriella. Of course, once that happened, Bryant convinced Mom to have a judge re-evaluate the visitation decree and had that limited. So I was pretty much stuck at home, always wondering when I would hear the sound of my door opening in the middle of the night."

A lump formed in my throat at the thought of what she had to endure. "I'm so sorry, Bri. I should have seen all the signs."

"You did," she replied. "You saw them, but I always yelled at you when you tried to bring it up. I covered it up and kept it from you. If I had said something, he wouldn't have been able to hurt Marley and then she wouldn't have…" Her lower lip trembled. "It's my fault she's dead. I could have prevented all of it if I had just stopped living in fear, like Marley finally did."

"We're not even sure it was him. It could have been something or someone else," I said dejectedly.

She grabbed the sleeve of her hospital robe and pushed it up, showing me the bruise. "I know you saw something similar on Marley's body," she said, referring to the marks with a crisscrossed pattern identical to that of her step-father's wedding band.

I simply nodded and she lowered her sleeve. "What happened yesterday?"

"It all started after we left the church. I was supposed to go home with my dad. As I was getting into the car with him, Bryant grabbed my arm and tried to yank me out. Right in front of my mother and half the church, he accused my dad of assaulting Marley. I knew he was trying to set my dad up again. They argued and, finally, my dad grabbed me and shoved me into the car. He knew what kind of monster Bryant was, even if he couldn't prove it. A father just knows, I guess.

"We got to my dad's house and were sitting there, both of us trying to hide our emotions over losing Marley, when Bryant walked in the house with a gun. He shot Dad in the shoulder, then grabbed me and hauled me into my bedroom." Her body began shivering from the traumatic experience. "I tried to fight him, but he's stronger than I am. He threw me against the dresser and I blacked out. The next thing I knew, he had dragged my dad into the room. He had already lost a lot of blood, but he was still conscious. He put a gun to his head and told me to swallow the pills. My dad begged me not to. Part of me didn't want to die, but I couldn't let him kill my dad. Then part of me wondered if Marley had finally found peace, and maybe if I swallowed the pills, I could finally be at peace, too."

Tears fell down her face once more and I embraced her, hoping that my gesture could make her feel loved.

"Don't ever think that, Bri," I begged. "Please. I promise you'll find peace, but when you're alive."

"I lost count of how many pills I took. Next thing I knew, I was waking up here last night with Bryant standing next to me and I freaked. I told the doctor that I didn't want him here and he kicked him out. My mom, of course, left with him, not caring that her daughter almost died. He's not allowed to come back here."

"You just rest. Take some time and decide what you want to do about making a statement."

"I already know what I want to do. I'm done remaining silent. I'm sure the police are going to want to know what happened. And when they come and ask, I plan on giving them a *true* story that they'll never forget."

# CHAPTER FORTY-FOUR

## *MEMORY*

*Cam*

SITTING ON THE MAKESHIFT stage in our school's gymnasium a week later, watching my fellow graduating class enter and take their seats, a strange feeling washed over me. I still couldn't believe it had been two weeks since the Jessamine Pageant. Everything was different, but at least I had answers. I felt relief that Marley didn't snap for some unknown reason. As a survivor of abuse, she didn't think she had any way out when she was brought back to that time of her life and subjected to the same trauma again. I missed my sister more than I could recall missing anything, but I felt vindicated knowing that the person responsible would face judgment for his actions.

"Today is a little bittersweet," Mrs. Pritchard, our faculty advisor, said. "What should be a celebration of the beginning of the next step in your life has been marred by tragedy. Miss Marley Jane Bowen showed all of us that one voice can get people to think, and isn't that what a class president should do? She should be here today, delivering her speech. Instead, we all had to say good-bye to this vivacious, beautiful, intelligent woman last week. In her place, her brother will deliver the speech she had written." She turned and nodded in my direction.

I stood up and made my way to the podium, my eyes scanning the faces of everyone I had spent the last seven years with, imagining that Marley's smiling face was among them. "Thank you to the faculty, board of trustees, parents, and my fellow seniors. Marley spent her last night alive writing this speech. I recall sitting on the roof with her, like we did a lot, as she jotted down what she wanted to say. When she wrote this, she already knew what she would be doing at the Jessamine Pageant. She was setting herself free. Free from her past and free from the silence. So here goes."

I glanced down at the notecards in front of me and adjusted my face, summoning the inner strength to speak my sister's final words. "Silence has been my life for as long as I can remember, but in silence, there is heartache. There is pain. There is suffering. I've worn a mask. We all have. I'm not the only one. No one knows how it started, but not one person sitting in this gym can say with absolute certainty that they are who they truly are.

"This town and society have dictated how we should act, what we should wear, what we should do, and I'm not going to do that anymore. Today, we leave this school for the last time and start on our new paths. We should celebrate in the fact that we all made it through high school." I paused, trying to get my emotions under control as I looked at the tears falling down the faces of many people in attendance. My eyes settled on my mama sitting with my aunt and uncle, and they all gave me an encouraging nod.

Returning my attention to the notecards in front of me, I continued, "We should learn to embrace and celebrate each other as individuals and not try to be cut from the same mold. My past has shaped me into the woman I am today, and I'm no longer going to feel ashamed of that person.

"On the first day of school of my senior year, my favorite teacher asked me who Marley Jane Bowen really is. I couldn't answer. I had no idea who I was. But throughout this year, as I began to slowly chip away at the mask I had been forced to wear, I've realized who I am. I'm someone with a voice. Someone who's suffered, but who survived, even when the odds were stacked against me. And that's who I plan to be every day for the rest of my life."

Sobs echoed in the gym and it took everything inside me not to break down and cry. These were Marley's last words and they needed to be spoken. "My wish for all of you is that you find yourself. Whether it be today, tomorrow, next month, next year, or ten years from now, I hope you celebrate in your journey to self-discovery as I have celebrated in mine."

I looked up from the podium. "I beg all of you to listen to my sister's words. Stop for a minute. Look in the mirror. Are you proud of the person staring back? All actions have consequences, no matter how insignificant you may deem them. You all know that my sister took her own life. You've heard that she just snapped out of nowhere and shot herself after killing the man that abused her nearly every night for three years when she was just eight years old. But that's not the whole story. Her autopsy report has indicated that, several hours before her death, she was assaulted rather brutally."

My eyes grew intense as I scanned the audience. The truth set Marley free and it was about to set Brianna free, as well, regardless that she had to miss graduation because she was still in the hospital.

"A week ago, Brianna Monroe allegedly also tried to

kill herself, but not before shooting her very own abuser. Or so you've been told. Both Brianna and Marley had similar bruising patterns. After an exam of Brianna's body, the authorities have determined that they were both assaulted by the same person. This week, I've heard the stories going around about what happened. Well, I'm here to set the record straight."

I paused briefly, preparing myself for what I was about to do. "Brianna Monroe didn't swallow those pills intentionally. A man held a gun to her father's head, threatening to pull the trigger unless she did what he asked. And he demanded that she take those pills, scared that she was finally going to tell the truth about her own years of abuse. This was a man we all trusted…that we all admired. Marley spoke of wearing masks, but Bryant Grayson wore the biggest one of all."

Gasps echoed throughout the gymnasium. "Brianna made a statement earlier regarding what happened, and the police, as I mentioned, were able to corroborate her testimony with physical evidence. He's now in police custody where he can't hurt anyone again. Silence, fear, and hypocrisy have caused more harm than good over the years. It nearly killed Brianna. It's probably damaged so many of you out there, too, but you're still scared to say anything. And it's taken my sister from me, from all of us, too soon. Please. No matter where your life takes you, remember the lesson that Marley Jane Bowen has taught us. Find your voice and don't be afraid to use it." I looked up at the ceiling of the gym as if talking to the heavens. "To the moon and back, Mar…"

I closed my eyes and heard several voices say, "From the stars to the ocean." My vision blurry from my tears, I was surprised to see my senior class standing up from their chairs and looking at the ceiling with me and saying

324

their final farewell to Marley Jane.

~~~~~~~~~~~~

A WEEK AFTER GRADUATION, as I was packing up the last of my things, a gentle knock sounded on my door.

"Come on in," I called out.

"Hey," an unexpected voice said.

"Brianna." I stopped what I was doing and met her at my door, leaning down to kiss her. She had been discharged from the hospital the day after graduation, returning home to an irate mother that was upset she had filed charges against Mr. Grayson. "How are you feeling?"

"Better. A lot better, actually." She nervously danced from foot to foot, glancing around at the boxes stacked in my room. "So, are you ready to leave?"

"I guess so. I hate to leave this place, but Marley's part of me. No matter where I am, she'll be there. I feel closest to her in this house, but I'll always have her with me."

She smiled in understanding as she fought back her tears.

"What's your plan now?" I asked, trying to cut through the tense atmosphere.

A look of hesitation crossed her face and she grabbed my hand, leading me toward my bed. "That's what I wanted to come talk to you about." She sat down and I followed. "I've decided to go live with my aunt down in Georgia. I'm thinking about taking a year off to just be for a minute. Clear my mind before starting college."

"Where in Georgia? I'll come visit whenever I can. Once I'm all situated at Mama's, I'll look at flights."

Brianna took a deep breath and turned to me, her chin quivering. "I don't think that's a good idea. I need to start

325

over. *You* need to start over, too. You have such a bright future. You need to live your life. Every time you look at me, you'll be reminded of your past."

"But I love you, Brianna."

A quiet sob left her mouth. "I love you, too. With all my heart. But we've both suffered too much. Whenever I see you, I'll always be reminded of everything I went through. And you'll be reminded of Marley whenever you see me. We'll never move on. There will be no future. You will always have my heart, but you're so pure and light, I'll only shadow your existence with darkness. I just don't see myself ever coping with my past if we don't go our separate ways."

I sat there and stared ahead, processing her words. "So this is what it feels like," I said solemnly.

"What?" Brianna asked, wiping her tears.

"Having your heart broken. It really sucks."

"I know," she quivered. "My heart's breaking, too. But we both need a clean break. You realize that, don't you?"

I gazed deep into her puffy eyes. "I hate to admit it, but you're right. It doesn't mean I have to like it, though." I leaned in and brushed my lips against hers.

"I'm really going to miss this," she murmured.

"Me, too."

She grabbed my face and deepened the kiss, all the anger, heartache, despair, and love we had experienced over the past year rushing forward as we kissed each other with more passion than either one of us had done anything in all of our years. She pulled away and leaned her forehead on mine, her entire body trembling through her sobs. "Have a good life, Cameron Michael Bowen. You deserve all the happiness that finds you."

Unable to say anything in response, I watched as Brianna walked out of my life, a strange feeling of emptiness washing over me. Needing to clear my mind, I climbed out of the window onto the roof and lay back, the Carolina sun hot on my skin. I closed my eyes and tried to feel Marley on that roof.

*"You're snoring, Cam. And drooling. You'll never get laid if you keep doing that."*

*I flung my eyes open at the sound of that voice to see that darkness had fallen. Looking next to me, I saw Marley lying on the roof. Maybe her death was just a dream.*

*"How are you here?" I asked. "You…"*

*"I know. You hear that sound? That's you still snoring even though you're talking to me. You're dreaming, Cameron Michael."*

*"Then I don't ever want to wake up," I choked out through my tears.*

*"I know. But you have to, Cam. You have to move on." She smiled the most beautiful smile in the world. "So, tell me. I'm dying to know."*

*My eyes grew wide.*

*"Whoops. Bad choice of words. Anyway, how did everyone like my graduation speech?"*

*"They really enjoyed it. I made a few changes, though."*

*"Yeah," she interjected. "I know. It's okay. I won't sue you for taking liberties with my artistic vision."*

*I chuckled and rolled onto my side, never wanting the dream to end. "I'm taking your advice."*

*"Oh yeah? What advice is that?"*

*"I'm going to help people. I'm heading to U.S.C. this fall instead of Georgetown."*

*"But you were so excited to get in there! Cam, you can't abandon that opportunity!"*

*"I'm not, Mar. I found a new opportunity…a new calling. Plus, I want to be near Mama. We kind of missed growing up with her so I hate to head to D.C. and have to leave her again. Plus, U.S.C. has a good psychology program."*

*She raised her eyebrows at me. "So you're in agreement that the world doesn't need another lawyer then?"*

*"I'll never admit that you were right, but you may have been on to something."*

*She began to pinch my side and I howled from the pain, thinking that maybe it wasn't a dream. Surely that would have woken me up. Then I felt the vibrations of my snores and knew this wasn't real.*

*"Okay! You were right!"*

*She released her grasp on me. "Mark this day down. After over eighteen years, Cameron Michael Bowen has finally admitted I was right. Just wait. In about two years, it will be in all the history books." She giggled.*

*It was silent for a moment as we both lay on our backs, like we always did, and stared at the sky.*

*"Hey, Cam?" she asked.*

*"Yeah?" I turned my head to look at her.*

*"Do you miss me?"*

*My entire body convulsed from my heavy sobs in response to her question. "Every second of every day. I still hear your voice in my head. I still have conversations with you where I hear what your answer would be. Like today when I was getting dressed, I could picture you lying on my bed, staring at me and asking if I was really going to wear what I had on. Don't worry. I changed. You were right. Navy blue and brown don't go well together. You always were the fashionable one."*

*"I do the same thing." I heard her take a deep breath, but didn't see her chest rise and fall. "I'm sorry about Brianna," she said softly.*

*"What do you mean?"*

*"That she wants a clean break. I'm sorry, but I get it."*

*"Yeah. I get it, too." I swallowed hard. "She's so sorry, Mar. She wishes that she had said something about what Mr. Grayson was doing sooner. If she did, then maybe…"*

*"I'm sure he'll go to prison for a long time," she interrupted, lightening the mood. "Hell, I'm sure he'll get a taste of his own medicine. He's a former judge! Those inmates will do a number on*

*him! They hate pedophiles!"*

I smiled at her optimism.

*"I'm sorry about Mr. Monroe,"* she offered. *"But don't worry. We're concocting another scheme to mess with the rich housewives of this town. Even from up here. Oh, Grams says hi. And she's not in pain anymore."* She turned to look at me, her chin quivering. *"Either am I, but I hate all the pain that I've caused everyone. You were right. I should have talked to you first. I never should have..."* She trailed off. *"I always was a little impulsive and dramatic, wasn't I?"* she joked.

*"I really want to hate you for what you did. I miss you so fucking much, Marley. My heart physically hurts."*

She nodded at me and wiped the tears falling down my cheeks. *"I know. It hurts me, too. But there's a reason for it, Cam."*

*"Then, by all means, please tell me what it is because I can't possibly see a reason for it all, Marley. I honestly can't."*

She looked around slyly as if trying to ensure that no one would overhear her.

*"What are you doing?"* I asked.

*"I could get into so much trouble if the big light finds out about this..."*

*"You mean God? He does exist?"*

She shrugged. *"That's one of the big questions, isn't it? You said it yourself. You're a firm believer in the light and that's what you are, Cam. And that's what you will be. Someone is going to come into your life that is going to need you more than I did. You're going to be her reason to live. You're going to be this girl's light in her otherwise dark existence. But, more importantly, she's going to become your light, too. Your purpose. Your higher calling. You'll bring her back from tragedy, despair, and torment. She'll be a survivor, and it'll be your beautiful heart full of light that makes her see that her past doesn't define who she is. By doing that, you're going to be able to save hundreds of women from having to endure unspeakable things. I needed to go... To keep them alive. That's the purpose."*

329

"How will I know?"

"You will. This course is already charted. It won't be an easy road for you, Cam. You're going to try to save every girl you come across, thinking that by helping them, it'll make up for what happened to me. But my course was charted, too. It was meant to happen." She paused briefly, her lips turning up slightly in the corners. "Just so you know," she said, her voice playful. "Your first born will be a girl. Feel free to name her after me."

"You know I will." It was silent for a moment before I asked the question I didn't want the answer to. "Will I ever see you again?"

"Oh, Cam," she exhaled. "You will. But not until it's time. I'll always be with you, watching over you." She wiped the tears that had fallen down her cheeks, her voice turning light. "Well… almost always. I won't be with you in the bathroom. You need to stop jerking off so much, by the way."

I shook my head as laughter and sobs rolled through my body.

"Let me go, Cam," she implored me. "You need to so that you can move on with your life. If you don't, you'll never be able to help everyone that you're meant to. Please."

I took a deep breath, hating the thought of ever letting my sister go, but I knew that I couldn't move forward if I didn't. "Okay," I agreed dejectedly.

"Can you do me a favor?" she asked solemnly.

"What is it?"

"Can you tell Doug that I said hi when you see him? I know he's worried about me. I just haven't been able to bring myself to pay him a visit yet. I don't know if I ever will."

I rolled my eyes. "Sure. I'll tell my best friend that my dead sister visited me in a dream and said hi. That won't put me the psych ward or anything."

"No. That won't. But you'll end up there eventually, the future Dr. Cameron Michael Bowen. You'll make a difference. And you'll save a lot of girls. You'll meet one girl who will make you forget all your pain. Don't worry. I'll send you a sign."

"A sign?" I asked. "What kind…?"

*She raised her eyebrows at me.*

*I nodded. "Got it. To the moon and back, Marley Jane."*

*"From the stars to the ocean, Cameron Michael."*

# EPILOGUE

## Twenty Years Later

*Cam*

PUTTING MY LEXUS IN park outside of my house just a few blocks from the downtown area of Fernandina Beach on Amelia Island, Florida, my heart was racing in my chest, brilliant blue eyes permanently ingrained in my mind. The most amazing, gorgeous, spectacular blue eyes that I had ever seen. Getting out of the car, I walked through the front door of my house and ran up the stairs, opening the window in one of the guest rooms.

It had been years since I had come out here, but something about the girl that fell into my life so unexpectedly made it seem like the right thing to do. And the way her body felt against mine as I carried her into her house after she passed out from getting over-served at a bar was unlike anything I had ever experienced before. There was this magnetism I felt and I had known her for less than twenty-four hours. I had no idea what to think. I needed my sister to tell me that I was just horny and that was why I felt this way, but that dream I had on the roof of my aunt and uncle's house was still fresh in my mind, even twenty years later.

Climbing onto the roof of my Victorian house, I leaned

back. "Hey, Mar," I said. "Is this your version of a belated birthday present, or just your way of smacking some sense into me? Or is this her? It's been twenty years, for crying out loud! Part of me thinks that you were just messing with me."

I sighed. "I get it. I know I've been a bit of a prick since, well…the past few years." I paused. "See, this is when you'd say 'since forever' so I'll just pretend you said it. And this is me rolling my eyes at your dig at me, okay?"

The smile disappeared from my face. "She's lost, just like you were. She's scared. But she's strong, just like you were. I wish you saw that." A tear fell down my face from the memory of my sister. "I just hope you're proud of the life that I've led. I owe it all to you, ya know. If you didn't do what you did, I would have probably just gone on to law school and be stuck working for some schmuck that decided what cases I would have to take. But you saw a different calling for me."

I shook my head, chuckling to myself. "I remember all those times you said I'd make a good therapist." My expression turned stoic. "Well, you were right, Marley Jane. I'm a damn good psychiatrist and it's because of you. Because I hate myself for not seeing the signs, for not stopping you from doing what you did, and for keeping secrets from you. I can't help but think…"

I stared off at the ocean that was visible over the roof tops. "I know, I know. You'd tell me I can't think that way, that it was going to happen no matter what because your course was charted, so let's just agree to disagree, okay?"

I continued to lay on the roof and watched the stars glimmer in the sky, remembering all the times in my youth that I would sit on the roof with Marley and make up new constellations. "I guess I just wanted to come and talk to you. I don't feel you like I do over at Aunt Terryn and Uncle Graham's house, but I still feel *something*. I guess I always kind of feel you around me. I'd like to think that you're watching over me...over all of us.

"You should see Meg and Jules. Meg got married after college and she already has her hands full with two kids. Julianne is still in med. school, but she goes home as much as she can. Uncle Graham is still running that crisis center for women he started in your honor. He found a purpose in your death, as you know, and left the church. I'm real close to him...and Aunt Terryn. She works at the center with him and they've really made a difference. Whenever I go home to visit, I help out there, too. I still see the guilt in their eyes. They're still shouldering the blame, but I think it was that guilt that forced them to reevaluate their current path and choose a new one. And a lot of people in that town did the same. It's definitely not like it used to be. They still have that pageant but, from what I hear, it's different. Oh, and Meg and Julianne were certainly not allowed to participate in any pageants. A lot of girls were pulled from all of it after you died.

"Let's see. What else would you want to know? Oh, Doug's still doing well. We've stayed in touch over the years. It took him a while to finally get over your death, and I still don't think he's completely over it, but he's moved on. I still see Brianna once in a while when I go home. It was hard at first because I was reminded of how much I miss you, but it's gotten easier."

I sighed, placing my hands behind my head and could almost sense my sister lying next to me, her eyes bright. "This is when you'd tell me to stop rambling and dish about the girl, isn't it?" I paused, as if waiting for Marley to reply. "Well, her name's Jolene, but she doesn't want anyone to know that. I like her. I really, really like her. She's running from something and I can't help but think that she was dropped in my life for a reason. Maybe this is the girl you told me about in that dream all those years ago."

The sky began to glow and I could tell that the sun was about to rise. "I miss you like hell, Mar. I can't help but think about where you would be if you were still here. Would you have gotten over your past? Or would it have eventually come back to haunt you? I guess we'll never know." I took a deep breath and began to raise myself off the roof. "Give Grams and Mama a hug and kiss for me, will ya?"

I was about to crawl back through the window when I noticed three streams of light fall into the ocean in the distance. My jaw dropped, remembering her promise that she would send me a sign when the girl that would brighten my existence came into my life.

Grinning in disbelief, I looked to the heavens. "You made your point. I get it. To the moon and back, Marley Jane…"

The End

# PLAYLIST

*Enter Sandman* - Metallica
*To The Moon And Back* - Savage Garden
*Free Falling* - Tom Petty
*Jane* - Barenaked Ladies
*Us Against The World* - Coldplay
*Dirty Diana* - Michael Jackson
*When I See You Smile* - Bad English
*Right Now* - Van Halen
*More Than Words* - Extreme
*Baby Did A Bad Bad Thing* - Chris Isaak
*Runaway* - Bon Jovi
*The Dreaming Tree* - Dave Matthews Band
*Keep Breathing* - Ingrid Michaelson
*Pay For What You Get* - Dave Matthews Band
*November Rain* - Guns N' Roses
*Bed Of Roses* - Bon Jovi
*Closer* - Nine Inch Nails
*To Be With You* - Mr. Big
*Silent All These Years* - Tori Amos
*Something I Can Never Have* - Nine Inch Nails
*Hate Me* - Blue October
*Burn* - In This Moment
*Janie's Got A Gun* - Aerosmith
*The Unforgiven* - Metallica
*Far Behind* - Candlebox
*My Immortal* - Evanescence

*Heart Of Marley*

*Nothing Else Matters* - Metallica
*The Freshman* - The Verve Pipe
*Tears In Heaven* - Eric Clapton
*Hold My Heart* - Sara Bareilles
*Send Me The Moon* - Sara Bareilles
*I Can Let Go Now* - Nathan East, Featuring Sara Bareilles
*That Year* - Brandi Carlile
*Sister* - Dave Matthews

# Coming Soon From T.K. Leigh

## Heart of Brianna
*Brianna's Story*
*Anticipated Publication 2016*

## Heartless
*Doug's Story*
*Anticipated Publication 2017*

## Heart of Light
*Cam's Story*
*Now Available*

## *HEART OF LIGHT EXCERPT*

*Read the rest of Cam's journey in Heart Of Light*

THUMP. THUMP. SHE COULD swear her heartbeat echoed through the vast hotel suite she had been living in longer than she cared to remember. Years of planning led her to this moment. Nothing could go wrong. If it did, she didn't want to think about what would happen. Her success depended on everyone playing their part...the head of housekeeping, the bus boy, the room service attendant, the girls, even poor Shelby.

She carefully tiptoed across the living room, carrying just the bare necessities she would need to get as far away as possible. Glancing over her shoulder at the couch where *he* was passed out from the pills the room service attendant had slipped into his food, she knew she didn't have much longer until he woke up. And she had no intention of being there when he did.

Looking out the peephole into the hallway, she prayed that Shelby was able to entice the two guards normally stationed out there to leave their post. She would never be able to repay her for what she was doing at that very moment...all to help her. A chill ran through her body at the thought, but the girls were right. She didn't have a choice. She had to get out.

Carefully opening the heavy door, she looked back at

*him*. Her heart raced when she saw him move slightly on the couch before he stilled again. She watched as his stomach rose and fell, the occasional snore sounding through her prison. Taking a deep breath, she glimpsed one last time at the man she used to look up to and admire. Now, every time she saw his gentle and attractive features...the chestnut eyes and strong jaw, the distinguished gray hair and broad shoulders...she saw him for what he really was. A monster that destroyed her very existence.

She crept into the hallway, thankful to be one step closer to her freedom. But she still had to get out of the hotel before anyone discovered that she was missing.

"You're five minutes late, Jolene, baby," an older black woman said, rushing up to her and pushing a laundry cart.

"I'm sorry. I tried to get out on time, but it took a bit longer for those pills to work on him," Jolene whispered as she crawled into the cart. "Probably from all the shit he does regularly." She took a calming breath as she covered herself with old laundry sheets and bath towels, the musty smell making her gag.

"It's okay, darling. We're almost done here. We'll get you out safe." Rosa pushed the cart down the hallway toward the service elevator.

"What's going on here?" a loud, booming voice called out.

Rosa looked up, trying to hide her nerves. "Just bringing these dirty sheets to the laundry downstairs, sir," she said, mindful of the gun peeking out of the large man's jacket. She hated working at that hotel, but she didn't have a choice. She was those girls only hope of escape.

"Isn't that supposed to be done in the afternoon? It's

340

past midnight."

"I know, sir, but we were short-staffed today." She shook in fear. No one was allowed on the top floor after nine at night. That was when *he* held his little poker games, auctioning the girls off to whomever offered the most money. It broke Rosa's heart knowing that, just beyond the hallway's walls, the girls were dying a little bit more inside.

"It's getting done now," she continued, her voice turning strong once more.

"Fine," the large man said, a scowl crossing his face. "Get on with it then. Don't make this a habit. I really don't want to involve the boss in this shit." He walked away.

Rosa breathed a sigh of relief and continued to push the laundry cart down the long corridor toward the service elevator. "It's okay, baby girl. Almost there," she whispered quietly as the doors opened.

But not quietly enough.

"Who are you talking to?" The large man spun around, running toward the elevator just as the doors closed, banging on the metal exterior in frustration. He had a bad feeling about tonight, particularly after noticing that Mr. Falconi's bodyguards were not stationed outside of his suite.

Grabbing his phone, he dialed a number. "Joe. It's me. Get someone down to laundry. Check the cart the maid is pushing." He hung up and walked in the direction of his boss' suite. Nervously, he knocked on the door.

"Boss, you in there?"

Nothing.

No response.

"Tony. It's Ralph. You got Jolene in there with you?"

Still no sound. No rustling. No movement.

"Okay. I'm coming in." He took a deep breath, hoping he wasn't interrupting anything between his boss and his girl. Grabbing his universal keycard, he slid it in the slot and slowly opened the door. His eyes grew wide when he observed his boss passed out on the couch in the living room, the room service tray scattered on the floor in front of him.

He drew his gun, scanning the suite for any sign of what could have happened.

"Jolene!" he yelled. "Where are you, princess?!"

He made his way toward the second bedroom, hoping that Falconi had instructed Jolene to take a client in there instead of one of the other rooms. His heart dropped when the door was wide open, the extravagant bedroom distressingly empty.

He ran into the room, checking everywhere for some sort of indication as to what could have happened. In the back of his mind, he knew that Jolene was gone.

Returning to the living area, he grabbed a bottle of scotch off the wet bar and poured himself a drink, hoping that Joe had stopped the bitch maid with the laundry cart. His mind raced, trying to figure out how to tell his boss that his girl was gone. He just hoped it wasn't too late to find her.

~~~~~~~~~~~~

"JUST A FEW MORE minutes, Jolene, baby," Rosa said, looking into the rearview mirror of the old station wagon at the still body covered with ratty blankets. "Patrick is inside getting your bus ticket, so you'll be free of this place in just a little bit," she explained, her chin quivering.

She was relieved that she got Jolene out of the hotel without raising any more suspicion. A bus boy that had helped Rosa from time to time was able to hide her in a storage closet leading to the loading dock before any of the boss' guys came to search the laundry cart. It all worked out just as they had hoped. Only a few people actually knew about what really went on in the hotel late at night, and even those who knew pretended they didn't. It was too dangerous any other way, but that didn't discourage Rosa. It was just by chance that she saw Jolene that day over a decade ago.

She wasn't yet sixteen when she first met her. She was sweet and had just lost her mama. Jolene had told Rosa all about how Mr. Falconi was a friend of her mama's and was granted custody of her until she turned eighteen. She seemed so excited to be able to live in the glamorous hotel on Michigan Avenue that Falconi used as a front for his less than legitimate businesses, mainly gambling and forced prostitution. Rosa had her doubts from the beginning, the girl's sparkling blue eyes reminding her of a ghost from years ago. Then poor Jolene turned eighteen and her life changed forever. She was forbidden from ever leaving the hotel again, locked in *his* suite. And it had been nearly ten years.

She had helped a few other girls escape in the past, but never the boss' girl. They said it couldn't be done, but Jolene was sweet and the other girls wanted her to be free. Now, she almost was. Once that bus left the station outside of Chicago with Jolene safely on board, she would finally be free…something she hadn't experienced in over a decade.

Rosa saw a tall black man walking, determined, toward the car, thankful to see her husband clutching the bus ticket in his hand. He opened the door, his breathing labored from the adrenaline coursing through his body.

"Everything go okay?" she asked.

"I suppose, if your idea of okay is half of your boss' men stopping everyone inside that place."

Rosa's eyes flashed toward the brightly lit building. "How did they figure out we'd be here? We chose this station for a reason, just in case they caught on. I was certain they'd check the one downtown first."

"I don't know, but they're questioning the ticket agents about whether anyone has seen her. They have her photo, for crying out loud! This could be bad."

"I don't have any other choice," a sweet voice rang out from the back of the car. "I can't go back there," Jolene sobbed. "Never again. I would rather die than have to…"

"Hush, Jolene, baby," Rosa said, keeping her eyes straight ahead. "We'll get you on that bus and out of here."

Patrick glanced at his wife. "Rosa, it's only a matter of time until they put the pieces together and realize we were behind all of it." His voice was full of concern…and fear. "Are you sure this is a smart idea?"

"Yes," she hissed. "It's the least I can do." A tear fell from her eye just thinking about what all those girls were forced to endure. "How would you feel if that was our daughter? Wouldn't you want someone to help her?"

Patrick hung his head in defeat. "I certainly would."

"Okay, then. Let's do this. You got the wig on, baby girl?" Rosa asked.

"Yes. I'm ready," Jolene responded, thankful that Rosa had thought of everything. She had packed some clothes from the lost and found at the hotel that fit Jolene perfectly. She had also grabbed an auburn-colored wig from her sister's hair salon that looked more natural on her than the blonde hair she was forced to have to make *him* happy. That's what he liked on her. Blonde hair and blue eyes.

"Okay, Jolene, baby, you know I love you. And I'm going to miss our chats, but you need to get far away from this city. I don't ever want to see you again, you hear?" she choked out through her tears.

Jolene nodded, trying to stay strong. She was so thankful for everything that Rosa had done for her. She never thought she would be free, and here she was, seconds away from never having to bend to another man's will for the rest of her life.

"Thank you, Rosa." She climbed out from under the blanket.

Rosa glanced back and the two women shared a look...a look that said everything Jolene wanted to, but didn't have nearly enough time to utter.

"Go, baby girl. Live your life and don't ever come back to this awful place."

Jolene wiped the tears from her cheeks and crawled out of the car.

Patrick accompanied her the short distance to the bus, turning to face her just outside of the door. He scanned the area for any suspicious activity, knowing that not only her life was at risk if they were caught.

"Here you go." He handed her a ticket. "Stay safe. And, as much as you may want to, *do not* let us know where you end up. There's an e-mail address on the back of the ticket. If you want to let us know that you made it somewhere and are safe, that's how you do it. Other than that, do not contact anyone directly. Do you understand?"

Nodding her head, she bit her lower lip, wishing she would be able to talk to one of the only friends that she felt she had, but she knew she couldn't. Once she arrived somewhere, she had to stay hidden. It was the only way.

She looked down at the ticket, wondering where she

was headed. Miami, Florida. At least she was going somewhere with no snow. Flipping the ticket over, she made out the e-mail address.

"Last call for Miami!" a man sounded on the intercom.

"Get going now," Patrick said. "Remember, don't take the bus to the end of the line. Get off somewhere before the final destination. It will increase your chances of never being found." He held out his hand for Jolene to grab on to so he could help her up the stairs.

She stared at it, slowly stepping back, a look of trepidation in her brilliant blue eyes.

Patrick shook his head and watched as she boarded the bus, wondering why every one of the girls he had helped escape cowered in fear of being touched. He could only imagine what they had suffered through to cause that reaction.

Less than a minute later, the doors closed and the bus turned out of the station with Jolene on it, heading south and away from all the horror and misery of the last decade of her life.

~~~~~~~~~~~

SENATOR DAVID MURPHY DISCREETLY left Falconi's luxurious Landmark Hotel on Michigan Avenue, making his way down the dark side alley where his driver was to pick him up. No one could know that he spent tax dollars going to the hotel, not when he had an apartment in the city that the taxpayers already provided him. People would get suspicious as to why he spent so much of his time there. He was a happily married man, after all. A scandal like this would ruin his career, especially when his entire campaign platform was based on re-instilling family values and the sanctity of marriage.

Some would say he could be called a hypocrite, but he was a man... A man with needs that had gone grossly unsatisfied most of his life.

When running for state office, his advisor recommended he start a family. He hated having to date and play the sweet, caring individual. That wasn't who he truly was. But voters loved a family man, so that's what he became, although he couldn't remember the last time he played catch with his son, or had a pretend tea party with his daughter. And his wife... Well, they hadn't been intimate in years. She wasn't nearly as adventurous as he needed.

He was thankful to have met Anthony Falconi early on in his political career at a fundraiser for an organization fighting against human trafficking. Falconi was a deeply religious man and contributed a substantial amount to his campaign. One night after his victory party for winning the race for state office, David enjoyed quite a few drinks with Falconi. Rather drunk, Falconi invited him up to his penthouse. That was the first time he saw Jolene. And it certainly wouldn't be the last. Once she turned eighteen a decade ago, he had been returning to Falconi's Chicago Landmark Hotel as much as possible for her, even after he won election to the U.S. Senate and was supposed to be in the nation's capital, expected to participate in mundane tasks such as solving the country's budget issues.

On that warm Chicago night in June, David made his way back to his government car, thinking about the immense pleasure he felt every time he had Jolene tied up and could do with her what he wanted...what he needed. He was startled when he heard the service door open and close loudly, followed by an echoing "Hush."

He slowly turned around, not wanting anyone to be

alerted to his presence.

"Come on, Jolene, baby. Free and clear, honey girl."

His eyes grew wide. What was going on? Someone was helping his Jolene get out of the hotel? The girls never left. They weren't allowed. He knew all too well what kind of operation Falconi was running and he supported it one-hundred percent, as well as the various charities that Falconi had established to prevent the very thing he was involved in. Senator Murphy didn't blame him for it. Falconi was a businessman, plain and simple. He saw a marketable need and he catered to the very distinct tastes of wealthy men. But Jolene... She was his. Senator Murphy felt a connection to her that he never had with any other girl, and it wasn't just because he had mortgaged his house in order to pay Falconi to be her first. *Money well spent,* he thought to himself.

His heart raced when he saw the head of housekeeping hide the tall, leggy blonde in the back seat of a station wagon. He clenched his teeth and fists, his blood spiking in rage and anguish at the thought of never being in the presence of Jolene again. Never listening to her sweet voice beg for mercy when she had misbehaved. Never getting his dick hard from the look of fear she had in her eyes. He needed Jolene in his life. She couldn't get away.

"Where to, senator?" his driver inquired.

Shaking his head, he snapped out of his thoughts, desperation taking over. "Follow that car. The run-down station wagon."

"Yes, sir."

The government Town Car turned off the alley onto Michigan Avenue, driving the streets of the city that David had called home for years. The Chicago skyline transitioned from magnificent hotels to smaller apartment buildings, most of them decrepit and in need of serious repairs. For the duration of the long drive, he made sure to keep the station wagon in his sight. His vision was a little blurry from all the scotch he drank earlier in the evening, but he had a mission. Follow Jolene. The thought of losing her sobered him up quite a bit.

After driving for a little over an hour, the car eventually pulled into a bus terminal.

"Stay close, but don't make it obvious," David instructed.

"Yes, sir."

He watched for several moments while the station wagon remained in a secluded area of the parking lot, an older black man getting out and running toward the station.

Almost immediately, he noticed a few of Falconi's men pull into the station, as well. They looked frantic as they held up a photo, approaching nearly everyone. David's mind turned calculating, thinking they must have realized that Jolene was missing and were looking for her, too. If Falconi's men knew that she was in a station wagon in that very parking lot, they wouldn't be questioning transients about whether they had seen the girl. This presented a golden opportunity for him. Instead of calling Falconi and having him forever in his debt, he had a new course of action. Follow her, and get what he always wanted... Jolene all to himself. He was giddy with excitement over the thought as he observed the black man walk Jolene, wearing an atrocious wig, to a bus.

As the bus drove out of the station, he looked at his driver. "I hope you're ready for a road trip. Follow that bus."

"Yes, senator."

~~~~~~~~~~~

ANTHONY FALCONI WAS STARTLED awake with a pounding headache in the middle of the night.

"Jo-Jo Bear! Bring me some aspirin!" he yelled out, wondering what kind of party he had with her the night before that would cause the room service tray to be dumped all over the floor. And if it was a party, how come he had no memory of it? The last thing he remembered was having a drink with that sleazy Senator Murphy after he had finished with Jolene and escorted her back to the suite. Once he had said his good-byes to the senator, he settled down in his suite for a late night snack, courtesy of one of the room service attendants.

"Jolene?! What did I just say?!" he shouted, his temper beginning to flare. He listened and didn't hear anything other than the whirring of the air conditioner in the suite.

Groaning, he raised himself off the couch, going in search of Jolene. "What the…?" His eyes scanned the guest bedroom, looking for any trace of the blonde-haired angel that should be in that room.

He ran to the door of the suite, his heart dropping when he found his two security agents were nowhere to be found.

"JOLENE!!!!" he thundered, not caring that he may be waking up some high-paying clients at that moment. It didn't matter. Jolene was gone. And someone was going to have to pay for that.

# ACKNOWLEDGEMENTS

When I was growing up, I always participated in a summer theater program for middle school and high school aged kids. I think that's where my love for all things dramatic has stemmed from. After I graduated high school, I went on to college to study music. But every summer, I returned home, having been lucky enough to be asked to join the staff of this theater program as its music director. And it was a position I held each summer until I started law school, encouraging kids to step out of their comfort zone for six weeks of their summer vacation. Each and every kid that I taught will forever have a place in my heart... One in particular.

Several years ago, I got an e-mail from the woman that had directed alongside me, telling me that one of the students that I taught had committed suicide. It was his senior year of high school. I never found out the details, but it was definitely a shock to me. He never had the lead in any of the plays, but that never stopped him from joining in on all the theater games we used to play. That made me realize that you never can tell what's going on in someone's life, despite outward appearances.

The same is true for so many people out there. I know this book may not have the happily ever after you all crave, but Cam's story goes on. And Marley's does, too, through Cam. This was a story that I needed to tell, to make people think twice before judging someone. To make people realize that it's okay to ask for help. It's okay to talk about your past, no matter what.

I've been navigating this crazy author world for the past year and, with every book, the number of people I need to thank increases. First and foremost, a big thank you to my wonderful beta readers... Lynne Ayling, Karen Emery, Lea James, Natalie Naranjo, Natasha Rochon, Stacy Stoops, and Kimberly Twedt... Thanks for taking the time to read through this book. I know the subject matter isn't the easiest to deal with, so I appreciate all your feedback. I promise the next book will be much lighter.

A big thanks to my street team, my very own angels, who go above and beyond in spreading the word about my books. Alexis Brodie, Anna Kesy, Brenda Mcleod, Cecilia Ugas, Cheryl Tuggle, Christine Davison, Chrissy Fletcher, Cindy Gibson, Claire Pengelly, Crystal Casquero, Crystal Solis, Crystal Swarmer, Danielle Estes, Donna Montville, Eann Goodwin-Giddings, Ebony McMillan, Erika Gutermuth, Erin Thompson, Estella Robinson, Jamie Kimok, Janie Beaton, Jennifer Goncalves, Jennifer Maikis, Jennifer Patton, Jessica Green, Joanna Haskins, Johnnie-Marie Howard, Katharine Cordy, Kathryn Adair, Kathy Arguelles, Kathy Coopmans, Kayla Hines, Karrie Puskas, Keesha Murray, Kim King, Kimberly Kazawic, Kimberly Twedt, Lea James, Lindsey Armstrong, Lori Garside, Lori Moore, Marianna Nichols, Meg Faulkner, Megan Galt, Melissa Crump, Melissa Miller-Mattern, Melissa Stickney, Natasha Rochon, Nicola Horner, Nicole Chronister, Pamela McGuire, Rachel, Fowler, Rachel Hill, Shane Zajac, Shannon Baker-Ferguson, Shannon Palmer, Shayna Snyder, Sherri Stovall, Stacy Hahn,

Stefani Tabakovska, Stefanie Lewis, Suzie Cairney, Sylvia Chavarin, Tabitha Stokes, Theresa Natole, Tiffany Reid, Tiffany Tyler, Tricia Crouch, Tracey Williams, Victoria Stolte, Yamara Martinez... Thanks for all you do for me!

To my parents and sisters... My amazing family... Thanks for providing me the inspiration, motivation, and the love of reading, without which, none of this would have ever been possible.

To my editor, the amazing Kim Young... Thanks for the time and effort you spent on this book. I know this one wasn't an easy subject matter for you to work on. I promise, the next book will be full of laughter instead of tears.

To my husband, your unyielding support means the world to me. I love you... To the moon and back.

Last, but by no means least, to my readers. Thanks for all your love and support over the past year. I never imagined that ten people would buy my books so the fact that my stories have spoken to you on some level is truly humbling. Thanks for the past year. Here's to many more years to come.

## *ABOUT THE AUTHOR*

T.K. Leigh, otherwise known as Tracy Leigh Kellam, is the *USA Today* Best Selling author of the Beautiful Mess series. Originally from New England, she now resides in sunny Southern California with her husband, dog and three cats, all of which she has rescued (including the husband). She always had a knack for writing, but mostly in the legal field. It wasn't until recently that she decided to try her hand at creative writing and is now addicted to creating different characters and new and unique story lines in the Contemporary Romantic Suspense genre.

When she's not planted in front of her computer, writing away, she can be found running and training for her next marathon (of which she has run over fifteen fulls and far too many halfs to recall). Unlike Olivia, the main character in her Beautiful Mess series, she has yet to qualify for the Boston Marathon.

Made in the USA
Charleston, SC
14 October 2014